D0097991

Praise for Lisa Brackmann

Black Swan Rising

"Lisa Brackmann's *Black Swan Rising* is a savvy, riveting thriller that's also deeply human, with characters who are as authentic as they are compelling."

—Lou Berney, Edgar Award–winning author of
The Long and Faraway Gone

"*Black Swan Rising* is more than just a thrilling read—it's also an unflinching examination of the corrosive effects of racism and misogyny on American culture."

—Chris Holm, Anthony Award–winning
author of *The Killing Kind*

"A raw and masterful mystery thriller that explores the real darkness of the human soul."

—Jonathan Maberry, *New York Times*
bestselling author of *Glimpse*

"Lisa Brackmann tells not just the harrowing story of two women impacted by a mass shooting, but the story of America's deadly love affair with guns."

—Bryn Greenwood, *New York Times* bestselling author of
All the Ugly and Wonderful Things

"*Black Swan Rising* cuts deep in a way that is all too distressingly believable." —Steph Cha, author of *Dead Soon Enough*

Rock, Paper, Tiger

"Fast paced and strikingly atmospheric."

—*Publishers Weekly* (starred review)

"Lisa Brackmann's novel gets off to a fast start and never lets up … Be prepared for a wild ride." —*New York Times*

"Timely and hip." —*Boston Globe*

"Lisa Brackmann's debut novel is as slick and smart as an alley cat."

—*Time Out: Beijing*

"A gripping ex-pat nightmare that unfolds with superb pacing."

—*Miami Herald*

"A gritty and intriguing tale of terror that draws in the reader with each page." —*Library Journal*

Getaway

"Brackmann strikes exactly the right mood in this frantic look at an ordinary woman who can't seem to claw her way out of the mess in which she's managed to land." —*Kirkus Reviews*

"A sinister tale of a vacation gone bad … Puerto Vallarta provides a lush backdrop for Brackmann's richly drawn ex-pat world, which is as eccentric as it is dangerous." —*Publishers Weekly*

"*Getaway* draws you in with the immediate force of its sensuous atmosphere, its living and breathing characters, its riveting plot— and most of all, with its sheer believability."

—Lene Kaaberbøl and Agnete Friis, *New York Times* bestselling authors

Go-Between

"The edgy plot never lets up, touching on the war on drugs, for-profit prisons, and nefarious nonprofits."

—*Publishers Weekly*

"While today's female-centric crime fiction has been swarmed with the kind of domestic noir made popular by *Gone Girl*, Lisa Brackmann continues to go her own way."

—*Los Angeles Review of Books*

"Nothing is as it seems in this terrific noir tale that channels Richard Stark's stories."

—Carole E. Barrowman for the *Minneapolis Star Tribune*

"A kick-a** thriller that's nearly impossible to put down."

—*Arizona Daily Sun*

"Brackmann takes the noir formula—things start out badly for a hapless hero and keep getting worse—and gives it a feminist reboot… A fun, smart, and fascinating trip."

—*Reviewing the Evidence*

Black Swan
Rising

LISA BRACKMANN

Black Swan
Rising

black swan \blak swän\ *n* A highly unlikely event that has
massive impact, and which seems predictable in hindsight.

MIDNIGHT INK
WOODBURY, MINNESOTA

FIRST EDITION
First Printing, 2018

Book format by Steff Pitzen
Cover design by Shira Atakpu
Editing by Nicole Nugent

Midnight Ink, an imprint of Llewellyn Worldwide Ltd.

This is a work of fiction. Names, characters, places, and incidents are either the product of the author's imagination or are used fictitiously, and any resemblance to actual persons, living or dead, business establishments, events, or locales is entirely coincidental.

Library of Congress Cataloging-in-Publication Data
Names: Brackmann, Lisa, author.
Title: Black swan rising / by Lisa Brackmann.
Description: First edition. | Woodbury, Minnesota : Midnight Ink, [2018]
Identifiers: LCCN 2018014114 (print) | LCCN 2018015422 (ebook) | ISBN 9780738759920 () | ISBN 9780738759470
Subjects: | GSAFD: Suspense fiction.
Classification: LCC PS3602.R333 (ebook) | LCC PS3602.R333 B58 2018 (print) | DDC 813/.6—dc23
LC record available at https://lccn.loc.gov/2018014114

Midnight Ink
Llewellyn Worldwide Ltd.
2143 Wooddale Drive
Woodbury, MN 55125-2989
www.midnightinkbooks.com

Printed in the United States of America

To my friends Christy Gerhart, Ebbins Harris, and Pilar Perez.
You've done so much to enrich my life.

THEY'D FOUND HER NEW email address.

YOU FAT SLUTTY CUNT WHY DON'T YOU GO SUCK A TWO-
INCH COCK

She stared at her laptop screen and shivered. The headquarters' air conditioning ran so high it was like being inside a refrigerator half the time. She'd complained to Natalie, the closest thing they had to an office manager, saying, "You know, given Matt's environmental focus, this isn't setting the best example," but Natalie had rolled her eyes fractionally and told her that she'd gone to the building manager and he'd promised to adjust the thermostat, but if they turned it up too much, then the tenants on the floor above them complained it got too hot.

The conversation replayed in her head, like a lot of conversations did.

You fat slutty...

All at once the noise of the office—the phones, the ringtones from everyone's cells, the conversations ranging from muttered to shouted, the TVs droning in the background, the clatter of heavy fingers on keyboards—seemed to recede, like she'd entered a tunnel and was leaving them all behind.

"Sarah, how are we doing on the CaliBaja page?"

She looked up. Ben stood there, wearing a carefully faded microbrewery T-shirt, his sandy hair curling at the collar.

"I … It's … I'll have it done by end of day."

"Cutting it close." He rested his palms on her desk and leaned in. Staring openly at her computer screen.

It's not there, she told herself. It's on your phone. He can't see it.

"The language is okay," he said. "It's maybe a little dry. The images … these are too stock. Too bland. We want something a little edgy but that isn't going to scare people."

He wasn't that much older than she was, but she felt like he was a lot of the time, like the line between your early twenties and late twenties was a huge divide. Or maybe he just knew how to *be* so much better than she did. Like being the communications director was no big thing, it was just something he deserved.

"Okay," she said. "I'll work on that."

"Make sure you emphasize job creation and economic impact on *this* side of the border, okay? Because that's what the people want to hear about."

She smiled and nodded, smiled a little too hard and nodded a little too much. "Right. For sure." Her cheeks twitched as he walked away.

She realized she was breathing hard. Her back and shoulders ached.

This chair is uncomfortable, she thought, and it's too cold in here. She stood up, shoved the chair back under the desk. Grabbed her phone and tucked it in her pants pocket, which was so shallow that half of the phone stuck out of it. But she was wearing business attire, not jeans and a brewery T-shirt. No one would take her seriously if she dressed like Ben, even on Beer Friday.

She walked out of the small maze of cubicles, past the ranks of long beige folding tables where a few volunteers sat phone-banking, past Natalie at the receptionist's desk directing calls beneath the campaign banner, down the beige hall to the building's lobby, and out the door, into the blinding sun.

Too hot.

The heat waves in San Diego almost always used to happen in September and October, people told her, but the weather had changed the last few years. Sometimes there were heat waves in March. May and June used to be gray most mornings into the early afternoons, but here it was, the beginning of May, and the temperature was in the low 90s and dry, with winds from the east and some stretched-out clouds too high up to bring any moisture.

She took off her jacket, a black blazer that matched her slacks, folded it, and sat down on the retaining wall that ran in front of the parking lot.

No one here knew who she used to be, she told herself.

The brewery across the street was rolling up its metal doors, opening for business. There were three or four breweries within walking distance of headquarters, in this neighborhood of long, flat featureless buildings, industrial parks, cheap office space. Plenty of options for staffers to grab a quick beer at lunch, or engage in more serious drinking sessions after work. "They're *tasting* sessions," Ben had said once, grinning, when she'd declined his invitation. She wasn't sure if he was serious or not, but she did know that beer was a major business here in San Diego—"the craft brewing capital of the United States; fuck Portland, they can't compete"—and it seemed to be okay, even encouraged, to go taste the IPAs, stouts, saisons, dubbels, and sours.

Not that she did.

She caught a whiff of chili oil from the dumpling restaurant in the next complex. That was another thing you could find in the area, Asian food. Chinese dumplings, Japanese ramen, Korean barbecue. There were two large Korean supermarkets not far from here, a Ranch 99 market too, Asian strip malls that had sprouted among the car dealerships and fast food chains and gentlemen's clubs, big box stores, parked semis, and medical buildings. All of these Asian businesses moving slowly west, pho place by Taiwanese bakery.

You hardly ever saw people walking around here though. The landscape was oversized and empty, a neighborhood built for absentee giants.

"This a cigarette break?"

She started. Turned. She thought she knew the voice, but it had never spoken to her directly.

Her boss. Representative Matthew Cason.

He stood there, suit jacket slung over one shoulder, blocking out the sun.

"I ... no," she stuttered. "I don't smoke."

"Shit. Oh well. Probably a good thing."

He was taller than average—always good for a politician—thick, dark hair shot with just a touch of gray, a square jaw with a beard that came in heavy and a nose just crooked enough to make his face interesting. She'd known that from seeing him on TV, at events, and, more recently, from a couple of his quick sweeps through the bull pen on the way to the campaign manager's office.

He sat down on the wall next to her. "I quit years ago. But I swear, if you'd had one just now? I'd be smoking it."

It was strange when someone you'd mostly seen on TV and at a distance suddenly sat less than a foot away, becoming three-dimensional. The reality of the person, his body, how he held himself—it wasn't the same on a screen. She was conscious of all kinds of things: the patches of sweat under the arms of his blue Oxford button-down, how trim his waist and belly were, that his eyes were on the green side of hazel and were staring at her.

"Today's been a clusterfuck," he said.

"I'm sorry to hear that." It seemed like the safest thing to say. Or did he want her to ask why?

Why do you care what he wants?

He's your boss, she told herself. Of course you care. You wanted to work for him. He's sitting right next to you.

Close enough to smell his sweat.

Her heart was pounding.

"What happened?" she asked.

He rolled his eyes. "Flight from DC was late. Missed a fundraiser. Almost missed another one. You're in Communications, right?"

"I...yes," she said, nodding.

"I don't remember your name."

You wouldn't know it, she wanted to say. "Sarah. Sarah Price."

"Right," he said. "Sarah Price." He was still staring at her. She thought he was going to do something, like shake her hand, but his hands stayed where they were, at his sides, grasping the edge of the concrete wall.

He kicked out his legs and sprung to his feet. Now he stuck out his hand. She took it. Warm, dry, slightly callused. He held on a moment.

"Great meeting you," he said, letting go. "I'm looking forward to your thoughts on the CaliBaja mega-region."

He might have smirked as he said it, but he was gone before she could be sure.

Of course he had that kind of charisma. Of course. It was how he got away with some of the stands he took, the things he said. She'd been hearing about his charisma since she'd started following his career during his first term in Congress.

It was just different, seeing it up close, aimed at her.

She hadn't gone to work for him just because of that. It was his policy positions, that he said smart things, and he didn't seem to measure every word by its potential to hurt or help; he just said what he thought.

And he was a vet in a military town.

You want to get into Washington, you pick your player. Matt Cason was a good bet.

But his first reelection campaign was going to be a bitch.

————

"I'm not going to make a speech. You've heard too many of them from me already, and we have a long way to go on this shitshow. And believe me when I tell you that it's going to be a shitshow."

The congressman—Matt, everyone called him Matt, even if they sounded self-conscious when they said it—sat in the middle of one of the long tables in the bull pen, hands on either side of his thighs, fingers curled over the hard rubber edge.

Same pose as when he was sitting next to her outside.

"We don't know for sure who we're going to be running against, but the amount of money our opponent is gonna spend on this race? We might break the record for a congressional campaign. Maybe four million by him, and that's not even counting outside money. All of which

I'm sure will be spent on positive ads talking about issues and laying out a constructive agenda to move the district and this country forward."

A wave of chuckles rippled through the room. Most of the senior staff were there, regardless of whether they were paid by the campaign, by the state party, or were outside consultants: Jane and Presley and Angus (The Troika, Ben called them), Tomás the field director, John the tracker, Natalie, who handled all the office stuff and answered the phones. There were a few junior staffers she recognized, Sylvia the constituency coordinator for one, and a couple of volunteers she didn't know.

She was still trying to figure out how everything worked.

"Yeah," Matt said. "Whoever ends up getting the nod, they're going to go negative. And they'll get the outside funding to bury us in this … negativity. So, what are we going to do about it?"

"Raise more money!" somebody called out. Laughter.

Matt gave a little fist pump. "Always." Then he shrugged. "You know what, fuck 'em. We don't put up with their shit, and we will hit them back hard. But we run our own campaign. We focus on our own game plan."

The stare. It was weird to watch. All this intensity, focused on someone, or something, but you didn't know what he was really looking at. What he was seeing.

"We are going to talk about real problems and concrete solutions, and we are going to articulate a vision. We explain things clearly without talking down to people. We talk about our goals, why we have those goals, and how we're going to get there. And we'll aim for the minimum ration of bullshit. Though I'm not making any promises on that one."

The obligatory chuckles.

He hopped down off the desk, the same choreography as outside.

"Right now? It's Beer Friday, and I'm in the mood for a beer. Who's in?"

———————

"You're coming, right?"

"I'm working on CaliBaja."

"I thought you were going to be done with that by now." Ben hovered by her desk, clasping his hands.

"I'm close."

He huffed out a sigh. "Matt wants to get to know everybody better, and you need to be there. He asked about you today."

She felt a little rush of adrenaline. That's good, she told herself. It's what you want, right? To get noticed?

"Okay," she said. "I just need a few minutes."

Ben leaned over her desk. "Look, I know you want to do issues. Just don't try to reinvent the wheel. If it's any kind of policy that could be considered a part of his public role, then the congressional staffers do the heavy lifting. If it's posted to his official website, you can use it. If he's in total synch with the state party or the DCCC on something, you can pull from them too. Most of what we're doing here? It's about crafting a message specifically for the campaign. Something that's going to pop, get people excited. It's about creating a consistent style and voice across all our social platforms."

"Right," she said.

He straightened up. "Just wrap it up and come over, okay? We can publish the page tomorrow."

"I will," she said. "I'll be there in fifteen minutes."

Probably more like a half hour, but Ben didn't need to know that.

There was a poster of a baseball player tacked to the wall across from her cube. A good-looking black guy with hazel eyes, wearing a desert-themed camo jersey and a cap with the SD logo on it, smiling and holding two puppies. She ended up staring at the poster a lot, when she wasn't sure what to write.

Maybe I should go to a baseball game, she thought. A lot of people working here did. She'd heard it was fun. And Matt was a big fan.

Just save the report, print out a copy, and go to the brewery, she told herself.

The phone rang.

She jumped a bit. It was the ringtone for her area, for Communications, a series of low trills.

Maybe Ben, wondering where she was. Except … he'd call her on her cell.

The person who emailed her, maybe he'd found her.

She felt like she'd been slapped. Her gut twisted, and she was sweating in the cold, stale air.

Why don't you go suck …

No, she told herself, no, don't be stupid. It's not him. They don't know who you are now. Just pick up the phone.

"Cason for Congress. This is Communications."

"Oh, good. I guess I dialed correctly." A man's voice, relaxed, maybe a hint of a drawl. Not young, not old. "Who am I speaking to?"

"Sarah."

"Sarah," he repeated. "Is your boss around?"

"No, I'm sorry, he's not. Can I take a message?"

"Hmmm." A pause. "That's all right. I can talk to you."

Oh, fuck, she thought. Not someone who wanted to talk. She'd gotten a few of these calls from people who wanted to talk, about things like HAARP and vaccines and Islamic terrorists crossing over the border from Mexico.

But she had to hear what he wanted to say before she could figure out how best to get him off the line in a hurry.

"How can I help you?" she said.

"This is more about me helping *you*. I know some things about your opponents that you might find interesting."

"Oh."

Oppo research was under Presley, who had a voicemail box here but only came into the headquarters for meetings. He was a consultant, Ben had told her, based in Los Angeles.

"I'm not really the right person for you to talk to," she said. "I can transfer you—"

"That's okay. Tell you what. Why don't you check the *LA Times* tomorrow? There's going to be a story in it you'll like."

"Okay," she said. "I'll be sure to do that."

He laughed, one solid chuckle. "Good. I'll give you a call tomorrow, after you've had a chance to read it. I'll be interested to hear your thoughts."

I can transfer you to a better person, she wanted to say, but he hung up before she could get the words out of her mouth.

Oh well, she thought. Odds were he wouldn't call back. He was probably just another crank who got off on punking people. He didn't sound like one of those, but then yesterday she'd fielded a call from a guy who'd sounded totally sane until he told her that California's drought was caused by geoengineering.

"Why would anyone want to do that?" she'd asked.

"Because they want us all to starve! It's all part of Agenda 21, don't you get it?"

"Right," she'd said.

God, people were crazy.

2

"Where've you been?"

Sarah slipped onto the open space at the end of the bench next to Ben. "Finishing the report."

Giant fans blew hot air through the little brewery, one of many that occupied industrial parks like this one, behind roll-up steel doors. They'd left the ceilings open, silver ductwork and electrical lines running from one end to the other. Large metal tanks and plastic barrels and kegs lurked behind the bar and taps.

"You need a beer," Ben said. There was a small goblet-style glass in front of him. The beer that was left in it was a deep, thick caramel, like maple syrup. "Belgium quad. It's really good. You want to try it?"

"I ... that's okay. I'll just get something light."

"They do great Belgiums here. Good sours too. And the IPAs are awesome, but this is San Diego, you have to do a good IPA."

He was talking a little fast, a little loud, three fingers of one hand tapping out an arpeggio on the base of his glass. Probably not his first beer, Sarah thought.

She didn't drink much when she went out. Of course, she didn't go out much anymore either. Sometimes she'd buy a bottle of wine and take it home and open it up in front of the TV. Drink more of it than maybe she should. She drank a whole bottle the first night she slept in her new apartment. But she was safe at home, at least.

"Maybe the saison—good fruit, nice spice, not too strong—"

"Why don't you share mine?"

It took her a moment to recognize him. The congressman—Matt—stood there, holding a long paddle-like board with small glasses stuck in a line of holes. He was wearing a T-shirt and shorts, which was so out of context that she hadn't been able to place him at first.

He didn't have to ask. Ben slid over to make room for him. She hesitated for a moment, then shifted to the outside of the bench. Better to have Matt in the middle. It would make Ben happy. She wasn't sure she wanted to sit between the two of them anyway. Matt and Ben would either talk over her or she'd be the focus of too much attention.

As soon as he sat, Matt turned to her. "I just got here too. I really needed to change."

He was wearing a faded T-shirt, like Ben. But not advertising a brewery. It was for the Padres, the baseball team, and it looked like a cheap shirt that had gotten a lot of wear.

"How goes the CaliBaja mega-region?"

No doubt this time, he was smirking.

Or maybe it was just a smile. Like it was their own private joke.

"I'm working on it," she said. "Trying to get it to pop."

Was that a strange thing to say? Did he get that she was joking back?

12

"I'm sure it will," he said.

She still couldn't tell.

Matt lifted up the first glass in his rack. "So this is supposed to be their flagship IPA. I've had it before. Have you tried it?"

She shook her head.

"Here." He held out the glass.

Don't. You never take a drink, ever, from a stranger.

Or even from a friend.

He was staring at her, smiling, all that intensity aimed at her, and if she hesitated a moment longer, it was going to look strange, awkward. He might ask questions.

The beer was fine, she told herself.

"Thanks," she said, smiling back.

She took a sip. An explosion of citrus and pine supported by a bitter bite.

"What do you think?" Matt asked.

"It's good," she said. "I mean, I like it."

"It *is* good. They won an award for it."

"Mosaic and Simcoe hops," Ben blurted.

Matt smiled at him. "So how many breweries do you think you've hit in San Diego?"

"I think it's eighty-three."

Ben's turn. Good. She'd have a little time to think about what she wanted to say to him. To Matt. It was always best to ask a question. Take the attention off yourself. People were usually flattered when you asked them questions.

Something about his legislative priorities for the next term, maybe?

Maybe he really was interested in promoting cross-border economic development. That one was tricky. If you weren't careful how you said it, people thought you were shipping their jobs to Mexico. Which sometimes you were.

"San Diego is majority minority, just like every other big city in California," Ben had told her. "But there's a strong nativist sentiment here. There's people who hate living on the border. All they care about is building higher walls. They'll tell you it's to keep the illegals and the drugs out." He'd laughed at that.

"Which is your favorite so far?" Matt asked.

Sarah turned her head. "What?"

"The beers. Which one do you like best?"

She still clutched the first glass he'd given her, nearly finishing it without thinking. "I'm sorry," she said. "I just drank this one."

For the first time, something in his eyes looked different. Like he'd turned off the high-beams for once. Maybe he actually *saw* her.

"Don't feel bad. It's a great beer. Let me get you another one."

It's okay, she told herself. It's just a beer.

She watched Matt wind his way through the barrel tables, someone in a Padres cap stopping him on the way, a huge smile on his face as he recognized Matt. The two clasped hands.

She couldn't see Matt's face, but she knew the lights were back to bright.

"So what do you think?"

She looked at Ben. He was just raising his glass to his lips.

"About what?"

The campaign? The beer? The CaliBaja mega-region?

Ben swallowed hard. Wiped his index finger along his lips. "Matt. What do you think about him?" His voice sounded nervous around the edges.

Was this some kind of test?

"I think he's great. That's why I'm working for him."

"Yeah. Yeah, me too." Ben lifted up his goblet and took a slug of beer, sweat beading on his forehead. Swallowed. "He likes you," he said, his voice flat.

She shivered a little. Managed a smile. "I think he likes everybody."

But she didn't think that was what Ben had meant.

"Hey, looks like Lindsey's entered the building," Ben muttered.

Lindsey, the finance director. Matt's wife.

She stood just past the entrance of the brewery, backlit by the early evening sun. But her figure was unmistakable: a little taller than average, long-limbed, with an athletic build. She played some sport in college, but Sarah couldn't remember what. Soccer, maybe? She looked like someone who spent a lot of time running up and down a field, anyway. Her head swiveled from side to side, scanning the room.

Matt had finally made his way back to the table, two beers in hand. "Here you go," he said, handing one to Sarah.

Behind Matt's back, Lindsey approached their table. "Hey," she said, giving Matt's shoulder a squeeze.

He flinched, turned, and smiled. "Hey." They briefly hugged, with a quick kiss on the lips.

Was it real, the affection? Sarah couldn't tell.

"Lindsey, I know you've met Ben," Matt said. "This is Sarah. She's also in Communications."

"Nice to meet you, Sarah." Lindsey smiled and extended her hand. Sarah took it. A hard grip, for a woman. She held on a moment. Sarah took in her hair, its layers and highlights, carefully styled to look natural, her face, slightly long and angular like the rest of her, a light sheen of makeup covering skin that had spent a lot of time in the sun.

Lindsey let go of her hand.

"You want a beer, Linds?" Matt asked, starting to rise.

"I'll go get one," she said. "I need to check out the menu."

So fucking typical.

"This would be a good time to roll a few calls," she'd said.

He'd flopped on the couch with a wave of his hand. "Let's not. It's late."

"It's eight fifteen."

"It's late. I'm tired. And I've had a few beers."

"Just three calls. They want to talk to you."

"Look, I've raised my quota for today, okay?"

And Matt had turned away, picked up the remote, and put on the baseball game.

"God dammit."

Lindsey didn't think he heard her over the TV. *"Padres lead the Mets, bottom of the fourth, with an add-on run just waiting out there on third ... "*

The TV took up half the living room wall. Matt had wanted it. One of their compromises. Funny, she couldn't remember what she'd gotten out of the deal.

She didn't want a fight, not now. But there was some sick part of her that couldn't help it. She stepped around the side of the couch, where he'd see her.

He looked up and muted the TV.

"That girl. That intern."

"Oh come on, Linds." He sounded tired. "I just met her. I don't even know her."

"Don't fuck this up, Matt."

She'd seen the body that girl tried to hide, beneath her Gap blazer and white blouse.

NEIGHBOR2NEIGHBOR/CLAIREMONT/NEWS_FEED

George Morales, Bay Park Morena

> GUNSHOTS FIRED? 3 MIN. AGO?

George Morales, Bay Park Morena

> ANYBODY HEAR GUNSHOTS? LIKE A BUNCH MAYBE A
> DOZEN? I'M SOUTH CLOSE TO OLD MORENA.

Reilly James, Clairemont Village

> DUDE ITS FIRECRACKERS LOL

Kate Czerny, Bay Park Western Hills

> AGREE ITS GUNFIRE

George Morales, Bay Park Morena

> HEARING COPTERS AND SIRENS NOW

Jessica McDonald, Overlook Heights

> ME TOO, A BUNCH OF POLICE CARS JUST HEADED DOWN
> THE HILL.

Reilly James, Clairemont Village

> LONG AS THEIR NOT SHOOTING AT YOU ITS NOT SERIOUS

Sarah heard the helicopters first, then the sirens. They seemed to be coming from different directions, converging down the hill from her. She grabbed her iPhone and opened Twitter.

She'd started following San Diego–related accounts when she'd first become interested in Matt: his account, of course, then the accounts of other local politicians, news outlets, government agencies, tourist attractions like the San Diego Zoo. By the time she actually

17

moved here, she'd added restaurants and breweries, sports teams, local influencers. That last category was the hardest to compile, but she thought she'd done a pretty good job, and she added new names every day.

If something was going on down the hill, it would turn up in her feed.

Hop Head @HopHead
IM AT @CROOKEDARROWBEER SOMEONE IS ON A ROOF SHOOTING PEOPLE OUTSIDE

Brett Untamed @BrettUntamed
WE WERE GOING TO OUR CAR AND A GIRL GOT SHOT IN THE HEAD RIGHT IN FRONT OF US AND THIS GUY TRIED TO HELP AN HE GOT SHOT

Hop Head @HopHead
THERE'S 1 GIRL HURT PRETTY BAD IN HERE SHE GOT SHOT BY THE DOOR AND WE CARRY HER IN AND ARE APPLING PRESSURE 2 SLO BLEEDING PLS SEND HELP

News 9 San Diego @News9SanDiego
ACTIVE SHOOTER ON MORENA BLVD.; MULTIPLE FATALITIES REPORTED.

Now a hashtag—#MorenaShooter

A couple of photos by Hop Head and Brett Untamed: Barrels stacked against the double doors, bloody towels pressed against a woman's stomach, blood staining the pressing hands. Now a few photos from outside, flashing blue and red police lights, what looked like a body lying in the street. It was hard to make it out, in the dark.

Who would be crazy enough to take pictures with someone out there shooting?

She opened Campaigner, clicked on the New Post box, titled it "Morena Shooter." Wrote: THERE'S AN ACTIVE SHOOTING INCIDENT GOING ON NOT FAR FROM MY APARTMENT, DOWN ON MORENA BLVD, NEAR THE CROOKED ARROW BREWERY. SUPPOSEDLY THERE ARE SEVERAL FATALITIES. THE HASHTAG IS #MORENASHOOTER.

She copied the links of a few of the best tweets. Pasted them in the post. Hesitated a moment, her finger hovering over the Priority box.

Some people probably knew about it already. They must. But no one had posted about it yet.

Has to be Code Red, she thought. It's a mass shooting, in his own district.

She labeled it Red and hit Send.

It never hurt to be first either.

———

A video from @CaseyChengNews9:

"We're told the shooter is on the roof of a building behind me." The reporter—a slight, pretty Asian woman with long, glossy hair—seemed very calm, her face pixilating and then coming back into focus. *"The police have instructed us to take cover, and my photographer and I are crouched behind a car right now. You can hear gunfire in the background. We've had reports of multiple fatalities but have not been able to confirm—"*

A sharp metallic spat. The reporter flinched. *"That was close."*

A male voice in the background. *"We'd better move."* The video panned to the cameraman briefly, a big Latino guy, then back to the reporter. She was the one taking this video, Sarah realized, holding the phone or the camera or whatever she was using in her hand, her arm stretched out enough to show the street behind her, beams of red and blue light sweeping over it.

"*All right,*" the reporter said. "*We'll keep you posted with the very latest on News 9 at eleven.*"

―――――――

Sarah sipped a glass of the beer she'd brought home in a small growler from the brewery. Ben had bought it for her, "Since you didn't get to try the saison." It tasted pretty good, but she liked the IPA Matt had given her better. She flipped through the local channels on her TV. Two of them were doing live coverage of the shootings. The others were late to the show.

"*The suspect has taken position on that roof, and the police have asked us to stay back, they say he is armed with a high-powered rifle, and unfortunately that's making it very difficult for paramedics to reach the injured―*"

While she watched, she checked Campaigner. There were several replies to her post now: THIS IS HORRIFIC. PRAYING FOR THE VICTIMS.

And then Angus: ASSUME MATT WILL BE MAKING A STATEMENT.

Presley: YES BUT SUGGEST WE WAIT UNTIL THERE'S A RESOLUTION.

Jane: AGREE.

She checked the Seen button. Most of the staff had checked in, with two notable exceptions: Matt and Lindsey.

There was a stream of new tweets with the #MorenaShooter hashtag.

One of them, from *@Haraguro93*, caught her attention. MY POV, it said. GOOD NIGHT FOR HUNTING CHADS AND STACYS.

Below that, a nighttime photo, it looked like. A photo of a rifle, looking down the barrel to a street below.

HAHAH, DREAM ON BETA FAGGOT, someone replied.

HOPE YOU GET A HIGH SCORE, wrote another.

Total shitpost your stupidity gives me asspain

Reeeeeeeee

Go cry about it on /r9k/ faggot

> **Haraguro93** @Haraguro93
> Hahaha fuck off normie cucks wish I could kill more of you #MorenaShooter

> **PacManButt** @PacManButt
> Don't joke about this shit the libcucks already trying to disarm us don't give them more ammo

> **Haraguro93** @Haraguro93
> Not joking asshole just watch time 2 rise & shine

She nearly dropped her phone when the trumpet fanfare that announced a Campaigner alert went off, and a black banner dropped over her screen.

Thanks Sarah for being on top of this. Matt.

She felt a brief flush of gratification that she'd done a good job, that it had been recognized. That she'd been seen, by Matt. The thought of what was happening on her Twitter feed quickly pulled her out of that mood, but she couldn't tell what she was feeling now, whether it was anticipation or dread.

What if Haraguro93 was for real?

He's probably full of shit, she thought.

She clicked out of Campaigner and went back to Twitter.

There was a new tweet from Haraguro93. A video. #MorenaShooter.

Her heart thudded hard. She almost didn't want to press play. What if …?

But of course she did.

That same shot of the rifle again. Except now, you could hear things. Some kind of loud, pulsing motor—a helicopter? Indistinct shouting. And there were lights. Blue and red lights that swept over the scene, almost lazily.

The shot panned around to a face.

"Hey, robots."

Young. Thin. Pale. The changing colors lighting up his features and then receding, leaving them shadowed.

"This is the best thing I ever did," he said. *"I just wish I'd gotten closer, so I could've seen their faces."*

The video ended. Sarah realized she'd been holding her breath.

FUCKER, LINDSEY THOUGHT, AS her foot hit the pavement. Asshole.

Don't land so hard on your heels. You're being sloppy.

She made herself slow down. Let her strides even out. Started to feel like her feet were pushing off from the ground rather than pounding against it.

Better.

He was still an asshole.

"Why do you have to pick a fight?" he'd said.

"You think I'm picking a fight? Is that what you think?"

"I don't know what else you'd call it."

"How about advice?"

"Advice? Give me a fucking break."

"You're running for office."

"I am so sick of this shit."

And he'd slammed out of the room. Driven off someplace, she didn't know where.

So she'd put on shorts and a T-shirt and her running shoes and set off through the neighborhood, and after a rough start was finally hitting her stride.

When the Campaigner alert went off, she didn't stop right away. She'd just started to feel good. Everything was flowing. And it probably wasn't important.

Besides, if Matt didn't care, why should she?

But as she ran, she kept hearing the alert in her head, the trumpet fanfare playing over and over.

"Shit."

She'd half stumbled on something—a slab of pavement pushed up by a tree root. A ficus. Why did people plant those things? she thought. Didn't they know better?

Her steps slowed without her thinking about it. She halted and stood for a moment, slightly bent, hands on her thighs, drawing in deep breaths until she felt replenished.

Then she unstrapped her phone from her arm and tapped on the app.

Christ. Of course it was an alert from that girl.

THANKS SARAH FOR BEING ON TOP OF THIS, Matt had written.

Asshole.

But as she skimmed the and tweets, it was clear that Sarah had been right to send the alert. Matt would need to respond.

You can't be mad at her for doing the right thing, Lindsey told herself.

She hesitated, then hit Recommend for Sarah's post.

DITTO, she wrote under Matt's reply.

HOLY FUCK HE REALLY DID IT #MORENASHOOTER

BETA UPRISING! #MORENASHOOTER

She'd drunk most of the beer in the little growler without realizing it while watching the Twitter feed, Campaigner, and the local news.

Haraguro93 was the Morena shooter, he had to be. You couldn't fake that video. Or you could, but not that quickly, not while it was going on.

"We are receiving reports that the shooter has been neutralized."

Neutralized. That probably meant killed.

"Police have confirmed that the shooter is among the dead tonight, in the worst mass killing in San Diego since the San Ysidro McDonald's massacre in 1984 ... "

Five dead, not including the gunman. Seven wounded, some with life-threatening injuries.

Matt sat on the couch, staring at the TV. The two anchors looked stunned, one of them tapping a stack of papers against the desk, straightening the edges for no apparent reason.

"Among the injured is News 9's own Casey Cheng. We're waiting for word on her condition."

Was he listening to the conference call at all?

He'd come back as soon as he'd gotten the alert, he'd told her. He hadn't gone far. "Just went to Rubio's for some tacos."

Which probably meant he'd gone to the Night Owl for a beer.

"We cannot politicize this," Presley was saying.

"Nobody's suggesting that." Angus. He'd been pushing for a statement ever since the thing had started. A levelheaded guy for the most part, but young, Lindsey thought. Every once in a while he'd get a bug up his ass about something and dig in his heels. Something he wanted Matt to do or say that wasn't practical. Like he believed the hype.

"We can't bring up gun control," Presley said.

"Why not? Your own polling shows a shift in public opinion."

"It's too soon."

"It's always too soon," Angus snapped back.

The way Angus sounded, Lindsey was starting to wonder if this was something personal for him.

Well, he was black. African-Americans tended to support stricter gun control, at least according to the last polls she'd seen.

"Anyway, I wasn't suggesting we bring it up directly. We can make a statement about working together to find ways to prevent tragedies in the future. Is that vague enough for you?"

"That'll work," Presley said. His usual, cheerfully neutral self. "Just remember, right now this is coming from Matt Cason the congressman, not Matt Cason the candidate. We reference the statement coming from the congressional office, we don't release one of our own."

"Agreed." This was Jane. Lindsey could picture her nodding slowly, not so much in agreement as it was to signal that a decision had been made.

"Are we all on the same page?" Jane asked. "Matt?"

"Yeah," he said, his eyes never leaving the TV screen. "Agreed."

"Good. Make sure somebody pings Ben as soon as we get the press release. We should put this out on Social right away."

———

REP. CASON STATEMENT ON MASS
SHOOTING IN SAN DIEGO

Tonight an unspeakable tragedy has struck our city. My thoughts and prayers are with the victims and their families. I want to extend my deepest gratitude to the first responders who risked their lives to come to the aid of the victims and protect our community. Make no mistake, this was an attack on our community, on our sense of safety, on the enjoyment we take in assembling and participating in the life of our city. As we learn more about the circumstances surrounding this dreadful, criminal attack, I plan to work together with my colleagues in Congress and members of our communities to find ways to prevent tragedies like this. America has seen far too many of them.

———

The office was buzzing when Sarah arrived.

"Jesus, I go there all the time."

Ben seemed genuinely shaken. He was wearing a Crooked Arrow T-shirt. "I don't know, just to show my support," he muttered. "They're an awesome brewery. Their Imperial Stout medaled in the Great American Beer Cup."

"Oh," Sarah said. "It's really sad," she added.

"Fucking MRA gun nut."

"Is that who he was?" Sarah asked. The coverage she'd seen this morning didn't have much background. Just a name: Alan Jay Chastain. Age twenty-three. Resident of Clairemont.

"Sure looks like it from his tweets. All that shit about Chads and Stacys? Libcucks? Beta uprising?" Ben rolled his eyes.

She knew what Chads and Stacys meant; she'd spent some time on the Urban Dictionary and Know Your Meme last night checking definitions. As far as she'd been able to determine, they were the equivalent of a jock and a cheerleader: the beautiful golden couple who were having more and better sex than you. MRA she'd already known. Men's Rights Activists with websites that told men how to get a woman to let them do what they wanted to her.

She knew about them.

"Normies?" she asked.

"Yeah, I'm sure there's some mental health issues, but I'm tired of people acting like being on the spectrum and not getting laid is some kind of an excuse to be a homicidal asshole."

His back was turned to her as he said this.

"So … how am I supposed to handle this on Social? I mean, what should I say about Matt's response?"

"Let's look for content in Matt's record about crime and violence, and we can totally tweet out quotes from the press release. Just be careful about anything having to do with gun control directly. They're a little nervous about that."

They. The Troika? Matt? Lindsey?

She decided not to ask.

You couldn't get inside if you acted too eager.

Still, it bothered her a little, not being included. She was the one who'd alerted everyone about the Morena shooter. She'd known it was important.

She could be doing so much more on this campaign.

"Also, we need to talk about how we're going to handle the Hauser thing."

"Hauser? You mean, Phillip Hauser?" The front-runner opposing Matt.

Ben turned to face her. "Yeah."

"What happened?"

He suddenly, unexpectedly grinned. "You didn't hear?"

She shook her head.

He was almost laughing now. "Oh, man. It's too good for me to try to tell you. Just go check out today's *LA Times.*"

Sarah booted up her laptop and logged on to the office network. It didn't take her long to find the story. It was right there, under California Politics on the left-hand side of the site's front page.

SAN DIEGO BUSINESSMAN TARGET OF DEPARTMENT OF JUSTICE PROBE

Indictments expected in bribery, money-laundering case involving Phillip Hauser, current Republican front-runner in hotly contested race to unseat incumbent Congressman Matt Cason (D).

Sarah stared at the screen.

"Pretty good, right?"

There was Ben, hovering over her in that way she wished he wouldn't.

"This looks serious," she said.

"Yep." He was still grinning. Sarah realized she was smiling too.

"You think he'll drop out?" she asked.

"I don't see how he can't. Even if he's not guilty … defending against something like this? The big money's gonna run from him like cockroaches in daylight."

"So you think it'll be Tegan?"

"Has to be. She's got an enthusiastic fan base and people willing to write checks."

"It's better for us, right? For Matt to be facing her instead of Hauser?"

"I think so. Tegan's too extreme for this district. Plus, she's a lightweight." He snickered. "Have you seen her? She looks like an aging cheerleader. I can't believe anyone takes her seriously. Best case scenario, we get a majority of independents, peel off some moderate Republicans or hope they're so disgusted by Tegan that they just stay home."

"And … we turn out our base." It was the thing you always had to say, she'd read. Because it was true every election, and you never knew if it would actually happen, especially for a midterm election like this one.

"Yeah. We don't do that, we're fucked. Because the people who like Tegan? They're motivated."

"So what *do* we say on Social?"

The phone rang, a series of low trills: the ringtone for Communications.

It was probably for Ben; it usually was, unless it was a random caller who somehow had gotten directed their way. But Sarah had a feeling that Ben liked it when she picked up. Like he had someone answering the phones for him.

"You want me to get it?"

Ben glanced at the Caller ID screen. No name, no number. "Sure, thanks."

She picked up. "Cason for Congress, this is Communications."

"Sarah. How are you doing this morning?"

A man's voice. Not young, not old.

She responded automatically. Politely. "Fine, thank you."

"You have a chance to look at the *LA Times* yet?"

The man who'd called yesterday. The one she'd figured was either crazy or punking her.

Check the LA Times tomorrow. There's going to be a story in it you'll like.

There were all kinds of ways he could have known about it. He could have been a source for the story. He might even work for the paper.

"Yes," she said. "Yes, I read it."

"What'd you think?"

"It was ... very interesting."

A chuckle. "That's one way of putting it. Your guy would've had a tough time against Hauser. The path's a little easier for you now, don't you think?"

"I couldn't really say. It's not my area."

"You're careful. That's smart."

Ben mimed a phone at his ear and pointed to himself. A question: *Should I take it?*

She shook her head and waved him off. The man had called for her, hadn't he? She'd find out who he was, what he wanted. Then she'd have a better idea of what to do with him.

"Just doing my job, Mister ... I'm sorry, what was your name?"

A pause. "Mr. Gray will do. Wyatt, if you want to skip the Mister. Whatever makes you comfortable."

Not his real name? That seemed to be what he hinted at.

"Mr. Gray. Would you mind telling me ... how did you know about that story?"

"I'm not really comfortable discussing that."

"Okay." She thought for a moment. If she couldn't find out *who* he was … "How about … why? Why did you call?"

He laughed. "I like your candidate. I want to see him do well."

"Oh. Well. We're grateful for your support."

Silence. She filled it. "Look, it's been nice talking to you, but I … I'd better get back to work."

"Sure thing, Sarah. I don't want to keep you from it."

"All right, then. I hope you have a great day."

"I'm planning on it."

Just as she was about to hang up, he said, "You know, I have access to a lot of information. Information that can help your guy. Would you be interested in a tip now and then?"

"Of course," she said, without thinking. And then thought maybe that wasn't the smart thing to say. She had no idea who he was. It could be some kind of trick. Some kind of ratfucking from the opposition. She'd read about things like that.

"But … I'm really not the best person for you to talk to. I do social media, mostly. I can put you through to somebody else, somebody who handles this kind of thing."

A pause.

"You know, I don't think I want to talk to anybody else. I think I'd rather talk to you. You're a good listener." She heard him exhale, like he'd suddenly moved closer to the receiver. "I can help you, Sarah. If I give you information, that makes you valuable. You'd like that, wouldn't you? Being valuable?"

Her heart was thudding hard in her chest. Of course she would. But she knew she shouldn't admit it.

"I'd like to help the campaign," she said.

"I promise you, you'll be helping the campaign a lot. But you'll need to keep this just between the two of us for now. Can I trust you to do that?"

She nodded before she realized that he couldn't see that. "I...yes. I guess that would be okay."

"Good. I'll give you a call in a couple of weeks, after the June primary. I should have something for you by then."

"That sounds great," she said. "Looking forward to it."

"Me too, Sarah. Me too. Just remember, this is between us. Okay?"

"Sure. Okay."

"Good. We'll talk soon."

After he hung up, she sat there, staring at the poster of the baseball player, not ready to look at her computer, not ready to do anything, her heart still pounding, her gut feeling like she was perched at the top of a roller coaster, just beginning the plunge. She wasn't sure how much of what she was feeling was excitement and how much was dread. Because depending on who this guy was, what he really wanted...

She might have found a way to get noticed. To be valuable, like he said.

Or she might have made a deal with someone who was out to sabotage the campaign.

And getting noticed...getting noticed meant being exposed.

If the campaign found out who she was, who she'd been...

She hadn't done anything wrong, but she knew that didn't matter. She'd be a controversy. An embarrassment. An unnecessary distraction. No campaign wanted those.

And if those assholes who'd ruined her old life found out about her new one...

They won't, she told herself. She was behind the scenes, where it was safe.

He calls, he offers information, you can check it out and then decide what to do.

She wasn't going to get in trouble for this. As long as she was careful.

4

THEATER SHOOTER HAD HISTORY
OF ERRATIC BEHAVIOR,
ANTI-GOVERNMENT SENTIMENTS

WICHITA, Kan. (AP)—"We may never know his exact motive," police chief says.

Not everyone was surprised when John Reynolds, 52, walked into a crowded theater lobby and opened fire, killing three women and one man.

"Not that I figured he'd do exactly what he did," says former neighbor Rory Murphy. "But that he'd do something, it doesn't shock me. He was an uncomfortable guy."

"'We may never know his exact motive'?" Ben laughed. He sat at the next desk over, reading the article on his iPad. "Jesus. Extremist literature at his house, a history of violence, especially towards women, and the theater he shoots up is running *See You Next Tuesday, The Musical*? Who are they fucking kidding?"

Sarah looked up. Ben stared at her, like he expected something. Maybe a response?

"Yeah. It's pretty laughable. It's not like anyone really cares."

"What?"

She must have mumbled it. She did that sometimes when she wanted to say something but was afraid to say it.

"Nothing," she said. "Just … it keeps happening, right? And everyone says the same thing, every time." She shrugged. She'd run out of words to say.

"Some people care," Ben said. He was still staring at her, his eyes big and liquid, like he was on the verge of tears.

What the fuck did he want, anyway?

"Hey, listen up." Angus had entered the bull pen. He clapped his hands. "Oppo's Tegan compilation video is ready. You could all watch on your own, but there's a few things everybody needs to be on the same page about."

"Everybody" meant Angus, Jane, Tomás the field director, Sylvia the constituent coordinator, John the tracker, and Ben and Sarah.

Two things about the invite list surprised Sarah. The first was that Jane was there. Ben might call Jane, Presley, and Angus The Troika, but so far Angus was the only one of the three that Sarah had ever really dealt with. Jane was remote, like some resident of Mount Olympus, even if her office was only on the other side of the bull pen. Now she sat at the side of the conference table, a thirty-something woman with black hair plaited in a single thick braid, her expression watchful, like she was always looking for mistakes.

The second thing that surprised Sarah was that she herself had been invited.

———————

"Of course I love our neighbors to the south. But there's a reason we have borders."

The last clip of the compilation showed Kimberly Tegan at an outdoor rally in some mountain boulder and desert scrub landscape—near the border, maybe?—in front of a backdrop of a couple American flags held outstretched by supporters. Bottle-blond with salon highlights, wearing tight jeans and a scoop-necked T-shirt with a faded American flag on the front.

"Borders help us to control what kind of country we have. Borders are about protecting American values and keeping us safe. So we need to protect our borders."

Maybe she did look a little like an ex-cheerleader, Sarah thought. She seemed young for her age, which was forty-seven. Not as attractive a candidate as Matt. A former realtor as opposed to a veteran.

But maybe not as bad as Ben seemed to think. She recited her lines with some authority, maybe even with some charisma. Said things that some people really wanted to hear.

Her husband owned a car dealership. He did well. Enough to help get her elected to a city council seat. For this run, she'd picked up some wealthy donors ready to contribute the max. More importantly, she had big money. PAC money. Dark money. The kind of money that could make you look better than you are, and make your opponent look worse.

"She'll run as a moderate," Angus said, easing his lanky body into a black vinyl conference room chair. "We need to prove her false, every chance we get."

The assistant campaign manager wore a pink button-down Oxford shirt, sleeves rolled up, since today the AC wasn't keeping the headquarters cool enough (layers, Sarah had learned). Angus was young, younger than Ben, but had been working campaigns since he was a teenager, "because I'm a big ole nerd," he'd once said. His hair was natural and slightly long, the old-school tortoiseshell glasses somewhere between professorial and hipster.

"We want to stay as positive as possible," Jane said. "There are PACs on our side that can go negative if that is their judgment. But we need to have answers for constituents who ask questions about Tegan. We tell them that of course Matt is committed to keeping our community safe. He's already literally fought for our country, and we tell them what else he's done and plans to do as congressman. But we will need to hit back at any negativity that's thrown our way. We will need to show that Tegan is too extreme for San Diego. We think she is particularly vulnerable among constituents with ties to immigrant communities, and we'll be looking carefully for evidence of that."

"We'll mine her city council record and every thought she's ever tweeted, but she can always say she's 'evolved,'" Angus said, with air quotes. "What we want is a fresh gotcha. Thus, Tracker John."

John lifted his hand in a mock wave.

"Our secret weapon," Angus added. "No one will suspect he's on our side."

Obligatory chuckles. John was a young guy in a pinstriped Oxford shirt, short hair, a little heavy, pale in the way that a white guy who worked indoors might be. His job was to follow the opposition candidate and record his or her every move. "He totally blends in," Ben told her once. "He has a collection of T-shirts. He'll bust them out depending on who he's tracking. He's got sports teams, bands, American flags, the Gadsden banner..."

Sarah wasn't sure if the DCCC or the state party paid his salary. Either way it meant the party and whatever PACs were on their side could use the material too.

"They want this seat, and they're willing to blow through the record for the most money ever spent on a congressional campaign to get it," Jane said. "We can't match it, but we can get close. We're counting on you guys in Social to create organic opportunities for buy-ins whenever you can."

Ben nodded quickly. "Will do."

How? Sarah wanted to ask. Kimberly Tegan spoke in code. In dog whistles.

Protect our values. Take our country back. Nothing she said in the video compilation was damning on its own, if you didn't want it to be.

5

THE BULLET HAD KNOCKED her to the ground. The burning came next, the excruciating pain, the wet, warm spread of blood on her back. "Casey," Diego had said, "we have to move. Can you get up? I'll help you."

She'd tried. She couldn't. One of her legs wouldn't work right. Diego had dropped his camera and hauled her to her feet. When that didn't work, he'd picked her up like she was a little kid. All the while she felt the drip drip drip, the warm blood, her blood, her life draining out of her.

The way she'd felt, that sense of her self dissolving...this was it, she'd thought, the end of her story, and she'd felt vaguely sad, too dizzy and faint to feel much of anything else.

Her parents would be so unhappy. So disappointed. No husband. No grandkids.

But she didn't die, which still surprised her. The bullet had cracked two ribs, nicked a kidney; there was some sciatic nerve damage that hurt like hell and made walking difficult (friends had brought her this awesomely tacky cane with a carved dragon's head they'd found on Convoy, and she was determined to use it), but three and a half weeks after the shooting, she was back in her own condo, definitely not dead.

"Can I get you anything?" Paul asked.

"Why don't we open that bottle of cabernet on the counter? The Rafanelli."

He looked concerned. "You sure?"

Casey felt a raw rush of irritation rise in her throat, threatening to come out as words. She swallowed it. "Yes, I'm sure. That's why I got the bottle out. That's why I haven't taken an oxy in four hours. Because I really would like to drink a nice glass of wine."

Well, *three* hours, but close enough.

Maybe not her best ever job of swallowing her irritation.

"Okay," Paul said, lifting his hands. "Okay."

Now he worries about me, she thought. Before The Event, she'd been pretty sure he was going to break up with her. They'd dated about five months, and in the last month, it had started to sour. *You don't take this relationship seriously*, he'd said. *It's clear you have other priorities.*

Meaning work. Okay for *him* to put work first, of course. His biotech company would cure cancer. Or make him pots of money, anyway.

Her work? It was trivial. He'd never said that, but she was pretty sure that was how he felt. She'd never asked, because she'd been afraid of what he might say.

There it was, the lovely *pop* of the cork, the *glug* of the wine poured into glasses. It scared her almost, how much she was looking forward to a sip. But without the oxy to blunt the throbbing in her

41

side, in her back, she needed something to stop her from screaming at him.

What's wrong with me? she thought. She'd been crazy about this guy, before. She'd cried when she thought he was going to break up with her. Taken a Lyft to a Gaslamp bar with a girlfriend and gotten good and drunk, moaning over him.

Now? She just wished he'd go home.

She was tired of Paul, his too-gentle kisses, the way he treated her like a wounded child, incapable of deciding or doing anything for herself. And the worst: How much he seemed to like her this way.

You're not being fair, she told herself. You're not thinking straight.

Paul came over from the open kitchen, two glasses in his hand. He placed one on the table next to Casey. She picked it up. It wasn't even half full. "Really, Paul?" she said.

"You don't want to overdo it."

Actually, she did. But he was probably right. He usually was. That was one of the things she'd found attractive about him at first, his quick certainty and competence.

Everybody always said they looked great together. He was trim and tan from running and tennis, and he always seemed ready to move—a body never at rest.

He sat down next to her on the couch and raised his glass. She lifted hers and felt a sharp twinge in her ribs.

"Are you okay?" he asked immediately.

"I'm fine," she said, gritting out a smile. She clinked her glass against his. She wanted that first sip of wine as much as she'd ever wanted anything.

It was every bit as good as she'd imagined, an explosion of ripe, black fruit and creamy oak.

"You don't think you're rushing things? Going into work?"

"I'm not going to *work*. Just into the station. To show everyone I'm okay."

Which she wasn't.

Nerve pain danced up and down her damaged leg like a ballet conducted by a Taser. The binding around her ribs that held her unruly organs in place itched around the edges.

She *wanted* to work. It was so frustrating. She'd been on her way up, on the cusp of breaking through to the next level. The bigger stories. The more serious subjects.

She'd handled the Crooked Arrow shootings, hadn't she?

Casey had watched the tape. She always did, why should this be any different? It was how you got better. She looked at it dispassionately, or tried to, evaluating her own performance. She'd done a good job. She'd been calm. Authoritative, even.

She couldn't ask for a better addition to her reel. Too bad she'd had to get shot to get it.

God, this wine tasted good.

In two days she'd go into the station.

What the hell was she going to wear? She'd been living in her baggiest sweats and most oversized T-shirts. Anything tight around her body seemed to set her nerves on fire.

"Are you sure you don't want me to stay tonight?" he asked.

"I'm sure." Maybe that sounded a little too eager. She reached over, placed her hand on top of his, and briefly wondered why she felt compelled to pretend. "Really. I'll be fine."

"Well … I guess I'd better let you get some rest."

She watched as Paul went into the kitchen, found the wine vacuum pump and rubber cork and pumped the air out of the bottle. After that, he came over and kissed her on the lips. Gently, of course.

"Is there anything else I can do for you before I leave?"

What she really wanted was more wine. But she knew the reaction she'd get if she asked him for that.

"I'm good." She smiled. "I just want to sit here a little longer and enjoy my view."

"I'll call you tomorrow."

She watched him let himself out. The door shut.

She was finally alone.

She'd gone straight from a week at the hospital to her condo, but she hadn't been alone for more than a couple of hours the whole time. Her parents had wanted her to come up to Diamond Bar and recuperate, but the thought of being in a car that long, not to mention being at her parents' house for any length of time…

They meant well.

Instead, her physician mom had come down here for five days, complaining the entire time. She was angry, Casey could tell, angry at Casey for the choices she'd made that had almost gotten her killed. Why hadn't she gone to med school, or law school? Why was she always off visiting crazy places on the other side of the planet? Why couldn't she just do something *safe*?

"That's not fair, Mom," she'd finally said. "I'm doing local news, in San Diego. Not reporting from a war zone."

Which, truth be told, was what she'd really wanted to do. Work for a big newspaper or magazine. Cover the big international stories. Wear a flak jacket from time to time, even.

"Print's dead," everyone told her. "You've got the right look for TV."

Meaning *pretty Asian woman*, she'd suspected. Someone decorative you didn't have to take seriously.

Okay, she'd thought. I'll use it, and I'll show them. Make it to CNN, or the BBC, or Al Jazeera.

But that wasn't how things had worked out.

"Well, law school would have been better," her mother had snapped. "You don't make enough money."

This was also true. Her parents had helped her finance this condo—partly, Casey was certain, because they wanted to tie her down to Southern California.

After a few days of snarling at each other, Mom used the *ayi* network to find a recent Chinese immigrant in San Diego to cook, clean, and follow instructions on how to change Casey's dressings and monitor her medications, who helped her into bed at night and to her feet in the morning.

Tonight was the first night Ruby would not be here since Casey had been released from the hospital. The first night Casey had spent alone since The Event.

And I'm glad, she told herself. She was so tired of always having people around. Of always having someone hovering over her. Finally, her space was her own again. She could enjoy the light bamboo floors, the clean white walls, the funky furniture she'd gathered from thrift shops and cheap importers, the souvenirs she'd collected on her travels. Could sit on her battered leather couch facing the giant picture window with the view of Lindbergh Field, gaze out at the runway with its Christmas tree string of lights, watch the planes take off and land.

The view made her happy, like it always did.

It was just that her little condo was so quiet now, without any friends visiting, without Ruby around, without Paul or her parents or her sisters. Just a hush of air from a slowly rotating fan. Distant traffic noises, like ocean tides.

The doors were locked. No one could get in. This was a safe place.

Maybe I should get a dog, she thought. A medium-sized dog. Big enough to offer some protection, small enough so that it would live longer. Big dogs died too young.

Maybe a cat.

Go to bed, she told herself. Take an oxy and maybe a Zoloft and fall asleep to the TV.

She pushed herself to her feet, the pain making her gasp. Reached for the hospital cane by the couch, hating its gray ugliness, the stupid rubber stopper at the end. I'm going to collect canes, she thought. I'll have different canes for different outfits, different moods. They will be fabulous, and I'll donate this one to a homeless shelter, or just throw it in the trash.

You will get better, the doctors kept telling her. It will just take some time.

6

CLINIC SHOOTING VICTIMS:
A NURSE'S AIDE, A COLLEGE STUDENT
AND A MOTHER OF TWO

LAS VEGAS (AP) — When Tanika Kennedy didn't come home in time for dinner, her mother didn't worry right away. "She's young," Georgia Kennedy, 42, said. "Sometimes she goes out with friends and forgets to call. I didn't think anything of it, at first." But when Georgia turned on her television to watch the local six o'clock news, she immediately feared that her oldest daughter might be in trouble.

"I knew she had the appointment. She told me she didn't need anyone to come along. 'It's just a check-up, Mom.'"

REP. CASON STATEMENT ON MASS SHOOTING AT CHOICES REPRODUCTIVE HEALTH CENTER

···································

These killings were not simply the actions of a mentally disturbed individual. We need to call it what it is: a terrorist attack directed at women's reproductive freedom. These kinds of attacks have been going on for decades, inspired by a twisted, hate-filled ideology that seeks to control women's bodies and women's choices.

Beyond that, there are more mass shootings in this country each year than there are days. There are common-sense actions we can take that won't solve the problem but that will reduce the carnage, measures that the vast majority of Americans agree upon, including most gun owners. The only thing stopping us is the political will to fight back against a weapons lobby that profits off mass slaughter.

————

"Please tell me there won't be cameras."

Diego snorted. "Come on, you *know* there's gonna be cameras."

Casey heard herself sigh. She meant it, truly. But realistically there was no way News 9 would not be recording this moment: her "triumphant" return to the station, accompanied by her Hero Photographer.

She was not feeling particularly triumphant. She looked like shit. She'd lost weight she could ill afford to lose. No amount of concealer hid the black circles under her eyes or her blotchy, ghost-pale complexion.

I should have had Marcie come over and do my makeup, she thought. God knows if she can make Craig's complexion look good, she could make me look like I'm not dead.

Diego steered the station's Highlander onto the Balboa Avenue off-ramp. Casey stared at the familiar strip malls, the auto dealerships, the gentlemen's club, sports bar, and Korean mega-supermarket.

"This was Jordan's idea, right? Having you pick me up?"

Diego shrugged. "Somebody needed to. Not like we wanted you taking an Uber."

Which didn't really answer the question.

"So it was Jordan's idea."

"He asked me if I wanted to." Diego didn't meet her eyes, but he smiled a little.

"Well, thanks for doing it."

"No problem."

She'd seen Diego since The Event. He'd come and visited her in the hospital; a lot of the crew had. She'd been really doped up on that occasion and vaguely recalled weeping like a little kid when she'd seen him. Her cheeks flushed, thinking about that.

She was pretty sure she'd thanked him then. Should she thank him now? What was the etiquette for a situation like this?

Do you send flowers to a guy who saved your life?

She studied him. A stocky, solid guy with a perpetual shadow of beard and spikes of thick black hair falling into crescent-shaped waves around his face. He was actually kind of cute, which she hadn't really thought before now—they hadn't known each other that long, had only worked together for a few months before The Event, and besides, she'd been totally preoccupied with Paul.

Why was she even thinking about this?

"So ... how are you?" she asked.

"Pretty good. They told me to take some time off, so I did. Saw a counselor like they told me to. Went down to Baja for a couple of days and chilled. Since I've been back they've had me on surfing bulldogs."

She snickered. That was their nickname for the more trivial end of the human interest beat.

"I'm surprised they're not having you filming me," she said. "So they could film you filming me. That would be ... meta."

Whatever that meant. She couldn't quite recall the definition of *meta*. Had she ever known it?

Diego laughed. "Sure, Casey. You want me to run it by them?"

It took her a long moment to figure out what "it" was. "No, let's not give them any ideas."

Hello, oxycodone, she thought. My new friend. She liked how it dampened the pain, the warm narcotic balm of it, but when she was on it, sometimes she felt like her thoughts were becoming disconnected, like they were a string of beads and the string had snapped.

She'd taken a Zoloft too. The thought of going into the station ... her heart had started racing just picturing it. Which was stupid. The station was a safe place. Nothing was going to happen to her there.

She really needed to get better and get off this stuff. She couldn't think straight, and she hated that.

Except ... what if she did get off the drugs, and there was nothing actually there? Just the Big Empty she'd been dissolving into when she got shot?

Could she go back to her job? Do stand-ups in front of car crashes and house fires and surfing bulldogs? Try to prove all over again that she was worthy of better things?

She didn't have much time to prove it. Twenty-nine was old to be at this point in her career. Because working in TV was like living in dog years. Medium-sized dog, at least.

Maybe Mom was right, she thought. Maybe I shouldn't have spent so much time traveling. I should have just gotten on that career track right away and stayed there. Not taken any breaks.

But she'd traveled after college. Traveled on her vacations. Traveled for six months after the round of layoffs that had eliminated her first on-air job in Sacramento, picking up cash writing travel pieces and teaching English. She almost didn't come back to take the gig in St. Louis, but she did. Asked for a couple of weeks "to settle things" when she'd quit that gig to take the job in San Diego. She'd gone to Peru that time.

You don't take anything seriously. Mom had said that to her more than once.

They pulled into the station parking lot, an asphalt expanse in front of a low industrial complex that looked like all the other complexes around here, regardless of what the businesses were: high-tech, brewery, auto customizer, Chinese bookstore, they all looked the same.

"You ready?" Diego asked.

"Nope."

There was a small crowd waiting for them. Craig and Elise, the evening anchors. Danise the weather gal and Dominic from sports. Tim, the assignment editor, and Gloria, the evening news producer. Jason from the live truck. They were the crew the night she'd been shot.

And of course a photographer. She wasn't sure who it was. She didn't want to look at the camera. Didn't want to watch him film her.

Diego helped her out of the car.

She emerged, leaning a bit on her gloriously tacky dragon cane. Lifted her free hand in a wave.

Everyone started clapping. Slowly, almost gently at first. Then harder and faster.

Casey smiled. Ducked her head. Wondered if she could crawl back into the car and go home.

Danise the weather gal moved first. Closed the distance between them and gave her a cautious hug. Casey had always liked Danise. Gorgeous, curvy, and goofy as hell.

"Oh my god, you cut your hair!"

"Yeah. I was tired of it."

Her long hair had been her signature. Black, glossy, cascading past her shoulders. A pain in the ass to take care of, especially after she got shot. She'd managed with the help of Ruby to make it to a fancy downtown salon yesterday. "Just cut it," she'd said. "I'm done." Now her hair hugged the line of her jaw, buzzed around the base of her skull. She kept running her fingers through it, feeling the short soft hair, like it was some kind of animal pelt.

"I love it!" Danise said. "It's really cute."

"Thank you, you're so sweet," Casey said.

Paul had loved her long hair. He wasn't going to like this, she was pretty sure.

A cat, she thought. I'll just get a cat. Or maybe two.

"Casey, it is so great to see you."

"You look wonderful."

"How are you feeling?"

The voices around her grew louder, then receded; she fought off a wave of dizziness that left her weak at the knees.

"You okay, Casey?" Danise asked, her voice somehow cutting through the buzz and the blur.

"Oh, sure, I'm fine. Just a little tired." She managed a smile. "So happy to see all of you!"

———————

Another one.

One of the monitors in Jordan's office was tuned to CNN. The slug in the OTS read: *Three Dead in Alabama High School Shooting.*

"You look great, Casey."

"Oh," she said. "Thanks. I'm feeling pretty good."

Jordan smiled, but he looked worried. He often looked worried. Shrinking budgets, shrinking ratings, and still expected to "aggressively drive growth in content across multimedia platforms including: digital, mobile, social media, and any new platform opportunities that may arise." (This was from his mission statement as news director.) No way she'd want his job.

He was a white guy passing forty and waving at fifty, balding and gut straining the buttons of his dress shirt, though she knew he worked out regularly. Stress, probably.

"Interesting haircut," he said. "It's ... a little angular."

He was still kind of a dick.

Was there a hair clause in her contract she'd missed?

"Yeah," she said. "Easier to blow dry."

"I am guessing we are still a ways away from you resuming normal work activities?"

She shrugged. "I'm not where I want to be yet. But I'm getting there."

"Well, take all the time you need. We've got a great fill-in from Tempe. Carly Nixon."

"I've seen her."

"Oh. Of course. Well, she's not on your level, but she's doing a great job."

"She's got a great look," Casey said. She stared past his head at the walnut bookcase where he showcased his Emmy, at the plaques and framed photos on the wall, then back to the bank of monitors.

"You just keep us posted," Jordan said. "Whenever you're ready to come back, of course there's a place for you here."

Extremist literature found in home of Las Vegas women's clinic shooter, read the crawl on CNN.

"You know," Casey said suddenly. "I'm ready to come back now. I mean, not my regular job, obviously." She laughed, suddenly feeling self-conscious. "I wish I could do it, but the fact is, I can't. But..."

Three Dead in Alabama High School Shooting.

She waved at the monitor. Her left arm, the one she could wave. It still hurt when she tried to raise her right arm up. "Another shooting. How many have there been since Morena? We just move on to the next one. I know this is going to sound..."

She suddenly felt herself on the brink of tears. "You know, people who get hurt, whose friends and loved ones die... they don't get to move on. And I was thinking..."

She leaned forward. Time for her pitch. The hint of tears might even help. "We suffered a major loss in this community. Seven dead now. Five seriously injured. And we've largely moved on from it in terms of our coverage. What do you think about a special report? A series about the long-term repercussions of a tragedy like this?"

Jordan crossed his arms over his belly. Thinking it through. "So the angle is... you?"

She smiled. "Who better?"

He was still thinking about it. Frowning now. First-person journalism wasn't the kind of thing they generally did.

"Just to be clear, I'll *report* the story. Not *be* it. Interview victims, their families. My own experience won't be the focus. I'll just provide … context. And empathy. I'll be able to frame the story in a way nobody else here could."

"What if there are points where we *want* to focus on your experience?" he asked suddenly. "Would you be willing to show the long-term repercussions for *you?*"

She hadn't expected that. The idea made her uncomfortable. If she showed people how she really felt, how scared she was sometimes, how angry, the kinds of thoughts that were running around in her head …

"Sure," she said, putting a bright note in her voice, just like she did to end her upbeat features. "I'm fine with that."

She'd pitched it, hadn't she?

Jordan finally uncrossed his arms. "It's an interesting idea. Let's toss it around. Rose might be a good person to get in the mix."

Rose was a good producer. Maybe Jordan was actually taking this seriously.

"Great," she said, putting some enthusiasm into it. "I can start doing research, work on the breakdowns."

"I haven't approved anything yet."

"That's okay. It'll give me something to do." She *was* enthusiastic about it, on some level. The level of *fake it till you make it.*

"We'll need a physician's note clearing you for limited duty."

She gave him a mock salute. "No problem."

Jordan studied her. Evaluating her fitness for the gig, maybe. "You really want to do this, Casey?"

"I do," she said. Because she really did, even if she didn't exactly feel it yet.

If something this shitty was going to happen to her, she might as well get a good story out of it.

———————

Casey Cheng News 9 @CaseyChengNews9
SO GLAD TO BE BACK WITH MY NEWS 9 FAMILY! SO GRATEFUL FOR ALL OF YOUR SUPPORT! YOU ARE AMAZING, SAN DIEGO!

San Diego Christine @SanDiegoChristine
LOVE YOU @CASEYCHENGNEWS9! WELCOME BACK!

Stans The Man @StansTheMan
STAY STRONG GURL YER AWESOME! GLAD TO HAVE YOU BACK ON THE TEE-VEE!

White Pride 419 @WhitePride419
SOMEONE SHULD SKULLFUCK YOU SLANT CUNT TOO BAD HE MISSED YOUR CHINK FACE #ALANJAYLIBERATIONARMY

7

SHE LOOKED GOOD, SARAH thought, that reporter who'd survived the shooting. Casey Cheng.

Sarah was taking a break from her database project. She'd agreed to help Lindsey go through a DCCC list to flag potential likely contributors outside the state. "We're looking for voters who donate outside their own district, who understand the importance of strategic donations for national party-building. We're also looking for voters with an interest in veteran's affairs, the environment, women's reproductive rights, and gun safety"—she counted them off on her long fingers—"all issues of strength for Matt. It's tedious, but I don't want to rely on email blasts that aren't properly targeted. It just turns people off, and we want them to buy in."

"Sure, will do."

Lindsey had actually smiled at her. Not a particularly warm smile, but a smile, anyway. "Thanks, Sarah. We really appreciate your help."

She doesn't like me, Sarah thought now. It didn't seem fair. She'd hardly interacted with Lindsey.

Probably because Matt was nice to her.

It wasn't her fault that Matt was nice to her.

I'll do a good job for Lindsey, Sarah thought. Maybe she'll like me if I do a good job.

But there were only so many hours she could spend looking at cross-tabs and entering data fields before she needed a break.

Seven a.m. Friday. The office was quiet.

It must have been adding names to the gun safety field that made her think of that reporter. Casey Cheng had been so calm, almost nonchalant on the selfie video she'd made right before she'd been shot. Like the danger hadn't been real to her.

She should have been more careful, Sarah thought. *She'd* made that mistake, assuming she was safe.

Sarah had done a quick Google search and found the top hit: a story and video on News 9's website.

"An emotional day at News 9 as our own Casey Cheng returns to the station for the first time since last month's tragic shootings."

There she was, smiling and hugging people and shaking hands. She didn't look that different, Sarah thought, except for the short hair. Slender, pretty, with dramatic brows and a broad smile, she seemed lively. Happy. As if the horrible thing that had happened to her hadn't marked her at all.

The phone rang. The ringtone for Communications.

"Communications, Sarah speaking."

"Sarah. Nice to hear your voice."

Sarah shivered, and then she knew who it was. Wyatt Gray.

"Hello," she said. "Is this Mr. Gray?"

"You can call me Wyatt if you'd prefer."

"Whatever you want."

"You need to stand up for what *you* want, Sarah."

She felt a sudden, brief surge of anger. "Mr. Gray, then."

He laughed. "Good for you. Mr. Gray it is. You had an easy primary, I take it."

They had. There hadn't really been much doubt that Matt would end up one of the top two finishers in California's "jungle primary." The other, predictably, was Tegan. The one woman who ran against Matt as a Democrat was far to his left, a registered Green until the primary. No money and no institutional support.

"We didn't take any chances."

"Good. You shouldn't ever get complacent. Got a pen?"

She felt around her desk, which was actually a table, with no drawers. Finally she found a pen that had rolled behind her computer. "Got it."

"I'm going to give you a YouTube URL. You ready?"

He read off a string of letters interspersed with a couple of numbers. She scribbled them on a legal pad.

"Now read them back to me."

She did.

"Good. I suggest you download the video. It won't be up on the site more than an hour. Probably less."

"How—" she began, and then she stopped herself. She could figure out how to download a YouTube video. There had to be apps for that.

"What is it?" she asked instead.

"Watch it. You'll see."

———

"Are we sure it's her?" Jane asked.

"Looks like her. Sounds like her." Angus shrugged. "And it sounds like something she'd say, if she thought no one was listening."

The video was shaky, the sound was muffled, and the apparent speaker's face was turned away from the camera part of the time. But what the video seemed to show was Kimberly Tegan at a garden party of some sort, wearing a butter yellow cocktail dress. A warm day, from Tegan's bare arms, in a big, beautiful yard with a glimpse of ocean. *"Oh don't get me started about Henry Echeverria,"* she said, glass of white wine in hand. *"I don't know what country he's really loyal to. He's one of these people, he won't be happy till we're part of Mexico again. Till we're part of Assland."* Laughter. *"Isn't that what they call it? Well, that's what it sounds like."* More laughter. *"Assland,"* she repeated, pausing to swallow some wine. *"That's what you get when you turn things over to Mexicans."*

"Assland" was Aztlán, Sarah knew. The name for the traditional Aztec homeland, real or mythical, and what some Chicano activists wanted to call a new nation for mestizos, a República del Norte that would encompass the American Southwest from Texas to California. She'd read about it in her Chicano studies class in college.

Did anyone take Aztlán seriously anymore? Sarah wasn't sure.

She'd had to Google Henry Echeverria. He was a labor activist who'd butted heads with Tegan when she was on the city council over raising the minimum wage. He'd already endorsed Matt this election cycle.

"Tell me again exactly what he said." Jane was staring at her again. Maybe she'd never stopped. Her eyes were a dark brown, so dark they were almost black.

They sat in Jane's bare office: Jane, Angus, Sarah, and Ben. Jane hadn't decorated it beyond a potted plant that probably came as part of the lease, and a couple of framed campaign photos—a younger Jane with various candidates. The most prominent was one of her

and Matt smiling and hugging each other in front of a sea of CASON
FOR CONGRESS signs, a rally from their first campaign.

Jane, smiling?

In the nearly two months that Sarah had been working here, she'd
barely glimpsed the inside of Jane's office before now. She'd longed to
be invited in. But this ...

Did Jane ever blink?

A trickle of sweat rolled down her back. "Just that ... he had some
information for the campaign. Something he thought might help. And
he gave me the URL and said I should download the video, because it
wouldn't be up there long."

"And that was it? He didn't say who he was working for? He didn't
give a name?"

Sarah shook her head.

She wasn't really lying, she told herself. She just was leaving things
out. Things like that he'd called before. That he'd wanted to talk to
her, specifically. That he'd told her not to mention any of that.

"You think it's a ratfuck?" Ben asked. A little too eager. Sarah was
starting to notice that about him now, that maybe he wasn't as confident as she'd first assumed.

"I think it would be easier to vet this if we had the purview," Jane
said. "As it is ... " She sighed. "It's the kind of thing I wish had gone to
one of our surrogates."

"We could show it to Henry," Angus said. "Let him run with it."

"The problem is, things like this always find their way back. Always. If we leak it, we're going to have to own it." Jane took off her
reading glasses and rubbed the bridge of her nose. "I need to think
about this."

———

"She's not gonna use it. Not unless we're really in a hole."

Sarah nodded. She understood why, or she thought she did. Still, a part of her was disappointed. A chance to have an impact, and it wasn't going to happen. "I guess we should hold fire unless we need it," she said. Be positive, she told herself. Show that you just want to contribute.

"Yeah. Hopefully, we won't." Ben drained the last of his saison. "Latino vote projections are way up as it is. Tegan's not popular with that community when they find out some of her positions, and Tomás is out there busting his ass making sure they do."

Sarah sipped her IPA. She'd drunk one to Ben's two, and the remains were getting warm.

"You want another beer?" he asked.

"Sure."

She'd surprised herself, agreeing to go out for a beer with Ben after work. The meeting in Jane's office had left her both drained and on edge. She'd thought about going to the gym, working out. That always helped. But when Ben asked if she wanted to go to the brewery down the block, she'd hesitated and then said, "Sure. Thanks for asking."

Maybe talking to him would be good. Maybe he'd have something else to say about the video, something he wouldn't say in front of Jane.

And maybe it's better that they don't use it, she thought. There's no way I can get into trouble if they don't use it.

"It's too bad though," Ben said after he returned with the beers. "I could just see the commercial." He spread his hands and made expansive finger quotes. "'Too extreme for this district. Too extreme for San Diego.'"

"What if we found out where it was from?"

Ben shrugged. "It would help, but I don't see how we can."

"If he calls again, I'll ask."

"What makes you think he'll call again?"

Ben stared at her across his beer. Was he suspicious? She felt herself flush.

"I don't know, I mean … he said he wanted to help. Maybe he has other information."

"If he does, let me talk to him. I'll see if I can pin him down."

He won't talk to you, she wanted to say. But of course she couldn't say that.

———————

Her car wouldn't start, and Ben's jumper cables didn't work.

They'd walked back to the headquarters' parking lot just after nine p.m. She'd thanked him for the beer and said goodnight, already looking forward to home and the local news.

Instead, the ignition clicked.

Ben rocked back on his heels. "Shit. Sorry. Must be something other than the battery. Or the battery's just totally dead."

"I guess." Her Hyundai wasn't new but it wasn't old either—less than five years.

"Want me to drop you home? So you can deal with it tomorrow?"

Her heart started pounding. She could feel the beat in her throat. "That's okay. I'll just call Auto Club. I wouldn't feel comfortable not having my car."

He shrugged a little. "Yeah, but if they can't start it, then you've just wasted the time. It's not like you can tow it anyplace tonight."

She hesitated. But he was right, she knew. "Yeah. Okay. Thanks. I appreciate that."

Still, she wished she'd just told him to leave, taken her chances with the tow truck. This area was deserted this time of night, but it didn't feel dangerous. Just empty.

It wasn't just the ones you didn't know that you had to worry about.

————————

"Cool little area," Ben said. "I didn't know this was here."

Her neighborhood was tucked away off the steep slope section of Clairemont Drive that led down to Mission Bay and the freeway—a series of hills and canyons, cul-de-sacs and dead-ends, quiet and easy to miss. She liked that.

"Oh? Where do you live?"

"Not in the district. I'm in Normal Heights."

"Oh. I guess that's ... probably more interesting than here."

Normal Heights was an older area of San Diego, near Kensington and North Park, with a lot of restaurants and an art house theater close by.

"There's more stuff to walk to there. That's the big problem with Clairemont and Kearny Mesa. They were designed for cars. It's hard to walk anywhere. I really like being able to walk to places."

His voice sounded tight. Nervous.

"Turn right here, then left. I'm on the left in two blocks."

The street where she lived had a few small apartment buildings and single-family homes that hadn't been updated and looked comfortably run-down. You didn't hear the freeway noise so much up here. Hardly any traffic. Just birdsong, blowing leaves, and the occasional helicopter.

"That's me." She pointed at one of the apartment buildings on the left, a row of cubes with wood slat and stucco facades, done in various shades of cream, beige, and tan.

Ben pulled his Corolla into the driveway, backed out, turned, and nudged the tires into the curb. "I can swing by and pick you up in the morning."

"That's okay, I can take a Lyft. This is out of your way."

"It's just a few minutes." He stared at her for a moment, and she thought, *You're not going to, are you?*

They were too close together. She could feel the heat radiating from him.

"If you change your mind, give me a call," Ben said. He sounded normal now. Maybe she'd been imagining things.

"Thanks," she said, opening the car door. "Thanks for the ride."

———

There was an email from her mother. Except that it wasn't.

JUST CHECKING IN, the subject line said.

HEY BETH, HOW'S IT GOING? YOU STILL LIKE TAKING IT UP THE ASS?
YOU STILL LIKE IT WHEN THEY CUM ALL OVER YOUR PIG FACE?
SOMEONE SHOULD MILK THOSE COW TITS OF YOURS YOU FAT
STUPID CUNT

She slammed the lid of her laptop shut, breathing hard.

After the first email, she'd switched to white-listing incoming mail. Only addresses she approved were supposed to get in.

How were they doing this? If they could spoof her mom's email address … did they have other email addresses? From her relatives? Her friends?

"Shit!" She grabbed her laptop, shook it, raised it up to throw it across the room.

But you can't do that, she told herself. You need it.

She stood there, trembling with rage. Waited for the anger to drain out of her, then gently put the laptop down on the coffee table. It needed to last.

I can't stand up any more, she thought. I'm going to pass out.

The couch. Right behind her. Her hand felt for the seat. She crawled onto it. Kicked off her shoes and pulled the afghan her aunt had knitted for her up over her hips.

Stop it, she thought. Just stop it.

———

She took a Lyft and got to work early the next morning. Called Auto Club. "Yeah, you need a new battery," the tow truck driver said an hour later. "We can have one delivered."

She couldn't decide what to do about her email account. There hadn't been any more of those emails yet, but there would be. There always were.

Change her account again? Have her mother write to her from a different address?

"You get your car going?" Ben asked. He'd paused by her desk on the way back from the kitchen, cup of coffee in hand.

"Yep, all fixed." She took a moment to meet Ben's eyes. He really had been nice last night. He got intense sometimes, but she was starting to think that it wasn't because of her, it was just how he was. "Thanks again for the ride."

"Not a problem. How's the website update going?"

Now he was all business.

"Good. Just waiting for some language on the environment page."

"Still?" Ben chuffed. "I'll nudge Presley. With all he's getting paid, he could try not dicking around on shit like this. It's not like we really need him to do it."

She watched his stiff, retreating back head over to Jane's office. Not in a good mood. Had something happened?

Her phone rang—Communications' low trilling ringtone.

"Communications, Sarah speaking."

"Sarah. How are you this morning?"

She recognized him immediately. Wyatt Gray.

"Hi, Mr. Gray. I'm fine. How are you?"

"Now, I know we agreed on Mr. Gray, but I really wish you'd call me Wyatt, so we're on the same level. This feels like I'm your teacher or something. I'm not calling you Ms. Price, am I?"

Had she told him her last name? She couldn't remember. "I'm okay with that," she said.

"Since you asked, I'm doing well," he said. "It's a beautiful day."

It was. The usual June Gloom had burned off early; it was sunny but not hot, the air gentle, the sky a muted blue.

"So you're in San Diego?"

"I do a lot of traveling."

Which wasn't an answer.

"What did you think of the video?"

"It was … definitely interesting."

"Useful?"

She hesitated. Don't tell him anything, she thought, the voice in her head so clear that she felt like she'd said it aloud.

But … if there was some way they could use the video …

"It would help if we knew where it came from."

"Ah. I see."

Silence on the line.

"It was a private event," he finally said. "That's why your tracker wasn't on it. And that's really all I can tell you. You don't expect me to burn my source now, do you?"

"No," she said. "Of course not."

So he hadn't been the one to record it?

"But I understand your position," he said. "You're careful. That's the sign of a smart campaign."

Was there anything she could say to that?

"We're trying to stick to the issues."

He laughed. "Right. Well, I'll keep an eye out for something you can use. You have a great day, okay?"

————————

She did a little online digging after they hung up.

A private event. She watched the video again. With that expanse of lawn and ocean view, if this was somebody's home, then it was somebody very rich. The event, whatever it was, looked fancy.

Something the newspaper society pages might cover?

She found it in the *Union Tribune*: a private party / fundraiser for a local cancer research center that had been held at a hotel overlooking the ocean. She scrolled through the photo gallery until she found the proof: a photo of Kimberly Tegan, wearing the same butter yellow outfit she'd had on in the video, smiling broadly for the camera, showing her bleached teeth.

Now what?

8

PHOENIX (AP) — A *GUNMAN WITH* alleged radical Islamist leanings
and armed with an AR-15-style assault rifle stormed a Phoenix movie theater
Friday evening in an attack that left 13 dead and scores more wounded, before
he was shot and killed by police SWAT teams.

———————

Excerpt from Rep. Matt Cason's statement on the House Floor,
News 9 San Diego:

"Islamist terrorism must be met with a firm response both at home
and abroad. At home we need to make sure that our law enforcement
agencies have the tools they need to identify the radicals in our midst.
That includes building good, cooperative relationships with the
communities from which these terrorists can come. It also should
include closing loopholes in firearms regulations that make it far too
easy for killers such as this to get their hands on military-style

*weapons and massive quantities of ammunition without any
questions being asked, even of those on terrorist watch lists. We
should also keep in mind that the worst act of mass violence in the
history of my district was committed by a young white man with
no discernable religious motive."*

*Statement by Kimberly Tegan, candidate for Congress, 54th District,
News 9 San Diego:*

*"My first priority as your Congresswoman will be to keep our
country safe from the scourge of radical Islam. We will strengthen
our immigration laws to keep Muslim terrorists out of our country.
And we will fight the terrorists where they live, so we do not have to
fight them where we live. There's no room for jihad in America."*

News 9 San Diego comment section:

*Tom P: The liberals will try to use this to confiscate guns. More gun-
free zones, that works so well! Idiots. I have the right to defend
myself and my family.*

*Dennis Z: What do you expect? We should turn in local jihadists
and redeem a reward for their disposal. Do what they do in Isreal,
bulldoze a mosque every time they kill a Christian.*

*Mary A: Pray for the victims. This is a Christian nation! Our
country is flooded with Muslims. Soon we will all live under
Sharia law if this keeps up!*

If there was anyone Casey had to interview for this series, it was Helen Scott.

The mother of Alan Jay Chastain, the man who'd shot her.

"I thought the idea was to focus on the victims," Rose said.

"Well, she's a victim too, right?"

Casey was pretty sure that Rose wasn't exactly buying that explanation. When she was being honest with herself, she had to admit that she didn't think of Helen Scott as a victim the same way that Mario Villa was a victim, or Darlene Fields, or Tamara Johns, or herself, for that matter.

Helen Scott hadn't been shot.

But she'd suffered the loss of a family member, hadn't she?

Close enough, Casey thought. Helen Scott was a compelling get, and that was what really mattered. She hadn't talked to anybody since her initial statement after the killings.

If she could pull this off …

Hello, local Emmy!

Rose took the last sip of her coffee.

"Can I get you a refill?" Casey asked.

"I'll get it."

Rose straightened up and hopped off the couch. She tended to move in bursts, Casey had noticed. She was a little chubby and wore her dyed black hair in subtle spikes, her clothes businesslike but on the edge, favoring saddle shoes and hoop earrings in double-pierced lobes. Not a person with ambitions of going on the air; Casey had once glimpsed an elaborate tattoo peeking out below her short sleeve one hot day during the afternoon meeting. Rose was shooting for assignment editor, executive producer, maybe news director at some point, Casey figured.

She brought over the carafe and freshened Casey's coffee.

"Thanks for coming over, by the way," Casey said. "Not being able to drive myself yet, it just makes things a lot easier."

"Not a problem. Your coffee's a lot better than the station swill."

She did make good coffee. Quality beans, burr grinder, in a Chemex, poured into a Thermos.

"You might as well enjoy the little things," Casey said.

Rose sat down. She didn't pay attention to how she sat, Casey noticed, just flopped on the couch. Funny, Casey thought. She'd long had to pay attention to such things. How she sat. How she moved. What her hair looked like. God, it was tiring. Such a performance.

"We'll have to run it by Legal."

"Legal? Why?"

"Because you're involved with Helen Scott. What if you decide to sue her?"

"How could I sue her? For what?"

"I don't know, say she'd supplied her son with the rifle."

"But she didn't," Casey said. "He bought it himself."

"But she could have encouraged him in some other way. Maybe she fed him hate literature. Maybe she encouraged him to be violent."

"There's no evidence of any of that. It's not like that kid who shot up a school with the AR-15 his mom bought him. She just ... she gave birth to him."

Casey tried to picture it. Thought about what it was like, growing a baby in your womb, pushing him out of your body, raising the kid, *cultivating* him ...

There was an expression for that in Mandarin, *peiyang haizi*. Raise your child with good habits, with some culture.

Maybe Alan Jay Chastain hadn't been raised with any of that.

"I'll tell her I don't want to sue her, I just want to talk to her. I'll tell her she's not liable for what happened to me, and I'll sign paperwork stating that. Give her a little peace of mind." Casey felt herself smiling. "An interview would be a small price to pay for that."

"Don't even think about making this a quid pro quo," Rose said sharply.

"Just a joke."

She'd meant it as a joke. Hadn't she?

Rose was staring at her. "So how do you want to approach this?"

"I'll call her myself. If she doesn't answer, I'll lay it out in an email, and after that, I'll knock on her door."

Rose opened her palms in lieu of a shrug, all the while shaking her head. "Why do you think she'll talk to you? She isn't talking to anybody, and you're not exactly going to make her feel comfortable."

"I can make her feel guilty," Casey said. It made her feel a little warm, a little happy, to say it. "And I'm kind of famous now. I can flatter her. People like her, at some point they're going to want to tell their story."

"People like her?" Rose scribbled a few notes in her Moleskine. "When you say that, who do you think she is?"

That was actually a very good question, Casey realized. It was funny, with the meds she was taking she'd sometimes lose track of things, like sentences or lines of argument, and definitely remote control units. Other times, everything felt slowed down to her, slow enough that she could grasp things that felt essential, that had always been passing by too quickly before.

"Maybe that's what we're trying to find out," she said.

Rose nodded and made a note. "Just be careful. Because if she thinks for a second that we're going to paint her as a monster…"

Casey had a sudden flash of footage she'd seen of Helen Scott: a middle-aged white woman gone thick through the hips, faded brown hair tied back in a ponytail, blinking rapidly as she ducked away from a sea of microphones.

"I don't think she's a monster."

But her son was.

"Why didn't you tell me he called? I told you to let *me* talk to him."

Ben wasn't as mad as she'd thought he might be. Mostly he seemed annoyed. But he'd been in a good mood before she'd told him. His face had lit up when she'd asked if he wanted to get a beer after work. Which worried her a little.

She wanted him to like her. Not to *want* her.

Still, telling him at the brewery had been the right way to do it.

"You were meeting with the Troika—I didn't want to interrupt."

Which wasn't exactly true, but close enough.

He heaved a sigh and swished around a mouthful of his sour. "Yeah, okay. Good call. And … good job tracking that down."

She'd spent most of the day trying to decide what to do. She'd thought about not saying anything at all. They still weren't likely to use the video, were they?

But thinking some more, one thing occurred to her: the video had come from an event that Tracker John didn't have access to. But somehow Wyatt did.

That seemed important.

So she'd saved the photo of Tegan in her yellow dress to her phone to show Ben. Told him about the party where it had been taken, and Wyatt's call.

"Sorry," she said. "But he's … a little strange. He didn't even want me to tell anyone that he was giving me this information. Which is kind of stupid. It's not like I know anything about him."

"He didn't tell you his name?"

She took a swallow of her stout to give herself a moment to think. She didn't know if Wyatt Gray was his real name. Thinking about it, she had a strong feeling that it wasn't. She'd Googled the name and hadn't found anybody who seemed like a likely match.

But still … he'd told her not to tell anyone. She'd already partly broken the rule.

But telling Ben his name, even if it wasn't his real name …

Maybe that wasn't a good idea.

She shook her head.

"Well, whoever he is, he's got some interesting intel, for sure." Ben finished his pint. "You think he'll call again?"

I'll keep an eye out for something you can use.

"Maybe," she said with a small shrug.

"If he does … we need to find out why he's doing this. What his motivation is. He could be trying to set us up."

"But whatever reason he's doing it, he's someone close to Tegan," Sarah said. "Or has access to someone who is."

That was what had finally made her decide to tell Ben, when she'd realized what Wyatt's knowing about that video really meant.

She needed someone else's take on this, someone else's understanding of the implications. She wanted to be important to the campaign, and she couldn't afford to hide the wrong things.

9

SURGING GUN SALES LEAD TO RECORD
PROFITS FOR US GUN MANUFACTURERS

WASHINGTON (AP)—Sales of guns have soared following a wave of mass shootings in the U.S. in the first six months of the year, according to a new study conducted by Gun Safety For U.S. "We found that demand has been driven by rising fears of terrorism and worries over stricter gun control legislation, in particular that certain kinds of firearms will be taken off the market entirely," said spokesperson David Monk. Sales of assault-style weapons such as the AR-15 have seen dramatic increases in the months following two high-profile mass shootings in which these weapons were used to kill a total of 47 people.

Rose left Helen Scott a voicemail making the proposal in general terms. "We'd like to assure you that the station is not pursuing any legal actions. This is about giving you a chance to correct the record, if need be. To tell your own story." She left a follow-up two days later.

Helen didn't return the calls.

Not exactly a surprise.

"If we can't get her, we can just go back to Plan A," Rose said. "Focus on the victims. Tamara John's parents are anxious to speak with us. They've gotten very active in the gun safety movement."

Casey nodded and sipped her tea. Rose had come over later in the day, so Casey had served the new harvest high-grade Dragon Well from Hangzhou that her sister had brought her back last month, in the proper clay pot. Because you might as well do it right.

"Well, I want to give them the platform," she said. "But I don't want to give up on Helen Scott. We've seen Tamara John's parents on the news. We haven't seen Helen Scott."

"This tea is like crack." Rose waved the steam rising from her cup toward her nose and inhaled deeply. "Okay, she's ignoring our phone calls. What do you suggest we do next?"

Casey thought about it. They knew where she worked—at a corporate records storage company in Mira Mesa. They knew where she lived—just off Clairemont Mesa Boulevard near Clairemont Square. But you couldn't really go to either of those places. Trying to catch someone going to or from work, entering or leaving the house … They could get some BS ambush footage of her not answering their questions. But you weren't going to get a conversation that way.

Casey had a sudden flash of Helen Scott outside her house, holding two dogs on a leash, struggling to pull them inside her house and slam the door shut against an onslaught of cameras.

"She has dogs, right?"

Rose nodded. "Two, I think."

"Well, she has to walk them. Can we find out where?"

———————

Being outside was weird.

Helen Scott took her dogs to the North Clairemont Community Park, a ten-minute walk from her house. Rose and an intern had staked out her house and observed her routine: Home by five thirty, fifteen minutes to change and get the dogs on a leash, out the door and on the way to the park by five forty-five.

Okay, it's not like you haven't been outside, Casey told herself. You've been outside lots of times. You've been to the station, to the doctor, to the physical therapy place, to the hairdresser, even a few restaurants.

But sitting here on this concrete bench under a sycamore tree, the foot of her cane scuffing at the packed dirt, it just felt different, somehow. More open. More dangerous.

Which is silly, she thought. There were kids kicking a soccer ball around. Smaller kids on the swing set, getting pushes from their parents. Teens playing basketball. Couples on the tennis courts.

Ordinary people in an ordinary neighborhood, going about their ordinary lives.

Of course, that's what those people at Crooked Arrow Brewery were doing too.

It was a pretty evening, still light. The marine layer had already moved in, making the air feel soft.

Who here might be carrying a gun? Casey wondered. That black teenager with the basketball? The middle-aged white man sitting at a table across the way, eating a Subway sandwich?

"You sure you don't want me to wait with you?" Rose had asked. "Get somebody else to watch her house?"

"No. Just text me when she's close. I need a little time to stand up." She wanted to be ready.

"Well, I'm going to be close by. You won't be on your own, okay?"

It was nice of Rose to be concerned, she thought, if slightly annoying. Helen Scott wasn't Alan Jay Chastain, and Casey wasn't a delicate flower.

Nothing was going to happen to her here. Was it?

Casey sighed. The truth was, she was glad Rose had her back. It didn't matter sometimes, how much she tried to boost herself up, to tell herself that things were okay.

They weren't. She wasn't.

Her phone buzzed. A text from Rose: SHE'S ENROUTE. I'M RIGHT BEHIND. DOGS ARE CUTE.

Good to know, Casey thought. Because getting attacked by dogs at this point would really suck.

You can do this, she told herself.

She'd been cleared to work "light duty." No prolonged standing, the doctor had cautioned. She'd told him she'd just be sitting, doing interviews.

They'd started stepping back on the opiates. She was still hurting a lot, but it was the only way she could convince him she was ready to go back to work. "Pain level is definitely improving!" He'd given her a prescription for another three months of Zoloft. "If you're feeling good, don't stop taking it all at once. We'll need to ease you off it. But if returning to work increases your anxiety, well … we'll need to re-evaluate whether you should be doing that."

"Oh, I'm not planning on doing anything that's going to make me anxious," she'd said, giving him her best smile, heart fluttering in her throat.

Another text from Rose: COMING THRU TENNIS COURTS.

Time to stand up.

One hand on the bench, the other on her cane (the boring, practical one), she pushed herself to her feet. Pain pulsed from her side, below her ribs, down her spine and leg and foot.

Maybe this was not the best time to be cutting back on the opiates. She needed to think straight, but it was hard to think straight when everything hurt this much.

Deep breath. Then another.

"Better now," she said aloud.

DO YOU SEE HER? I'M RIGHT BEHIND.

Casey focused on the path that ran past the tennis courts. And there she was: Helen Scott, wearing baggy sweats, two midsized dogs straining at their leashes in front of her.

YEP, GOTCHA, she typed.

Showtime.

She waited for Helen to draw closer. The woman looked exactly how she remembered her from the TV appearance, the lines of her eyes and cheeks and mouth pulling down the flesh of a face constructed in slabs, her washed-out brown hair in a ponytail, as it had been before. Not a lot of makeup, but a slash of old lipstick that was a fluorescent shade of coral.

The dogs were a floppy-eared Aussie shepherd mix and some sort of beagle/hound. They seemed friendly enough. Casey hoped.

"Ms. Scott?"

Helen flinched. Drew back and stared at her. With recognition, Casey wondered, or just the expectation of an attack? She couldn't tell.

"I'm sorry," Casey said, "I don't mean to disturb you. I just..."

Helen yanked on the dogs' leashes and started to wheel away.

Fuck it, Casey thought, I *do* mean to disturb you. She stepped in front of Helen, in front of the dogs, trying to keep the pain that shot down her leg from showing on her face. The dogs barked and wiggled, tails wagging.

The shepherd mix jumped up, its paws landing hard just above her hips. She gasped, seeing nothing but white for a moment, doubling over, one hand clutching her cane, the other braced on her thigh.

"Casey! Hey, you okay?" It was Rose, whose arm circled her shoulders.

"Oh, sure. Sure, I'm fine." She managed to straighten up. Pasted on a smile. "Just, the dog. The dog caught me in a bad place. It's okay."

"He's just friendly," Helen said. "He didn't mean anything." She sounded frightened.

"Maybe you better sit down," Rose said.

Casey shook her head and faced Helen. "Do you recognize me?"

From the expression on Helen's face, Casey couldn't tell. She looked scared. Hopeless. Or maybe just tired.

"Your son shot me."

She could hear Rose let out a little groan. Maybe she shouldn't have said that.

Dial down the blunt, cowgirl.

"You're the reporter," Helen said. "I didn't recognize you with the short hair."

"Right, that's me." She forced a smile. "Look, Ms. Scott, I'm not here to harass you. I don't want to cause you any trouble."

"I got your phone calls," Helen muttered. "If I'd been interested, I would have called you back."

Casey took a step forward. The dogs wagged their tails and the shepherd mix tugged hard on the leash. She lurched back, nearly stumbling.

"Santos, *sit!*" Helen hissed.

"It's okay," Casey managed. "He's a cute dog. I wish I could play with him."

For a moment, she could see a crack of sympathy in Helen Scott. She pushed on. "I just want to talk to you. I just want to understand why. Why this happened."

"I don't *know* why it happened!" Helen said, and then she began to sob, standing there stiffly, taking in shuddering breaths, one hand covering her face, the other clutching her dogs' leashes.

Casey felt two things at once: an impulse to hug her, and a sincere regret they hadn't brought cameras.

10

CHICAGO (AP)—An altercation at a party that escalated to *armed violence led to the shooting deaths of two men early this morning in Gage Park, police officials said.*

———————

"Mom, it's no big deal. Just … "

The last thing she needed was to get into it with her mom right now. Sarah took a deep breath.

"Just use a different email address, okay? So I know it's from you and not … Russian spammers or whatever."

Her head throbbed. It had been a busy morning, getting the flyers, emails, tweets, and Facebook events created, scheduled, and promoted for a series of fundraisers and house parties, plus reminders about the community fair that Matt was attending this weekend. And since the office was officially closed tomorrow for July 4th, she had even less time than usual to get everything done.

"I have to go," she said into her cell. "I'll call you later."

She didn't want to change her email address again, not yet. So far they'd only spoofed her mom's address. To have to call up all the people she'd white-listed, tell them she was changing it again ...

She was so sick of it.

Though if it hadn't happened, she probably wouldn't have had the money to do what she was doing now. Wouldn't have been able to come to San Diego, rent a place, work her way up from volunteer to staffer, and it wasn't like she was making a lot on the campaign.

I deserved that money, she thought.

She had to keep telling herself that.

The office phone rang—the Communications trill. She picked up the handset.

"Communications. Sarah speaking."

"Sarah. It's Wyatt. How are you doing?"

"Fine," she said. "How are you?" She felt better, actually—the little rush of excitement when she heard his voice had cleared her head. Maybe Wyatt would give her something really good today.

"Well, I don't have a lot of time to chat right now, but I've got some news. You're going to have an independent running on your left."

Well, this might not be good, but it was big.

"Who?" she asked.

"Not sure. They don't have to file for another six or seven weeks, till late August. But there's going to be some money behind them, Sarah. Big money. Enough to cause you some problems. You better get ready for it."

"Thanks for the heads-up," she said. "But Wyatt ..." She drew in a breath. She wasn't used to confronting people. "It would really help if you told me where you're getting this information. And why you're sharing it with me."

"I told you, I'm not burning my sources. And I like your guy. I want to help him win." He sounded amused. "Is that so hard to believe?"

"He called again," she told Ben, when he came back to his desk.

Ben sighed through his teeth. "And he'd only talk to you?"

"He doesn't want to talk to anyone else," she snapped back. "And no, I don't know why that is."

"Okay, okay." Ben held up his hands like he didn't want an argument. "What did he say?"

She told him.

"Shit. We'd better take this to Jane."

———

Jane's response was to take off her glasses and massage the bridge of her nose. "Well, that would suck," she said.

"Do you think he means Kat Oren?" Ben asked. "I mean, if it's for real?"

Kat Oren had been their primary opponent, the former Green.

"If it's for real … no. She wouldn't do that. She's got her eye on a city council run next time out, and now that she's in the party she wants to stay here. Hey, we win this thing, maybe we'll even help her."

"We'll still win," Ben said. "Somebody to Matt's left, in this district … they *can't* win." He sounded like he was trying to convince himself.

"No, probably not. But they can wound," Jane said. "I imagine that's the point—to try to peel away enough support to tip this thing to Tegan."

She suddenly focused on Sarah—that merciless stare of hers, the one that seemed to measure everything. "And we have no idea who he is, the guy who's calling you? Or what he wants?"

Sarah shook her head. "I asked. He just says he wants to help Matt."

She was telling the truth. It felt good to do that, for a change, like a knot in her belly had begun to dissolve.

———————

The house was about as ordinary as it gets: a beige one-story stucco ranch from the late fifties or early sixties, as almost all the houses in this neighborhood were. Some were nicer, better kept up, some had minor updates, like new windows, and a few had second stories added. Some looked a lot worse. "That's a rental," Helen Scott mentioned, waving at the run-down, weed-choked house on the corner. "Nothing but trouble. I think they're heavy into meth."

The irony of this, that so much more trouble had come from her own house, seemed to escape her.

The dark brown trim on Helen's house had started to fade and peel. The lawn was mostly crispy grass and weeds, but neatly trimmed. There were odd, red splotches on the grass and dirt near the front door. "I had a couple cute dog statues there," Helen Scott explained. "But somebody tossed red paint on them. I cleaned it all up as best as I could and put the dogs in the backyard." She said all this without much emotion.

"Let's make sure to get some B-roll of that," Rose said to Diego in a low voice.

Diego nodded. Panasonic on his shoulder, he panned around the yard.

This was okay, Casey thought.

She realized that it had only just now occurred to her how normal this felt, being out in the field with Diego and Rose. She wasn't nervous like yesterday in the park, wasn't panicked; she was just taking it all in, looking for good angles.

Now that she'd had the thought, she'd stepped outside herself again, was watching her own actions, gauging her responses, feeling the muscles between her shoulder blades twitch.

But for a while she'd been in that familiar flow state, that groove she loved.

If I can feel it at all, I can feel it some more. She smiled briefly, the thought warming her.

"Ms. Scott, thank you so much for opening your home to us," she said.

Helen shrugged. "I don't think you'll find anything very interesting."

On the surface, she was right.

Like the exterior, the inside of the house was slightly shabby, tidy, and bland. Nothing stood out, Casey thought. Not the industrial fabric couch, not the faded beige carpet worn down by a decade or two of use, not the framed blue dog poster on the wall to the left of the flat-screen TV.

Not a lot to shoot here.

They set up the interview with Helen and Casey on the couch, knees angled forward so Diego could get them in a two-shot now and again as well as separate shots of them both without a lot of movement. Mostly he'd focus on Helen Scott. Too bad they couldn't have two photographers, but that would blow the budget. Casey knew her real-time reaction shots weren't so important anyway, as long as they got her looking concerned enough times to intercut as needed, and she knew how to cheat her angle to make things easier on Diego.

She could hear the dogs in the backyard, the jingling of their collars, an occasional playful growl. We should get some footage of the dogs, she thought.

"Can you tell us a little about Alan? What was he like?" Casey kept her voice soft, as though she actually had some sympathy for the little asshole monster.

"He was … quiet. I guess a little shy." Helen Scott sat stiffly, her hands rigid on her thighs, like she didn't know where else to put them.

"Did he have many friends?"

"Oh, sure, he had friends. High school friends, and a couple from the community college."

"What kinds of things did they like to do together?"

"They … " Her eyes flicked back and forth, like she was scanning the room for answers. "They just went out sometimes. To movies. Played video games. He spent a lot of time chatting to them on his computer."

She doesn't really know, Casey thought.

"Maybe when we're done, you could give us a few of their names? We'd love to talk to them too." She leaned forward, her best earnest pose. "We're trying to understand what Alan was like, Ms. Scott. What might have driven him to do what he did. With stories like this … a lot of times the person gets lost. We just see the crime."

Helen nodded rapidly. Stared at her hands.

"What was Alan like as a young child, Ms. Scott?"

"Shy, I guess you could say. He was always shy. Things scared him." She smiled a little. "He liked to stick close to me. It was hard for him at first, when he went off to school. But a lot of kids are like that, right?"

"Right. It's a normal thing, not wanting to leave your mom." Of course, Casey had been one of those kids who couldn't wait to go to school, but no need to mention that. "Did Alan enjoy school? Did he have any favorite subjects?"

Helen sighed. "He was up and down with it. He had a hard time paying attention sometimes. He liked to draw, so I tried to get him in art classes when I could, but you know how it is with the schools—all those tests the kids are always taking, and he didn't always do so well on those."

"He was going to community college, wasn't he?"

She shrugged. "You know, off and on. Mostly he was working these days."

"At Highsmith's, right?" Highsmith's handled estates sales. They had a two-story warehouse down on Morena. "Looks like a giant thrift store," Rose had said.

On their go-to list.

"Right. He seemed to enjoy it. That's what he told me, anyway."

"And ... was he seeing anyone? Dating at all?"

"Not recently. Not that he told me about anyway. He did keep some things to himself." She laughed, one hard chuckle. "Obviously."

"But ... he did date? At one time? Because some of the things he said, on Twitter, about women ... "

If a man rapes a slut in the forest and nobody sees it, does she make a sound? Hahah, joke, you can't rape a slut!

Casey kept her voice soft. Gentle. "It sounded like he wanted something from them that he wasn't getting."

"I don't know anything about that," Helen said, her voice sharp. "I never saw *anything* like that. I just thought, he's shy. He didn't seem that interested. You know, not everybody cares so much about it. It doesn't have to mean anything."

"It" meant something to *him*, obviously, Casey thought. But was there any point in saying that?

"What about his father?" Casey asked. "Did Alan—?"

"Wasn't in the picture," Helen snapped.

Well, *that* door sure slammed shut in a hurry. No one had been able to find out much about David Chastain, just that he'd worked in construction and had died of an opiate and alcohol overdose two years ago in Oklahoma City.

How to get Helen Scott to open up again?

A loud, raspy meow, almost a screech. Casey flinched. Another meow. A long-haired black and orange calico cat padded into the living room from the hallway, heading straight to the couch. The cat sat down on her haunches at Casey's feet and looked up at her. Loudly meowed again.

Helen smiled a little. "That's Cleo."

Cleo stood, stretched, and wound around Casey's ankles. Casey extended her hand. The cat sniffed, then rubbed its head against her fingers.

"She's very friendly," Casey said. To prove the point, the cat jumped up on the couch.

"She didn't used to like strangers, but now she's old, and anybody who pays attention to her is her friend."

Petting her, Casey could feel the cat's backbone, disguised by the thick fur.

"Alan loved that cat," Helen said. "I guess that makes sense, they practically grew up together. Cleo's seventeen. I found her in a dumpster when she was a kitten. So Alan would have been six or so."

Casey snuck a glance at Helen Scott. Her eyes were glassy with unshed tears.

I should say something, she thought, but she couldn't think of anything to say. She continued to pet the cat, and it suddenly occurred to her, *he* petted this cat. He touched the fur I'm touching.

"He liked the dogs too. But the cat was special. He ... the night before ... "

Casey felt the room grow still. She knew that Rose and Diego felt it too, that they were all connected, suspended in this moment. Keep petting the cat, she told herself. Just let her talk.

"It was just ... " The older woman drew in a breath. "Alan had Cleo on his lap, and he sat there for a long time, petting her. And then he just picked her up all of a sudden, and put her down on the couch next to him, and he said, 'She's old. She's not gonna be around much longer.' And then he told me goodnight and went to bed."

Helen swept her fingers across her eyes. "I guess that was him saying good-bye."

It wasn't that weird that a twenty-three-year-old would live with his mom these days, especially not in Southern California, where housing was expensive. Casey's youngest sister had been out of college for a year and still lived with their parents.

Of course her youngest sister was just a little spoiled and annoying, as opposed to being a mass murderer.

"There's nothing much to see." Helen gestured toward a closed door on the side of the short hall. Casey knew how these houses were organized: one or two bedrooms on the side, the master bedroom at the end. Funny, she thought, how little privacy there was in these old tract houses. Everyone was so close together. Like the first house she remembered from when she was a little kid, before her parents made enough money to upgrade. She'd been in high school by the time they did, grateful for the extra space, which meant she could sometimes sneak a boyfriend into her bedroom when her parents were at work, without her little sisters finding out.

Somehow, Alan Chastain had stockpiled weapons here. Had planned a massacre without his mother having a clue.

That is, if you believed her.

Helen opened the bedroom door and switched on the light. Casey stepped inside. Diego followed her, camera on his shoulder.

The bedroom was painfully neat. A twin bed with a plain dark blue quilt. Not much on the walls, one framed painting and a few posters, also framed. Bookcases, a desk and bureau, all made out of old, solid wood, mismatched and scarred in places.

Probably got them from his job at the estate sale store, Casey thought.

The police had to have been here. She looked for the signs. Was that fingerprint powder, on the corner of the desk?

The surface of the desk was devoid of clutter—just a blotter and a coffee cup holding pens and pencils. No computer.

"You mentioned that Alan liked to chat with his friends on his computer," Casey said. "Is it in a different part of the house, or did the police—?"

"It was a laptop. I don't know what happened to it. He took it with him sometimes. They think … I don't know, that he must have gotten rid of it, before."

"Did the police take anything, Ms. Scott?"

"Not much. A couple sketchbooks. Some clothes out of the closet. Some … " She seemed to shake herself. "There were some things in the closet. Some … ammo and … accessories."

"And you never noticed any of those things? You didn't know he had an interest in guns?" She kept her voice soft. As much as she wanted to accuse, to scream, she kept the bite out of it.

"He liked guns the way everybody likes guns," Helen said. "I knew he'd gone out and plinked some cans before with friends. I didn't know he owned all of that. He was twenty-three years old, I wasn't going to come in here and spy on him." Her arm swept up in a sharp, jerky wave. "Art. That's what I knew he liked to do."

She was gesturing at the painting that hung above the desk. "That's one of his. I framed it and put it up, after. He wouldn't have put up one of his own paintings. He would have been embarrassed."

Casey took a few slow steps over to the desk. Leaned on her cane and studied the painting.

A watercolor, she thought. Of some docks at sunset, with sailboats moored at them, the harbor and the downtown city skyscape behind them, orange and yellow light from the sunset reflecting off the glassy towers.

"Nice, isn't it?" Helen said.

It *was* nice, Casey thought. Even beautiful. Too dramatic to be precisely peaceful, but still . . .

Casey nodded. She ran her fingers along the surface of the desk, feeling the old wood's slightly uneven finish. "He was very talented," she said.

"Otherwise I just fixed the room back the way it was before the police came," Helen said behind her. "He liked things neat."

Diego would want a clear shot of that painting, Casey thought. Rose was probably whispering in his ear about it right now.

She slowly moved away from the desk. She was getting tired, waves of pain radiating from her side down her leg and up into her shoulder. Just a little bit longer, she told herself. Just pretend you feel okay. Then go home and lie down.

At the end of the desk was one of the bookcases. Casey had always loved snooping among people's books. You could find out a lot about a person, and nobody questioned your doing it. Not like going into bathrooms and checking out their medicine cabinets. Which she'd also done on occasion.

Action figures. Mostly anime characters. Never her thing, so she couldn't say who or what they were supposed to be. A row of smaller metal figurines: Painted soldiers. Vikings. A couple were Nazis.

Color me not surprised, Casey thought.

Some manga on the shelves, along with other American comics collections. A bunch of smaller paperbacks—something called *Men At Arms*. Casey opened one. A series of paintings of American Revolutionary War soldiers on both sides of the conflict. He had a couple dozen of them, everything from Ancient Macedonian Fighting Men to Irregular Armies of the Modern Middle East.

"He used those for some of his drawings," Helen said.

Casey continued to look at the books. Photography books of landscapes and cities. Animals. The kinds of references that would be useful for an artist, she guessed. A few novels: fantasy stuff, mostly. One title caught her eye.

True Men Will Rise. Another graphic novel from the size. She pulled it out.

Definitely a graphic novel. On the cover was a tall, silhouetted figure in a long coat, standing on the crest of a steep hill, staring down its flank, the lights of a big city below and in the distance. To his left, something burning atop a tall pole: not a cross, but a circle with two crossed lines inside of it, a starburst in its center.

At the bottom of the hill, shadowed men, maybe a dozen, some shouldering rifles, others carrying pistols, were starting to climb up it.

To attack him?

No, Casey thought. To join him.

True Men Will Rise. Created by George Drake.

"Huh," Diego said. Casey was aware of the camera's lens focusing on her, on the graphic novel she held.

Rose peered over from the doorway. "Let's get a shot of that on the desk," she said in a low voice.

Casey wondered why. She placed the graphic novel on the desk and stepped back to give Diego room. Waited a moment to ask her question. Diego would want to get Helen's reaction, if she had something interesting to say about it.

"Do you know anything about this book, Ms. Scott?"

She just shrugged. "He loved comics, ever since we went to Comic-Con when he was a little kid. He used to like to draw them. I think he hoped to get into that business at one time."

"What happened?"

"What happened with everything he did." Helen sounded suddenly, impossibly weary. "He just … gave up."

———

"I loved that guy, before he went nuts," Diego said.

"George Drake?" Rose asked.

"Yeah."

They were in the Highlander on the way back to Casey's condo. It was after eight, and she was ready to crawl into bed. But it had been a good shoot, she thought. While a part of her hated to humanize the little motherfucker, she had to admit she could allow for a tiny drop of sympathy, especially for his mom. Helen Scott didn't seem like a bad person. Just somebody who'd been knocked around by life and who still kept trudging forward. Maybe with blinders on—how else could you keep going sometimes? But she hadn't seen what was happening with her own son, in her own house.

"What's the deal with the comic book?" Casey asked.

"You haven't heard of George Drake? Really talented writer/illustrator, but he went off the deep end. The stuff he writes now, he's practically endorsing fascism."

Diego snorted. "Practically?"

"Okay, wait, you guys are both nerds?"

"I'm more of a geek," Diego said.

Not a surprise Alan Chastain would have something like that comic, then. What was more surprising was how little else there was. No overtly extremist literature beyond the graphic novel, if that even counted. No laptop. No hint of what he'd planned on his Facebook page. If he'd been on Reddit or 4Chan, she hadn't been able to find him. Which didn't necessarily mean anything—he could have used different user names, and besides, there were so many dark corners of the internet where he could have hidden.

He'd left a few clues on Twitter, before the rampage: Tweets about bitches and sluts, about "ghetto" attitudes ruining the country. About hating himself and feeling useless. About feeling trapped—*if I was a rat I could chew my leg off and get away.*

You went by the number of people saying things like that on the internet, you'd be tripping over dead bodies on the street.

Maybe there was no answer. Maybe there was no "why." Just the Big Empty, calling one of its own home.

"You okay, Case?" Diego asked. "You got quiet all of a sudden."

"You saying I talk a lot?" she said lightly. She knew that she generally did. Something to remember when she needed to show she was okay. Smile, and make small talk.

"I'm fine. Just tired."

11

FROM: CASEY CHENG

TO: ROSE ARMITAGE

WHAT ABOUT THIS FOR SERIES TITLE, OR IS IT TOO CORNY?

"THE SHOOTERS AMONG US—A NEWS 9 SPECIAL REPORT"

ALSO, PULLED THIS BITE FROM A NETWORK PACKAGE FROM MAY, CAN
WE ARRANGE TO USE?

*CHYRON: Professor James Ferrer, UCSD Global Health Gun Violence
Working Group*

*FERRER: Mass shootings of the kind that get the lion's share of media
attention are a very small percentage of gun deaths in America—we have to
stop looking at these incidents as the template on which we base our gun
policy, because they are relatively rare. We can't just look at one aspect of
this problem. It is multifaceted and complicated, and we need to come up
with a variety of strategies to effectively address it.*

———

Thomas Ricci's sigh was audible through the phone. "Okay," he finally said. "You come down, I'll talk to you. You can talk to the other employees too. We've got nothing to hide. Just ... can you keep it on the down low? I don't want to freak out the customers." Then he laughed. "Though truth is, we've had more people showing up here since the thing with Alan. Pretty sad, right?"

But typical, Casey thought. She was just taking Diego; no need for Rose on this shoot. Rose had other stories to work on, and there was no hit time for their package yet.

It was such a luxury, having this amount of time to work on a story, something she'd never experienced before. One of the benefits of getting shot. Also pretty sad.

She'd polish up her script based on what they got today, and with any luck they'd cut something together tomorrow. And if Jordan and Gloria liked it, they'd do a few days of promos and slot it in a prime spot on the six o'clock news.

Of course they're going to like it, Casey thought. She'd gotten Helen fucking Scott on camera, talking about her son. No one else had done that.

We'll wrap this one up and on to the next, she thought, as Diego pulled the car over to the curb about a block up from Highsmith's. She was getting back into the flow, she could tell, the fog clouding her brain burning off, the pain receding to the background.

"What are you smiling about?" Diego asked.

"Just ... we're kicking ass on this, aren't we?"

"Pretty much."

And it felt good she thought. *She* felt good.

Nearly ready for surfing bulldogs, even.

They'd use a GoPro for the interior shots of Highsmith's, if Ricci would let them shoot in there at all. Casey wasn't sure they'd even need the footage. A bunch of old furniture, who cared?

"Alan worked on the thrift store floor, primarily."

Ricci looked to be in his fifties. Graying hair, weathered face, and forearms that suggested he spent a lot of time outside when he wasn't buying and selling dead people's belongings. They sat in his small office, which, if Casey had to guess, was decorated with items plucked from various estates, most with Tiki themes—mugs, statuettes, some retro surfing prints on the wall.

"What kind of employee was he?" Casey asked.

"Reliable. Meticulous. Most of what he did was sorting and shelving. He worked really hard trying to keep things in some kind of order. I'll be honest, there's a lot of junk up there and new stuff coming in all the time, but he did his best to keep it neat."

Casey thought of Chastain's room, of its tidiness and lack of clutter. His mother had said she'd put things back the way he liked them. Well, being neat doesn't mean you're crazy. And even if he was OCD or what have you, that didn't make you go out and shoot people.

"Did Alan have any close friends on the staff?" she asked.

"Not that I know of. He seemed to like working on his own." He shook his head. "It's the biggest cliché, right? Quiet kid, kept to himself. Never caused any trouble."

Until he did.

All the other employees said variations of the same thing. He was quiet. He worked hard. We went out for beers after work once.

Nothing earth-shattering, but good for a couple of quick hits.

After, she decided to poke around a bit as Diego shot some B-roll. Physically, she was still feeling good, the best she'd felt since The Event. Maybe she could get a better sense of what the creep's workday here had been like.

Downstairs was the "estate" section, the bulk of it taken up by furniture. The store was big, bare-bones with concrete floors, undecorated save for framed paintings and prints on the walls that were also for sale. Most of it didn't look particularly special: the kind of matching bedroom sets you bought on sale at a low-end department store. A few customers wandered around, checking out the prices. Two workers in red T-shirts, guys she'd already talked to, hauled boxes into a freight elevator.

In the center of the floor there was a square of counters with a cash register and some glass display cases. Jewelry. Watches. Were those wedding rings?

She kept walking. On the other side of the display counters and cash wrap were ranks of industrial shelving filled with ... stuff.

Lamps. Figurines and statuettes. Souvenir ashtrays. Dolls. Vases and pitchers. Hamilton Mint plates. Clocks. Old cameras. Glass and ceramic vases. DVDs and CDs. Portable heaters. Boom boxes. Cat-shaped bookends. Cloisonné salt and pepper shakers. A couple of clay busts that she guessed were the work of high school art students. Matching mugs signed *Dave* and *Laura*, decorated with twining flowers and hearts. Oversized nutcrackers, an Elvis and a Santa Claus. A giant bottle of champagne—what was it called, a double magnum?

Bought for a celebration that never happened, she thought.

All this *stuff*, cleared out of dead people's homes. What among these objects had been meaningful to their owners? What was just random clutter that had built up over time?

If I'd died, what things of mine would have ended up on shelves like this?

Her side had started to throb. She really didn't want to look at any more of it.

But I should go upstairs, she thought, and see where the little asshole worked.

———

Upstairs were rows of low metal shelves sitting on worn linoleum, overflowing with more stuff. San Diego Padres giveaways, bobbleheads of players that were long gone, old hats and cheap gym bags and backpacks with cracked vinyl trim. Broken-up sets of cheap dishes, giveaway glassware, bins of mismatched silverware, pots with the lid knobs missing, piles of clothing, old shoes and battered toys and cheap skateboards. Dust was everywhere—on the stuff, on the shelves, in the closed air.

How could you possibly keep this in order? Had there ever been any order to begin with?

I have to get out of here, she thought. Get outside. Go lie down.

She decided to wait for Diego in the Highlander. Quarter after four and I'm done for the day, she thought. She walked slowly up the empty block toward the car.

The marine layer was coming in, June Gloom on schedule. Shorts and zip-up hoodie weather.

I'll go home, get into my PJs, and call for some takeout, Casey thought. Maybe Thai. Or maybe pizza. Pizza actually sounded wonderful.

Another good thing about stepping back on the oxy: her appetite returning.

They'd parked the car in front of a gourmet coffee roaster, closed now. Too bad, she thought briefly, she could use some good beans. She got out the key fob for the Highlander and heard the lock click open.

"Hey, are you Casey Cheng?"

Her heart slammed in her chest, and she almost dropped the fob. She turned, off-balance, half stumbled, felt the car door at her back.

"Sorry," he said. "I didn't mean to scare you."

White guy. Mid to late twenties. Stocky, even a little overweight. Brown hair cut short. A sprinkle of pink acne across his cheeks.

She straightened up, gripping the cane tightly. He wore sunglasses, so she couldn't see the intent in his eyes.

If he takes a step closer, scream. Hit him with the cane. Right in the nuts.

"The street's so quiet," she said. "I wasn't expecting … wasn't expecting anyone."

He gestured down the block, toward Highsmith's. "Were you talking to them about A.J.?"

"A.J.?"

"Alan Jay. That's what he liked to be called. Alan Jay or A.J. Not Alan Chastain."

"You knew him?"

He nodded. "Yeah. I work at the Quik By. He'd come over for sandwiches."

Her heart was still pounding hard. "It sounds like you two were friends."

He shrugged. "I guess, maybe. We ate lunch together sometimes."

Do your job, she told herself. "We're putting together a story about Alan. Would you be willing to be interviewed?"

She could read the hesitation in his face, even behind the sunglasses. But there was eagerness too. Like there was something he wanted to say.

"Because I know there was more to him than … than what he did. We'd like to find out who he really was."

"I don't know," he said.

"You wouldn't have to be on camera if you don't feel comfortable with that." They could film him in silhouette, maybe. Or worse comes to worse, she'd just quote him in a voice-over or stand-up.

He shifted back and forth. "I guess I'm not really comfortable talking about him," he finally said.

"Well, look, let me give you a card." She had several stashed in her blazer pocket. You never wanted to fumble around in a purse in situations like this and give them too much time to turn it down. "Just email or call if you decide you'd like to talk. We can handle it any way you want."

He took the card. Looked at it a moment and shoved it in his pants pocket.

She glimpsed a tattoo on his forearm. A circle with two crossed lines inside, like a plus sign, with a little star in its center, woven lines snaking around the inside of the circle. Where had she seen something like that before?

"What's your name?" she asked. "So I'll know it's you?" She smiled at him. A little extra charm never hurt.

"Lucas," he said. "My name's Lucas. I'll think about it." He smiled back, a little awkwardly. "I promise."

He probably won't call, she thought, watching him cross the street, heading toward the convenience store. Which on the one hand was too bad. She thought he was telling the truth, that he really did know Chastain and was friendly with him. She had a feeling he might even have something interesting to say, something beyond *Alan kept to himself and was a hard worker.*

And he'd approached her, hadn't he?

Which led her to the other hand: the panic she'd felt when he'd surprised her. She rarely sweated like this, the drops rolling down her back, soaking her blouse, collecting around the abdominal binding she still wore. She leaned against the car door, feeling utterly drained.

I am getting better, she told herself. It's okay and understandable to be a little jumpy. You don't always know with strange men, what their intentions are. And if he really was Alan Chastain's friend, who knew what he was like?

Lucas who works at the Quik By. Easy enough to remember. Worth a follow-up if there was time, she thought. As much as even thinking about that made her stomach lurch.

————————

He had one good beer left in the fridge, a Sculpin. He wasn't a big drinker anymore. Tonight was the right night to have it.

He popped it open and sat down on the couch. "Here's to you, A.J.," he said, lifting up the bottle. He took a long pull. It tasted so good.

It was so fucking tempting. It would have been easy.

He felt around for the master control unit and found it between the couch cushions. Switched on the TV. A Viking show on the History Channel; that would work.

She'd been right there. *Right there!* It would have been awesome to finish what A.J.'d started. To fucking shoot that stuck-up cunt between her slant eyes.

Or better—in the gut. So she'd have time to bleed out and feel her pain, feel her life ending.

The Vikings were attacking an Irish village. The battle scene wasn't half bad for the History Channel. Plenty of extras. Lots of swordplay and real-looking blood. Some good deaths. The decapitation looked a little fake though.

His hand grasped the grip of the 9mm SIG PRO in the concealed carry holster tucked in the front of his work khakis. Nobody knew he had it. It was against the law. Against company policy. Which was bullshit. Convenience stores got robbed all the time. If someone came into his store with a gun, he wasn't pushing any alarm, he was shooting the motherfucker.

Not that he'd have to worry about that for much longer.

Killing that bitch would have been stupid. She was too high-profile, and he would have been right in the frame.

But he knew he needed to practice. Find a target he could hit and not get caught. So he wouldn't hesitate when it was time to rise.

12

DRUG DISPUTE SUSPECTED IN CLAIREMONT AMBUSH SHOOTINGS THAT LEFT TWO DEAD

Two area men were shot to death last night as they shared beers around a fire ring at an apartment complex recreation center. Witnesses reported a single male, described as a white or Latino man in his twenties, fleeing the scene after fatally shooting Riley James, 23, and Elray Harrison, 21, at approximately 1:20 a.m. Drug paraphernalia and large amounts of cash were found on the victims' bodies, leading to speculation that a drug deal gone awry might have motivated the murders.

Families of the victims, however, argue that James and Harrison may have been drug users, but they were not criminals and did not otherwise engage in illegal activities.

"Riley was a nice kid," his uncle Colum James told reporters. "Maybe not set on his course in life, but he meant no harm to anyone. I can't see him getting involved in something like that."

Elray Harrison's mother, Arminta McCann, agrees. "Elray didn't engage in violent behavior, not ever. He wasn't that kind of man."

———

They'd gotten some great stuff at Helen Scott's.

Casey had known it while they were filming, she could just tell; she'd gotten that buzzing feeling that let her know when she'd plugged into something good, something real.

But seeing it again, on her laptop …

Damn. It was really good.

"We've got enough of that painting we can use it for a voice-over," Rose said in her ear.

"Yeah, I like that."

Rose was at the station. Casey sat in her living room. The plan was for her to do the edit after they hashed it out—it wasn't like she had anything else to do, and Rose had plenty. And she wasn't a bad editor. One advantage of the one-man-band jobs she'd done in the past. Shooting, writing, and editing your own pieces—she'd learned a lot. Though it was hard work doing the whole job on your own, even dangerous at times. She'd had her camera stolen once, when she'd been shooting a stand-up and had the camera positioned across the street.

She thought about that night at the brewery. If she'd been by herself …

"What do you think about the Drake book?" Rose asked. "Worth getting into? It's a little obscure, but … "

The cover of *True Men Will Rise,* the graphic novel by George Drake with its supposed fascist themes, was up on the screen now: the man in the long coat, the burning circle atop a tall pole.

A circle with two crossed lines inside of it, a starburst in its center.

"Shit," Casey said. "Any way you can get me a copy? Today?"

A little Googling ID'ed the circle with the cross inside. It had different names: the Bolgar Cross, the Sunwheel, Woden's Cross, a common symbol that dated back to Neolithic times. The cross without the starburst was used now by Pagans, Native Americans, and, sometimes, neo-Nazis and white supremacists. *The overwhelming use of most versions of the cross is non-extremist*, an anti-hate website informed her. *Care must be taken to judge its use in context.*

The starburst was an original element as far as she could tell, added by Drake.

It looked like the tattoo she'd glimpsed on Lucas's arm, the clerk at the convenience store who'd claimed to know Alan Jay Chastain.

"I've got to try to talk to him."

"What's the approach?" Rose asked.

"I don't know, show him the comic? Ask him about the tattoo? Grill him about his relationship with Chastain?"

"I don't think we can just ambush him. All of this, the tattoo, the comic ... we don't really know what the connections are or if there even are any."

"So we find him and ask him for an interview. There's time, right?"

A hesitation on the other end of the line. "Look, Jordan's going to want to see something soon. Like tomorrow. We've got enough here to put together something really solid."

"Can we just ... can we just make an attempt to interview this guy? If we can't, we can't. But I think it's worth a try."

Another pause. "Okay. If we can get something from him today. A commitment at least."

"Great. I'll go there right now. I can use a GoPro and take an Uber or something."

"*No.* Are you *kidding?*"

"Well, I know you're busy, and I'm sure the photographers are already booked."

She could hear Rose take in a deep breath.

"Casey. Listen. You are not going to go confront a guy who you just told me might be an extremist who claims to be friends with a mass murderer who almost killed you. Do you hear how crazy that sounds?"

"You said we have to move on this today. Who else is going to do it?"

"Just … hang on, let me think." Now Casey heard her exhale. "Okay. Let me see if I can find out if he's working and what time he gets off."

"You're going to call? We don't want to scare him off."

"Look, I know how to bullshit people on the phone, okay?"

Casey realized her pulse was racing. Calm down, she told herself, and stop being a bitch. "I know. Sorry. I'm just … I'm tired of not being able to do my job the way I used to. And I want … " The words stuck in her throat. It was all she could do not to cry.

Don't you dare, she thought.

"I want this story to mean something," she said.

"I hear you. I'll see what we can do."

God, I sounded utterly unhinged, Casey thought. It's just a story on a local news show. She wasn't going to change the world with it. She wasn't going to make much of a difference at all.

None of this means anything.

Don't go down that road, she told herself. Just don't. Do the work, and stop acting crazy.

If none of it meant anything, she still needed to do *something*. And she was only going to get so much mileage for being one of the little fucker's victims.

Rose called back fifteen minutes later.

"He's not there. He called in sick this morning." Her voice sounded ... strange. Casey couldn't pinpoint the emotion in it.

"Did you get a home address? A last name?"

"No. The guy I talked to was not into sharing data."

"But if we go there, to the store? Do you think ... ?"

"I don't know." Rose managed a slight chuckle. "You've got me thinking all kinds of things. Like, should we call the police?"

"The police? What, and tell them about a comic book and a tattoo?"

"That a friend of Alan Chastain's has changed his routine and called in sick. Because that's what they do before they go off."

Casey felt something crawl up her spine. No, she told herself, that's just your fear. It's not real.

"Or he has a cold. Or food poisoning."

"It's not like this guy is a source. We have no obligation to protect him. If he's ... if he's up to something, arguably we have a moral duty to report it."

"And if he's *not* up to something? We want to screw up his life by reporting him to law enforcement?"

"I don't know," Rose repeated. "Look, you're the one who said you thought there was something off about him and he gave you the creeps."

"We're gonna get laughed out of the cop shop if we call this in. You think they're going to listen to my *feelings*? Nobody cares about that." She knew she sounded angry. She *was* angry.

"*I* listened," Rose said. "I'm going to talk to Jordan."

"Fine. And after that, what we should be doing is trying to find this guy. How's about that for moral duty?"

"I'll call you back," Rose said, and hung up.

"Shit!"

Casey stared at her phone for a moment, then chucked it against a couch cushion.

You need to stop acting crazy, remember?

But she wasn't proposing that they do anything dangerous. Just go to the store. Get his last name. See if they could find an address, or a phone number. *Talk* to the guy.

What was the point of giving a totally sketchy tip to the police, who probably wouldn't do anything about it anyway? The point was to get the story.

———

They were right. It wasn't so hard when you knew you were doing the right thing.

He'd picked that nigger and that piece of white trash because no one would give a shit if they got popped. He'd seen them around, he knew what they were like. Sitting out there for hours by the barbecue pit, vaping weed and drinking tallboys. Playing music so loud in the beater pickup the white guy owned that his windows rattled when it drove by.

Not all blacks were niggers; he didn't think that. Some were good, hardworking people. Christians. But a nigger was a nigger, and he knew one when he saw one. And that white guy? A nigger-lover. Even worse.

They weren't adding anything to the world.

13

THEY WERE BACK, AND they weren't going to leave her alone.

WE'RE CUMING FOR YOU YOU FAT CUNT AND WHEN WE
FIND YOU WE WILL PUT A BAG ON YOUR PIG-FACE &
FUCK YOU WITH A BAT TILL YOU SPLIT OPEN AND
BLEED TO DEATH YOU STUPID COW

Change the email. She couldn't take the chance. She'd be okay as long as they didn't find out her new name. If *that* happened...

Don't think about it. Just lift.

The little gym was roughly halfway between the campaign office and her apartment. Sarah had taken a midafternoon break, because she knew by the time she got done working tonight, it would be too late for a good workout.

The gym was basic, but it had everything she needed, and not much in the way of attitudes. A nice neighborhood place with a range of ages and fitness activities. There were treadmills, cycles, and stair-steppers.

An activity room offered yoga and Zumba classes, but she didn't care about those. She cared about the two power cages, the hex bar, and the benches.

She was doing bench presses. Her favorite lift. Five reps at 95 pounds. Her PR on the bench was 120, but she wasn't going anywhere near that kind of weight without a spotter.

She finished her fifth rep and placed the bar on the rack. Slid out from under it and sat up. She needed water.

"Hey."

She looked up. Matt Cason stood there, in one of his faded Padres T-shirts, patches of sweat staining the neckline and underarms. He looked her up and down. "I didn't know you lifted."

How would you? she thought. But she didn't say that. Instead she just nodded and said, "I like it."

"Me too."

She could tell he lifted, looking at him now. His triceps and delts were cut. She'd already known his abs and glutes were tight from the way his suits fit.

He gestured at the rack. "You still have sets?"

"Just two short ones."

"Going up in weight?"

"Yes." She managed a smile. "That's the plan."

"Need a spotter?"

She almost said no. She wasn't comfortable with that, with him.

It's just a spot, she told herself. And you want him to pay attention to you. To like you.

"Sure. Thanks."

She added five-pound weights to each side. 105 pounds, three reps. Lay back down on the bench as he positioned himself behind her. Knew that his crotch was right above her head.

"You want me to hand you the bar?" he asked.

"Not for this weight."

She placed her gloved hands on the bar, just where she liked them. Took in a deep breath, let it out, tightened up her abs and her glutes and her quads, and took in another breath. Lifted the bar off the rack, set her shoulders, and held it there for a moment. Brought it down.

One. Two. Her arms trembled.

Three.

Rack it.

Behind her, Matt snorted a laugh. "You made that look easy!"

Was he being condescending? She didn't think so. He sounded like he actually meant it.

"Thanks. It wasn't too hard." She sat up and sipped water from her bottle. Matt came out from behind the bench and stood at her side.

"What's your PR?"

"One twenty. Two reps."

"I bet you could do one twenty-five."

"Maybe."

He grinned. "You wanna try?" Matt slid a ten-pound weight onto his end of the bar. Sarah loaded hers on the other. Grabbed a clip and jimmied it onto the bar to hold the weights in place.

"You don't need clips," Matt said. "I'm spotting you, you're not going to dump the weights."

She felt angry, then embarrassed, or maybe it was the other way around. "I like using them."

Matt shrugged and smiled. "Better safe, yeah. You're right."

Then a flood of gratitude. Just for being listened to.

You're so stupid, she thought.

She positioned herself on the bench. Placed her hands on the bar. Squared her shoulders. She could feel Matt's presence behind her, the heat of his body, smell a slight tang of sweat.

Focus, she told herself. Focus.

She tried to boost the bar off the rack. It didn't seem to budge, almost like it had stuck on the rubber. Crazy that just five pounds more than her max felt so much heavier.

"You want me to hand it to you?"

She hesitated. "Okay," she said.

Matt put his palms under the bar and lifted it up. She could see his face above hers. He was smiling, his forehead damp with sweat. She placed her hands on the bar, his hands bracketing hers.

Deep breath. Tuck your shoulder blades in your back pocket. Abs and glutes tight. She nodded. Matt let go of the bar.

She held it there a moment. Brought it slowly down. Pushed up, as hard as she could, still seeing Matt's face above hers, even when she closed her eyes.

Her arms shook. She could not straighten them, and they shook harder. She felt her arms start to collapse. She was going to lose the weight.

Matt grabbed the bar.

"You okay?"

She kept her eyes squeezed shut. "Yeah. Fine. Just didn't have it."

"You want to try again?"

No, she thought, I don't. I just want to go away. Hide someplace. Never come out.

But fuck it, first she'd try to lift this weight.

She huffed a couple of fast, deep breaths. Positioned herself. Hands on the bar. Shoulders, abs, glutes, quads.

"Ready?"

"Yeah."

He let go. She locked her arms, squared her shoulders. Lowered the bar. Started to raise it, her arms wobbling.

"Come on, come on, you got this! You got this, Sarah!"

Fuck it, she thought. Fuck it! Get the fucking bar up.

With one last push she locked out her elbows. Held the bar a moment. Started to rack it and hit the rubber bumpers. Matt's hands appeared again on either side of hers. Steered the bar into the rack.

"That was awesome!"

She sat up. He clapped her on the shoulder. "Man, you are *strong*. How long you been lifting?"

"Over two years."

"I bet you can get to a hundred fifty on this within a year, no problem."

She managed a smile. "Maybe. I'll keep trying, anyway."

If he'd seen her two years ago …

She hadn't been fat. She had to keep telling herself that. She'd been round. A little chubby. With large breasts that had made her blouses gape and her T-shirts cling to her in a way that had brought stares and catcalls ever since she was fourteen. She knew some girls liked that attention, but it had always made her uncomfortable. She'd been a bookworm, a nerd. When strange men would tell her to smile, most of the time they'd startle her because she'd been thinking about something else, unaware they'd been watching her.

She learned. By her junior year in high school, she'd adapted. She bought clothes that hugged her curves and told herself to be happy when men stared. Told herself to remember to smile.

Like she was smiling now.

Matt was staring at her.

"You coming to the fair tomorrow?" he asked. Matt was supposed to make at least an hour and a half of it, presenting community commendations, meeting constituents, and shaking hands. They'd pushed out another round of emails, tweets, and posts about it this morning.

She shook her head. "Probably not. There's a lot of work to do at the office."

"Come on, you should come. Tell them I need you for social media. Which I do."

She hesitated. Ben wouldn't like it. Ben was planning on going himself. She was supposed to hold down the fort.

But Matt was the boss, wasn't he? The person who had the last word.

"Okay," she said. "Sure. I'll tell them."

———

"Well, Jordan agrees with you. He doesn't feel that what we have warrants going to the police."

Casey had been trying to pace while she waited for Rose's call. She really liked pacing when she was angry or just pent-up. But she couldn't really pace since The Event. Instead, she had to focus on walking twelve steps. A slow pivot. Twelve more steps. Then side-steps the length of her living room to the picture window, and back to the bar that separated her living room from the kitchen.

Look, Ma, no cane!

"Good to know," she said. "So I'm going to Quik By?"

"*We* are going to Quik By. Google says I'll be at your place in twenty-two minutes. Can you get ready that fast?"

"Yeah, Rose. I can get ready that fast."

Bitch, she thought, tossing the phone against the couch cushion.

———

Five minutes into her ride with Rose in the station Prius, Casey needed to break the silence.

"I have to apologize to you," she said. "I know I'm…" She struggled to find the words. She was angry, that's what she was, swinging from anger to a kind of hollow despair and looking for some safe landing in between. But she couldn't say that. "My emotions are running a little high. I appreciate your concern, I really do. And your help with this. I know it's above and beyond."

Rose chuffed out a sigh. "Look… Casey… you're being a trooper here. You haven't complained about how you're feeling once. And Jordan's got some enthusiasm for it, he really does. But you need to understand…" She shook her head, keeping her eyes on the road. "From his perspective, you have celebrity because of what happened. He thinks there's viewer interest because of that. But it has an expiration date. People *do* move on, just like you said in your pitch. They'll move on from this and they'll move on from you. I'm sorry to be so blunt."

Casey wanted to shrug. It was nice of Rose to be honest, but it wasn't like she hadn't known this already.

"That's why I'm impatient," she said.

"Glad we're on the same page."

"So what's the deal? Jordan gives me this package, we see what the response is, if it's good, we do another one, if not, we move on?"

"Pretty much."

"If it tanks, will he move on from me?"

"It's not gonna tank."

"But if it does… when we're done… you think I'll still have a job?"

Rose hesitated. "I don't know how this kind of thing works in terms of HR policy," she finally said. "I think he wants to keep you on. I don't know what happens, eventually, if you don't recover to the point where you can do your old job. Or if you decide that it isn't something you want to do."

"Fair enough," Casey said.

It *wasn't* fair, really. She'd been doing her job when she got hurt. But what else could she say?

———————

There was a single clerk at the Quik By. A guy in his thirties, black hair, brown eyes, olive complexion.

"What's the plan?" Rose had asked.

"Go in, buy some cheesy snacks if there's other customers, wait for them to clear out if we can, talk to the guy."

One customer waited at the checkout counter, buying lottery tickets and a bag of Doritos. Casey decided to forgo the cheesy snacks. She approached the counter with a bottle of water instead.

"Hi," she said brightly, giving him what she hoped was a friendly but not too broad smile.

Don't overplay this, she told herself.

"Okay, that will be two nineteen." He had an accent Casey couldn't quite place—Turkish? Albanian?

She handed over the money. "Thanks." She hesitated. "So, I'm a reporter with News 9. We were hoping to speak with Lucas—I gather he isn't here today?"

"No. He's not working."

"Maybe you can help me."

He pushed the register drawer shut, not meeting her eyes. Not wanting to help, that seemed clear.

"Lucas said that he knew Alan Jay Chastain. The Morena shooter. I guess they had lunch together a few times. Did you know him too?"

Now he looked up. Glanced around. Noted Rose hovering in the background. "I saw him. I didn't know him."

"But Lucas said he did. Do you know if that's true?"

He shrugged. "Maybe they talked together a few times. I don't know. We don't work together much."

"The thing is … Lucas had said that he might be willing to talk to us about Chastain. And we're under a deadline here. I'm wondering … is there any way you can help us get in touch with him?"

He shook his head. "I can't give you that information."

"Sure, understood, and I wouldn't ask for that." Which was a lie, of course. She'd asked for things that people weren't supposed to give her plenty of times. "But would you be willing to give him a call? Drop him an email? Just to let him know we're following up?"

The clerk looked down at the counter. "No," he finally said. "He wouldn't like it if I did that."

There it was. A hint. A crack in the wall.

"Look," Casey said. "We don't have any cameras here. No recorders. This is all just between us. I'm wondering … is there something about Lucas that concerns you? That worries you?"

The clerk bunched his lips.

"Do you think he might be dangerous?"

He didn't say anything for a moment. Instead, he stared at the counter. Like he'd seen a spot there. "You can't tell him I told you this," he mumbled.

"We won't. We promise."

He met her eyes. Then it came out in a rush: "He isn't a nice guy. He says things sometimes. Then he says, 'It was a joke! Can't you take a joke?' I don't always think it's a joke. I think he means it. He has a gun, he carries it all the time."

And he'd stood no more than two feet away from her. He could have shot her down on the street if he'd wanted to.

Casey felt her gut hollow out. And something else.

Score!

"Why didn't you report him? For carrying the gun?"

"He said he had permission. His uncle, you know, he owns a couple of these stores. That's why he has this job. And I better not make trouble for him, because I won't like what happens." The clerk shook his head. "I don't know what's true. I don't know if any of it is. I just know he's an angry guy."

14

HIS NAME WAS LUCAS Derry.

Tony, the clerk, gave them what they needed. "Don't worry, he won't know," Casey told him. "With his last name, we could get that information on our own. It just would take more time." Which was generally true, when it came to addresses. Finding a renter could be a pain though. And cell phone numbers were even harder.

"Jesus," Rose said, as she started up the station Prius. "You flat-out lied to that guy."

Casey shrugged. "I only half lied. And if Lucas is dangerous? Then it was the right thing to do." She punched the number into her phone. It went to voicemail: *"Leave a message. I'll call you back."*

"He's not picking up."

"Listen, we can't just go knock on his door."

"We can't? Then why'd we bother to get that guy to tell us where Lucas lives?"

"Because ..." Rose slumped back against the car seat. "Casey, this is insane. The fact that that guy was willing to hand over Lucas's personal information? That was a real risk. He's scared of him. You should be too."

"Who said I'm not?"

"Let's at least call the station and see if we can get a photographer, Diego, or—"

"Why, so he can get shot instead? It doesn't make a difference *who* knocks on the door if somebody has a gun and wants to use it. Unless the station's invested in body armor." She smiled as she said that. Though it wasn't a bad idea, really.

"So *you* want to be the one to get shot?"

Casey let out a long sigh. A part of her really did want to knock on that door. Confront the Big Empty. Show it she wasn't giving up. And get a fucking story that would blow everyone away.

"No."

"So, what *are* you suggesting?"

"We do a drive-by. See if it looks like anybody's home. Look for a helpful neighbor. At least get some footage of his place so we'll be first, in case ..." Casey shuddered. "In case he does go off."

———

Lucas Derry lived in one of the many apartment blocks that lined stretches of Clairemont Drive and several blocks behind it. Impossible to tell from Google Streetview where his apartment actually was.

An intern back at the station had run a quick public records search that turned up nothing. Which didn't mean much. Lucas was a young guy. If he'd had problems as a juvenile, they'd have no way of knowing.

"Well, this isn't going to cut it," Casey said. She'd gotten in the back seat and aimed her GoPro out the window to get the front of the horseshoe-shaped complex. Old stucco and wood-trimmed buildings from the early sixties with crosshatched, peeling beams, like someone had tried to overlay a European cottage on a cement box. Old-style lettering labeled it THE CLAIRE-VIEW.

"What do you want to do?"

"See if they have assigned parking and if there's a car there. Get a shot of his door."

After that, she wasn't sure.

Rose drove the Prius around the corner of the long block and parked, putting another apartment complex between them and where Lucas lived. "Give me the GoPro," she said.

"What? No. This was my idea. I'll do it."

Rose held up her palms. "No fucking way. We shouldn't even be here. There's no way I am letting you anywhere near him."

"But—"

"Don't argue with me about this. If he's there, if he's watching, he won't recognize me. But you? He knows exactly who you are. Besides, I can run away. You can't." Rose stretched out her hand. "Give me the GoPro."

Casey handed it over. "I'm backing you up, then," she said.

———

There was a driveway between the two apartment complexes that led to a small parking lot bordering the canyon. A low cinderblock fence separated it from another parking lot and the open end of the horseshoe of the Claire-View. From there, Casey had a pretty good view of the courtyard. It looked like most if not all of the apartments were accessible from there.

"Text me when you figure out where his unit is," she said.

Rose nodded. "Will do."

Casey watched Rose slip through the gap in the cinderblock fence and cross the second parking lot.

This was stupid, Casey thought. She's going to get hurt and it will be my fault for being stupid. I shouldn't have pushed this. We should have called the police.

But, but, but. Calling the police in a situation like this? When they didn't really know if Lucas was a threat? That wasn't right either. They had no proof. Just an uncomfortable encounter, a clerk who didn't like the guy, a comic book, and a tattoo.

If you didn't think you had enough to report the story, then you couldn't go to the police with it.

That's what we're trying to do, Casey told herself. Get enough to report the story.

She leaned against the cinderblock wall and watched Rose talk to an old man sitting in a lounge chair in the courtyard. He pointed toward a second-story unit. Rose started to walk across the courtyard.

A text came through.

Got it. #204, back building, upstairs. Mr. Avakian here says Lucas is a dick. Paraphrasing.

Hahah, Casey typed. Be careful or I will hurt you.

Don't worry. Avakian doesn't think he's home.

Casey could see Rose enter a stairwell. Then she couldn't see her anymore.

Please be right, Mr. Avakian, Casey thought.

Behind her, she heard shrieks of laughter. Little kids, she was almost positive. She turned, and there they were: six years old, maybe, two Latina girls, one wearing a stained Supergirl T-shirt, the other in a pink dress, running down a path that led deeper into the complex.

Looks like nobody here, Rose texted.

Good.

126

You will laugh when I show you the door. OMG this guy is a tool.

Can't wait.

One of the girls screamed.

Casey flinched, like someone touched her with a cattle prod. She squeezed her eyes shut and clutched her phone. It's playing, she thought. They are just playing. Nothing is wrong.

She opened her eyes. She couldn't see the girls. She took a few stumbling steps across the parking lot, toward the other complex. Regained her balance and walked as quickly as she could.

Nothing is wrong.

As soon as she reached the paved path, she saw them. The one in the pink dress had a tiny Nerf football that she aimed at Supergirl's head. They screamed some more, laughing like little banshees.

Relief flooded her like a warm narcotic.

Something caught her eye to the right. A heap of color—flowers?—at the base of a light post near a barbecue ring and a Weber grill. Other objects she couldn't make out. A bottle, maybe.

She slowly made her way toward it.

Flowers. Teddy bears. Candles. A couple of tall beer bottles—Stone Ruination and Ballast Point Sculpin—and an empty bottle of tequila. Two photos in plastic slipcovers, a young white guy and a young black guy.

It was a memorial, the kind of thing you saw on street corners where someone was hit by a car. Or shot down by a gang. It was always weird when you saw ones that had been up for a while, how the flowers browned and objects faded in the sun, got windblown, grayed by dirt or smeared by rain.

This one was new, the photos crisp, the flowers fresh.

Casey felt cold prickles gather on the back of her neck, a swarm of tiny spiders' legs dipped in ice.

AM AT YARD OF OTHER COMPLEX BY BARBECUE AREA IN BACK NEAR CANYON. GET OVER HERE ASAP.

Ben wasn't happy about it. She could tell by the way his head pushed back, the tightening of his jaw and lips. "Okay," he said. "If that's what Matt wants. I can handle things here."

"We could both go," she found herself saying. She felt sorry for Ben, she realized. More than that: she didn't want him to be mad at her. Even if Matt liked her, having Ben mad wouldn't help her position in the campaign.

Ben shrugged. "Not sure there's anything for me to do there. Unless you think we need two people on Social."

She didn't, really. It was a community fair at a local park, a belated Fourth of July celebration. It featured food trucks, a few booths for service organizations including the police and the fire departments, an on-site electronics recycling vendor, a booth for urban trees and tips on xeriscaping, solar panel vendors, rec center sports teams taking sign-ups for youth baseball and dodgeball for grownups, and a bouncy castle and pony rides for the kids. There would be a band or two, a couple of massage chairs, and a tai chi demonstration. A lot of red, white, and blue bunting. Face painting and balloon animals, probably.

Matt's part in all this was to give a brief speech and hand out a commendation to the local fire station and EMS for their part in aiding the victims of the Morena shootings. The district home office would have a booth as well, with a few junior staffers giving out information about the district, who was who in Matt's office and how to find help, government and private resources available to residents, volunteer opportunities in the community, times when Matt was in San Diego and holding open house events for interested constituents. The booth staffers could not hand out campaign literature or do any obvious electioneering.

"If somebody asks about volunteering on the campaign, by all means get their information," Ben told Sarah. "Hand them a button, even. We just can't actively solicit that at a noncampaign event."

Matt would also take time for a meet and greet at the fire department booth. It was always fire season in Southern California, and the SDFD liked to take advantage of any opportunity to reinforce good fire prevention practices. Matt would listen to people's complaints and tell them the best way to protect their homes from wildfires.

"They do a demonstration showing people how to use fire extinguishers, have these big old gas flames shooting up you get to extinguish," Ben said. "We just need to make sure we get shots and maybe footage of Matt doing that. Great GIF material. Representative Cason dousing the flames of whatever."

"Maybe you *should* come, then. So we can get it from a couple different angles."

Ben shrugged again. "I'll see how things are going here."

He was still mad at her, she could tell. It's not my fault, she thought. She hadn't been the one to make the decision. But that didn't seem to matter. It never did.

———

"Well, fuck me."

Rose stared at the memorial to the two dead men, Riley James and Elray Harrison. "I thought this address sounded familiar, but I didn't connect why."

"Do you think ... ?" Casey began. She couldn't complete the sentence.

"I mean, how do we know? We've got this string of coincidences and no way to prove any of it's tied together. And ... why? What's the motive? It's just senseless."

It was as though Rose was talking to herself, trying to work the puzzle, the conundrum of what to do about any of this.

"So was what Alan Chastain did up on the roof," Casey said. "He killed people he didn't know. He didn't have any connection to them. Or no one's found it yet, anyway. He just went up there and killed people. He tried to kill *me*. Because I was there. No other reason. Or maybe he thought it would be fun to bag a TV reporter."

"You think Lucas Derry is killing people for fun?"

Casey thought about it. "I don't know. I just think if he is, I mean, if he *is* killing people ... we don't know what the reasons are. Like Chastain. We think he's one of those guys who just goes off and starts shooting. Maybe there's some other motivation, and we don't know what it is yet."

Let there be a reason, she thought. If there was a reason, you might be able to fix things somehow.

A breeze from the shadowed canyon came up, fluttering the photos and the flowers.

"What do we do now?" Rose asked.

———————

He knew he shouldn't have called in sick. You were supposed to stick to your routine as much as you could, not give anyone any clues. But after the high from last night and the thought of what lay ahead tomorrow ...

130

Lucas just couldn't face going back into that shithole of a store and doing that stupid, worthless job for one more minute. Fuck that place. The pay was shit. The job was boring. The other workers, most of them were useless trash, a bunch of fucking mud people. On his last full day of freedom? Maybe his last day on earth? Why should he have to spend any of it with them?

Instead, he decided to have some fun. Finally got his second tattoo. Went to the range and practiced shooting. Treated himself to an excellent steak and lobster dinner, something he couldn't really afford, but what the fuck difference did that make now? Saw a movie he'd been wanting to catch, in a theater instead of waiting for it to come online. Went to a massage parlor and got a hand job from a cute little Thai masseuse. It was too bad that he couldn't fuck her too, but on the other hand, would you really want to put your dick in that? Who knew what else had been in there?

It bothered him that he hadn't been able to fuck many women in his life. He *should* have been able to, but most of the girls he'd met were such bitches. Always wanting someone "better," some alpha asshole who'd treat them like shit but they'd still cream over. It wasn't fair.

Fucking sluts.

After tomorrow, everything would be different. If he lived, he'd be worshipped by the ones who understood what was at stake, who understood what he'd done for them. He'd have all kinds of ladies sucking up to him too, he'd bet, all those dumb bitches who fell in love with convicted murderers and even married the assholes.

Maybe there would be a few who'd finally see who he really was.

If he didn't make it, he'd die knowing he'd done the right thing. Something big. Something important that everyone would remember.

He wasn't sure if he believed there was a better world waiting for him on the other side, but when it came down to it, there was no fucking point in continuing to live the way he was living.

Lucas pulled the Saran wrap off the new tattoo on his left forearm, still red around the black Gothic letters, dots of scabbing here and there where the artist had gone a little deep.

"Those who will not fight in this world of strife do not deserve to live," he said, lightly running his fingertips over the inked words.

15

UNFUCKINGBELIEVABLE.

Lindsey grasped the back of the couch and squeezed the cushion as hard as she could. It was either that or break something.

Sometimes Matt was such an ungrateful SOB that she wanted to claw his face. She'd put her life on hold for him, and *this* was how he responded.

She'd resigned from the law firm. It had just gotten too complicated with Matt in Congress. Yes, a lot of people wanted access to her, thinking that meant access to him. But with the potential for conflicts of interest, the attacks made on her during his first campaign because of her work, it just wasn't worth it anymore.

They'd miss the money she brought in. Neither of them came from money, unlike the majority of Matt's colleagues in Congress.

But they were doing all right. She'd paid off her student loans. Matt's military benefits had covered his. They'd bought a modest house in a middle-class Clairemont neighborhood before Matt's election.

Refinanced and remodeled it. Not her dream house, not by any stretch, but they could afford it without her income now, and the remodel looked good, taking what had been a stucco box and turning it into a two-story Craftsman-style home with a rooftop deck and views of the bay and canyon. They had some money saved. And she would go back to work, after this election was over. She just wasn't sure what she wanted to do. What made *sense* to do under the circumstances.

So she'd taken on the fundraising role. She hated it. An endless, thankless task, and she didn't think she was very good at it. She lacked Matt's easy charisma, she knew. But she'd raised a lot of money regardless.

And Matt? He acted like it was an imposition on his time. Like a sullen teenager asked to do homework he didn't care about and she was the teacher insisting that he do it. Or worse, his mother.

And he wondered why she didn't want kids.

"Look, I've got to go, Linds," he'd said. "I don't want to show up late to the fair and have to run out of there soon as I've finished speaking."

"Five calls, Matt. That's all I'm asking. We sit down and do it now, and you won't be late."

"You know what, I would actually like to take a little extra time to talk to the people I represent, okay? If that means my priorities are fucked up, then fine." He'd left with a stomp and a slammed door.

Fine back at you, she thought. If *he* didn't care, why should she?

Still, she made a couple of the calls herself—people she knew somewhat and didn't feel too terrible calling. Sharon asked again about nailing Matt down on a date for her fundraiser, and Lindsey didn't have an answer for her yet, but that couldn't be helped. "I'll get Matt to commit," she'd said. "Soon, I promise. His schedule is just a

little complicated right now. But I know he really wants to do this."
She'd rolled her eyes as she said it.

Liar.

After that, she changed for the event. Casual, she'd been told. Bright green capris and an embroidered Mexican blouse, she decided. A relief not to get dressed up in political wife drag, for once.

The park was a quick seven-minute drive from their house. She had to circle around a few times to find street parking. The lot was full, a chunk of it taken up by three food trucks. Good attendance, it looked like. Booths were set up in a rough quadrangle between the trees. Kids waited in line at a bouncy castle, several fencing with balloon swords. There was a small stage at the far end where Matt would speak. Right now a group of mariachis played, except the song was by Nirvana. Lindsey smiled.

Matt hadn't been wrong, she had to admit. She wasn't late for his speech, but she'd gotten there right before it was supposed to start. He wouldn't have had the time he claimed to have wanted to meet with constituents.

Of course, if he didn't raise enough money to compete in this election, he wouldn't be able to meet with his constituents at all.

Lindsey crossed the parking lot and made her way past the food trucks, breathing in the scent of frying onions and meat from the taco truck, thinking maybe she'd have a couple of tacos after the speech, just relax for a little while. Maybe she and Matt could slip away for an hour or two, go have a drink together and some time to themselves. Not talk about the campaign. Just be together. They hadn't had enough of that in the last couple of years, not at all. Maybe if they made some time for each other, things could be better again.

When she was close enough to the little stage to see Matt, she almost laughed at her own stupidity.

There he was, a big smile on his face, standing next to that girl, Sarah, the palm of one hand resting for a moment on her shoulder and giving it the slightest of rubs. Sarah was smiling too, her cheeks suffused with the rosy glow of sexual attraction. Don't try to tell me that's not what it is, Lindsey thought.

This was what he'd wanted. Not time to meet with his constituents. Oh no. Just time to hang out with this girl with big tits who gazed up at him with her worshipful smile.

"Fuck this," Lindsey said. She turned on her heels and walked away. He could fucking do this without her.

————

Ben was right. Matt dousing the flames was going to make an awesome GIF.

The firemen had turned the gas up high, so the flames were big. White shirtsleeves rolled up, sporting comfortably worn khaki chinos and a mustard yellow and brown Padres hat that shaded his eyes but didn't hide his grin, Matt swept the nozzle of the fire extinguisher back and forth, dousing the gas flames with bursts of white foam.

It was a great visual. She was glad Ben had decided to come along and get it from another angle.

"Definitely, you should try it!" Matt told a teenage girl. "It's a good thing to know how to do." He handed her the fire extinguisher. Then he turned to Sarah.

"How was it?" he asked, moving close to her so he wouldn't be overheard.

She tensed. She couldn't help it. She could feel the solid presence of his body next to her. She wanted to feel relaxed and confident around him, a grownup woman he'd respect, but instead she was more awkward than the girl who was now wielding the fire extinguisher, laughing as she snuffed out the gas flames.

"It was great," she said. "I already posted a GIF."

The way he looked at her, the way she felt around him, it was like being enveloped in a great, buzzing electrical field.

You can't even think about that, she told herself. It would be a disaster.

But the way she felt ... she hadn't felt that way for a long time. Like he'd turned a key and unlocked something inside of her.

Don't, she told herself. Just don't.

"Ready for the speech?" Matt asked Sarah.

She smiled. "Sure," she said.

———

The speech was short. Matt presented official commendations to fire and EMS personnel up on stage, thanking them for their courage and dedication to the safety of the city. Then he paused. He'd taken off his cap at the beginning of the speech. You could see his eyes clearly now. They were glistening. Not exactly teary, and maybe it was just from the glare of the sun.

"I just want to say what an honor it has been for me to serve this community. You know, I've been a lot of places in my life, and I can honestly say that there isn't a better spot in the world than right here. And it's not just because of our weather. Or our beer."

A few chuckles.

"It's because of you. All of you. Your tolerance and your strength. Your willingness to come together as a community as a response to a horrible, criminal tragedy."

Sarah wondered how the community had actually "come together." Was there any real evidence of that? What did it even mean?

It sounded good, though, and he delivered it well.

"You stared at the face of intolerance and hate, and hate blinked," Matt continued. He waited a moment, then smiled. "I'm here for the next hour or so to talk to you about your concerns, your ideas, what you'd like to see from me in Washington and how we can all continue to create positive change in our city, together. We don't have to agree on everything. But let's keep talking." He waved toward the booth from the district office. "Hope to see you over there, maybe after you've had some tacos and fresh-squeezed lemonade!"

Ben fell alongside of Matt and Sarah as they made their way to the booth. "Pretty sure we have an oppo tracker," he said in a low voice, pointing to their right, at a young white man wearing a polo shirt and neat khaki shorts who carried a small video camera. "I spotted him during the speech."

Matt snorted. "Let's see them make something of that."

"I'm guessing he's more interested in the meet and greets. Better chance of something going south."

Matt lifted one hand in a Boy Scout salute. "I promise to be on my best behavior. Sarah here will keep me on track. Right, Sarah?"

She could feel herself blush. "I'll do my best."

———

It would have been so awesome if he could have completed the mission while that motherfucking traitor was up on stage. Right in the middle of his stupid speech. It would have looked so fucking cool, like a scene from a movie.

But it would have been stupid. He needed to get closer.

And this would be even better, in a way. Let that asshole alpha shit and the stupid little cunt hanging all over him see who he was, look him in the eye, before he did it.

Tegan's tracker wasn't even trying to hide it. He stood right there in his polo shirt and Top-Siders recording the meet and greet by the district office booth. "You have any questions?" Matt said, giving him a big smile. "I'd love to hear from you."

Next to him, Ben snorted.

A good crowd had gathered around Matt, who stood in front of the booth, shaking hands. Sarah stood off to one side so she could record him too. He was so good at this, so comfortable, making eye contact, smiling in a way that looked real. And he *listened*.

She decided to just let the video roll, see what she got. She held up her phone and touched Record. People came and went. Asked questions about more federal funds for the trolley, about cleaning up the bay, about what to do about a run-down house on the block and airplane noise from Miramar. Nothing special.

A man pushed his way to the front of the crowd. Twenties. Shaved head. Black T-shirt and sagging cargo shorts, eyes hidden behind dark sunglasses. "Hey! You! You're supposed to be a big hero? Well fuck you. All you've done is shit all over real Americans!"

Matt's posture changed. He let go of the hand he was shaking. Stepped forward. Held up his hands in a way that was both a signal to calm down and back off, legs slightly bent, like he was ready to fight if he had to. "Okay," he said. "Why don't we talk about it? Tell me what your problems are. Let's see what we can do about them."

The man stood there, breathing hard. Sarah could smell alcohol fumes coming off him in waves, carried in his breath, in his sweat. "I'm a vet, like you," he said. "I came home to no fucking job. I can't even get a job at a fucking McDonald's. You let Mexicans and rag-heads into this country instead of taking care of our own first. What the fuck, man?"

The crowd scattered back a few feet, leaving the man facing Matt in an empty circle.

Sarah glanced around. Saw an event security guard talking into his radio. Another came trotting over. Matt lifted a hand in warning. *Stop.*

She'd seen an SDPD squad car in the parking lot. Had they called the police? If she moved, would that just set the guy off?

She kept recording.

"I know it's hard when you come home," Matt said. "You're on the other side of the world where things are so different, and your head's on a swivel all the time. Then you get back here, in just a few hours. To this. Where everything's the same, but you're not." He gestured at the park. At the bouncy castle. You could hear the children, laughing and screaming, guitar chords as the next band warmed up. "People are out here, having a great day, having fun, and it makes no fucking sense to you. You're still on alert. And you don't get how these two places can even exist at the same time."

The man was still breathing hard. He nodded, fractionally.

"I know it can be infuriating, the red tape and the bullshit and having to wait to have some bureaucrat tell you to stand in another fucking line and fill out another goddamn form. I get it. I dealt with some of the same shit when I came home. But I had people in my corner. And I want you to know, you do too. I'm going to put you in touch with someone from my office who can help you, okay? We'll get your information, and I'm going to tell them who you are, and we're going to see what we can do. No promises I can find you a job. But I promise we're going to do our best to help you."

140

The man's shoulders slumped. All the fight seemed to have gone out of him. "Okay," he said.

A light tap on the shoulder. It was Ben, who'd moved alongside her. "You getting this?" he mouthed. She nodded.

Matt stretched out his hand. After a moment, the man took it. Matt placed his left hand on top of the man's. Grasped it. Said something so quietly that Sarah couldn't hear it. The man nodded, face tilted down, staring at his shoes. He might have been crying.

They stood there, the two of them, like there was no one else around.

Matt looked up. Met Sarah's eyes. One brow lifted fractionally—a half a smile. Almost a wink, like, *Can you believe this?*

Like it was their own private joke.

"Congressman?"

Sarah looked over and saw a young man in a black windbreaker. Stocky. Sunglasses. That was all she saw, before the gun.

16

SHIT! HE'D HAD A clear shot, and then that crazy asshole got in the way, and he couldn't wait any longer, rent-a-cops were already here, and a real cop heading this way at a run.

Now or never.

Now.

———

Shots. Someone, something, slammed into her and she fell, and there were more shots, and screams, and then the shots stopped and the screams continued, someone was lying next to her, moaning, and she opened her eyes and saw Matt, blood covering his face like a mask, his fist driving into the face of a man on the ground, over and over. She thought she heard a snap of bone, like when you cracked a chicken wing, as blood gushed from the man's nose, his mouth, she could hear him choking on his own blood, and Matt kept hitting him, his eyes wild, his lips drawn back in a snarl.

17

SHE WENT RUNNING. THAT was one of the only things Lindsey could think of to do when she felt like this. Well, one of the only things that wasn't stupidly self-destructive.

It was just after two o'clock. She generally liked running earlier in the morning or right around sunset, but the weather was good now: partly cloudy, with a cool breeze, enough humidity to make the air feel soothing on her skin.

Slow down, she told herself. If she started out too fast, she would burn out before she even got going, and the way she was feeling now, she needed to run a good long time. Just exhaust herself. Sweat it all out, the rage, the hurt, until she stopped feeling anything, just her feet hitting the sidewalk, her muscles carrying her along, the cool air on her skin, filling her lungs. In and out.

Goddamn it. What the fuck was she going to do? This ... she couldn't keep doing this. They'd been together twelve years, maybe that was long enough. She could still have a kid, if she wanted one.

Well, maybe. Thirty-six years old, that didn't leave much time. But not with him. He was so fucking unplugged, it was like they existed in parallel orbits, never really connecting.

The way he looked at that girl ... for all she knew he was already fucking her. He was always looking. Looking for someone younger, someone prettier, someone more exotic, more dangerous, someone *different*. That was the main thing. The novelty. That he could turn it on and take what he wanted. If he wanted to. That was the other thing. She wasn't sure he even followed through anymore. It was enough that he knew he could.

She decided to run up into the Western Hills, the section of Claremont above Bay Park. The hills were punishing, but she was in the mood for that. Which was stupid. Why should she punish herself? What had *she* done wrong?

Still, the hills were a good way to push herself. Just focus on getting up the hill. One foot after another. Stop thinking about all this shit.

She jogged up Milton, passing the back of the car dealership off Morena. That car dealership had long irritated her. It thrust into a residential neighborhood, the huge lot where new cars were parked cutting off direct routes to the other side of it for blocks. You'd try to get through the neighborhood, and if you calculated wrong, you'd run into a literal brick wall. Dead-ends.

Tegan's husband owned car dealerships. That was where her money came from. Not this one, she didn't think. Too bad. She'd love to hammer them on the negative impact poor planning like this had on neighborhoods. The city of San Diego had an ambitious climate action plan that was supposed to encourage walking, biking, alternative forms of transportation, to get people out of their cars. And here you were, forced to go blocks out of your way because of a huge car lot where the cars weren't even moving. Just sitting there.

When she got to the top of Milton, she paused to catch her breath and take a long drink of water. The views were beautiful up here. She could see the bay straight ahead, Fiesta Island, the Strand, the marine layer nestled against the ocean beyond, waiting to roll in as the sun went down. If she ran another block or two, she could see the harbor and Point Loma. On a clear day, the Coronado Islands.

She felt calmer now. Exhaustion would do that. Hang tough for the campaign, she told herself. Wait till the election is over before you do anything. You owe him that.

But did she, really? When he wasn't willing to do the work that needed to be done?

You owe the country, then, she thought. God knows Matt, for all his faults, was a better choice to represent the district than Kimberly Tegan.

Which way now?

North was a small park with trails where she sometimes liked to run. The only real problem with it was no bathroom. South was Teco-lote Park, which would be a longer run. But there were bathrooms, and if they were locked, there were restaurants and breweries close by where she could stop in if need be. Maybe she'd have a drink at the bar down on Morena where she and Matt used to go. The High Dive specialized in craft beer (of course), and it was a friendly place, with burgers and tacos, old-school pinball games and Tiki decor. They'd hang out there, split a plate of happy hour Gorgonzola fries, drink a few beers, play some pinball.

We used to have fun together, Lindsey thought. She started running south.

The route took her down and then up a hill and into a canyon. It was an odd neighborhood, a mix of newer tracts, expensive homes, and older houses and apartments, some of which were really run-down, the kind of thing you expected to see in a slum. Clairemont was like that, though. It varied from block to block, sometimes from house to house.

This particular canyon seemed almost cut off from the larger neighborhood. The houses here were oddly spaced and mismatched, not part of any planned development. There were mature trees, RVs parked on vacant corners, a couple of junked cars. The canyon walls left much of the area in shade. It was quiet down here too. You could hear muffled traffic from the freeway, but only if you listened. No children playing. Just a distant leaf blower.

Lindsey stopped for more water. Across the street was a large house, two stories with a balcony. Gray streaks ran down the white stucco walls. The big gravel driveway yard was parked up with vehicles: two new Beemers, a Jeep, an ATV, a vintage Indian motorcycle, and a powerboat on a trailer. Two German shepherds patrolled the large front yard, which was mostly patchy grass interwoven with weeds.

Weird, Lindsey thought. The slightly run-down, overly large house, like a stucco plantation, and all the expensive cars.

A blond woman came out the front door wearing a white blazer and a bright orange blouse. Thin, in decent shape, Lindsey thought. A few years older than she was.

Shit, was that Kimberly Tegan?

Lindsey ran through the facts that she had in her head, and realized that, yes, Kim Tegan lived in this neighborhood, and yes, that absolutely could be her.

She tucked her water bottle back in her fanny pack. The last thing she wanted was for the opposition candidate to think she'd been spying on her.

The woman was walking toward one of the Mercedes when she looked up and saw Lindsey. Her face changed. It was hard to identify her expression behind the sunglasses. It was more the tilt of her head, a kind of wariness. Then, something else. A decision made.

Tegan strode across the street, closing the distance quickly. "Aren't you Lindsey Cason?"

"I ... yes."

"I think you know who I am, right?"

"I ... well, I don't think we've actually met. You're Kim Tegan?" Lindsey waved toward the street she'd jogged down. "I was just out running." Stupid thing to say, but it was true, and the optics on this weren't great.

She couldn't place Tegan's expression. The sunglasses Tegan wore blocked access to her eyes.

Tegan seemed to shake herself for a moment, like a dog or cat who'd gotten unexpectedly wet. "I guess ... you haven't heard?"

"Heard what?"

Her phone rang just then. "Pressure Drop," the ringtone she'd assigned for anyone having to do with the campaign. "Excuse me," she said. She unstrapped her phone from her arm. Jane.

"Hello?"

"Where are you?" Jane asked right away. That was Jane. She didn't like to waste time.

"I'm out running. Why?"

"Tell me where you are."

"I'm ... " She'd jogged down here a few times before, but she hadn't ever noted the exact address. "I'm in Clairemont, in Bay Park or Western Hills, I guess. What's going on?"

For a moment, she heard nothing. Then, an intake and exhalation of breath. "Lindsey, there's been an incident. At the park. A guy with a gun and … we don't really know what happened."

"A gun?"

"Matt's hurt," Jane said. "I think … we think he's okay but I don't know for sure. People are dead."

"What?" This didn't make sense. Her ears were buzzing, and then there was an empty sound, a dull roaring. "What … what happened?"

"I need to know where you are, Lindsey. We'll send a police car to pick you up."

"I'm … " She looked around, trying to find a street sign. Wasn't there some way she could share her location on social media? Through Facebook, or Instagram? On a Google Hangout, or even through Chat?

All those apps, they wanted to know where you were.

"I don't know," she said. "Matt's okay?"

"We think so. Look," Jane said, "I want you to take a deep breath and see if you can find an address. The police need to come and get you. They want to make sure you're safe."

"Safe? What do you mean?"

"Can I give you a ride someplace?" Kimberly Tegan asked.

"I … "

Tegan rested her hand on Lindsey's shoulder. "It's not a problem. You just let me know." Then Tegan patted her hip. "Don't worry," she said. "We're protected." She hitched up her bright orange blouse a few inches. The edge of a black elastic band with flirty pink trim was just visible above the waist of her pants—a holster, the butt of a pistol in easy reach.

18

NEIGHBOR2NEIGHBOR/CLAIREMONT/NEWS_FEED

Scott Larson, West Central Bay Park

GUNSHOTS FIRED?

Scott Larson, West Central Bay Park

I'M HEARING GUNSHOTS AND HELICOPTERS, CAN'T TELL
FOR SURE BUT THINK IT'S AROUND CLAIREMONT
DRIVE AND THE PARK.

Scott Larson, West Central Bay Park

ANYONE HAVE ANY INSIGHT?

———

Standing in front of the makeshift memorial to Riley James and Elray
Harrison yesterday, Casey had finally agreed it was time to tell the
police. She hadn't sat easily with the decision since then. She wasn't
willing to go on the air and call Lucas Derry a killer—that was what

the standard should be for contacting law enforcement—but the way everything had added up ...

Could she live with herself if they didn't say anything, and the worst happened?

"So, I called Helton," Rose told her. He was one of the detectives on the Morena shootings and had been on their list to interview for the series. ("We go with the personal angle, right? What was it like, investigating a crime like this, a mass slaughter? Does he still think about the victims?") Helton hadn't said yes yet, but he had said maybe.

She'd found Rose at her desk in the newsroom after the morning meeting. Casey had missed it because of her PT appointment, but then, she hadn't made a morning meeting since The Event. She was still on light duty, officially.

But it was time, she thought. No reason not to go to the meetings. There was work she could do here. She could go out on stories if they weren't too physically challenging, she'd already proved it with the Chastain package. Reasonable accommodation, didn't they have to provide that?

Looking around the room, at the monitors that seemed to fill up every available space on desks and on walls, at the cubicles cluttered with photos of people's kids and spouses and partners, water bottles, food wrappers and half-eaten bagels on paper plates, cameras, at a Dejero GoBox ready to go, spare battery packs, at the wall of photos and cards and clippings and the shelf of Emmys, the battered filing cabinets and furniture that looked like higher-end Ikea stuff that had fallen out of the truck a few times, everyone plugged in and working ... she could *feel* the place, the whole thing. The parts she didn't like—the strange politics and often trivial stories and the sometimes brutal schedule and the surprisingly shitty pay—and the parts she loved. Getting out there. Seeing something she hadn't seen. Telling a story the right way.

"What did you tell Helton?" Casey asked.

"I just laid it out. What happened and what we know. What other people said about him. A screenshot from the footage I got of Lucas's apartment door."

The door. In another context it might have been funny.

It was covered with stickers. One with an assault rifle that said, *You Can Live Scared—Or Be Prepared*. Another praising the Second Amendment—*America's Original Homeland Security*. Then, *Ideas Are Bulletproof. Enemy of the State*. And *Got Liberty?*

And finally, *Do Or Do Not, There Is No Try*, with a silhouette of Yoda.

"So what did he say? How did he react?"

Rose shrugged. "He said they'd look into it."

"Did he mean it?"

"Who knows? But I made him promise if we were right that we'd get confirmation ahead of any presser."

"You think he'll honor that?"

"Again, who knows? But if he doesn't, we still have an angle. We're the first to make the connection between Alan Chastain and Lucas Derry. Plus, you were stalked by a killer."

Casey supposed that had to count for something.

Rose looked away, as though she were embarrassed. "Also, I left out the comic book."

"You did?"

Another shrug. "For now. It's pretty tenuous, and if Helton screws us over, we still have something no one else has."

———

SD Baseball Mom @SDBaseballMom
Cant believe what I just saw guy shooting at
@RepMattCason and Cason beat the shit out of
him Im shaking

San Diego Police Department @SDPolice
Active shooter incident at Mid-Clairemont Rec
Center, Stay away from the area. Media: Don't
call for updates at this time, more to follow

———————

They were meeting in the small conference room just off the newsroom about the Helen Scott package, about Lucas Derry, what made sense to run, and when. If they got confirmation on a connection between Chastain and Derry, they had something cut together that would only take a few tweaks before it was good to go. In the meantime, did it make sense to hit with Helen Scott as planned?

"I vote we promo a couple more days," Gloria said. "There's no urgency to get it on tonight. Let's build it."

"Slow night tonight though," said Chris, the six o'clock newscast's director. A new guy, he'd come in since the Morena shooting. "We'll run short without it."

An intern—Casey couldn't remember her name, she was new too—stuck her head in and said, "Active shooter incident at the Mid-Clairemont Rec Center, multiple casualties, Congressman Cason's there."

You could feel the room go on alert, everyone suddenly tense, upright, focused on the intern's bright face, her excitement.

This was the shit they all lived for.

"Where'd you get that?" Gloria snapped.

"Twitter and Facebook, SDPD's confirmed."

"I'll go," Casey heard herself say.

Everyone's head swiveled toward her: Rose, Jordan, Gloria, Craig and Elise, Chris.

"I don't think—" Rose began.

"I can do it."

"You're sure you're up to it?" Gloria asked.

She *wasn't* sure, but she forced a smile and said, "Yeah. I am."

Jordan and Gloria exchanged a look. Then Gloria nodded. "Go for it."

Blood really did smell like metal. Like the old, dirty pennies she'd collected in her piggy bank when she was a kid. Like metal and raw meat.

The person lying next to her was Ben.

She couldn't see where he was shot, at first. His head, his torso, she couldn't see any blood. Then he'd rolled over onto his back, and she saw his leg, soaked in blood, blood pulsing from his thigh, pooling on the ground around it.

"Somebody do something," she said, and she couldn't make her voice loud enough over the screams and the shouts, two policemen yelling for everyone to stay down, surrounding the man that Matt had beat up, planting a foot in his back and cuffing his hands, Matt sitting on the ground looking dazed.

Finally, she did the only thing she could think of to do: peeled off her black blazer, wadded it into a ball, and pressed it against the wound on Ben's leg. He let out a high-pitched cry, weaker than she would have thought given how much it must have hurt, but he was so pale, and there was so much blood.

"Help's coming," she told him, but she didn't know if it was. She thought she heard sirens.

She looked up for a moment. More police arriving. And something else. Someone, a man with a camera, aiming it at her.

———

News 9 San Diego @News9SanDiego
BREAKING: GUNFIRE AND MULTIPLE CASUALTIES
REPORTED AT @REPMATTCASON COMMUNITY EVENT
IN CLAIREMONT

———

The videos were coming in as fast as the police, several uploaded as squad cars and a tactical team arrived at the scene.

Most of them weren't very good, taken at a distance after the gunfire had stopped. But there was one that stood out. Someone, *@SD-BaseballMom,* had been live-streaming on Periscope just before the shooting started, capturing Cason speaking to a man who looked like he might be drunk or drugged. *"I promise we're going to do our best to help you,"* Cason had said. A moment of silence, someone yelled, *"Congressman!"* and then a gunshot, and another, and screams. The camera POV jerked and swung, catching a glimpse of a stocky guy in a black jacket and sunglasses, holding something dark in one fist, then a flash and another gunshot, and a plunging blur as the phone hit the ground.

Casey watched it on her phone as they sped to the park in the live truck. "Shit," she said. "*Shit.* It looks like *him.*"

"Wait, what?" Rose twisted around in the front seat. "What are you watching?"

"Video of the park shootings. I think it's Lucas."

"Are you sure?"

"It's a Twitter video and I'm watching it on a phone, I *can't* be sure."

But she'd managed to freeze the video on the man. The shooter. It was him.

"Shit," she said. "Can we call your detective? There has to be some way we can get a positive ID."

"I'll call. You've got a stand-up to do," Rose said.

Right, Casey thought. Get as close as she could get to the crime scene, the yellow crime tape, the flashing sirens, the police securing the area.

She shuddered, thinking about it.

They'd gotten close that night at the brewery. They were looking for a good angle, and they'd found one. She'd thought it was okay, and the police hadn't stopped them, maybe because units were still arriving, still setting up a perimeter.

Too close.

You can do it, she told herself. You want to work. Even if you aren't fast on your feet, you can still do the job.

Besides, she knew that park. No tall buildings anywhere close to it.

It won't be dangerous, not this time.

Clark Went @ClarkWent
SOMEONE JUST SHOT MY CONGRESSMAN, @REPMATTCASON. HOPE HE MAKES IT

SanDee @SanDeeinSD
CANNOT BELIEVE THIS IS HAPPENING AGAIN, THIS HAS TO STOP, GET GUNS OFF THE STREET!

Pepe Got Your Number @PepeGotYourNumber
GO AHEAD GET RID OF YOUR GUNS MOAR FOR US LOL #ALANJAYLIBERATIONARMY #AJLA

Liberty Tree 17 @LibertyTree17
CRIMINALS WILL ALWAYS FIND GUNS, SADLY.

Truth Is Glorious @TruthIsGlorious
SORRY @REPMATTCASON YOU KEEP PUSHING PEOPLE
TOO FAR THEYRE GOING TO PUSH BACK #ALANJAY-
LIBERATIONARMY #AJLA

Melody @MelodySoulSinger
#PRAYFORSANDIEGO

————————

Casey Cheng, brave survivor, reporting from the latest massacre.

Of course they wouldn't say that. But she knew that was how Jordan was thinking about it. About her.

What's *my* excuse, she thought?

"Casey, hit time's in thirty seconds." That was Chris. The show director's voice faded in and out in her ear. She fiddled with her IFB.

It was a beautiful day. Perfect blue sky. A gentle breeze. In front of her, three other stations' live trucks. To one side, a reporter from CBS setting up; to the other, the park's half-pipe and skateboard park. Empty now, cleared by police.

Behind her, a phalanx of squad cars, red and blue lights pulsing, and a matte-black SWAT vehicle that looked like it had been shipped from a war zone. Next to them, ambulances—one had pulled away, sirens wailing, while they were parking the van. Knots of bystanders gathered by police barricades.

It would make a good backdrop.

News 9 had been first, getting here in just under twenty minutes after they'd given her the green light to go. That made her happy, in spite of everything.

"Case? Can you hear me?" Chris again.

"You okay, Casey?" That was Gloria. She'd be sitting next to Chris in the booth in her producer's chair, back at the station.

Casey took in a deep breath. Focused on Diego in front of her.

Accompanied by her Hero Photographer.

How was he doing? He'd been quiet in the van, but then he generally was.

"Yeah," she said. "Yeah, I'm good."

It will be fine, she told herself.

"Witnesses describe a scene of terror and chaos as a gunman opened fire on a crowd of people gathered for a meet and greet at a community fair with Congressman Matt Cason," said Elise's voice, live on camera back in the studio. "Witnesses" were mostly tweets and posts from Twitter and Facebook. "Terror and chaos" seemed safe enough to say, under the circumstances.

"Okay, we're in the double box," Chris said.

She was on, a split-screen graphic with Elise on screen left and Casey on screen right.

"Our own Casey Cheng is at the scene. Casey, what can you tell us about what happened?"

"You're out of the box, Casey."

Back in the booth, they'd cut away from the two-shot and the studio, and now what was going out was just Diego's shot.

It was all on her now.

"Elise, details are scarce at this moment but I can confirm that there are multiple casualties. Police have told us that they believe we are no longer in an active shooter situation, but they aren't taking any chances and are searching the area as we speak."

("Yeah, he's down," a cop had told them. The "search" part was obvious—police poured into the park, some with dogs.)

"If you look behind me and to my left, you can see the search in progress."

She watched as Diego panned away from her and zoomed, trying to get a shot that would sell the search.

"And Representative Cason, any word on his condition?"

Rose's voice came in hard and fast over her earpiece. "Hey, I've got a witness who says Cason took out the shooter himself. Says Cason walked away from it. He'll talk on air."

That ought to make for one hell of a campaign ad, Casey thought.

"Go for it," Gloria said in her ear.

"Nothing confirmed," Casey said, "but we're hearing from witnesses that Congressman Cason may have played a role in subduing the gunman, and that he was able to move under his own power, so the hope is that his injuries are not serious. I want to repeat that this is unconfirmed, but we should have more information for you on that shortly."

Chris in her ear: "Elise, on you till Sharp Hospital's up."

"All right, Casey, we'll be waiting to hear from you," Elise said. *"We're continuing with our live coverage of the shootings at Congressman Matt Cason's event at a Clairemont park community fair."*

"Social media OTS is up, Elise. Casey, you're out."

"We're getting a lot of tweets and posts from the scene," Elise was saying, *"and though we cannot vouch for the accuracy of everything that's been posted, here are what witnesses are reporting. A warning: some of this content may be graphic."*

"Can you get over here?" Rose again. "We're behind the rec center."

———

"He just pounded on him! The guy's face looked like hamburger at the end. I got photos, you can see."

Rose tilted her head toward the rec center. "Police are taking witness statements inside. But Mr. Stewart here wanted to talk to us first."

Lucky us, Casey thought.

"Yeah, I bailed," he said. He was barely out of his teens, if that, a long, lanky kid with baggy cargo shorts that hung off his butt and a T-shirt from the Clairemont Surf Shop. He stuck his hand out at Casey for a quick shake. "I'm Gio."

She put on a smile. "Hi, Gio, I'm Casey. It's great to meet you."

"It's great to meet you too! I watch you all the time. It's so cool you're the ones seeing these first."

Casey's smile felt frozen in place. It was a nice thing to say, she told herself. Not something to be afraid of. Not like with Lucas.

"Can she take a look?" Rose asked.

"Sure." He handed Casey his camera, a Canon PowerShot. "I got some good stuff."

Casey started clicking through. Winced and swallowed hard. "You did," she said.

Zoomed-in close-ups of Matt Cason, his face covered in blood, hand clutching the jacket collar of a man on the ground. If that was Lucas, you couldn't tell from the photos. The kid was right, the man's face was a mass of swelling and blood that no longer looked like flesh on bone, just raw, misshapen meat.

"Have you posted these yet?" Rose asked.

He shook his head. "No WiFi."

"We can take care of that. Just let us show them first. On-camera interview, photo credit, and we can pay you a licensing fee for their use—it won't be a lot, but you'll still own them. Deal?"

"Yeah," he said, grinning. "Yeah, I really want to be a photographer, or maybe a reporter, you know?"

"These are pretty brutal," Casey said quietly, while Diego showed Gio Stewart his News 9 camera setup.

"They can do a black bar on Douchebag's face if they don't want to show the whole thing. That's up to Chris. The shots of Cason ... " Now it was Rose's turn to smile. "These are fucking killer."

Casey had reached the last image on the camera. This one was of a young blond woman crouched by a man's body, pressing a wad of fabric against his blood-soaked thigh. Her white shirt was smeared with blood, and it had popped open so you could see the top of her bra.

She was looking up, her eyes huge, staring directly into the camera's lens.

———

News 9 San Diego @News9SanDiego
UNIDENTIFIED BYSTANDER AIDS SERIOUSLY WOUNDED VICTIM AT #CASONSHOOTING—NEWS 9 EXCLUSIVE
KASD.US.WGU9X

Jack @JackAMole
NICE TITS LOL #CASONSHOOTING #AJLA

19

SHE CALLED MATT'S PHONE. He didn't pick up.

"Ping me when you get to the hospital, I'll meet you in the lobby," Jane had said. "I'll probably beat you there by ten, fifteen minutes."

"Did they have any information for you?" Tegan asked.

"No. Just that ... someone was shooting people at the park. And Matt's at the hospital."

"I'm so sorry." Tegan steered her Beemer onto the 5 South. "Well ... just so you know ... we can't be sure it's true, but I did see a tweet right before we left that said your husband took down the shooter himself."

"A tweet?"

"I know, it's not a lot," Tegan said.

The traffic was light. But even on ordinary days, Lindsey always felt stressed when she came around that huge cement curve and merged onto the 8 East from the 5. Mission Valley was so poorly designed. They'd built it in a flood plain, around a river that disappeared during drought so they could pretend it wasn't there, sacrificed the best farmland in the county for car lots and hotels and shopping malls and, more recently, condos. She hated how inefficient and ugly it was, how wasteful.

Funny, Lindsey thought. These were thoughts she had every time she drove this interchange, like wheels falling into a well-worn groove. And for just a moment, the familiar litany was actually a comfort.

Tegan cut over into the third lane, squeezing the car into a faster-moving box on the freeway. "I'm hoping and praying for the best for you," she said.

"Thanks. I appreciate that."

Tweets, she thought. I'll look for tweets. Lindsey unlocked her phone. Should she check Campaigner first? Well, Sarah was at the park, she seemed to be on top of these things.

God, you're a bitch, Lindsey told herself. Sarah could be dead for all she knew. People were dead, Jane had told her that.

She opened up Campaigner. She'd had the thing on mute since she'd left the park. Red Alerts: news on the shootings posted by Jane and Angus. Nothing about Matt's condition, or anyone else's. Jane had tagged Matt, Sarah, and Ben: PLEASE CHECK IN!

Tegan shook her head. "We're living in crazy times. There are people who do things and you just can't understand why. I don't know whether it's craziness or evil. A lot of times I think it's both."

There were multiple tweets about the shootings tagged with Matt's handle. Two stood out.

News 9 San Diego @News9SanDiego
WITNESS: @REPMATTCASON TOOK DOWN
CLAIREMONT SHOOTER EXCLUSIVE MORE TO COME
#CASONSHOOTING

SD Baseball Mom @SDBaseballMom
Cant believe what I just saw guy shooting at
@RepMattCason and Cason beat the shit out of
him Im shaking

Lindsey stared at the screen. A picture formed in her head. She knew if she closed her eyes, she could play the whole scene.

———

That was quick thinking.

I don't know if he would have made it here if you hadn't done that.

He's still very sick.

It's too soon to predict an outcome.

Sarah found herself in the main lobby of the hospital. She wasn't sure what she was doing there. She'd ridden in the front seat of the ambulance that took Ben. She didn't have any other way to leave the scene—Ben had driven both her and Matt from headquarters.

For some reason, when she closed her eyes she could still see the dashboard of the ambulance. A low-end radio and a glove compartment, with GPS mounted on the dash.

What should she do now?

The hospital lobby was soothing and spacious, done in earth tones with mood lighting. A grand piano stood in an alcove. No one was playing it.

She sat down on a padded bench by the piano and got out her phone.

She'd texted her parents first thing, in the ambulance on the way here: There's been a shooting in the park but don't worry I'm fine. They'd called back immediately, but she didn't answer. Instead she texted back, I'm not hurt, I'm fine, but I can't talk now. Will call as soon as I can.

I should call them, she thought, but she didn't want to. She could already hear their voices, the concern, their rising panic. She couldn't take that right now. Just thinking about it made her feel like she was sinking back into who she had been before.

Mommy, Daddy, please come take care of me.

Something bad happened.

It wasn't my fault.

Tell me everything will be okay.

She couldn't go back to being that person. She'd worked too hard to get away from her.

Instead, she opened Campaigner. She'd heard alerts go off but they'd been background noise.

From Jane: @MattC @SarahP @BenK Please check in!

I'm at the hospital, she wrote. I'm not hurt. Ben is in ICU. Someone needs to call his parents. Matt is here too. He has some injuries but he—

She didn't know how to put it. "Nearly killed the person who was shooting at us so I think he's okay"?

She'd seen the paramedics trying to slide a tube down the man's throat, searching for an airway in a mass of mangled flesh and blood, broken teeth and bone.

She felt a rush of anger, the first thing she'd really felt since she'd gotten in the ambulance.

Serves him right, she thought. She hoped he died.

Matt has some injuries but they didn't seem serious, she typed and hit Send.

———

He texted her as she got out of Tegan's car. I'm okay. Just banged up a little. XOXO Matt.

Lindsey found Jane in the ER waiting room. "Come around from the frontage road," she'd said, "you'll miss the press that way."

It wasn't hard spotting Jane. The ER lobby was small, more of a waiting room, the vinyl chairs in facing lines against opposite walls, the lights a harsh fluorescent. Jane sat near the reception desk, texting on her phone, thumbs skittering on the virtual keyboard. She stood up when she saw Lindsey. "Don't worry," she said first. Then, "Let's go outside."

They walked a few yards away from the ER, over to a large planter with a palm tree and a couple birds-of-paradise, where the reporters camped out by the main entrance couldn't spot them. Behind the planter, cars drove by on a frontage road, the blur of freeway traffic beyond it. She caught a whiff of moldy cigarette butts, though she was pretty sure you weren't supposed to smoke here.

"Matt's down in Imaging," Jane said. "He's conscious and he's ambulatory, and that's all they'd tell me. But I think it's good news."

Lindsey could feel some of the muscles in her neck and back start to relax. Relief was blood, she thought, flowing where it was supposed to.

She nodded. "He texted me and said the same thing."

"Thank god." Jane let out a deep breath.

"Did you ... did you get my Campaigner alert?"

She'd forwarded the tweets from News 9 and SDBaseballMom to the core staff, hating herself as she'd pushed Send. Because how could she be thinking about this *now*? What was wrong with her?

They needed to know, she thought. It meant that Matt was probably okay. As for the rest of it ...

"Yeah. Yeah, I did. It's ... " Jane rubbed her forehead, her eyes closed. "It's more good news, really. I mean ... not that any of this is good. But, under the circumstances ... " She suddenly reached out her arms and pulled Lindsey into a tight hug. Lindsey hugged her back, feeling Jane's wiry, compact body against hers.

They'd known each other for years, but they rarely hugged.

"Did you get Sarah's alert? About Ben?"

"Yeah."

"One of the interns from the district office too. I don't know how bad she's hurt."

"Oh, god."

"I know. It's ... " Jane let go of her and swiped her fingers over her eyes. "I called Angus and filled him in. He's handling press and looping in Presley."

"Okay. Good."

You have to tell her, she thought. "Look ... I think he needs to get on top of this News 9 story."

Jane frowned. "What's to get on top of? If it's true he took down the shooter, that's nothing but good for us."

"It's ... it's what images they might have. In case ... well, the one woman, San Diego Baseball Mom, she said he beat the shit out of the guy. That can look ... "

A fist smashing into a face. Blood gushing. An eye, puffing up, swelling purple.

"It just might look ugly."

Jane nodded, her eyebrows drawing slightly together. "Okay. I'm guessing they've already called us, so we should be able to work it. The bottom line is, Matt's a hero. He took down a killer. No matter how many casualties there were today, it could have been a lot worse if he hadn't stepped in." She stopped, drew in a breath, let it out, and closed her eyes. "Jesus," she muttered, sitting down on the rim of the cement planter, in a gap between the beaky orange flowers of two birds-of-paradise. "I'm sorry, this is just ... "

"It's okay," Lindsey said. "We need to be thinking this way."

Jane looked up. "Why?"

"Because Matt..." Her throat closed. "He has a temper. He's done some things."

For a moment, Jane just sat there, her mouth slightly open, as if she was waiting for the right words to emerge from a place she didn't know. "I know Matt gets mad. I've seen that," she finally said. "Are you... are you talking about something else?"

Lindsey sat down next to her. "It wasn't me." Which was mostly true. "And it was years ago."

"Okay." Jane stared straight ahead. "Nobody's going to blame Matt for taking down a killer," she said, seeming to test out the words. "Nobody. He's a hero." Now she turned to Lindsey. "Look at me, okay?"

Lindsey did. Jane's eyes were bloodshot, the lids puffy. She could still do that particular trick of hers, though, the one where she would stare at you like she could read your mind, and she'd know if you were lying or telling the truth.

"What happened in the past, it's not relevant to what happened today. I want you to tell me about it, but whatever comes up, whatever they say, Matt is a hero who took down a killer and saved people's lives. That is how we respond to the media. Unless you really have a reason to disagree."

"No. I don't." She stood up, legs and back aching. I'm still wearing my running clothes, she thought. She was starting to itch beneath the sweaty band of her sports bra. "We better go inside."

A sudden trumpet fanfare: the Campaigner alert. Lindsey and Jane both reached for their phones.

From Angus: NEWS 9 POSTED PHOTOS FROM THE PARK. YOU'D BETTER TAKE A LOOK.

"Are you okay?"

Sarah opened her eyes. She was so tired. She thought if she just closed her eyes for a few minutes, she'd have the energy to figure out what to do. Take a Lyft home, probably.

"You're not hurt, are you?"

It was an older woman, maybe a volunteer, a frizzy gray-haired lady with glasses around her neck and a pear-shaped body.

"No," Sarah said.

"I'm sorry to have bothered you. It's just your blouse ... "

"My blouse?" She looked down at her white shirt, noticing the bloodstains for the first time. "Oh," she said. "It's not mine. I mean, the blood."

Jane found her a few minutes later.

"Sarah. Thank god." Jane sat down next to her and put her hands on her shoulders and gave them a gentle squeeze.

Sarah started to cry.

"I know," Jane said. "We're going to get you out of here." She pulled something out of a shopping bag—a large, long-sleeved T-shirt with *San Diego CA* written across it.

"Put this on," Jane said. "We can go out the back, we should miss the press that way."

"Why ... ? Oh." The blood on her shirt. She kept forgetting about it. "How did you know I needed it?" she thought to ask.

Jane gave a quick, brief shake of her head. "We can worry about that later."

Did that mean there was something to worry about?

———

"I'm fine," Matt kept saying. "I'm fine." He patted Lindsey's back as she rested her head on his shoulder. His sweat had a sharp, sour edge to it.

Finally, she let go of him.

He didn't look fine. He sat on the edge of the hospital bed, wearing a gown. His head was bandaged and his arm was in a sling, his wrist and hand splinted. It was his eyes, though, where you could really see it. It had been years since she'd seen his eyes look like that. Like he wasn't seeing anything around him. Like he wasn't really here at all.

They'd put him in a private room in the hospital wing. A policeman stood by the door. "Just a precaution, ma'am. Nothing to worry about."

She wiped her eyes with the back of her hand, found a tiny box of rough tissues and blew her nose.

She wanted to ask about what happened but wasn't sure how. She could try to draw him out, but if she pushed too hard, she knew what the results would be.

Just leave it alone, she thought. Wait until he's ready to talk.

Which might be never.

"I saw some crazy stuff on Twitter," she finally said.

Matt laughed. One short, hard snort. "When you say crazy, what are we talking about here? The guy that came up to me in a park and started shooting?"

You should have left it alone, she thought.

"Matt ... I'm sorry ... You've been through something horrible, and I shouldn't have said anything, I just ... "

"Speaking of crazy ... there was this head-case vet whose hand I was shaking when some *asshole* fucking *shot* him." His good hand gripped the hard plastic side of the bed. Now he was present, all right. Lit up with building rage.

"I'm not trying to start a fight. I want to help, just tell me how."

"Then there was a little boy, a kid who went to the park with his mom and dad to ride a fucking pony and get his face painted. I saw him on the ground with blood pouring out of his head."

A knock at the door. A big man in scrubs entered without waiting for an answer. "Hello, I'm Doctor Parviz, I'm the hand specialist."

For a moment, Matt stared at him, his eyes big and bright, a flare of red on his cheeks. She watched him struggle for control, then smile.

"Hi, Doctor. Thanks for seeing me. Yeah, feels like I did a number on it."

"You did."

Parviz grabbed a chair by the seat and pulled it over next to the bed. He carried a large iPad. "Here," he said, unlocking it with his thumbprint and tilting it so Matt could see. Lindsey glimpsed an X-ray of a hand and wrist. "You have what is commonly referred to as boxer's or brawler's fractures of your fourth and fifth metacarpals. You see here, the jagged ends of the bones? With this degree of misalignment, we can try to reduce the fractures manually, but you may require surgery. You've also got a partial tear of the scapholunate ligament in your wrist. That should resolve with splinting and rest, but we will want to keep an eye on it."

"Okay," Matt said, nodding. "Sounds good. What's next?"

"I want to do a quick consult with the attending physician and see if you need to be admitted. I don't think so, but with the head injury—in case that is more serious than it is currently presenting—we'll want to monitor you closely after the administration of any narcotics, which you will want when I try to reduce the fractures. In any case, as your physician probably explained to you already, you'll need to be monitored at home."

"You get all that, Lindsey?" Matt asked, smiling. Their eyes met for just a moment and then it was as though his gaze glanced off hers, like he couldn't stand to look at her.

"I think so," she said. "I'll make sure to talk to the other doctor."

When Parviz left, he closed the door behind him. They were alone again, for however long that would last, before the next doctor or nurse or policeman came in.

Or Jane. She should have let Jane have the conversation with him. You're so stupid sometimes, she thought.

"I'm sorry," Matt said.

"No, it's my fault. I should have just let you be."

"It's gonna be a shitstorm, right?"

"I don't know. Probably." Definitely, she thought. With those photos out there, Social was going to blow up. "We'll deal with it. You didn't do anything wrong."

He cradled his injured hand in his good one and seemed to study it. "I lost it." His voice was flat. "I just wanted to keep hitting him. I only stopped because the cops pulled me off."

Finally, he looked up at her. The anger had drained out of him, and he looked empty of anything else. "He killed a little kid, Linds. Am I supposed to feel bad?"

She felt something she hadn't felt in a while, a sudden, fierce emotion that she couldn't even name, a chemical surge of protectiveness and connection.

"No. No, you have no reason to."

She sat down in the chair Parviz had vacated. Put her hands on Matt's bare thighs and gently massaged the muscles beneath her fingers. "You took down a killer. You're a hero."

20

STALKED BY A KILLER— A NEWS 9 EXCLUSIVE

(BEGIN VIDEO CLIP: MONTAGE OF MORENA SHOOTINGS NEWS FOOTAGE, CHASTAIN PHOTO INSERT, CASEY AT CROOKED ARROW)

ELISE MENDOZA, NEWS 9 ANCHOR (V.O.): Casey Cheng had more than a usual interest in the background and motivations of Morena killer Alan Jay Chastain. She herself was badly injured in that incident, one of the worst mass shootings in San Diego history.

CHENG (IN STUDIO): Yeah, I think it's fair to say I'm a little invested in this story (LAUGHS). I guess a part of me hoped that if I could make sense of why he did it, I could make better sense of what happened to me. I pretty much had to tell myself to think of it as something like this big storm that came out of nowhere, washed over me, and moved on ... An act of nature.

(BEGIN VIDEO CLIP: DERRY PHOTO INSERT, EXT. HIGHSMITH'S, QUIK BY) MENDOZA (V.O.): But meeting Lucas Derry on the street

near Alan Jay Chastain's last place of employment caused her to question her past assumptions.

(END VIDEO CLIP) CHENG (IN STUDIO): He approached me when I was getting into my car. He said he recognized me, and that he was a friend of Alan Chastain's. And I'll admit, he made me a little jumpy. Just … there was something off.

(BEGIN VIDEO CLIP: INSERT TRUE MEN WILL RISE *COVER)* MENDOZA (V.O.)*: But it was a comic book of all things that led Cheng and the News 9 I-team to dig deeper …

"This is fantastic, guys," Gloria said.

Jordan nodded. "I'm comfortable going with this."

"You don't think we're burying the lede a bit?" Casey asked.

Gloria shook her head. "You'll be live on set with Craig and Elise, they'll intro you and the story, you guys do a few lines of cross talk. We'll run it after the main package on the Cason shootings, including your exclusive with our witness. There will be plenty of context."

Everyone sitting around the conference table seemed good with that. Everyone but her.

"It just feels like there's a lot of … *me*," Casey said.

Gloria laughed. "Yeah, it's pretty much the Casey hour tonight. But look, you've earned it. You guys have done a fantastic job."

Casey smiled. She knew she should feel good about this. Great, even. How many times did a story like this fall into your lap working in local news?

Though she supposed getting shot first took it out of the "falling into your lap" category.

There was barely time to recut the segment, in any case. Hit time was less than an hour, nine minutes into the six o'clock news. She needed to do hair and makeup, change into the blouse hanging in her locker that she'd wear at the anchor desk.

At least they'd filmed the studio segments in the newsroom, instead of at her condo or against some gauzy scrim. It made her feel slightly more like a reporter. Slightly less like some local celebrity.

A subject.

"Okay, guys. Just want to make sure we spread the credit around. As far as I'm concerned, Rose and Diego both should be getting airtime."

Rose held up her hands. "Hah! No way. That's *your* job, hon."

―――――

"What did your cop say?" Casey asked her on the way to her locker.

"'Thanks for the tip,' basically. I told him about the True Men graphic novel connection. I don't know if he took it seriously or not."

"I bet he does. We were right about Lucas."

And he'd repaid that favor by calling Rose five minutes before the press conference announcing the park shooter's identity took place. They'd gotten it on the air before anyone else.

"Yeah," Rose said. "What he said was, two mass shootings that might be related, trying to kill a US congressman, that meant the FBI was getting involved, and he'd let them know about the comic book." She laughed. "It sounds ridiculous every time I say it."

Still, it was worth giving Helton the heads-up, show they were willing to keep trading information. Building up that kind of goodwill with a well-placed police officer never hurt.

They'd been careful not to make any definitive claims in the segment. Just that Lucas's tattoo had reminded Casey of the cover of *True Men Will Rise.* And that the man who'd claimed to be the friend of a mass murderer then went out to commit his own killings.

This wasn't how Sarah thought she would see the inside of Jane's house.

She'd hoped that she would become part of the core staff. Be invited over for strategy sessions. Ben had been invited before. *Yeah, I had drinks over at Jane's last night,* he'd said, so casually.

Now he was in the hospital, and he might not make it, and she was here, and she was only here because of what had happened at the park.

If Ben hadn't been shot, would she be here at all?

Jane lived in Clairemont, which surprised her. She would have pictured Jane in some other kind of neighborhood, something nicer, or older, or more distinctive. But here was her house, a small tract home overlooking Tecolote Canyon just off Clairemont Drive, in a part of Clairemont that wasn't fancy at all.

"The bathroom's here," Jane said. "Do you want to take a shower? Get out of that shirt? I can bring you something short-sleeve. And ... pajamas or sweats or something."

"That would be great," Sarah said. She did want to get out of these clothes, out of the bra with straps cutting into her shoulders, the black pants that had been too warm for a summer's day.

The blazer with Ben's blood all over it ... what had happened to that?

"Maybe you should sit down first," she heard Jane say.

She shook herself. "I'd really like to shower."

"Okay. I'll get you some things."

Sarah stood in the shower for what felt like a long time. It might not have been. She realized, finally, that she'd lost track of where she was for a while, just letting the water fall on her body.

I shouldn't waste water, she thought. California has cyclical droughts.

She got out of the shower, dried off, and dressed in the clothes Jane had brought—a soft Padres T-shirt and long cotton knit shorts. She didn't put her bra back on. Like her white shirt, it too was crusted with dried blood.

What do I do with these clothes? she wondered. She finally laid them down on top of the closed toilet.

When she came out of the bathroom and into the living room, there was another woman in the house who held Jane in an embrace, a taller woman with a halo of frizzy red hair. "I'm fine," Jane was saying. "I'm fine." She sounded a little irritated the second time she said it. "Char, I wasn't even there."

When the two broke apart, Sarah could see that the second woman was pregnant.

"Sarah, this is Charlotte," Jane said. "My wife."

Charlotte rushed over. She wore a wild, floral-print dress and necklaces strung with silver and chunks of turquoise and glass beads, and her arms were decorated with tattoos of flowers, filigree, a feathered quill and inkpot, and a cartoon Wonder Woman that looked like it was from World War II. "Oh, sweetie," she said, clasping Sarah's hand. "Welcome to our home. How about if I make you a margarita?"

Jane ever so slightly rolled her eyes, smiling a little as she did. "Charlotte is a drama professor at UCSD," Jane said. "In case that wasn't obvious."

"You hush," Charlotte said, heading into the kitchen.

Jane has a pregnant wife, Sarah thought. It was hard to absorb. Not that Jane was gay, but because she'd never thought of Jane having a life outside the campaign at all.

The kitchen was separated from the living/dining room by a bar and a row of cupboards on either side. Knotty pine in the kitchen and painted white wood with glass panes on the bar/dining room side. Older white linoleum tiles in the kitchen and dining area.

"Are you hungry at all?" Jane asked.

Sarah shook her head.

"When was the last time you had something to eat?"

She tried to remember. A protein shake in the morning, before the event. A Luna Bar at the park, maybe?

Jane gestured toward the couch. "Sit. I'll get you something."

Sarah sat. It was a long, poufy leather couch that faced a wall of bookcases, framed photos, and a large TV. To her left were sliding glass doors that led out onto a fenced deck. Below that, the canyon: clumps of sage and other shrubs, a few trees, brown and gold earth between and around the desert green plants.

There was nothing fancy about the house. The furniture was mix and match. The walls needed paint.

Sarah stared at the photos interspersed among the books on the wall opposite. Families at holidays. Jane and Charlotte hiking. Friends having dinners and picnics. Then one that caught her eye: a selfie of Jane and Matt, wearing baseball hats, at a ballpark, the two of them grinning and showing teeth, Matt holding up a beer, both of them looking younger.

From the kitchen she heard the sound of a cocktail shaker and ice.

"Salt or no salt?" Charlotte called out.

Sarah thought about it. She couldn't decide. "Salt," she finally said, because salt was the normal thing to do, wasn't it?

Charlotte came out with a drink in a tumbler. "Rocks," she said, putting it on a coaster on the coffee table in front of Sarah. "I hope that's okay. Blended is an abomination."

"Thank you," Sarah said. She sipped. Cold, almost tart, lime with a honeyed alcohol bite.

"I want one of those so much," Charlotte said. "I use good tequila and fresh lime."

A minute later, Jane appeared with a platter of cheese, salami, and hummus. "We'll need this to absorb one of her margaritas."

"Should we order pizza?" Charlotte asked.

"Let me … let me talk to Sarah about that."

"Okay. I've got some work to do in the office."

Sarah knew that was code. Jane wanted to have a private conversation. She sipped her drink. Thinking, a few more sips and I'll feel better.

Jane sat down on the couch next to Sarah. Close but giving her space. "You're not from San Diego, right?"

"No. I moved here from Connecticut." To work on the campaign, she almost said. But that would have sounded strange, wouldn't it? To move to the opposite coast for what had started out as an unpaid internship?

"Do you have relatives or friends in town?"

Sarah shook her head. "It's okay, though," she said. "I'll be fine."

"Well, there's no reason you can't stay for some pizza, then, is there." Not a question.

What Sarah really wanted to do was go to her apartment and crawl into bed. But I'm here, she thought. At Jane's house. A place where she'd wanted to be.

And maybe it was better not to be alone right now.

"Sure. Thanks, that would be great."

———

Jane had a pizza place on speed dial. "One veggie, one meat, is that okay?"

After she'd ordered, Jane went into the kitchen and returned with her own margarita and a large tumbler. "Top off?"

"Thank you."

Jane sat. Took a long sip of her drink, seeming to stare at it. "Look, you do Social," she finally said. "I know you get how it works. Right now, there are some photos and videos circulating of what happened in the park."

"Right," Sarah said, nodding. Of course, there would be. Plus, she'd put up that great GIF of Matt using the fire extinguisher. She wondered if it had gone viral, given the shooting.

"Some of the pictures..." Jane's dark eyes met hers. "You were there. You saw what happened."

Sarah nodded. When she closed her eyes, she could see it still: the man with the gun, Matt's fist driving into his face, Ben's blood all over her.

When she opened her eyes, Jane was still staring at her, with an expression that might have been concern.

"They've probably gone viral," Sarah said.

Jane nodded. "Unfortunately, they have. And...I just want to give you a heads-up...there's one of you. Sadly, it's attracted some trolls."

All at once she felt a rushing in her ears, like the air was being sucked out of the room. "What was I doing?"

"Helping Ben. There's the internet for you." Jane let out a sigh, shaking her head. "What you did was really heroic. Don't let a few trolls get you down."

"What are they...what are they saying? Do they know who I am?" Her voice sounded shrill in her own ears. She told herself to breathe.

"They're just saying the kind of stupid shit that frustrated basement dwellers say on the internet, that's all."

Sarah got out her phone. "What's the hashtag?"

"Sarah—"

"What is it?"

Jane hesitated. "Cason shooting," she said. "And some other ones, I don't know. There's just … a lot of ugliness attaching itself to this, and then with the shooter claiming to be a friend of the nut who shot up the brewery … "

There was the photo, from News 9. She barely recognized herself.

NICE TITS LOL

I'D FUCK IT.

IN THE ASS OR WITH A BAG ON ITS HEAD?

WHO IS THIS CUNT ANYWAY?

PROBABLY @REPMATTCASON'S JIZZ JAR

Her hands shook. She gripped the phone harder.

"I'm so sorry," Jane was saying. "Don't even look at it right now, okay? We'll deal with it, I promise."

"There's nothing you can do about it," she heard herself say. "They won't stop. They'll just keep going."

"Some of them are also threatening a sitting US congressman." Jane's voice was hard. "Believe me. We will deal with it."

"I guess that's more important than them talking about raping me," she blurted out.

You could see it on Jane's face, a moment of acute embarrassment, like she couldn't believe she'd said what she'd said. "Oh, Jesus, no. I'm sorry. Of course it's not. It's just that, the FBI or whoever's handling this will focus more attention on it because Matt's involved." She stopped in midgesture. "Fuck," she muttered and took a big gulp of her margarita.

Jane set down her glass with a thunk. "You're right. Yes, the authorities will take the threats on Matt's life more seriously than they'll take the threats on you. He's a congressman, and someone tried to kill him. You understand that, right?"

Sarah thought about it. She supposed she did. She could smell the gunfire just now, hear the shots echo in her head.

Rape threats were just something some men said to women, she told herself. Most of them didn't follow through. And most of the things they were saying now weren't even threats. Just … what were they? Desires?

"You've had an awful experience today," Jane said. "And what's happening online now—nobody should have to put up with that. You need support from other people, and I want to make sure that you have it. A counselor who specializes in this kind of thing. We'll take care of it."

Which part of it? Sarah wondered. Seeing someone getting shot right in front of you? What was happening to her online? What had happened to her before?

"In the meantime … is there someone we can call? A friend or a relative? A boyfriend?"

She'd stopped talking to so many people when she'd become someone else. And the few friends she kept in touch with, it wasn't like she talked to them about anything important. Mostly they texted about what was going on in that moment. Trivial stuff. She stayed connected with them on Snapchat and Facebook, but she never posted anything of her own. Just "liked" and gave thumbs ups and occasionally said "Congratulations!" and sent birthday cake emojis.

She knew she would have to call her parents, but the last thing she wanted to do was tell them about any of this. She couldn't take the edge of hysteria in her mother's voice, the anger in her father's.

"There's no one," Sarah said. "There's no one I can talk to."

"You can talk to me."

Talk to Jane? The remote, all-powerful Jane? She didn't look like that now, though. If anything, Jane looked kind.

It was tempting. Just to tell the truth, for once. But if she did…

Would they keep her on the campaign?

"So, do you like baseball?" Sarah asked.

"What?" Jane looked confused.

"I just… the photo." She pointed to the wall. "The one of you and Matt. And this shirt." The one she wore, with the Padres logo, the swinging friar. "I… I never really followed baseball."

"Oh." She could see Jane's shoulders relax and sink down, a hint of a real smile. "Yes. I love it. Matt and I are baseball buddies. We've been getting season tickets together for years."

"Lindsey isn't a fan?" Sarah wasn't even sure why she asked. She felt sneaky asking it, somehow.

"She likes it. Just not as much as Matt and I do. Look, Sarah…" The relaxed shoulders, the smile, were gone. "The police will want to talk to you. Just to take a statement. I held them off at the hospital, because I couldn't see the urgency, and with the shooter in the ICU, neither could they. But they will want to talk to you. As for the press—"

"I don't want to talk to the press," she said, and she knew she sounded panicked.

"I understand. But *you* need to understand how this works. That photo of you… it's a great photo. Dramatic. You're credited with saving a life. And you're young and pretty. Believe me, people are going to want to know who you are. You might be better off getting ahead of it rather than waiting for them to come to you. Issue a statement, maybe do one interview. There will be a couple of stories and then they'll move on to the next thing."

"I can't," Sarah said. "I just can't." She stared down at her drink. I want to go away, she thought. Go away and hide.

"We don't need to talk about this now," she heard Jane say. "Let's just focus on pizza. And there's a game on if you want to watch. Personally, I find baseball therapeutic."

Maybe she should. If Matt and Jane were fans, maybe it made sense to learn about the Padres. It would give her something safe to talk about with them.

"Sure," she said. "That sounds great."

21

CASEY STARED AT THE high-res photo of the girl from the park, the one who had helped the wounded man. She'd loaded it onto her laptop, along with the other photos Gio had taken.

"She's probably one of his staffers, don't you think? Black slacks, white blouse—she's not dressed for a fun day at the park."

"Yeah, and I'm pretty sure the guy she's helping works for the campaign too," Rose said. "The deputy campaign manager told me they had an injured staffer when I talked to him this afternoon, you know, making the case that was part of why Cason went all Hulk smash on Lucas Derry. So let's start there instead of the district office."

She and Rose sat in the small conference room after the debrief of tonight's six o'clock newscast. It had gone well. Everyone said so. Her first time sitting at the desk, stage left, where the sports anchor generally sat, exchanging lines with Craig and Elise. It was all pretty scripted, except for one moment after they'd run the package, when Craig had said, "Casey, in all my years of doing broadcast news, I can-

184

not think of anything quite like this story, the way that it's intersected with you, with one of our reporters. You've encountered two killers. How are you feeling about all this?"

For a moment, she'd gone blank. Stared into the stage lights and the dark of the studio beyond that. How was she feeling about all this? It was just a big black hole.

"Well, it's … a strange feeling," she'd finally said. "I prefer to be *reporting* the news. Not being it."

Afterward she got so many congratulations that she felt like she should pop open a bottle of champagne.

When I get home, she thought. If she had the energy. This was the longest she'd worked since The Event, and she was so tired, completely depleted of whatever fuel it was that had kept her going today. Her muscles, her bones, ached.

"I'll follow up with him," Rose said. "He wants to spin this thing, so maybe he'll decide to play nice with us. I'm pretty sure the campaign wants to downplay those photos. Though I'm not sure why." She laughed. "Cason may have beat the living shit out of a guy, but there's no way you can call him a wimp after that, right?"

"Right." You could question his fitness to serve, maybe. Call him unstable. But how many people would really blame him for what he'd done to a man who'd tried to kill him, who'd killed innocent people out for a fun day at the park?

"I'll keep at it," Rose said. "You, my dear, are done for the day."

"I can help," she said, even though she really wanted to be done.

"Go home. We need you here tomorrow, and you look like you're about to drop. Let me just see who I can find to drive you."

"No, that's okay. Everybody's crazy busy. I'll call a Lyft."

She went into the restroom, changed out of her nice blouse, hung that back up in her locker. She'd take it to the cleaners after she brought in another one from home. The way things were going, today might not be the last time she'd make a last-minute unscheduled appearance in-studio.

That's a good thing, she told herself, heading back into the newsroom. It meant she was a draw. Greater prominence led to bigger stories. That was what she wanted, wasn't it? To tell the important stories?

It wasn't just about ego. It was about telling the public things they needed to know. Maybe it was corny, but she believed in that, in those principles you learned in your beginning journalism class: journalism's first obligation is to the truth; its first loyalty, to citizens.

She hoped she still believed, anyway.

She'd swing by Rose's desk on her way out the door to say thanks and good night. As exhausted as she was, a part of her didn't want to leave. There were two other people who understood the craziness of today: Rose and Diego. Who else could she talk to about it?

Speaking of, she could see the back of Diego's head over the outer cubicle wall, putting him where Rose's desk was. No one else working here had that dark, curly hair.

When she got past the wall, she saw that Diego stood behind Rose's chair. His hands were on her shoulders, giving them a quick, gentle massage. Her head tilted up to his, and he leaned over and kissed her on the cheek.

When had *that* happened?

"Hey, guys," she said.

Diego straightened up. "Hey, Case." He was smiling.

"Didn't I tell you to go home?" Rose said. She too was smiling.

Casey stood there for a moment. A part of her felt pissed off. Like she was being excluded, somehow. Like Diego was *her* hero photographer.

She looked at the two of them, and thought, Don't be a bitch. They're happy to see you. More to the point, they're *happy*.

"I am out the door," she said. "See you guys tomorrow."

————

She almost didn't stop in the lobby to pick up her mail. It could wait, she thought, and her unit was closer to the garden entrance.

On the other hand, the lobby had the elevator, and who was she kidding, she couldn't make it up three flights of stairs right now.

Sitting on the floor by her mailbox in the lobby was a bouquet of white flowers. She could see the card emerging from the tissue paper around the vase, the black cursive letters: *To Cas—*

She almost left the flowers there. She didn't want to bend over to pick up the bouquet. She knew it would hurt.

And white flowers … she shuddered.

Not that she was superstitious. She was pretty sure her condo had mediocre *feng shui* at best. But white flowers …

Those were for funerals.

Don't be a baby, she told herself. If you weren't Chinese, you probably wouldn't think of white flowers that way. Just that they were pretty, and went with a white wedding dress, which plenty of her Chinese girlfriends, not to mention her middle sister, had worn to their weddings.

Bracing herself, she bent over and picked up the bouquet.

"*Shit.*"

Thanks, sciatica, she thought.

She carried the bouquet over to a small marble table that lived in the little lobby and placed it there so she could get a better look.

Mostly carnations and baby's breath, in a plain ceramic vase. The kind of thing you'd buy in the supermarket.

She pulled out the card. *To Casey Cheng, welcome back!* it said.

No sender. No business address on the card either. Maybe whoever it was really *did* buy them in the supermarket.

Okay, she thought. No need to freak out here. Authorized delivery services had their own entrance code, and if this wasn't from an authorized delivery service, a helpful neighbor might have brought the flowers in.

Still.

I'll just leave them here, she thought. She didn't want to try to juggle flowers with her backpack ("No purses till you're healed, and nothing heavy, period!" the physical therapist kept telling her), her mail, her keys…

The lobby could use some flowers.

She'd take the card though. Just in case.

Just in case what? But she didn't want to think about that right now.

Once inside her condo, she dumped her bag and mail on the couch and somehow managed to get into her pajamas, thinking, oxy? Wine? Vape pen?

Glass of wine. And maybe vape pen. She was aching and wiped out, for sure, but it was manageable. She hadn't felt the need for an Oxy since … since the night they'd interviewed Helen Scott.

I'm finally getting better, she thought. Time for a toast to me.

It kind of sucked that she'd be celebrating alone tonight.

You could text Paul.

Oh, was that a good idea? She hadn't seen him since she'd started working again, had put him off the few times he'd texted, not that he'd made much of an effort to push back. He had a lot going on too, he'd said.

I should just let it die a natural death, she thought.

Instead she got out her phone.

Hey what are you up to? Crazy day today—I'm opening good wine. Feel like coming over?

No response.

Oh well, she thought. She'd give it a few minutes and then open the bottle. In the meantime…

Of course she had the regular news broadcasts scheduled on her DVR, and she'd used her phone to start recording Channel 9 when she was in the live truck on the way to the park, to catch the breaking news and the live shots she knew she would be doing.

There would be lots of footage to watch. A lot of footage of herself.

She opened up the wine, a reserve Rioja she liked, and poured herself a glass. Slowly sat down on the couch—this was where she still needed her cane, to get up and down after a day like today. She rested the cane against the couch and patted the handle. She'd taken to calling it Trusty.

She sipped the wine and contemplated the remote. She wasn't ready. Or she was tired of watching herself.

Netflix?

Sitting on the coffee table was a thick manila envelope, messengered over from the station two days ago. It took her a moment to remember what it was. She opened it. Three volumes of the graphic novel series True Men Will Rise. On top was the issue they'd seen in Alan Jay Chastain's room, the one with the cover of the lone man on the hill, the armed mob climbing up to meet him.

I should read these, she thought. She'd only had time to skim the one before they'd recorded the segment; Rose had done the heavy lifting on the script in any case.

She flicked on her reading lamp and grabbed the top comic book.

22

"**OKAY, SO, THE INFIELD** fly rule is, basically, if the batter hits a fly ball to the infield, it is an automatic out if there are less than two outs and runners on first and second, or the bases are loaded."

"Why?" Sarah asked.

She and Jane sat on the couch that faced the living room TV. Charlotte had claimed the recliner to one side: "My mother bought this for us. At first I was all, why would I want an old lady chair? Then I entered my third trimester."

"Because the infielder could choose to drop the ball on purpose and get a double or even a triple play," Jane explained.

"Oh," Sarah said, though she still wasn't sure she understood.

"I don't get it either," Charlotte said. "Usually I binge-watch Netflix in another room when baseball is on."

Jane groaned at the TV. "Bases loaded and they couldn't score one run."

Charlotte took a last bite of pizza. "Which I hope you won't think is terribly rude if I go and do now." She pushed back the leg-rest on her recliner and rose, a little awkwardly, and crossed to where Sarah sat. "If you get too bored, you can join me," she said in a mock whisper.

"She gets pretty tired these days," Jane said as Charlotte disappeared down the hall. "And hot. I had to put a wall unit air conditioner into the bedroom for the heat waves." She shook her head. "She's due in early September. Timing's not the best for me, but she's not teaching fall quarter, so—"

The Campaigner alert went off. Sarah flinched, and suddenly she could hear the gunshots again, the screams, smell the metal tang of bullets and blood.

Jane patted her pants pocket as if to confirm it was hers, and pulled out her phone. Unlocked it with her thumbprint. Her eyebrows bunched as she read. She grabbed the remote and muted the TV.

"News 9 has already called Angus to ask the name of the staffer who aided the injured man, who they've also IDed as staff."

"Did he—?"

"No, not yet. He wanted to check in with me and with you first." Jane sat up straight. Gave Sarah her intense stare—the one that meant she was measuring you, and that you needed to pay attention. "Sarah, I will be completely honest with you here. This is a local TV news I-team, not exactly Woodward and Bernstein." A pause. "I assume you know who they are."

"Of course." She knew about Watergate, and Deep Throat, and the Pentagon Papers. She'd studied American political history.

"It's entirely possible that if they can't identify you in a day or two, they'll give up and move on to the next dumpster fire. But on the other hand, these guys apparently knew the name of the killer before the police did, so I can't promise you that they will. If we offer them something, we might have a better shot at controlling their narrative."

"I don't want to be on television!"

"I understand. But ... you're part of a big story. This is national news. There might be other people who will want to talk to you."

CNN. Fox News. The networks. The big papers. The tabloids. They wouldn't stop.

"They'll find out who I am." Sarah felt sick, the pizza sitting in her stomach like wet cement.

"If they decide to look? They probably will. Sarah ... "

Sarah looked up. Jane's level gaze was still fixed on her. "Is there a particular reason you're worried about this?"

Sarah shook her head, too quickly, she realized.

"Because I understand that some people like to be in the public eye, and some people prefer to be behind the scenes. I had to learn to deal with the public aspect of my role. It's not easy for some of us."

A pause. She's waiting for me to say something, Sarah thought.

It was so tempting to tell her the truth.

"If there's something else going on, you can tell me," Jane said. "We'll handle it."

No, you won't, Sarah thought. You'll fire me.

"News 9 ... is that the reporter who got shot?" she asked instead. "Casey Cheng?"

"Yes. She covered the park shootings today. And they ran a special report tonight, I haven't had a chance to watch it yet." Unexpectedly, Jane grinned. "I thought baseball was a better choice."

"So you have the special report? And some of the other stories?"

"I have the lead story about the shootings and most of the earlier live coverage. But Sarah ... " Jane shook her head. "Do you really need to watch that? You were there."

"I want to see it."

Jane glanced at the TV. The Padres were losing by six runs. "Okay," she said. "If you're sure you want to."

Sarah watched it all. It wasn't as bad as she'd thought it would be. Like Jane said, she'd been there, and nothing could be worse than that.

The hardest part was seeing that tweet, the photo of her crouching by Ben with the blood on her shirt and hands, knowing that it had been retweeted time and time again, that there were people all around the world who had seen it now, who were making comments, judging her, wondering who she was.

It's just one photo, she told herself. I don't look the same way I used to look. Maybe no one will recognize me.

"Have you heard anything about Ben?" she thought to ask.

"Still in the ICU. With the blood loss I guess there's some organ damage, and they're just trying to get everything stabilized. I'm going to head down there in about a half hour and spell Angus."

"Angus is there now?"

"Yes. Ben's parents should get here tomorrow morning, but ... we just thought someone should be there in the meantime."

In case Ben died. Sarah knew that was what Jane meant.

"I could go too."

"Sarah ... If you don't want to talk to the press, that's not a good idea. Matt's still there, and there's reporters staked out waiting for him to leave or make a statement. We can't count on sneaking past them again."

"Oh."

Should she talk to the press? Do what Jane suggested, agree to one interview, hope they'd leave her alone after that?

Not now, she thought. I can't.

"I should go home." She was suddenly so very tired. Her body felt impossibly heavy, sinking into the couch like a dead weight.

"There's no need for that," Jane said. "You're exhausted. Stay here. We have a guest room."

Sarah nodded. "Okay. Thank you."

She was too tired to argue, and the truth was, she didn't want to be alone.

Hey! Was on plane, just landed at SAN. Was in SF for meetings. Still up for that wine? Car's at airport, won't take me long.

Casey glanced at her glass. It was still half full. She'd been focused on the graphic novels, taking notes on her iPad as she read. She'd gotten through the first two. Still had number three left.

She could say she was too tired now, which wasn't far from the truth. But it had only been forty minutes since she'd texted Paul, and if anything, she had more energy now than she'd had then.

Besides … a little celebrating might be nice.

Yes, if you don't mind me in my PJs - See you soon!

Twenty minutes later, Casey was deep into the third volume of True Men Will Rise. By now the heroes—the "True Men"—had been assembled from their various walks of life: an unemployed factory worker, a policeman, an Army vet, a farmer. The list went on. Mostly men, mostly white. There were some wives and girlfriends—the farmer's wife depicted as a crack shot with a rifle, the policeman's girlfriend raped and killed by a gang of Mexican thugs, and one or two people of color among the True Men. Just not very many.

As for the True Men themselves, they rose to take back America from the grasp of the oligarchs, from terrorists, illegals, and criminals. To return America to its core values and rescue it from social decay and decadence, back to a time when an honest man could earn enough with his two hands to provide for his family. The villains who opposed them lurked in dark and dangerous cities, in the halls of power, in guarded, gated compounds: a scheming woman senator, a gay man who molested teenaged boys, a cowardly black police chief. It was the farmer who started the uprising, when his farm was foreclosed on by an uncaring and corrupt bank, and in an act of desperation, he retaliated by shooting at the officers who'd come to serve the foreclosure notice (only to frighten, not to kill). He and his wife held off an increasing number of sheriffs and deputies until he was wounded and she was finally shot dead by a sniper.

Women did not fare well in these comics, Casey noted.

He was rescued from the hospital where he was under police guard by a mysterious man named Slade, who turns out to be a former Army ranger who had lost his squad in a busted mission, betrayed by a conniving, cowardly State Department official under orders from higher up.

Betrayal. Almost all the heroes were betrayed in some way. And the revenge they took in response was righteous and just.

The doorbell rang. It took her a minute to get to her feet. Her legs, her back, were stiff, and the spasms that hit when she straightened up made her gasp.

You overdid it today, she told herself. But you're still getting better.

By the time she reached the door, the spasms had eased up. Good, she thought. Maybe she could manage a smile for Paul.

She was looking forward to seeing him, she realized, feeling a flush of anticipation she hadn't felt in a while. Not since the first few months they'd dated. She'd really enjoyed going out with him before the arguments about priorities and not taking the relationship seriously. Before The Event.

And anyway, she'd had about enough True Men for one night.

Paul stood there, holding a flat blue and gold box. "Hey," he said. He smiled, but there was something tentative about it. He stepped inside, and she closed the door.

After a moment, he leaned down and kissed her on the lips. She could taste a hint of peppermint.

It felt good. Better than she'd expected.

"Ooooh," she said, looking at the box. "Is that chocolate?"

"It is."

"And I have red wine open. Perfect!" She gestured toward the couch and hobbled over to the kitchen to get a clean glass for him.

"It's what I could get at the airport," he said, sounding almost apologetic. "But they tell me it's local." He took her hand and stiffened his arm as she lowered herself to the couch; he was strong enough that she could use him for support.

He sat next to her. She poured the wine. They clinked glasses and sipped. He leaned in and kissed her again. This time she kissed him back, and at first it was gentle but she could feel the teeth beneath his lips, and as their tongues touched she felt a rush of pleasure spreading in little warm waves through her body.

It had been a while.

They broke apart. "Shit, I think I spilled some wine," Paul said.

"Well, don't worry about the couch." It was an old wood and cowhide thing she'd found at a secondhand store; she just threw Mexican beach blankets over the more battered spots.

"I'd better get a paper towel or something." He got up and went into the kitchen.

"If I open the chocolates without you, does that make me a bad person?" They'd had bagels and burritos at work, but it had been a long day.

"Go for it." He came back with a wad of wet paper towels, rubbing a patch on his suit pants and then wiping a section of leather cushion.

"What's this?" He'd picked up the volume of True Men she'd been reading. "You studying up for Comic-Con?"

Now the wave she felt was irritation. "I guess you missed the news."

"I was in meetings all day about the latest round of funding, so yeah, not a lot of time for news."

"You didn't get an alert about Matt Cason?"

He frowned. "The congressman? Yeah, but … what does that have to do with anything?"

Don't be a bitch, she told herself. If he'd been in meetings and on planes all day, he most likely wouldn't know anything beyond that someone took shots at a congressman. He wouldn't know about a special report on a local news program that talked about a comic book.

"He's okay, right? I did hear that much."

Five people weren't okay, she thought. Two were dead, three were injured, two critically.

"Yeah. He's still in the hospital, but the doctor said it was primarily to monitor for concussion. They might even discharge him tonight."

Saying that, she felt a sudden rush of adrenaline. I should be there, she thought. Maybe she could get a quote from him.

"Somebody said he took down the shooter himself, is that true?"

She nodded. "It looks that way. We have witnesses and photos. No statement from him yet."

"*We*? Were you working on this story?" He sounded almost incredulous.

"Well, yes. Because of my series on the Morena shootings. I met the shooter a couple of days ago. He's a friend of Alan Jay Chastain. Or said he was. We still don't have confirmation of that."

"Wait. You met the shooter?"

Try to keep up, she felt like saying. But that wasn't fair, and she knew it. They hadn't really spoken in weeks. Just a few texts that had dwindled to none.

"It's a crazy story," she said. "Just crazy." She hesitated. She knew what he'd thought of her work before: Trivial. Not real news. Surfing bulldogs.

And this? If it *was* real news, would that even make a difference? Her work would never be as important as what he did, would it?

"I have the segment and footage from the park on the DVR. Do you want to see it?"

"Sure," he said, his eyebrows pinched, his mouth set in a straight line.

Not exactly a show of enthusiasm, but she'd take it.

When they finished watching, Paul didn't say anything. He sipped his wine, still frowning.

"So?" Casey asked. She knew she sounded a little anxious. Eager. Wondering what he thought about what he'd seen. What he thought about her work. About her. Today had been so strange. She suddenly wanted to talk to him about it, to tell him what her day had been like, and to have him listen.

"That's ... some crazy stuff," he finally said.

"Yes, isn't it? I mean, the comic book! Of course maybe there's no direct connection, but what a weird coincidence, and it makes for a great … I don't want to say *hook*, because it's not strong enough for that, not yet, but as another way to tie the story together, it really works."

She stopped talking. Paul was staring at her. She thought his expression might be disbelief.

"He could have killed you." He sounded angry.

"Yeah. I know," she said. Because she did know. She'd thought about it ever since the park. Even before that, when she saw the memorial in the barbecue pit at the apartment complex, she'd thought about it. It was why she'd agreed they should call the police. Not just because she was convinced Lucas had killed those two young men.

Because he could have killed me.

She shrugged a little. "Apparently he had bigger targets to shoot."

"I don't get it, Casey. I don't get it. You … you almost died. And you're acting like … like this is no big deal."

"No, I'm not," she said. "I get it, okay? I just can't spend too much time dwelling on it, that's all."

"You need to be more careful."

"How? I was just doing my job. I had no idea it was going to be dangerous for me to walk to my car after shooting interviews at a giant thrift store."

That shut him up.

"All my life I've been hearing people tell me how everything I want to do is dangerous. And it's shit like this! Walking down a street by myself. Going out on my own at night. What if I told you I wanted to be a foreign correspondent? Cover stories in conflict zones. I shouldn't do that?"

"It's more dangerous for you. That's just reality."

She laughed. "Really? A man with a gun can kill *you* as easily as he can kill me."

Paul closed his eyes for a moment. "I worry about you," he said.

Why am I so angry at him? she thought. She shouldn't be. But she couldn't seem to help it.

"I care about you, Casey. Or I'd like to, anyway. I'm just not sure if you even want that."

Well, did she? It was a good question, she realized.

Why had she been so obsessed with this man before? She thought about it. He was attractive. Okay, sexy. He was smart, successful, and driven.

Paul checks all the boxes, Casey thought. Was that enough? What did they really have in common?

"To be honest with you? I don't know. I'm … in a place where I'm trying to figure out a lot of things. I understand if you don't want to wait for me to do that."

He sat on the couch, jaw working.

"I'm going to go," he said abruptly, standing up.

"You don't want to talk about this?"

"Why? It's not like anything I say is going to change your mind."

What just happened? she thought, watching the door close behind him.

24

Fifty days ago today we lost #AlanJay. Let's celebrate his memory with a day of action. Tell us how you're celebrating #AJLAAction-Day #AJLA #TrueMen

Followed girl thru TJ's. When she stopped I stopped. When she moved I moved. Stood behind her in line & rubbed against her ass. Scared her shitless LOL! #AJLAActionDay

Dirty-dicked the office bitch's lunch and watched her eat it #AJLAActionDay #AJLA

My goal: Doxx that slut from Cason's office #AJLAActionDay #AJLA #CasonShooting #TrueMen

"I'm sorry to leave you here like this." Jane wore one of her serious outfits, the one she used for pressers, a black suit with a black blouse and a single strand of oddly-shaped pearls. "I have to get back to the hospital for Matt's statement."

"That's okay," Sarah said. "I'll be fine."

She'd slept well, which surprised her, only waking up when she heard Jane and Charlotte's voices in the hall. By the time she'd pulled on her borrowed sweats, Charlotte had left for a morning class at the university and Jane was on her way out the door.

"Coffee's on the counter," Jane said. "Help yourself to anything in the fridge. I'm told you can't go wrong with cold pizza."

"Thanks for having me here," Sarah said. "I really appreciate it."

Jane grabbed a small travel Thermos she'd filled with coffee. "You don't have to thank me. This whole situation…" She shook her head a few times. "Anyway, please stay here as long as you'd like today. As mentioned, there's pizza, and I'm sure we have some beer."

"Thanks, but… I should get home. And change. So I can come into the office. I mean…" She hesitated. She knew how it might sound. Like her question about whether Lindsey liked baseball. "There must be a lot of work to do. With Ben in the hospital."

Jane's expression shifted, her eyes narrowing. Sarah couldn't read the emotion behind it.

Maybe she'd said the wrong thing.

"There is." Jane gestured toward the barstools, pulling one out for herself. Sarah sat across from her.

"I've got about three minutes before I have to leave, and that's not nearly enough time to discuss this. But yes. There's a lot of work to do, and no Ben to do it. I just don't want you to feel obligated." She sighed. "Sarah, you've been through a horrible experience. I meant what I said about getting you some counseling. If you need to ... regroup and heal, go home and spend some time with your family ... "

"You want me to leave," Sarah said.

"No." Jane sounded surprised. "No, not at all. With Ben out of commission for the time being, we've got a big hole to fill. But you don't need to try to power through this like nothing happened."

"I know. I'm not. I just ... "

She knew she wasn't okay, not really. Not just because of what she saw yesterday, not just because of that awful feeling of pushing down on Ben's leg, of feeling his flesh and bone and the blood all over her hands, her shirt.

It was the rest of it. That tweet. Her photo all over social media. What that meant.

But if she didn't work, what then? Would they fire her? *Then* what would she do? Go home? And do what?

No, she thought, I can't. I can't go back to who I was.

But she couldn't tell Jane any of that.

"I'd ... I'd feel better being there. With all of you."

"Okay." Jane was giving her that look. Studying her. "Just realize ... the likelihood is, there will be media at headquarters. We're a national story right now, and it's something we're going to have to deal with for a while. I know you don't want to talk to the press, but they will be hard to avoid. Especially if you're filling in for Ben. He handles some of those calls."

"I'll talk to Casey Cheng."

If News 9 were the ones most determined to track her down, maybe it made sense to try to control their narrative, as Jane had advised. To give them what they wanted, so they wouldn't have a reason to keep digging.

"Are you sure about that, Sarah? You don't have to talk to anyone if you don't want to."

"I'm sure."

Jane said all the right things, and maybe she even meant them, but there was something she *wasn't* saying too, Sarah thought.

There was work to be done, and she was the best person to do it. But she needed to show she could handle the pressure. That she could handle the press. And at least Casey Cheng knew what it was like to be a target.

"All right," Jane said. "Angus will put the two of you together. Let me know what she has in mind. I doubt if it's anything complicated, just the usual eyewitness statement: what did you see, what did you do, how did you feel. We can do a little role-playing at the office, if you think that would help." She rose. "Sorry, I've got to get to the hospital. Take your time coming in. There's no need for you to rush."

After Jane left, Sarah poured herself a cup of coffee from the carafe on the counter. It felt strange being in Jane and Charlotte's house without either of them here, like she was spying on them without meaning to. I'll wait for Angus to call, she thought, and then I'll get a Lyft and go home. It was too bad she couldn't just go straight to the office, where she'd left her car, but she couldn't go to work in borrowed sweats and a Padres T-shirt, could she?

The house was feeling stuffy, and it looked like a beautiful day outside, the sky a deep, cloudless blue. She opened the sliding glass door that led out to the backyard. There was a newspaper on the counter—an actual, physical newspaper—and she grabbed that to read. Maybe it would be nice to catch up on the news without worrying about the next alert, the next trending story. The next threat on Twitter.

She sat down on the couch to read. She was finishing a story about the art scene in Tijuana when she heard the voices.

Young. Male. Speaking in low voices. Coming from the backyard.

She stood, heart slamming against her ribs. Don't be stupid, she told herself. There's no one in the backyard. She could see the yard clearly.

She heard the voices again. Whispers. Laughter. From the house next door, maybe? She couldn't tell for sure, but she thought the sounds came from behind the house, not next to it. Was there a house behind this one?

She moved quietly outside.

The backyard had a cement patio and narrow crescent-shaped yard spooning it, box planters with tomato plants growing on tower trellises, big clay pots holding flowers and succulents.

And no, there wasn't a house directly behind this one. Instead, there was a chain-link fence marking the rim of a canyon. The canyon dropped steeply down, the slopes covered with sage and grasses and scrubby trees. The fences to either side were solid wood and tall, for privacy. But there wasn't anyone to see you straight ahead, unless people were out in the backyard on the other side, and they would be pretty far away.

Laughter again, abruptly cut off. A rustling in the bushes. She stared down the slope but didn't see anyone. Just a rabbit, bursting out into the open for a moment before it scrambled into a clump of sunflowers.

There were coyotes in the canyons, people said.

She stood there for a minute and listened. Heard only the faint rush of traffic coming from a busy street somewhere that was out of her sight.

25

MATT CASON WOULD MAKE a brief statement in front of the hospital some time late this morning.

"You don't have to cover this, Casey," Gloria had said. "We can send Hunter. I'd rather have you working on the next segment of the special report."

Whatever that was. With everything that had happened, did it even make sense to interview the families and victims of the Morena shooter? It would be better if they could take a closer look at the connections between Alan Jay Chastain and Lucas Derry, but was there anything to tie the two together beyond Lucas's words and a comic book?

"I want to."

She needed some time to figure it out, and besides, whatever the original intentions had been with the series, she *owned* the Cason shootings now. She wasn't about to give that to Hunter or anyone else if she could help it.

Maybe she could get an interview with Cason. Give him a chance to respond to those images.

She sat in the front seat of the station Prius after her live shot to wait for Cason's appearance, a light, asphalt-scented breeze blowing through the open windows. They'd talked about taking a live truck, but the assignment editor figured a Dejero was good enough for this: "Presser, static shot, he talks for five minutes and that's it." The van cost more to use, and besides, the Prius was easier to park.

They'd lucked out and found a parking space on the road in front of the hospital complex paralleling the freeway while the other stations' trucks were still circling the block.

Diego had staked out a prime spot in front of the hospital entrance, where they'd been told Cason would speak. Which was a good thing, because this was shaping up to be a crush. All the local stations had sent people, and she was pretty sure she'd spotted journos from CNN, Fox, and MSNBC, along with a network guy from CBS. Print was out in force, from here and out of town—was that a WaPo reporter?

This story was blowing up, and that was exactly why Casey had wanted to be here. She'd had a feeling. How could it not? A would-be political assassin connected to a mass shooter? A congressman who'd taken out his assailant with his fists? And all those awesome photographs and videos.

We own this, she thought. No one else had come close to getting what News 9 had gotten.

"Matt should be making his statement in about a half hour." That was the campaign manager, Jane Haddad, a dark-haired woman with an intense expression who'd come out to address the scrum while they were setting up.

Casey felt bad leaving Diego standing out there by himself. It was a hot day, and there wasn't any shade where he'd set up. But standing that long was an ordeal for her, and they both knew it.

She had her iPad out, with the idea that she'd brainstorm. Make some notes anyway. What would the next segment be? What made sense as a follow-up to what happened yesterday?

Her cell rang, a snippet of a song by Florence and the Machine—Rose's ringtone.

"Hey, what's up?"

"The girl from the park, the campaign staffer. Her name's Sarah Price. She wants to talk to you."

———

"This is the only interview I'm going to do."

The voice on the phone was young. Hesitant. Almost flat. Like the emotion had been drained from it, or was somehow disconnected from the words.

Well, she'd had a traumatic experience yesterday, Casey thought. She was probably still in shock. Or maybe she was just shy.

"Understandable," Casey said. "Thank you for trusting us with it."

"I want it to be short."

"All right." Dang, Casey thought. She'd hoped there might be enough to Sarah's story to warrant making her the focus of the next segment. But it would still be a scoop, and there were plenty of other people on the Cason campaign who'd been affected by the park shootings.

"And ... I really only want to talk about what happened in the park. I mean ... that's what you wanted to interview me about, right?"

"Well, that's what prompted us trying to get in touch with you, so yes, we'll focus on that. But I'd like to talk to you a little bit about your work on the campaign, how you got involved, that sort of thing."

"I'd really rather not talk about personal stuff."

Casey found herself leaning forward in the car seat. Interesting. She hadn't thought those topics were particularly personal. They were just background. "Could I ask why?"

A pause. "It's just… did you see what people are saying about me? On those tweets?"

Now she heard emotion. An edge of panic, choked back like a bridled horse.

"Oh," Casey said. "Yes. I'm so sorry that happened to you."

"*You* posted the photo."

Was that anger?

What should I say? she wondered. It was a powerful image that captured a moment. It was an exclusive. That kid photographer will be up for awards at the end of the year. Of *course* we posted it. We're kicking the ass of every other station in town on this story. Hell, we're kicking the ass of the *nationals* on this story.

I can't say that, she thought.

"We did. It was news. Look…" Don't lose control of this conversation, Casey told herself. "I understand. You've been through a horrible experience, and we don't want you to do anything you're not comfortable with."

An unexpected snort. "I'm not comfortable with any of this."

Fair enough.

"I really am sorry," Casey said. "I get tweets like that. It's just what happens to women on the internet sometimes, and… it's not fun."

Casey waited for Sarah's response. At first there was none, other than a sharp sigh. Then finally, she spoke.

"Yeah. It's not."

———

"They'll let us shoot there?" Rose asked. Casey could hear a snippet of voice-over in the background—maybe Rose was in the edit bay at the station.

"So far I haven't heard a no," Casey said.

"That would be awesome. We could open with some general commentary about how the shooting's affected the campaign, see if we can grab anyone else for a quick bite."

"Maybe we'll get a couple good lines out of Cason today. That would round it out." She tapped a finger on her virtual keyboard. "It's weird," she said. "I don't really get why Sarah's giving this to us. She seemed very upset that the photo's gone viral. If I didn't want that kind of attention, why would I want to help the people who put it out there?"

"Well, why is she upset?" Rose asked. "Is it a specific privacy thing? Or just a general, 'I'd rather not have my personal trauma retweeted a few thousand times' deal?"

"She mentioned the trolls, but ... I think it's more than that."

Something about Sarah Price seemed off. Anyone who was that eager to tell you what she was willing to talk about had something she didn't want to discuss.

"This story's really bringing out the trolls, that's for sure," Rose said. A slight hesitation. "Have you looked at your Twitter account today?"

"No ... I should, I've just been too busy. Figured I'd be tweeting from here."

"There's some pretty ugly stuff."

Casey shrugged, though of course Rose couldn't see that. "I'm used to it. Haters gonna hate and all."

"Yeah, I know, but … this is a little extreme. They're using the AJLA, the Alan Jay Liberation Army, hashtag, and there's a lot of them."

She felt a shudder rise, pushing against her skin from the inside. "Oh, poor little loser boys in their mommy's basement," Casey said, trying to keep it light.

"I'm sure that's most of them. Look, let's talk about it after you've wrapped there."

Casey knew Rose well enough to guess that Rose didn't want to distract her before the press conference. Which should be happening in about ten minutes, if Jane Haddad's estimate was correct.

I should tweet anyway, Casey thought. *I'm here at Sharp Hospital, where we expect @RepMattCason will be making a statement soon.* Something like that. Snap a photo of the hospital entrance to include. And she could get some video of Cason on her phone for immediate upload to Twitter, Facebook, and Snapchat.

She got out her phone and opened Twitter.

"Thank you all for coming."

Matt Cason wore a crisp blue Oxford shirt that looked a little too big for him—maybe so his splinted arm and hand would easily fit through the rolled-up, unbuttoned sleeve. He was freshly shaved, his hair neatly combed, his expression calm and thoughtful, looking nothing like the wild-eyed man who'd beaten a killer into a coma with his fists.

He stood behind a portable lectern, flanked by his wife, the campaign manager, and several uniformed police officers. There were a lot of police here, Casey noticed, ringing the perimeter, keeping watch.

"First, I want to express my deep appreciation to all the first responders, the police and paramedics and other emergency personnel
whose prompt actions undoubtedly saved lives yesterday."

> IT'S #AJLAACTIONDAY, ANYBODY WANNA FIND OUT
> WHERE THAT UGLY WHORE @CASEYCHENGNEWS9
> LIVES AND CELEBRATE IT WITH HER? #AJLA #TRUE-
> MEN

> BET HER CUNT LOOKS LIKE A FORTUNE COOKIE LOL!

> HEY @CASEYCHENGNEWS9 NEXT TIME WE WONT
> MISS, THIRD TIMES A CHARM BITCH #AJLAACTION-
> DAY #AJLA #TRUEMEN

Don't think about that now, Casey told herself.

Cason paused for a moment. Drew in a deep breath. "I'll be honest, I can't believe I'm standing here right now, talking about another
mass slaughter of people in our community. I can't believe that a man
I was hugging a moment before *died* right in front of me. That one of
my staffers is fighting for his life in this hospital. That a little boy out
for a fun day at the park was shot to death for no reason at all. This ... "

He closed his eyes. Shook his head. Next to him, his wife, Lindsey,
squeezed his hand and then put her arm around his shoulders. Cason
stood there silently a moment longer, his eyes still closed. Finally he
opened them.

"This is what happens in a war zone," he said. "Not ... not in a
prosperous democracy. Not in our city. It defies comprehension."

There were just so many of those tweets. Death threats. Rape
threats. Racist insults. The majority with the #AJLA hashtag. A few
with #TrueMen.

Probably because of the segment, Casey thought. It made sense they'd want to hit her with that as well.

They're a bunch of losers, she told herself. All talk.

She shifted back and forth in place, then leaned on Trusty the cane. The sciatica was really acting up again, shooting down her leg. The bottom of her foot burned. She wished she could try to stretch, but the crowd was tightly packed; she was surrounded by reporters and photographers and a few curious hospital visitors and staffers, pressed up against the yellow belt line separating Cason from the crowd.

Next to her, Diego zoomed in on Cason. They were at the front of the scrum, close enough to the lectern to see him clearly, the dark circles under his eyes they hadn't tried to cover with makeup. On purpose?

"As for my own behavior, I'm not proud of it," Cason said. "I was angry and I was scared and he needed to be stopped."

Something—someone—jostled her from behind, bumping into her shoulder blade, poking against the small of her back. An overeager photographer? Whomever it was kept pressing against her.

She spun around, sending fresh bolts of pain through her back and down her leg again.

A young white man stood there, tall, broad-shouldered, wearing sunglasses, a baseball cap, jeans, and a navy hoodie, his hands jammed in the front pockets.

It wasn't cold.

"I lost control," she heard Cason say. "I don't feel good about it."

She could feel her heart slam in her throat.

"Sorry," the man whispered. He was smiling.

Oh for fuck's sake, was that a hard-on? Did that really just happen?

"I don't really know if there's anything else I can say."

Casey stared at the young man a moment longer. Nodded. Then turned her back on him and faced the lectern, the muscles between her shoulder blades twitching.

He's just an asshole, she told herself.

Or maybe he didn't mean it. Maybe it was his hands she'd felt, the hands stuffed in the hoodie pocket. She couldn't see if anything else was going on. The hoodie covered his crotch.

Cason was still standing at the lectern, his eyes tired, slowly shaking his head. His wife whispered something in his ear.

There's nothing wrong, he's just an asshole, he didn't mean it, stay alert, if he has a gun, a knife, anything, you can run forward, the barrier won't stop you, that's your escape route and the police are there—

"Thank you again," Cason said, and then he turned away, his wife's hand on his back, passing Jane Haddad the microphone as three police officers surrounded them, and they retreated into the hospital.

Casey's hand went up, along with everybody else's, but her mind was a blank. She didn't know what to ask Cason if he *did* call on her.

He's just a guy, he's not here to hurt you—

"Congressman! Congressman!"

"Matt will be happy to take your questions a little later," Haddad said. "Right now he has an appointment with a physician."

Casey glanced quickly over her shoulder. The man was gone.

"What's his health status?" someone yelled out. Gabrielle from News 12?

"He's fine," Haddad said.

"The head injury?" someone else shouted.

"Minor. Medical observation was just an excess of caution. I'll have more for you later." Haddad turned to follow Cason.

"Is he considering withdrawing from the race?" Gabrielle again.

That stopped Haddad in her tracks. She turned back. "No. Absolutely not. There's no reason for him to." And with that she strode off.

"Hey, Case, you okay?"

Diego. She could feel his solid presence next to her.

"Oh, sure, I'm fine. Just a little hot. The sun ... it's bright."

26

COME AROUND TO THE BACK, Jane had texted. SOMEONE WILL LET YOU IN. As soon as Sarah pulled up to headquarters she saw why: media vans and cars had gathered there, waiting, it seemed, for something to happen. One of them was from News 9.

Jane herself opened the door. "Thanks for coming."

They walked down the hall that led to their office suite. "The News 9 people are here."

"I saw them."

Jane paused for a moment by the restrooms. "Are you sure you want to do this?"

Sarah nodded. "I'm sure."

She wasn't, not at all. But she wanted to stay on the campaign. Ben's job was open right now, and this was a way to prove herself.

I don't look the way I used to look, she told herself. And she didn't think anyone would recognize her voice. No one had ever much cared about what she had to say.

Casey Cheng was taller than Sarah had expected—maybe an inch taller than she was. But she was slender, even a little frail—the aftereffects of the shooting, maybe. Her hand trembled slightly as it grasped the head of the cane; the skin around her eyes seemed almost translucent beneath the camera-ready makeup.

I could bench-press her, Sarah thought. Which made her feel better, somehow. Like she wasn't the weak one in this situation, as weak as she felt.

"Hi, Sarah, thanks so much for agreeing to talk to us." Cheng smiled in a way that sparkled. You'd forget about any frailty, seeing that smile. She stuck out her hand for Sarah to shake. Her grip was firm, confident. "I know it's not an easy thing to do."

It seems easy enough for you, Sarah wanted to say.

"You can set up in my office," Jane said. There was no other place in the headquarters that was remotely private. Everyone tried to act like things were normal as the big Latino cameraman from News 9 took shots of the headquarters, of Tomás doing vol-calls, trying to round up a few more volunteers for phone banking and canvassing, of Sylvia working on her laptop.

But nothing was normal. There were the news crews ringing the parking lot, the police car parked at the curb. Inside, a volunteer taped sympathy signs and cards to a blank wall, and someone had sent over several bouquets of flowers, teddy bears, and heart-shaped balloons.

Ben would be here if things were normal.

Ben was doing better, Jane told her. They were still worried about his kidneys, but he was doing better. His parents had flown in from

Michigan and they were at the hospital now, so at least he wasn't alone.

Sarah wished she were doing this someplace else, but where? Not at her apartment. Not at the station—the last thing she wanted to do was walk into a newsroom. Headquarters at least was familiar. Comfortable.

She wished she wasn't doing this at all.

As they walked into the office, Jane rested her hand on Sarah's arm for just a moment. "If there's any point where you're not comfortable, just stop," she said in a low voice. "You're under no obligation to answer everything they might throw at you."

Sarah nodded, but she could feel the beginning of panic, her heart speeding up in her chest, the cold sweat prickling up on her skin. "I thought they were just going to ask me about what happened in the park."

"Exactly. So if she goes off on some fishing expedition? Just stop. If you're not sure what to say, don't say anything. I'll be there, and I'll get them off you."

Jane stared at her, and Sarah had the oddest feeling that she was trying to communicate something important, but Sarah wasn't sure what.

27

SARAH PRICE WAS SO young. That was Casey's first impression of her. Not that I'm ancient, she reminded herself. But Sarah could still be a student. Her face was so smooth, there was something almost unfinished about it. She was vaguely pretty in a bland way, solidly built, with curves that her boxy navy blazer and white blouse couldn't hide.

There was a loveseat-sized couch in Jane Haddad's small office. They set up there, Casey and Sarah at either end, and Casey had a sudden flash of the interview they'd done with Alan Jay Chastain's mother, Helen Scott. They'd sat on a couch like this, knees angled toward each other. There'd been that old cat, the one with the loud meow that just wanted to be petted.

Focus, Casey told herself. "Okay, Sarah, are you ready to get started?"

Sarah nodded.

They'd closed the blinds for some level of privacy. Jane Haddad stood by the door like a guard, or maybe a watchful aunt in charge of her niece's virtue. I would not want to tangle with that lady, Casey thought.

She turned to Sarah and smiled. "I'm just going to ask you a couple of background questions to start. Okay?"

Sarah hadn't been relaxed to begin with, but Casey could see her visibly tense up. A small, tight nod.

"So, your name is Sarah Price. Can you tell me how old you are?"

"Twenty-three."

Older than she looked.

"And where are you from?" .

"Connecticut." She shifted around on the couch. "Why are you asking me these questions? I thought we weren't going to talk about personal things."

The idea was to relax the interview subject, get her talking about easy topics and build some trust so she'd be more comfortable when the hard stuff came up. Obviously it wasn't working.

"No, it's helpful to have a little background for our records, that's all." Casey smiled. "So, you're twenty-three, working for the campaign, I'm guessing you're out of school?"

Another quick, fractional nod. "I just got my master's."

"What did you study?"

"Political science and public policy."

"So, obviously you're interested in politics."

"From a policy perspective."

"You mean, not as a candidate."

"Right."

"And what motivated you to get involved with Congressman Cason's campaign? Were you living in San Diego, or ..."

Another uncomfortable shift. "I was looking for a candidate whose policies I could get behind," she said after a brief pause. "And … it's an interesting district. One of the few that's really competitive. I wanted to see how that affected policy making, the impetus it creates toward crafting consensus. Or do you just push the limits of acceptable discourse for the district, do what you want and focus on your ground game and getting out the vote?" She smiled a little, almost chuckled, and for the first time seemed genuine. "I mean, you have to do that anyway, no matter what. And our opponent is such an extremist, Matt comes off looking like a moderate regardless of his positions."

Matt. There was a slight flush to her cheeks as she said his name. And she never said whether she lived in San Diego before she got involved in the campaign.

Well, Matt Cason was a good-looking guy and charismatic as hell. I'd do him, Casey thought, except for that whole "he's married" part. Though the rumors were that hadn't always stopped him in the past. Regardless, Sarah Price was not just some starfucker crushing on a candidate. She was smart.

"So, why politics?" Casey asked. "What is it that drew you to this field?"

"I want to make a difference." She said it as though that should be obvious. "I want to help create positive change."

Perfect, Casey thought. She could already hear the V.O. in her head: *"Sarah went to work on Congressman Matt Cason's campaign to make a difference in people's lives."* Then Sarah: *"I want to help create positive change."* Casey: *"She never planned on actually saving a life, during one of the darkest days in recent American political history."*

Something like that.

"Sarah, can we talk about what happened yesterday?"

Sarah drew in a breath. Closed her eyes. Nodded.

"You accompanied the congressman to the park. What was your job that day?"

"Handling social media. It wasn't a campaign event, but he thought there might be some good material for Social."

"So ... were you recording the event?"

They couldn't be that lucky, could they?

————

"Good stuff," Diego said, as they walked to the car.

"Definitely." It really was, Casey thought. Sarah mostly had spoken in that hushed near-monotone of hers, so when her emotions did break through, the contrast was powerful.

The smartphone footage Sarah had shot? The confrontation between Cason and the guy who'd said he was a veteran? Went right up to the moment when Lucas Derry pulled out a gun and started shooting.

And no one had seen it but News 9.

"Sure, you can use it," Sarah had said, after huddling for a few minutes with Jane Haddad. "It's not like we can." Casey wasn't too surprised they'd agreed. The footage made Cason look good, the kind of thing a campaign would turn into an ad, if it weren't for what had happened next. They wanted to try to use Casey and News 9 to get positive coverage, and in this case, she was willing to play along: *"In this exclusive video obtained by News 9 ... "*

Damn, this was turning out to be a good day.

Her phone rang—Florence and the Machine. Rose.

"You free?"

"Yeah. And you won't believe what we got."

"Tell me at lunch. I'm starving."

"We're going to want to hit with it tonight," Casey said. "And we'll want to start teasing it as soon as possible. Believe me."

"We've got time. We can get started at lunch."

Rose sounded worried, Casey thought. Now what?

28

Casey Cheng News 9 @CaseyChengNews9
EXCLUSIVE: TONIGHT AT 6 INTERVIEW W. CAMPAIGN
STAFFER WHO SAVED LIFE OF HER COWORKER PLUS HER
UNSEEN FOOTAGE OF THE #CASONSHOOTING KASD.US.
UCA9Z

————

"Casey, we *have* to report this. I mean, maybe there's no real connection, maybe it's all just these little turds' idea of lulz, but we can't take the chance."

Casey focused on her ahi and yellowtail sushirrito. She didn't want to have this conversation.

They'd met at a restaurant on Convoy. Diego dropped her off on his way back to the station, where he'd pick up another assignment. She could have gone back to the station with him, but clearly, Rose hadn't wanted to have this discussion there, and anyway, the restaurant was close to work. A casual place, distressed wood and aluminum counters, tucked in a strip mall between one of her favorite dumpling restaurants and a Chinese travel agency, across the street from the Jaguar dealership. Casey had been there for a feature she'd done before The Event, on *a culinary trend that's sweeping San Diego—sushi, or if you prefer, poke, meets burritos.* The segment had her taking a bite and proclaiming, *"I can find no downside to this trend, Elise!"*

Well, they really were good.

Casey sighed. Sure, she'd been a little freaked after reading those tweets and when she'd encountered that creep at Cason's presser, but now she just wanted to move on. "I don't want them to use this as an excuse to pull me off the story. I mean, what if they decide it's too risky to have me in the field?"

Rose put down her sushirrito. Swallowed the bite she'd been chewing. "Look, Casey, no story is worth your life. It just isn't."

"We're talking about tweets and hashtags, not … not credible threats."

Next time we won't miss.

Third time's a charm, bitch.

Rose got out her phone. Unlocked it with her thumb and swiped down to find a story on her lock screen. "Have you seen this?" She slid the phone across the table.

Casey picked it up. Breaking news on CNN.

4 Wounded By Explosive Device At Women's Soccer Game in Virginia

She skimmed the rest. "The guy who did this claims it was a prank that got out of hand." Her voice cracked, and she knew it was a tell. She couldn't even convince herself.

"Sure he does. And maybe it was. It's still a *prank* that hurt four people, two seriously."

"Okay. That sucks, but what does it have to do with me?"

"People are retweeting it and passing it around social media with that AJLA hashtag." Her fingers curled to make air quotes. "And AJLA Action Day."

"Are any of them using the True Men hashtag?"

"Not that I saw."

"I want to keep an eye on that. If the only people who are using it are responding to *me*, then it's probably just a ... a sick joke. Not part of some larger, I don't know, conspiracy?" She laughed a little. It sounded so crazy when you said it out loud.

"A joke." Rose stared at her. "Those are death threats, Casey." She kept shaking her head, like she couldn't believe she was having to say these things. "You need to get your head on straight about this."

Casey felt that anger rising from somewhere deep in her gut. It wasn't fair. It wasn't right. Always being told *It's too dangerous. You shouldn't. You can't.*

"Okay, fine, we'll call the cops, or the FBI, or whoever's handling this now," she said. "But let's not panic over stuff that probably isn't anything actually worth worrying about, okay?"

"This is not panicking. This is just saying that maybe it doesn't make sense for you to do things like a presser for a Cason statement. Anyone from the station can cover that. We can still use the material for our series. There's just no reason for you to be out in public exposing yourself unnecessarily while all this shit is going on."

Casey supposed Rose had a point. "All right," she finally said. "But if something big comes up? I'm not going to hide from these creeps. That's what they want. To make me too scared to do my job."

Rose sighed. "Okay. Agreed." Her phone buzzed. Rose picked it up and thumbed it open. "Text from Detective Helton," she said. "Looks like there's no need to call him. He wants to talk to you."

29

MONDAY. SARAH SAT AT her desk, wondering how she was going to get a handle on all the feeds.

Someone—Angus or Presley—had put up a few tweets and posts Saturday and Sunday. Her half day yesterday had been taken up by Casey Cheng and the FBI. A hastily assembled statement about how they were "devastated," a few lines from Matt about how he would continue to represent San Diego, that the campaign would go on. There was a video of Matt's hospital press conference from a local news station. Thank god the photo of her and Ben in the park hadn't been posted. She didn't think she could take that.

There were many comments and replies. Most of them were supportive.

"Take screenshots of any responses you get that are threatening," the man from the FBI had said. "And please don't delete them unless you absolutely have to. They're probably nothing to worry about, but we may want to track some of these users."

Did they really intend to?

"Of course we'll be monitoring the accounts as well. Please be assured that we take this very seriously."

Maybe they actually did, since Matt was involved.

She scrolled through the comments on the Facebook page, feeling her shoulders, her jaw, her stomach, everything tense up, clenching like a fist.

> WAIT TILL CRIMINAL MATT CASON GETS HIS ASS THROWN IN JAIL HE IS CROOKED AS THEY COME

> CASON'S A THUG. I LIKE THAT IN MY CONGRESSMAN!

> CASON AND HIS PALS SCRAMBLING TO MAKE IT LEGAL FOR ILLEGALS, CHILD MOLESTERS AND RAPIST TO VOTE....#TRUEMEN WILL PUSH BACK

I shouldn't have to do this, she thought, why are they making me do this? Then she remembered, no one was making her do it. She'd agreed to it. This was part of the job, and she'd wanted the job.

At least they weren't talking about *her*.

The News 9 segment hadn't turned out too bad. Casey Cheng had done what she'd promised—focused on what had happened in the park. Sarah's face wasn't even in it that much, except for when she'd talked about Ben—they'd used a lot of what she'd said as a voice-over. The footage she'd given them from the park had helped with that. There was only so much time in a local news segment, and of course they'd want to use the stuff she'd shot, stuff nobody else had seen.

Just like she'd thought they would.

The FBI man was unhappy that she'd shared the footage with News 9. "Material like that is evidence," he'd said. "Releasing it publicly can taint it."

How? she'd wanted to say. The recordings showed what they showed. The speech Matt had given to thank first responders. The compassion and kindness he'd shown toward an unstable veteran. Henry James Olivier was his name. He'd never been in combat, as it turned out, or in any kind of dangerous posting. Booted out on a bad conduct discharge, problems with drugs and alcohol.

She remembered just now how Matt had looked at her when he was comforting the man. That half smile. Like the two of them were sharing a secret.

Her phone rang. The ringtone for Communications.

She hesitated.

You have to answer it, she told herself. It's your direct line. It's probably okay.

She picked up the phone. "Hello, Communications."

"Sarah?"

She thought she recognized his voice, but she wasn't sure. She waited for him to say something.

"Sarah, it's Wyatt. Wyatt Gray."

He didn't sound quite like himself. There was a strange edge to his voice that she hadn't heard before. Something strained and uncertain.

"Hi, Wyatt."

"Sarah, I'm so glad you're okay. I saw the news like everybody else, and … it's just terrible. I am so sorry."

"It's okay, I'm fine," she said, automatically. Because he almost sounded like he thought it *was* his fault, somehow. But it couldn't be his fault. Could it? She could hear a deep inhale of breath.

"Listen, there's a couple of things I need to tell you."

"Okay, I'm listening."

"The first is, the things in Cason's past? They're coming out."

"What things?" she asked.

"His kicking the shit out of that punk made him look strong." A laugh. "People, you know? They're pretty sick sometimes. So, your opponent, the folks behind her, they will look for ways to turn that against him. I'm surprised all that didn't get dug up the first time he ran, but no one thought he'd win that one, they didn't take him seriously till too late. Didn't do their homework."

"What things?" she asked again.

A sigh. "Jesse Garcia. Maybe your campaign manager already knows, but tell her."

She scribbled down the name. "Okay."

"Second thing is, they're gonna go after his service in Anbar, try to swift boat him with it." A pause. "You do know what a swift boat is, right?"

"Yes," she snapped. Just because she was young didn't mean she was ignorant. "Turn your opponent's strength into a weakness."

A chuckle. "You're smart. I knew you were."

"How do you know all these things? Why are you doing this?" she blurted out. She just couldn't take this today. It was too much.

"I'm a concerned citizen with access to some data, that's all."

Suddenly her thoughts slowed down. Don't feel this now, she told herself. Think.

There weren't that many possibilities. He could be someone close to Tegan's campaign, a mole, or have a source there. He could be a ratfuck from Tegan or her allies. But so far his information had been good.

Or, he could be a third party, "with access to some data."

"Who do you work for?" she asked.

231

"I can't discuss that."

"Why not?"

"Because I can't." He sounded angry. Which was a first.

"So why do you want to help Matt? If that's what you're really doing?"

"Because things have gone too far," he finally said.

What has gone too far? she wanted to scream. But there was a part of her that had already had an idea, even if it wasn't what he meant.

Everything. Everything had gone too far. She had the sense that they were all rushing toward some cliff, being pushed there by something dark and angry that she couldn't quite see, only sense.

"You're talking about Tegan," she said. "That her politics, her positions, they're too extreme."

A weary laugh. "Yeah, Sarah. Pretty much."

"You're some kind of whistleblower then?"

"Look, I'm taking a risk calling you." Now he sounded angry again. "What you need to do is listen to what I said and try to get out ahead of it. You can, but you all are going to have to act quickly, before their narrative gets set in stone."

"Fine," she said. She was angry too. "Is there anything else?"

"There is." A pause. When his voice came back, it was low and urgent. "You're going to get outed, Sarah. They know who you are."

30

"WELL, THANKS, MS. CHENG. This is very interesting."

Casey nodded, not trusting herself to speak.

Helton wasn't bad, but this FBI guy, Kendrick, was the sort of man who really pushed her buttons: dismissive and condescending.

They sat in the small conference room: Casey, Detective Helton, Agent Kendrick, and Mika, the station lawyer, whose job wasn't to help Casey but to make sure the station's interests were represented.

"We're feeling a sense of urgency because of the possible connected nature of these events," Helton had told Casey on the phone. He had a mellow surfer accent that tended to undercut any sense of urgency, but Casey took him at his word. They'd agreed to meet at the station at three that afternoon—Mika had a slot available, and there was no way the higher-ups would let her meet with the police without an attorney present.

She hadn't expected Kendrick, and at first, she figured his being there was a bonus. Maybe she wouldn't be able to quote him for the record, but they couldn't stop her from saying that she'd met with the FBI as well as SDPD.

But she sure wasn't getting much material out of this. A bunch of nonresponses and boilerplates, uttered by a man who clearly wasn't all that interested in what she had to say.

Helton and Kendrick were both white guys, Kendrick in his forties, Helton maybe a few years younger. Kendrick had a tight haircut and a crisp white shirt stretched across his gut, his face freshly scraped and smelling of aftershave. Helton was rangy, his hair a little longer, with the kind of faded-tan face that came from spending a lot of time outside, just not lately. His eyes were gray and dark-circled. She liked him better than Kendrick, and not just because of his sad eyes. *He* wasn't being a dick.

She'd gone through everything that had happened: The interview with Helen Scott, finding the comic in Alan Jay's bedroom, the encounter with Lucas Derry, his tattoo. The visit to Derry's workplace and apartment. The stories in those comics. The hashtags and the threats.

"We're familiar with the material," Agent Kendrick said. He seemed bored. "And of course we take the threats against you seriously and we will be investigating them thoroughly." He inclined his head a fraction in Helton's direction. "Detective Helton will be your point person for that, given that he's local. I know he's got some recommendations for you about managing your personal safety."

Helton nodded slowly.

Kendrick rose from his chair. "I need to get to my next interview, but thank you again for your time. Please do call us if you run into anything else."

There was a moment of silence as Kendrick headed for the door.

"We came in separate vehicles," Helton said, leaning back in his chair as Kendrick's hand twisted the doorknob.

If Kendrick heard him, he didn't acknowledge it. The door closed behind him.

"About your concerns for Casey's safety," Mika said. "We'd really like to hear your take on it."

Of course Mika would, Casey thought. Probably concerned about the station's liability if they put her in a situation that could potentially expose her to danger above and beyond the normal expectations of her job.

"Well, there's still a lot we don't know," Helton said. "Though we do know our boy Lucas harbored some hostility toward her."

I'm right here, Casey was tempted to say. "How do you know that?" she asked instead.

Helton reached into his suit's breast pocket and got out his phone. He pressed his thumb to unlock it, swiped a few times, then pushed it across the table to her. "That's inside Lucas Derry's apartment."

Casey took the phone and looked.

Of course, she thought. Lucas had to have one of those Walls of Crazy—photos, clippings, stickers with white power slogans, all of it taped and tacked to a dingy beige wall.

"Swipe to the next one," Helton said.

She did. A close-up of a section of the wall. Her photo, her head and torso. She was holding a mic, smiling, against a background of blue sky and beach and palm trees. A station promo shot.

Lucas had graffitied it with red pen. A penis and balls, the tip of the cock touching her lips. An explosion of red on her chest.

"He's not much of an artist, is he?" she said lightly. She pushed the phone back to Helton.

"No, not so much."

"What is it?" Mika asked.

"Lucas had a bit of a crush on me, apparently," Casey said. "But hey, it's not like he's a threat to me now."

"That is true." Helton took the phone, clicked to the lock screen, and put it in his pocket.

Mika looked up from her iPad. "So in terms of Casey's personal safety, what are you suggesting?"

Helton turned to Casey. Making sure she was paying attention, she guessed. "We recommend that for now, you avoid scenarios that put you out there when you don't need to be. Especially into situations where you don't have a lot of control. Crowds. Uncontrolled access. If you're interviewing people in a place that's relatively secure, that's not so much of a concern."

Casey smiled. "You sound like my producer."

"Rose? She's a smart lady. You should listen to her."

She could feel herself tense up, that anger she'd been carrying around since The Event close to the surface. Don't be stupid, she told herself. There was no point in being angry at Rose and Helton. They weren't the ones who'd nearly killed her. That guy was dead, and his asshole buddy not much better.

"Good advice. As long as I can still do my job."

"What about home security?" Mika asked, taking notes on her iPad.

Helton turned to Casey. "What kind of housing?"

"Condo. Secure entrance. Underground parking."

"Okay. That's good. Take reasonable precautions. Watch yourself in the parking garage, those can be easy to gain entrance to. Check your car for anything that seems out of place. Practice situational awareness. They train you guys in that?"

"We have seminars," Mika said.

Casey had been to one. The station did its due diligence, ever since the killings of the reporter and the cameraman on live TV a couple years ago.

"Okay," Helton said. "I can give you some additional pointers if you'd like."

"I would. I could use a review."

Mika swiped her finger across her iPad and flipped the cover closed. "Casey, let's you and I schedule an ASAP meeting with Jordan and Gloria to discuss this, all right?"

The news director *and* the evening news producer. Casey wasn't sure if this was a good sign, or not. Being considered high-profile was one thing. Getting labeled a pain in the ass was another. "Will do."

"So," Mika said. "I think we're good for now. Unless there's anything else?"

Helton shook his head. So did Casey.

She'd much rather talk to Helton one-on-one anyway. Casey turned to him and smiled. "Walk you to your vehicle?"

————

Outside it was pleasant, with patchy clouds. Late afternoon. The June Gloom that came most late afternoons or early evenings into July didn't always make it to Kearny Mesa, but you could feel it coming today, rolling in from the ocean, gentling the air even in the station parking lot.

They walked as far as the first light post before Casey said, "So … about my personal safety … I'm not really that worried. I've had plenty of trolls since I started doing this job. I think that's all they are. Trolls."

They stopped walking. Helton nodded, seeming to scan the lot for his car. Maybe he was scanning it for threats. "Odds are you're right.

237

But with all that's going on, there's nothing wrong with saving yourself some stress when you can. You gotta do what you gotta do, but if you don't have to, don't do it."

Casey nodded. It was frustrating, but he was probably right.

He was looking at her now. Gray eyes staring out of a tanned face. Maybe he actually was a surfer. "In terms of the threats ... I'll be honest with you—this online stuff, we're still getting a handle on it. But we take it seriously. We'll do our best to track down the worst of these assholes. It just might take some time."

"Okay," she said. "I understand this isn't easy."

She thought for a moment about the interview. About Kendrick's dismissive attitude. Why not take the chance? Maybe he'd bite.

"Special Agent Kendrick didn't seem to take anything I said very seriously. I suppose I could have misread him."

Helton cracked half a smile. "He's a very busy, important man."

She half smiled back. "So ... who takes the lead in an investigation like this? The SDPD or the FBI?"

"There's also the Capitol Police, they're investigating as well."

"Capitol Police?"

"Charged with protecting members of Congress. They've got a budget." That hint of a smile again. "In answer to your question, it's a cooperative relationship. The FBI has the national databases and we provide the on-the-ground realities."

"I see. So, what do *you* think? About those on-the-ground realities? Like the hashtags. The comic. True Men. I mean, I've read those comics, and well, they're a little disturbing. In context."

"We did find copies of the comics in Derry's apartment. A complete set. I'm reading them now. Never thought I'd get paid for reading comic books, but hey, this is San Diego, home of Comic-Con."

"And ... ?"

"We're still working on this, but so far, the first appearance of that True Men hashtag in relation to the 'Alan Jay Liberation Army'"—he made air quotes around that—"has been since your story was broadcast."

"The ones related to me."

"Yeah. Those. And some others not related to you."

They had to have been posted since lunch, the last time she'd checked Twitter. Was it just the hashtags? Or had there been incidents?

She felt that hollow dread gathering in her chest, her gut.

"Do you mind?" she said, indicating her phone.

"Go right ahead." His gaze was level. "You probably should know."

There were more than she would have thought.

Some of them weren't too bad. #TrueMen are taking back this country from globalists and banksters #AJLA. Real women prefer #TrueMen not cucks. #AJLA.

Of course they got worse: #TrueMen will show feminist cunts there place #AJLA. Make America White again #TrueMen #AJLA.

And there were more directed at Casey.

Whatever. She could take it.

But this one, this one was bad.

The tweet linked to a news story about an attack on a mosque in Michigan that had happened an hour ago. Someone had driven by with an explosive device—a grenade, probably—pulled the pin, and thrown it into a small crowd that had gathered outside the entrance before prayers.

#TrueMen will defend America against Islamic terror. Remember #PhoenixCinemaMassacre #AJLA.

She looked up. Helton had unwrapped a stick of gum. He popped it in his mouth, still watching her. "You see the mosque attack?" he asked.

She nodded. "Yes. I mean … what's the likelihood that this is, I don't know, some kind of actual movement? Or if it's just trolls attaching a trending hashtag to an unconnected incident?"

"Too soon to say."

"Of course." She swiped back to the search page.

1 New Notification

She didn't want to look. She wasn't sure if she could take it, another threat, some crude insult, 140 characters of stupidity and hate.

She touched the link.

We know who @RepMattCason's little slut really is. And she will pay for what she did #TrueMen #AJLA.

Below that, the photo of Sarah Price in the park.

"Here's the thing." Helton's voice seemed to echo in her ears. "It's out there now, but maybe that's because you put it out there."

31

SARAH SAT AT HER desk, frozen in place. She could hear phones ringing, people making calls in the bull pen, but with Ben gone, the cubicle next to her was empty. Still, she lowered her voice.

"How do you know? Who *are you?*"

"I'm on your side, Sarah," Wyatt said. "Please trust me on that."

"Why should I?"

"If I'd wanted to cause trouble for you, believe me, I could have. But I don't."

It still sounded like a threat.

"You've got the same enemies you had before, and I'm not one of them," he said. "But when it gets out ... there'll be some blowback on the campaign. You *know* there will be."

She could feel the panic build and rise in her chest. She thought she might scream. She wanted to slam her fist against the desk, throw the phone across the room, something, *anything*, to get these feelings out of her body, emotions so strong they felt like they'd taken shape into solid *things*.

"What do I do?" she managed.

"I've been thinking about it. Running scenarios. Cason's kind of a dog, I'm sure you've figured that out by now. You could feed into that whole narrative, and yeah, there's still people out there who care about that kind of thing."

"I'm not … I haven't … "

"Okay, Sarah, okay, I believe you. Just watch yourself. It can't even *look* like you did. But if you keep your nose clean, my take is that there's only so much it can hurt the campaign. I mean, they hate Cason anyway, obviously. It's just going to amp that up some."

"'They'?"

"I don't have a name for it yet. I don't even know if there is a name, or how organized it is. The same kind of guys who hate you so much have fixated on him, like he's the big jock screwing the cheerleader they've always wanted to screw. You know what I mean?"

She nodded, though of course he couldn't see that. But she did know what he meant. She had an idea of it, anyway. "I should just quit," she said.

But then who would do the work, with Ben in the hospital?

"Your call, Sarah. If you quit, they'll play it like something went on between you and Cason, and you *had* to leave. It's gonna be a shitstorm no matter what you do."

She stared at the poster of the baseball player on the wall by her cubicle. They'll know who I used to be, she thought. Was it worth it, trying to stay here and fight, having to face their stares, their pity? Their judgment?

The humiliation, all over again. It would never end, no matter what she did, no matter who she became.

242

"Either way, you need to look out for yourself. What's going on now, it's unpredictable. Chaotic. I don't like the way it feels." That last sentence he seemed to be saying to himself, not her.

"What do you mean?" she asked.

A long silence. "You know what a black swan is, Sarah?"

"An unpredictable event that has a massive impact."

He laughed. "Should have figured you'd know. I'm not sure I agree with the theory, totally. Me, I think sometimes what seems like an unpredictable event is something that, well, we should have seen *that* coming. It all makes sense, in retrospect. We just couldn't see the pattern, the consequences, at the time. You know what I mean?"

"That's part of what a black swan is," Sarah heard herself say. "The event is inappropriately rationalized after the fact."

Wyatt laughed. "Okay, you win." She heard him sigh. Was that ice clinking in a glass? "People do some pretty unethical things to get power. To keep it." A snort. "Bet you're shocked to hear that."

"I'm not," she said.

"I know you *think* you're not. Hey, when I was younger, I thought I was pretty cynical. Turns out I was naïve. I still participated in the process. I thought I knew how things worked, but I didn't."

A long silence.

"You were talking about people doing unethical things," Sarah finally said.

"Yeah. Yeah, I was. Well, some people, what they do to keep power is they feed people's anger. They make all kinds of promises they don't intend to keep, but if they keep people angry enough, most of them will accept any bullshit excuse if that *excuse* feeds their anger too. Just blame it on something they're afraid of. Or they hate. Tell them somebody's taking what's rightfully theirs. Appeal to their rage.

There's a whole big infrastructure out there, ginning up rage. Does a bang-up job of it too."

Maybe he was drunk, she thought. He *sounded* drunk, now that she thought about it, the words tumbling out of his mouth a little looser, a little louder than usual.

"Wyatt," she said, "I was a poly-sci major and I have a master's in public policy. I know the kinds of politics you're talking about. We studied them. The Southern Strategy. Rustbelt Resentment."

He laughed. "Okay. So maybe you do. But here's what you need to understand. Sometimes what happens is, they really fuck up. They open up a crack, and it's not the light that gets in, it's something dark they can't control. Or contain. That's what sets the black swans loose. And once those black swans start flying … you don't know what's coming home to roost."

32

MATT'S GOOD HAND CLUTCHED a beer bottle. His wounded hand rested in its cast on a stack of pillows on the couch. The cast would only stay on for three more days—they liked to get the casts off quickly with hand injuries and start therapy, Dr. Parviz had told them, before the bones could calcify and the hand stiffen.

The Padres were on, an away game in Washington, DC. It was the top of the third, and they were winning by five runs with two men on and one out. Thank god, Lindsey thought, because Matt was in a shitty mood—the Padres winning took a little bit of the edge off.

You can't blame him for that, she told herself. He had every right to be angry and depressed and traumatized and ... whatever else he was. His bad moods were deep and layered; a lot of the time she only excavated the first few levels.

This was different. It wasn't the annoyance of making fundraising phone calls, it wasn't the fights over how he looked at other women, or the way he checked out when he didn't want to deal with something difficult or boring.

She thought about what happened in the park. People dead. Matt's face. The blood everywhere.

Somebody tried to kill him. I should have been there.

And it wasn't over. The Capitol Police had assigned a "protective security specialist"—a tall, thick man with a shaved head named Morgan whose job it was to accompany Matt wherever he went and who currently was sleeping at the Best Western on Clairemont Drive. ("Sorry, I don't want him in our guestroom," Matt had snapped.) There was a squad car parked in front of their house, where it would remain "until we get a more complete threat assessment." The police had even suggested a hotel, but Matt had refused. "We have an alarm system and a high wall," he'd said. "And I've got a gun."

She hadn't known he'd kept it.

She shuddered.

You don't get to lose it, she told herself. You aren't the one who saw what he saw.

You aren't the one who beat a man nearly to death, either.

He deserved it, she told herself. The world will be a better place if Lucas Derry never wakes up.

But god, those photos. The look on Matt's face. The rage.

"You want another beer?" she asked.

He was refusing painkillers, in one of his self-punishing moods. She had no doubt he was in some pain, with the surgery only this afternoon. He could have a beer at least.

He nodded. "Just one more."

But it was good he was moderating himself. He could get angry when he drank too much.

A double play ended the Padres' half of the inning. "Oh for fuck's sake," Matt muttered. He hit the mute button for the commercials.

Lindsey put the cold beer on the coffee table where Matt could reach it. She sat down next to him, on the side with no injury.

"Do you want to talk?"

He took a last swallow of the old beer. "I don't think you want to hear it."

Lindsey felt herself go suddenly cold, felt her heart thumping in her chest. If he'd fucked Sarah, she didn't think she could take it.

"You can tell me."

Whatever it is, just get it over with, she thought.

"I don't want to do this anymore."

She was suddenly so tired. "Okay," she said. It was funny, how little she felt. Maybe she didn't want to do it either.

"I go to DC and I hate it. The atmosphere's toxic, and nothing's getting done." He snorted. "Nothing good anyway."

Lindsey almost laughed. *So* not what she was expecting. But she didn't laugh, because he was actually talking, and she owed it to him to listen.

He took a long pull of the cold beer. "It's not normal politics. There's no compromising. It's war." He drank deeply. "And I'm tired of fighting."

The game was about to start again, the Nationals' half of the inning. Matt reached for the remote.

"Matt, wait."

His hand dropped to the couch.

"Are you saying you want to quit?"

"I don't know. Maybe."

You shouldn't be angry, she told herself. He's been through a lot. "If you need to drop out because of what happened at the park…I understand, I really do, and no one would blame you."

"And if it isn't?"

"Then why did you decide to run for reelection?" She tried to keep her voice calm, to make it a genuine question, but it sounded like an accusation, and she knew it.

"I don't know. That's what a 'rising star' does, right? I mean, that's what *you* wanted me to do."

She couldn't swallow the anger now. "Oh, don't you put this on me. I didn't make you do this. You're the one who wants everyone to love you. Not me."

He covered his face with his good hand. "Yeah," he said, without heat. "Add that to my list of fuckups." He picked up the remote and unmuted the TV.

33

"Jesse Garcia and Anbar." Jane let out a sigh and closed her eyes for a moment, her fingers pushing up her glasses so she could rub the bridge of her nose. "Okay. Thanks, that's good to know."

Jane and Angus had been watching something on the TV when Sarah walked into her office, heart still pounding from Wyatt's phone call. A press conference with a backdrop of water and palm trees. Somewhere on Mission Bay, she thought, but she wasn't sure. She still didn't know the city that well.

The man frozen in front of the microphones looked familiar. Good-looking. A few years older than Matt. Wavy brown hair past his ears that was streaked with gray and sun, big brown eyes, the kind that invited you in. I should know who he is, she thought.

It came to her suddenly—that TV show when she was a kid, the one about the American family who lived in Botswana. He played the dad, the heroic and kind veterinarian at the wildlife sanctuary.

"Is that—?"

"Jacob Thresher," Angus said. "Yep." He jerked a thumb at the screen. "Meet our independent challenger." He aimed the remote at the TV and backed up the recording. Pushed play. Thresher moved and started talking.

"I want to support our troops in the ways that really matter." Thresher knew where to look, not right at the camera but just to one side of it. Deliver a line, and then look to the other side. *"What that means is not sending them off to be maimed or die in misguided imperial adventures. It means not supporting corrupt industries that are getting rich off their suffering."*

Angus paused the DVR, laughing a little. "Does he really think that's going to sell in San Diego? Home of, oh I don't know, the largest concentration of military and federal employees in the United States?"

Sarah nodded. "One out of every five jobs, right? If you look at the ripple effect, I mean." She'd done her homework.

"Twenty-three billion dollars in direct spending. Ten percent of the local economy. I mean, it might go over okay in Ocean Beach, but in this district? In Clairemont?"

"It's not about a winning message," Jane said. She sounded tired. "It's about a message that will drain off enough votes for Tegan to slip by us. We're going to need polling and we're going to need oppo. Here's hoping the party is in a generous mood." She turned her gaze to Sarah. "So, your ... your contact, Wyatt. Did he say when Tegan's campaign plans to deploy their little grenades?"

"He wasn't sure. He said the timing was tricky. Just that we needed to get out in front of it."

"Good advice." Jane stared down at her desk. Sarah had the sudden thought that her stare would burn holes in the blotter if she held it long enough.

"That reporter from News 9," Jane said. "She might be a good channel to get our messaging out."

"Casey?" The idea made Sarah uneasy, though she couldn't say why.

"Yeah." Jane smiled in a way that did not reach her eyes. "You give them access, they want more. They tell the story you want them to tell, you give it to them. That's how this works. And I like the story she's telling."

Jane's phone rang. The ringtone was "Take Me Out to the Ballgame." Matt?

"I need to take this," she said. "Sarah, why don't you take a break? Get some air, some dinner. We'll talk more later."

You need to tell her, Sarah thought. There's a third bomb. You can't just put it off until it all explodes.

She knew that, but it was still a relief that she didn't have to tell her right now.

———————

Five p.m. Sarah wasn't really hungry. When she was younger, she'd eat to soothe herself. She'd gotten a lot better about that in the last couple of years. Instead, she'd train. Lift weights. After, she could have a protein shake, and some of those were pretty good. Even decadent.

Today, her stomach just hurt. Her body ached. Everything was tight, tensed up, like the world was pushing against her and she had to push back, just to stand still.

Maybe she should research Jesse Garcia and Anbar, see what she could find out. But she wasn't sure if she could focus, and besides, Jane had told her to take a break.

Later, she thought. I can take a break later.

I should go to the gym, she thought. But was there really enough time for that? What if something came through on Social? On one of the feeds? On Twitter or Facebook, Snapchat or Instagram?

Don't spiral, she told herself. Don't. You know what happens when you do.

She started driving before she decided where she wanted to go: to the hospital to see Ben. She wanted to see how he was doing, before it all came out.

If it comes out, she thought. Maybe Wyatt was wrong. *He* knew, she was pretty sure; she didn't think he was bluffing. But maybe "they," whoever they were … maybe that whole thing was bullshit.

You're kidding yourself if you think that's true, she thought.

It was inevitable this would come out. She'd always known that, as much as she tried to wish it away. She just hoped she'd have more time. That she could keep pushing the consequences down the road, until they wouldn't matter so much.

How long had Wyatt known about her? she wondered. Had he investigated her after she started taking his calls? Or had he known from the beginning and sought her out?

————

"He's stable enough now that normally anybody who wanted to see him could just walk in," Angus had told her today. "But because of the whole situation, they're checking people first. You're fine," he'd added, before she could ask. "I figured you'd want to see him after things calmed down a little."

They'd moved Ben from the Intensive Care Unit to Progressive Care this morning, which was very good news, Angus had said. "Things keep going this well, he'll be in a regular unit in a day or two."

She entered through the lobby where she'd waited for Jane, was it just two days ago? It seemed impossible to believe. But there was the grand piano, the warm wood paneled walls, the tastefully lit coffee shop.

When she got to Ben's unit on the fourth floor, she paused for a moment at the nurse's station. Should she ask someone if it was okay for her to be here? What if Ben was sleeping? I should have called first, she thought.

Too late for that. She followed the signs on the wall to his room.

The door was open. Two people were inside, she could see them sitting on a couch and chair by the foot of the bed. Middle-aged. The TV was on, the sound muted. She thought the man was watching it. The woman read a magazine.

"Hello?" she said in a low voice, in case Ben was sleeping.

They looked up.

"Can we help you?" the woman asked. She didn't sound very helpful.

"I'm Sarah. I'm ... a coworker. From the campaign."

"Hey, Sarah." Ben's voice. Weak, but recognizably his. She stepped inside the room. She could see him now. He wasn't quite sitting all the way up, but the head of his bed was raised so that he could make eye contact.

"Hi." She stood there for a moment, feeling awkward. Now that she was here, she didn't know what to say. The middle-aged couple—they had to be his parents—didn't help either. Neither of them said anything. Their expressions were unsmiling, almost hostile, especially the woman's.

"These are my parents," Ben said. "Glenn and Susan."

The two of them stood. In a way they reminded her of her own parents. Glenn wore a golf shirt and Dockers; Susan, bright blue capris and a short-sleeved floral print shirt. Both of them pale, like they didn't get outside much, both a little heavy around the middle. The kind of people who lived in a newer house in a suburb somewhere, who had newer cars. Upper-middle-class white people. They were what "normal" was. Or had been. Suddenly they looked strange.

"It's so nice to meet you, Sarah," Susan said. "You're the one who helped Ben, aren't you?" Not hostile after all. Just exhausted and worried.

"I tried to," Sarah said.

"Thank you," Glenn said. "Thank you for trying."

The three stood there, Susan with her hands clasped in front of her, until Glenn stretched out his arms and hugged Sarah stiffly around the shoulders, and then Susan did the same.

"Thank you," Susan said after an awkward pat. "I know that must have been really frightening."

Sarah nodded and swallowed hard. She didn't want to think about it right now.

Glenn seemed to notice. He rested his hand on Susan's arm for a moment. "Hon, you want to go grab a bite to eat? Give these two a chance to catch up?"

Susan hesitated, like she didn't want to leave Ben alone with Sarah. Finally she nodded. "That's probably a good idea. Can we bring anything back for you, Sarah?"

"I'm fine, thanks."

Susan leaned over the bed and kissed Ben on the forehead. "We'll be back in a few, honey."

"Take your time," Ben said.

He was still very pale, his skin the color of putty, the beard stubble on his face so dark against it that it looked like scratches of ink on paper. He had an IV going into one arm, a tube hooked around his ears and looped under his nose, prongs in the nostrils delivering oxygen.

"It's good to see you," he said after his parents had left.

"I'm sorry I didn't come sooner. Things were ... " What should she say? What did he know about the last few days? "There was a lot of press, and things got pretty crazy."

"Yeah. Yeah, I'm sure things were crazy."

How much had he been told? Jane had been with him, and Angus. Matt had visited too. But he'd been so much sicker then.

"How's Matt doing?" he asked.

"Out of the hospital. He had to have surgery on his hand, but aside from that he's okay."

"Good." Ben closed his eyes. She thought he might drift off. Maybe that would be for the best. She hadn't really thought about what she should say to him. Just that it would be nice to see him, before ...

"How's Social?" he asked.

"It's ... busy."

Ben managed a laugh. "Yeah. I bet. Anything trending?"

"Well, I'm still trying to get things up and running after ... after what happened."

He closed his eyes again. Maybe this time he really was drifting off. The room was silent, save for the hum of machinery and the soft whisper of oxygen.

"What is everyone not telling me?" Ben finally asked. "Everyone keeps saying things are okay. I asked my folks to bring me a charger for my phone and they 'forgot.' Look, I know it's bad. I know people died. Just tell me."

He was going to find out eventually, she thought. "How much do you remember?"

"The guy with the gun. Pushing you out of the way. Getting shot."

She felt it then, the sudden shock, the body slamming into hers. He'd pushed her out of the way?

"I didn't know." Her voice came out in a whisper.

Ben didn't say anything.

"I didn't know," she said again. "I'm so sorry."

"There's nothing to be sorry for," he said, with some of his old irritation. "It's just how it happened."

It could have happened that way. There was no way to know. None of the videos, none of the photos, showed exactly what had happened.

She tried to think about angles and trajectories and if his account made sense, and gave up.

You can't make this your fault, she told herself. He could have gotten shot no matter what he'd done, and she might not have been hurt either way. It didn't change that he'd tried to help her, and she'd tried to help him.

She nodded. "Thank you," she said.

Ben shrugged. "So tell me what's going on."

"Matt nearly killed the guy who shot you."

"Really?"

"Yeah."

He grinned. "That's awesome! Why didn't they want to tell me that?"

"Well, there's photos … and … they're just ugly, that's all. And there's a lot of trolls commenting."

"Fuck them. Who cares?" It might have been her imagination, but it seemed like some color came into his cheeks. "Matt's a fucking hero! Let them try to label him a liberal wimp now."

"Yeah," she said, nodding.

He couldn't understand, she thought, how on edge everyone was. The phone calls. The death threats. But he didn't need to know about that right now. Didn't need to know about the photo of her crouched by his side. Or Jesse Garcia and Anbar—not that she knew what those were about either. Or Jacob Thresher, their new independent opponent.

Should she tell him about Thresher?

"I'm so glad you're feeling better. Everybody misses you a lot."

"Just give me a couple of days. I'll be back."

Looking at him lying there, the color faded from his cheeks, she doubted it would only be a couple of days.

Her phone rang. The ringtone she'd assigned to important contacts.

"Go ahead," Ben said, closing his eyes.

It was Casey Cheng.

Sarah had pocketed the reporter's card at the end of the interview, thinking, *Why would I want to talk to you again?* But she'd entered the information into her phone anyway, just in case. Now with what Jane had said, about using Casey to get their message out, she was glad she did.

"Hello?"

"Hi, Sarah, it's Casey Cheng. From News 9. Would you ... would you have some time to meet?"

"When?"

"As soon as possible. Now, if you have time."

Sarah thought about it. She was supposed to be taking a break. There was nothing to stop her from meeting Casey before she went back to the office.

"Sure. If we could meet somewhere in Kearny Mesa."

"That's good for me too."

Perfect, Sarah thought. She'd PM Jane on Campaigner first, let her know about the meeting, promise that she wouldn't say anything about Jesse Garcia or Anbar. She wouldn't know what to say anyway. Explain that she just wanted to see what Casey wanted, work on establishing a relationship that the campaign could use, like Jane had said. Show she could be an asset to the campaign, in spite of who she was.

34

CASEY TOOK A LYFT to a place on Convoy she liked, a small Korean gastropub, cute but not fancy, with tiny lantern lights strung above the distressed metal-clad bar. "It's a bit hard to find," she told Sarah on the phone. "It's in the little strip mall across the street from the Lexus dealer. Just look for the big 'TOFU HUT' sign, and this place is right next door. I like it because it's quiet enough to hear ourselves talk." Also because this time of night she knew it was not likely to be crowded. She found a table at the very back of the long, narrow room, hidden in shadow, framed by more of the tiny lantern lights.

She spotted Sarah as soon as she walked in the door, in spite of the dim lighting. Not so much because she was a blond white girl in a pub mostly frequented by Asians but because of her posture, the way she moved—stiff, wary, unsure of the space she occupied.

Had she ever seen Sarah look comfortable?

Casey pasted on a smile and lifted her hand. "Thanks for meeting with me," she said after Sarah had sat down.

Sarah nodded. "What did you want to talk about?"

No foreplay with this one.

The waiter approached with a platter and a paper cone in a wire frame, plus Casey's mojito. "I got us some snacks," Casey said. "Do you want to order something else? Something to drink?"

Sarah hesitated. "Maybe a beer."

"We're featuring Alesmith this month," said the waiter, a wiry guy with spiked hair and purposefully nerdy black glasses. "We've got the double IPA, 394 Pale Ale, the English nut brown ale, the barley wine, and the Speedway Stout."

"Which of those isn't too strong?" Sarah asked. "I'm driving."

"I'd try the 394 if you like IPAs."

"Great. I'll try that."

"So, you like beer," Casey said.

Sarah actually smiled. "I'm learning to. One of the guys—" She stopped. Shook her head a little. "People at the office really like beer. Matt even takes us out sometimes." Her cheeks ever so slightly flushed.

"Beer is a big deal in San Diego," Casey said, watching her. "I really need to learn more about it." She gestured at the food. "Please, have some."

"What is it?"

"Popcorn chicken and a kimchi quesadilla."

Sarah stared at the platter. "I don't think I know what that is," she said. She seemed not just embarrassed, but as though she'd failed somehow.

"Hah, yeah, it's a little weird," Casey said, trying to make it light. She wanted Sarah to feel comfortable; she needed Sarah to trust her. "But if you like spicy food, it's really good."

Dammit, she thought, I should have picked a different spot, somewhere Sarah would feel more comfortable. Like maybe an Outback Steakhouse.

"Okay," Sarah said. "Thank you. I was supposed to get some dinner. I haven't done it yet."

Casey dished her a slice. She watched Sarah cut her quesadilla into small bites, chewing each one carefully, following with sips of her beer.

"This is really good," Sarah said.

"Glad you like it."

I'll let her eat for a bit, drink some beer, Casey thought. Let her get settled before I talk to her, tell her what I saw. Before the ask.

Sarah beat her to it. "So, what is it you wanted to talk to me about?"

Casey swallowed her mouthful of mojito. She hadn't worked out her approach yet, how she wanted to angle this. Then thought, this is not a person who angles. She's being direct; I might as well be too.

"I know you're concerned about trolls," Casey said. "And there've been some new ones since the segment aired yesterday."

"I know. I've been on the social media feeds all day." Sarah served herself another piece of kimchi quesadilla. Apparently she really did like it. "I figured there would be. It's not as bad as yesterday at least."

"When was the last time you looked?"

Sarah's brow wrinkled. "I guess about two hours ago?"

Casey drew in a breath. A part of her had hoped that Sarah had already seen it. That it really wasn't a big deal. Because as much as she wanted whatever the story behind that tweet was, there was something about Sarah—that wariness and discomfort, the lack of emotion, or maybe it was emotion constantly suppressed—that made Casey think there was something deeply injured in the center of her.

"There was one that posted a little over an hour ago," she said. "It worried me. I wanted to make sure that you saw it."

Sarah put down her knife and fork. "Okay. Do you want to show me?"

Casey got out her phone. She'd taken a screenshot of the tweet in case it had been removed, but it was still there. She held it out to Sarah.

Sarah took the phone and read. Something flitted across her face, a ripple of some emotion: Fear? Disgust? Casey wasn't sure.

"Right," she said.

"Is this … is it for real? Do you know what they're talking about?" Casey asked, as gently as she could.

"Sure I do." It was one of the few times Casey had heard something resembling humor in her voice, a bitter laugh that sounded like it belonged to a much older person. Sarah put the phone down on the table. "Now you're going to ask me if you can interview me about it, right? So I can set the narrative. Craft the messaging."

"Yeah." Because there was no point in trying to deny it. "But only if you want to. Look, Sarah, I meant it when I said I was worried. This whole True Men thing … I still don't know if it's real. But there are people doing violent things, and they're using this tag to brag about it. *Someone* is anyway."

Sarah took a long sip of her beer and then another, blinking rapidly. Blinking back tears? Then she put her glass down. Something in her face changed, turned blank and hard. "If I give you this story, then it has to be on my terms. I only want to tell it once. You can record it. But you can't show it or post it until I say so."

"Okay," Casey said, thinking, *probably* okay. They could hold it for a reasonable amount of time. Even if someone broke the story first, assuming there was an actual story to break, if they had the segment in the can and ready to go, it wouldn't be too bad. They'd have an exclusive from the source.

"Though to be honest with you, there are no guarantees that we'll ever broadcast it," Casey said. "That's up to the news director, not me."

Sarah smiled, a big broad smile that made her look very young. "Oh, you will."

35

OF *COURSE* **THEY WOULD.** Sarah had no doubts. It had been a big story, one that had broken nationally. Not for long; it faded out of the news pretty quickly, because nothing lasted long in the public's consciousness anymore unless it was constantly repeated.

But there was the video. And though the video had mostly been scrubbed from the internet, there was the image from that video, and there would always be that image, it would never go away.

That was what scared her the most, that it would never go away. That it would follow her for the rest of her life, and she'd never get any real distance from it.

She'd changed her name. Changed her hair. Changed her body, lost weight and transformed the baby fat into muscle. Kept her head down, didn't date, hardly socialized, went to grad school and got a master's degree. Was on the path to doing what she really wanted to do in spite of everything.

She'd thought she could stay hidden a while longer. Even when they'd found her email address, they still hadn't known where she was. *Who* she was.

But there was still *the image*, and it was catching up to her again. Maybe she could have outrun the emails, but the shitstorm now? It was too big, too strong. It had killed people in the park. Put Ben in the hospital. And now it was howling on social media, looking for more blood.

"We can go to the studio and tape it right now," Casey said. "We're ten minutes away at most."

Sarah nodded. Because at this point, she just wanted to get it over with.

Maybe it was for the best. Maybe it was time to stop carrying this thing around, time to stop wrapping it in layers of silence that had grown hard and too tight, to the point where she couldn't ever just breathe deep and exhale it all out.

Just let it go, and face the consequences.

"I have to talk to my boss first," she said. She owed it to the campaign to tell them ahead of time. Before it came out on Twitter.

"Jane Haddad?" There was no mistaking the avid note in Casey's voice, the way her eyes brightened and focused.

You've got to be careful with her, Sarah reminded herself. She'll use whatever she can, whether you want her to or not. "I'm supposed to go back to work tonight. I can't just walk out on my job to do an interview."

"Okay, sure, understood," Casey said.

She did a good job of disguising her impatience, Sarah thought, but it was still there.

"I'd like to do it tonight if we can. I just need to talk to my boss first."

"We can totally do that. Just text me. I'll make sure there's a crew ready to go."

When Sarah got back to the office, Jane had already left. That was not normal.

"Do you know where Jane went?" Sarah asked Natalie.

"No. She left right after you did. Just said she had to go and to forward her calls." Natalie seemed to focus on her laptop, not meeting Sarah's eyes. "Something's up."

Sarah sat down at her desk, her heart pounding hard. Was it something about Matt? About Anbar or Jesse Garcia, whatever the story was?

About Ben?

Had they found out about her?

She grabbed her phone and opened Twitter, her fingers fumbling on the virtual keys. Typed in Matt's handle. Tried #CasonShooting, #TrueMen, and #AJLA too.

Finally, she typed in her old name.

Nothing new.

Sarah let out a breath. Whatever was going on with Jane, it probably wasn't about her.

She opened up Campaigner on her phone. Found Jane on the chat list and opened up a private conversation. HI JANE, I AM BACK AT THE OFFICE, she typed. SOMETHING IMPORTANT HAS COME UP THAT I REALLY NEED TO TALK TO YOU ABOUT AS SOON AS POSSIBLE. SORRY FOR THE INCONVENIENCE.

She labeled it high priority and hit Send.

A minute went by. Two. Then the alert and a reply: IS THIS VERY URGENT?

Sarah hesitated. She didn't want to bother Jane. But it was. YES.

A pause.

AT HOME, Jane said. DO YOU REMEMBER THE ADDRESS?

––––––––––

The police car was parked in front of Jane and Charlotte's house.

If it was really bad, she wouldn't have replied to me, Sarah thought. If it was really bad, she wouldn't have told me to come over.

Jane answered the door. "Police are in the backyard," she said, before Sarah could ask.

"What—?"

"Eggs, dog shit, garbage, and graffiti."

"Harmless pranks, I'm sure," Charlotte said from the couch, taking a sip of a drink from a tall glass. "They were very interested in raping dykes, from the notes they left." She patted at the couch. "Please, sit. Jane can get you an iced chia lime tea."

Sarah sat. She thought Charlotte looked even more pregnant than she had on Saturday. Maybe it was the T-shirt she wore.

"The police should be gone soon," Jane said from the kitchen. Sarah heard the clink of ice cubes on glass. "I can clean up most of it tonight. The graffiti will have to wait for tomorrow."

"Sweetie, just … let's call someone and have them do it. There's no reason for you to."

Jane came over to the couch, carrying a tall tumbler with a greenish liquid. "It actually tastes good," she said, putting the glass on the coffee table in front of Sarah. "I'd rather do it myself. It's too risky to hire someone. I don't want this … I don't want this getting out. I don't want to give it any more oxygen."

267

They might have taken pictures, Sarah almost said, and there's nothing you can do about it. But she didn't say that. "I'll help you," she said instead.

Jane shook her head. "No. No, there's no need for that."

"I want to."

Jane shook her head again. "I can do it—" she began.

Charlotte cut her off. "Honey, one of these days you're going to have to learn to accept help when someone offers it to you." She turned to Sarah. "Thank you. We'd really appreciate your help." Then she looked at Jane. "See how easy that was?"

"Then *you* are not helping," Jane said, pointing at her.

Charlotte lifted up her glass of iced whatever it was. "My plan succeeds."

———————

The backyard smelled like rotten garbage and dog shit. The garbage was heaped in piles against the sliding glass door and the back fence, spilled across the yard, emptied out of big plastic bags that had been split open. The cement patio was sticky with eggs, the yolks bleeding into the whites. The dog shit was in paper bags that had been lit on fire.

They'd sprayed graffiti on the stucco wall of the house and the interior of the fence.

"They probably came up from the canyon and climbed the fence," Jane said. "Easiest way to get into the backyard and not be seen." She shook her head. "We have motion-activated lights but those don't do any good during the day."

The realization hit Sarah like a blow. "Oh my god. I ... the day I was here ... I thought I heard voices behind the fence. I meant to tell you. I didn't see anything but—"

"Sarah." Jane reached out and rested her hand on Sarah's for a moment. "Please don't worry about it. There are kids down there all the time. And that's probably who did this anyway."

"I meant to tell you ... I just ... "

"Had other things to think about." Jane let out a deep breath, looking pale and drained in a way that Sarah had never seen her. She went over to a Rubbermaid cabinet and retrieved two pairs of gloves, brooms, and a box of lawn-sized trash bags. "I don't want to try tackling the graffiti," she said. "Just ... if we can get the garbage bagged up so I can hose off the patio."

"Sure."

The garbage was rancid. One of the bags had held what looked like old fryer grease. There were vegetables and rotten scraps of meat and things that had started to liquefy.

"This isn't even our trash," Jane said as she swept some up into a garden dustpan. "Looks like it came from a restaurant." Sarah held a bag open while Jane dumped the pan-load into it. "So they not only dumped our garbage all over the place, they stole somebody else's and brought it with them. Hauled it down into the canyon and schlepped it up here. I mean, what kind of people do that?"

I could tell you, Sarah thought. "Did the police find anything?"

"Apparently they were smart enough to wear gloves. I think the technician got a couple of footprints though."

"At least they're taking it seriously," Sarah said. The smell of the garbage was making her gag.

"After what happened this weekend, I guess they have to." Jane took the bag from Sarah, tied the ends of it together, and tossed it into the black trashcan.

"What are you going to do?"

"I'm taking Charlotte to a hotel tonight," Jane said, grabbing another trash bag from the box on the picnic table. "Maybe we'll spend a couple of days with my mom after that. There's no way I want her here by herself. She's the one who came home today and found all this. I'm not letting something like that happen again."

Then Jane stopped what she was doing. Paused, garbage bag in hand, straightened up, and fixed her gaze on Sarah.

"But you had something you needed to talk about. I'm sorry. I'm a little distracted. Was it about what Casey Cheng wanted?"

"Yes," Sarah said. She could feel her heart pulse in her throat. "Can we sit down?"

36

"Why does it have to be now?"

"I don't know, because it does," Casey said. "Hang on, let me step outside."

She could understand why Rose was less than thrilled by the prospect. It was closing in on ten p.m., Rose had already gone home, and who knew how long this might take?

She'd hung out at the gastropub, limiting herself to the one mojito and then switching to tea, reading news and typing notes on her iPad. Now she stood outside the pub, drifting over to the blue neon lit entrance of the vape shop, trying to convince Rose that it was worth going to interview Sarah now, for a segment they couldn't even show until Sarah said it was okay.

She just had a *feeling* about Sarah, that whatever her story was would be worth the wait.

Or, that's just what you want to believe, she told herself. You want a backstory that lives up to that photo of her in the park. Something that would push the series even higher. Keep this streak, this momentum going.

"Do we even know what it's about?"

"She didn't want to say. She said she only wanted to tell the story once."

She could hear Rose's scoff in her ear. "I don't know, Case. This sounds like some weird manipulation to me. Maybe she liked being on the news more than she thought she would."

"Could be. My take is that she's trying to exercise what little control she's got over all this."

A pause on the other end of the line. Rose was thinking it over, Casey knew.

"Fair enough," she finally said.

Excellent, thought Casey. I'm right. She feels it too. "If it's a bust, I'll buy you guys dinner."

"She says she'll buy us dinner," Rose said, presumably not to Casey.

"What restaurant are we talking about?" she heard Diego say in the background.

Were they living together?

"Okay, we're in," Rose said. "I'll call the powers that be and give them a heads-up."

———

"Just come to my apartment. You can film it so no one will know where I live, right?"

Sarah lived in a part of Clairemont called the Western Hills, in the south, on the border of Linda Vista. The hills and canyons made the streets irregular, and very dark in places. Casey wished they hadn't taken a station car. If someone had followed them here …

No one's followed us, she told herself. Don't be paranoid.

"See if you can get her to tell you *something* before we start," Rose said as Diego parked the Prius. "So we can at least take five minutes to brainstorm some questions."

The apartment where Sarah lived was on the second floor above the garage. Casey led the way up the exterior stairs, needing to lean on Trusty the cane for the last few. Stairs were still a problem. The pain up and down her back and butt and leg were doing that taser thing again. Vape pen, she thought, as soon as I get home. She pushed herself upright, struggling to put on a smile.

Sarah waited for them on the landing. She looked different than Casey had seen her before, wearing a Padres T-shirt with the interlocked SD and the swinging friar and a pair of snug workout shorts. She obviously worked out, there was muscle on that frame.

"Hi, Sarah," Casey said, smile in place. "Thanks for having us. You remember Rose and Diego?"

"Sure. Come in."

If she wanted clues to Sarah's personality, she wasn't seeing them in her apartment. A couple of framed prints, things like the famous Seurat painting and a Chat Noir poster, some Ikea-type furniture, a solid but battered couch. A little clutter in the small kitchen, a plate, a cup, and a beer bottle on the counter.

"Nice apartment," Casey said.

Sarah shrugged. "It's a sublet. None of this is mine."

"We need to swing the couch around," Diego said. "Room's too narrow to get a good angle where it is."

"Sure." Sarah picked up one end of the couch, Diego the other. She did it easily, Casey noted.

"So, you're a Padres fan?" Casey asked while Diego set up a light stand and his tripod.

For a moment, Sarah looked confused. "Oh. The shirt. That's not mine either." She laughed. "It belongs to my boss. I borrowed it after the park. I really need to give it back to her."

They were almost ready to start. Might as well ask her, Casey thought. The worst that could happen is she'll say no and we'll be flying blind.

"Look, Sarah . . . I know you only want to tell your story once, and I respect that. But in order for this to be a good interview . . . it would really help for me to have a little background, so I can think about what to ask."

Casey thought she could see that ripple of indefinable emotion on Sarah's face, a little wave that came and went.

"Google Beth Ryder," she said. "If you don't know who that is already."

Beth Ryder. It sounded familiar, but Casey wasn't sure why. She got out her phone, opened up Google, and started typing.

"Oh," Rose said behind her.

Rose always did type faster than she did.

Beth Ryder. Of course.

There were enough stories like this that they tended to blur together, but Beth Ryder's had more staying power than most. It hit all the beats: college freshman, the debate about sexual assault or consent, the presence of a video and what it showed—especially what it showed.

God, that video, Casey thought.

There had been a trial, a lawsuit, threats. Long feature stories in print and on TV, several of which were nominated for awards. Casey couldn't remember if they'd won. A few follow-ups for several years after, and finally, nothing.

Beth Ryder was no longer trending.

Casey looked up from her phone. Sarah stood there, waiting, almost tapping her foot.

"So, is that enough background for you?" she asked.

Casey nodded.

37

THE VIDEO: A BEDROOM, dim lights, trance music on a Bluetooth speaker. She's on the bed with the boyfriend she'd just started dating a month ago, and they are undressing each other. She's a little chubby, voluptuous. You see her breasts as he frees them from her bra. Then he awkwardly slides off her underpants.

They'd been drinking. There's a loud snort of laughter, the person holding the smart phone, and the man-boy on the bed looks up, focuses on the camera.

"You assholes!" he says, grinning. "I didn't say you could come in here."

"What's going on?" slurs the girl.

"Nothing," he says, and he does something that makes her gasp, turning to look at the camera as he does. The camera zooms in jerkily. You can see her face clearly. Some news sites published that image as a still, with black bars covering her eyes.

And that's where the narrative bifurcates. Did it hurt? Was she enjoying it?

"I don't remember what I was feeling," Beth Ryder had said during the trial.

A second man-boy enters the frame, already naked, cradling his half-erect cock in one hand.

"That's pathetic!" says the voice behind the phone, laughing.

The second man-boy turns to the camera and flips him off, stroking his penis, taunting him. He too climbs onto the bed. The girl seems to smile, or maybe grimace. "Is that Harley?" she asks, slurring her words. It's hard to hear her. Hard to tell what the emotion is in her voice. "What are you doing here?"

———————

"Do you want to change your clothes?" Casey asked.

Sarah seemed to think about it. She shook her head. "No. My good blazer … I don't have it anymore. I like this T-shirt."

Casey wasn't sure what Sarah was talking about, but the Padres shirt wasn't a bad call. It draped nicely, showing her curves and cut arms, and a little hometown sympathy couldn't hurt.

"Okay," she said. "Then let's get started."

They sat on the couch, the same basic angles they'd used in her previous interview. Part of the Chat Noir poster intruded into the frame, but with a little bokeh blur it would look good.

"Do you want me to call you Sarah or Beth for this?" Casey asked.

"Sarah. It's my legal name now."

"Okay, Sarah. Let's start with that. What led you to change your name?"

"I was just tired. Tired of the harassment. The jokes. I mean, 'Beth Ryder.'" Sarah managed a laugh. "You can imagine what that got to be like."

"But news organizations generally don't report the names of sexual assault victims."

"Sure, most of them don't. But their friends … they knew who I was. Everyone on campus did. And once my name got onto the internet … everyone knew."

"And when you say 'harassment,' you mean something more than jokes."

"Yeah. Constant phone calls and emails … some vandalism … rape threats. Death threats. There was at least one invasion board coordinating it."

"Invasion board? Can you explain that?"

"You know, they're chat boards. And they like to try to ruin people's lives. Especially women's lives." She shrugged. "They pick a target and they go after you. I don't know why they do it. They just do. For the 'lulz,' that's what they say. They even called a fake police report in so a SWAT team showed up at our house. I'm sure they thought that was hilarious."

"Why do you think they were doing this, Sarah? What was their motivation, going after a person they didn't even know?"

"They hate me," Sarah said. She said it without much emotion. Just a statement of fact. "They thought I ruined these guys' lives … and I mean, they got off easy. Second-degree sexual assault. Nine months."

"Even with the video?"

"*Especially* with the video. They used it to argue that I'd consented. Well, I'd consented to sleeping with the guy I was dating. I was too wasted to consent to the rest of it. But they said I wasn't 'incapacitated'"—here she made air quotes—"and to the extent that I was, I'd done it to myself."

"But what about *posting* the video? There's no question they did that without your consent."

"Their attorney argued intent and mitigating circumstances. Because they'd put it on Snapchat. It was supposed to be private, and then it was going to disappear. Except it didn't. It got out. He even said that to me. 'That was just for me and my friends. Not for anyone else. Sorry.'" She mimicked him, a slightly whiny, deep voice, which surprised Casey. She'd never seen Sarah so animated before.

"I had to admit on the stand he'd said that, and then they used it as a defense. That he hadn't intended it to get out and that he'd shown remorse. Besides … " She shrugged. "Posting stuff like that is a misdemeanor in most states, if it's even a crime at all. And it's funny, if it hadn't been for the video … I don't think I would have done anything about what happened. I don't think I even would have told anybody. It was bad enough what they did, but then they had to *brag* about it?"

"And the harassment didn't end after the trial?"

"No. It got worse. Especially after the civil case. I guess I went from being a slut to being a whore." Another short, bitter chuckle. "I didn't even want to file it. I figured there was no way I'd get that much money, and why go through it all again? What was the point? But my dad … he was so angry. He wanted some kind of revenge, I guess. I ended up with enough for a college fund, basically. With a little left over so I could move out here and work on the campaign." She turned to the camera. "Thanks, guys. I appreciate the opportunity."

Casey could see it in Sarah's eyes, the tight rein she'd kept on her emotions starting to slip. Keep her on track, Casey thought. She suddenly didn't want to see Sarah melt down, even though it might make for good television. Sarah couldn't afford to lose it. Neither of them could. This wasn't ending anytime soon. Casey was certain of it.

She swallowed hard and cleared her throat. "Sarah, given your past experiences with harassment … given your employment by a Cason campaign that's seen an attempted assassination and a lot of negativity on social media … what do you think will happen, once the public finds out who you used to be?"

Sarah didn't say anything for a long moment. Her eyes lost that anger, that tight external focus. She seemed to draw inward, shutting off those feelings once more. "I don't know," she finally said. "I'm pretty worried about it."

38

"OF COURSE I DIDN'T fire her. What kind of hypocrites would we look like if I fired her for being a victim?"

Jane was as heated up as Lindsey had ever seen her. She paced around their living room while Matt and Lindsey sat on the couch. Well, she had good reason to be upset, with what had happened at her house on top of everything else.

"I understand where you're coming from," Lindsey said. "I really do. But the fact is, she lied to us about her identity."

"No, the *fact* is, she did not. Sarah Price is her legal name. It was her legal name for her second two years as an undergraduate and for the master's program that she referenced on her resume, along with her think tank internship and volunteer campaign work. She had no legal obligation to disclose who she was before that."

"Maybe no *legal* obligation, but come *on*, Jane," Matt said. "Shit like this gets out."

"Yeah, Matt. It does. Like Jesse Garcia and Anbar." Jane sat down in the club chair catty-corner to the couch.

Matt's cheeks flushed. "Anbar is total *bullshit*, and you know it."

Maybe the anger was good, Lindsey thought. Maybe that would get Matt's head back in the game.

It's not your job to push him up that hill, she thought.

"It's complicated bullshit," Jane said. She sounded calm again. "We need to come up with some preemptive messaging that boils it down to something simple. And it can't sound defensive. We have to turn this into a positive somehow."

"Have you looped Presley in?" Lindsey asked.

"Not yet. I want to make sure we're on the same page first. I don't know how much Presley knows about this. We didn't ask him to do a deep oppo dive on you, just to come up with the obvious lines of attack so we could be ready with rebuttals. Once we tell him … it gets into the party ecosystem."

"Fine," Matt said abruptly. "I didn't do a fucking thing wrong, and I'm happy to discuss it."

"And Jesse Garcia? How could you not tell me about that?" Jane fixed her gaze on him, as though if she stared at him long enough, he'd be forced to make eye contact. Instead, he seemed to study his injured hand.

"I'm sorry," he finally said. "It was a long time ago, I was a lot younger and I was really fucked up. Which you might remember about me."

Jane smiled slightly. "That I do."

The two of them finally shared a look. Coconspirators, Lindsey thought. Jane had known Matt longer than she had. They'd gone to high school together. They'd been best friends for years. They had an intimacy between them that Lindsey had never breeched.

Good thing Jane's gay, Lindsey thought. Though she'd never been entirely sure just how intimate their relationship had once been. Better not to dwell on that.

"So we come up with some messaging and deploy as needed," Lindsey said. "At least we had a heads-up."

She just wanted this conversation over with. She needed to go for a run, do something to tire herself out or she'd never be able to sleep, but with the police still watching over them and as late as it was, the best she'd probably be able to do was hit the treadmill in the garage.

"What about Sarah?" Jane asked. "That story's likely to break first."

"Does she even *want* to keep working for us?" Lindsey asked. "After what happened ... and if she stays with the campaign, she's just going to get more attention. Are we even sure that's not what she wants?"

As soon as she said it, she felt the weight of her words, what she'd implied, and in the silence that followed she asked herself, Is that what I really think? That girl who's hiding herself in boxy blazers and sensible shirts?

"I'm not sure she's decided," Jane finally said, watching her. "She offered to quit if it would be better for the campaign."

"Would it be?" Matt asked.

"I could make a case either way."

Matt turned to Lindsey. "What do you think, Linds?"

Both of them were looking at her, Matt and Jane, and there was something oddly similar in their expressions, something measuring more than questioning.

"Oh, so *I'm* the one who has to make the call?" She was suddenly very angry, and fuck it, she had a right to be. "*You're* the candidate, not me."

Then Matt did something unexpected. He reached across with his good hand and placed it on top of hers. "I'm sorry, hon. I don't mean to lay this on you. I just want you to feel comfortable with the decision, and I know you're not a big fan of hers."

"It's not that I'm not a fan, I just ... " *Don't want you fucking her.* "I don't want any more drama than we're already looking at, because I don't know how much more the campaign can take."

"Understood," Jane said.

How much did she really understand? She drew in a deep breath. "Okay. Let's leave it up to Sarah. If it's going to be bad either way, we might as well let her make her own choice."

Matt smiled at her. "For what it's worth, I think it's the right call."

Lindsey smiled back and hoped she wasn't making a big mistake.

———

She could hear cheers from the living room TV, even with the office door shut. It was a home game, so that meant something good for the Padres. Lindsey never had understood why a simple thing like a baseball game could make Matt so happy, but she'd long stopped asking about it. Baseball made him happy, that was enough.

Then, silence. That must be the end of the game. She glanced at the computer clock. 10:49. Late for a game. Maybe it had gone into extra innings.

A tap on the door. It cracked open.

"Hey," Matt said. "I'm going to bed."

"Okay. Be there soon."

The door closed. She turned back to her computer, deleted a few more emails. The lights in the office were low, and she yawned, thinking, *I should shut this down and try to get some sleep.* But she was exhausted and wired, a bad combination.

Sarah Price was Beth Ryder. Jesus Christ, she thought. If things weren't bad enough before, and now this.

Of course she remembered the Beth Ryder case, that it had been more than usually ugly, that there'd been a notorious video. Jane had mentioned the harassment Beth … Sarah … had experienced, how it had been organized and persistent. If *that* started up again …

Lindsey opened up Google and typed in *Beth Ryder*. Better to know what might be coming than pretend it didn't exist.

A half hour later, a headache had settled in behind her eyes. God, this was depressing. All of it. They were just kids, really.

And Beth Ryder. It was strange, Lindsey thought. Maybe because so many of the articles didn't use her name, but no matter how much she read, Beth Ryder remained indistinct. Undefined.

She was a kid, Lindsey thought again. She kept clicking, all the while thinking, enough. What was the point of reading further? She knew what she needed to know.

And then she found the video. A version of it, anyway. For a moment she stared at the screen, her finger hovering above her mouse.

You shouldn't look. There's no point. It's not right.

But of course, she did.

She knew it was real. Of course it was real. Those were real people doing those things. Having them done to her. That was Sarah Price. Someone she had interacted with for months. Someone she would most likely see tomorrow.

What's wrong with me? she thought. I shouldn't be watching this. It's disgusting. It's …

Her groin started to pulse, and that was the worst thing of all.

She quickly closed the browser and shut down the computer.

In the bedroom, the lights were off, save for a nightlight on her side of the bed that Matt had left on for her. She stripped off her clothes, draped them on the chair. They usually slept naked, especially when the weather was warm. Recently she'd found herself wondering if this habit was one of the reasons they were still together, if it had kept them close, in spite of all the time they spent apart, in spite of everything.

She switched off the nightlight and slipped into bed next to Matt, wanting to reach for him, but he was already asleep.

39

CRAIG BROOKES, NEWS 9 *ANCHOR (ON SET)*: Matt Cason returns to the campaign trail, just days after a shooting at a community fair that left three people dead and two seriously injured. Casey Cheng is live from Cason's campaign headquarters with this News 9 exclusive.

CASEY CHENG (EXT. CASON HEADQUARTERS): An emotional day at Cason Headquarters as Congressman Cason visits staff and volunteers for the first time since an attempt was made on his life on Saturday.

(BEGIN VIDEO CLIP: INT. CASON CAMPAIGN HEADQUARTERS: SERIES OF SHOTS, CASON MAKES THE ROUNDS. TEARY VOLUNTEERS AND STAFF HUG HIM. ANGLE ON SARAH PRICE, WHO STANDS OFF TO ONE SIDE IN THE BULL PEN. CASON SEES HER AND APPROACHES. THEY HUG. CLOSE ON THEIR FACES. BOTH ARE TEARY-EYED.)

PRICE: (inaudible)

CASON (low voice): It's okay, Sarah. We're so glad you're here.

ANGLE ON CASON IN FRONT OF THE BULL PEN, SPEAKING TO THE ASSEMBLED STAFFERS AND VOLUNTEERS.

CASON: This has been a very challenging time, for the families and loved ones of the victims in the park. For our family here. For the city of San Diego. And … it's going to take some time for us to heal … but … I promise you, I'm here for you. I'm going to work as hard as I possibly can for you and for this community … (WIPES HIS EYES) We'll get through this.

CHENG (EXT. CASON HEADQUARTERS): But the challenges for the Cason campaign aren't over. If you look behind me (CAMERA PANS), you'll see armed security guards guarding the entrance to the headquarters. Given the continuing threats made to Congressman Cason and now to other members of his staff, they feel that they simply have no choice.

BROOKES (IN STUDIO): A very sad state of affairs. We'll be checking in with the Tegan campaign to see how they're coping with the situation later in this broadcast.

"Who knows?"

"Angus," Jane said. "Matt and Lindsey, of course. I've pinged Presley, but we haven't spoken yet."

Matt knew. He'd known when he'd hugged her.

And Lindsey … as if Lindsey didn't already hate her enough.

Sarah and Jane huddled in Jane's office. It had been a crazy morning, with Matt coming in and News 9 covering it, plus the ongoing circus outside.

Matt had left, on his way back to DC. The media left with him, but the headquarters was crowded with volunteers, which surprised Sarah some. "We're not going to let this scare us," one of them had said, an older woman with gray hair and a tanned face who looked like she hiked a lot. She was one of the regulars. Rachel, maybe?

Sarah wondered if they came out of loyalty, or out of excitement.

She shivered a little, thinking of how Matt had hugged her, the way his body had felt against hers, the way he smelled: his freshly laundered shirt, the spicy scent he wore that couldn't quite cover the slight musky tang of his sweat.

"We're so glad you're here," he'd said.

What did he think of her now? What did he see when he looked at her?

"Look, we all feel the same way," Jane said. "It really is up to you. We'll support whatever decision you make."

How did she feel? Could they all see it on her face, the desire?

You're not allowed to feel that.

"I'd like to stay, for now. If you don't think it will hurt the campaign."

Jane's expression was neutral. "So far, you've been an asset." Now she smiled, as though she'd just remembered she should. "You're doing a really good job, under really tough circumstances. Just know that you can come to me anytime. Okay? You don't have to go through this all on your own."

Sarah nodded. "Thank you," she said.

She thought Jane was sincere. When she'd told Jane the truth yesterday, Jane had reacted calmly. "Thank you for telling me," she'd said. "I understand why you kept this a secret. I'm sorry you felt you needed to."

"Would you have hired me if you'd known?" Sarah had asked.

Jane had paused, seeming to really consider. "That's a good question. But we did hire you, and you're not going to be judged on this. What happened to you wasn't your fault," she'd said.

She thinks she means it, Sarah thought. But Jane didn't look at her the same way now, no matter what she said.

Sitting at her desk, Sarah wondered how long she had, before the True Men did whatever it was they had planned. How long could she just be Sarah Price, before everyone would look at her and see Beth Ryder?

40

THEY JUST WON'T STOP.

Casey stared at her phone. Of all the horrible tweets and posts and emails she'd received, this one ...

This one was the worst.

"Diego's still looking for parking," Rose said, sitting down at the table. "I had him drop me off so we could order."

Casey nodded. "Good plan." The Shanghai Saloon closed at eight thirty, so they had less than an hour to get their dumpling fix. She liked the place even though it was kind of cheesy: a big restaurant with a black chalk wall, a kung fu mural on the wall behind the bar, a rickshaw in the middle of one of the seating areas, and Chinese lanterns lining another. It was close to work, the dumplings were good, and they had fancy cocktails and plenty of craft beers.

"That was some moment with Sarah and Cason, wasn't it?" Rose said, like it was a particularly juicy bit of gossip. "Do you think he knows? Do you think she told them?"

"She said she was going to."

"Hey."

Casey looked up from her phone. Rose rested both elbows on the table, fingers weaved together, staring at her. "You okay? What's going on?"

Nothing, she almost said. What was the point? The threats were nothing new.

She sighed, opened the email she'd sent Detective Helton, and clicked on the link inside it. Slid the phone across the table.

"Jesus Christ," Rose said.

They'd used an archival photo from the Rape of Nanking. Casey thought she even recognized it: A dead, naked Chinese woman, her limbs splayed out, a bayonet shoved into her vagina.

ME SHOW YOU GOOD TIME CASEY CHINK. JUST YOU WAIT

"Did you ... you're going to tell Helton, right?"

"Already sent."

"Oh man, this sucks."

"Something to drink?"

The waitress, young, tattooed, with a deep purple streak in her hair, had her order pad out. This was not a place where the waitstaff hung around while you made up your mind.

"Pitcher of 394 Pale Ale," Rose said. "Three glasses. No arguing," she said to Casey.

Why not, Casey thought. She was done for the day, and anyway, beer went well with dumplings.

"Hey." Diego slid into the empty chair next to Rose. "I had to park all the way down by the auto customizing place where the pot dispensary is."

"Casey's getting death threats again," Rose told him.

"In point of fact, they haven't stopped," Casey said. "They just get worse every time I'm on the air."

"That is seriously messed up," Diego said.

"Casey, what do you want to do? I mean ... this is scary."

It was more than scary. It was exhausting. Tensing up every time she opened her email or her Twitter account or her Facebook page or the comments on News 9's stories. Looking over her shoulder every time they went out, and checking her surroundings once, twice, three times wherever she went. Making sure no one had followed her to the gated entrance of her building. Waking up to every unexpected sound that made it through her double-paned windows.

"Well, there's two choices," she said. "Doing my job, or not. I choose to do it." She shrugged. "So I'm just going to have to put up with this."

The waitress had returned with their beer. She put the glasses on the table and poured three pints.

"Cheers," Casey said, lifting her glass. They clinked.

"Casey, this isn't a binary choice," Rose said. "You're getting the flack because of the stories we're doing. These, these Alan Jay people ... they're crazy. Or they're assholes, I don't know. But if this is dangerous, you don't have to keep doing it."

"Are you kidding me, Rose?" Here was something that cut through her exhaustion. She felt a rush of some emotion—anger? excitement? "These stories, they're making our reputation. We're getting prime slots, we're getting heavy promo, and now we have an inside channel to Cason's campaign. I get that they're using us to get their messaging out, but it's great stuff, and nobody else has it. When we release the Sarah Price interview? That's more national coverage, for sure. It's worth the ... the inconvenience of getting trolled on Twitter by some little shithead losers."

Rose started to wag her finger, but it was more than that, Casey realized. Her hand was shaking.

"You know what, Case, this isn't just about you. Diego is out there with you on nearly every shoot you do, and he can't look behind him, he's got his eye on the viewfinder and he's watching *you*. Somebody could come up behind him while you're shooting and ..." Her voice broke. "This whole thing, these assholes we've been covering, they're scary. Maybe most of them are trolls, but the things they say ... and some of them *shoot* people."

"No kidding," Casey said, raising her glass to her lips.

"Oh, shit, that came out badly." Rose fished around for something in her backpack and pulled out a package of Kleenex.

"Hey, we could always go back to surfing bulldogs," Diego said. "Everybody likes surfing bulldogs."

"Surfing bulldogs are stupid and sad," Rose said, sniffling. She circled her arm around him and for a moment, leaned against his shoulder. "You know English bulldogs are so genetically deformed from overbreeding that their heads are too big to fit through their mothers' birth canals? C-section. Every single English bulldog is delivered via C-section."

"Look, I'll be fine," Diego said. "These assignments, it's mostly the three of us anyway, and I know you guys've got my back." He kissed Rose on the cheek. "We're doing good work. If it's up to me, which it's not, I say we keep doing it."

Rose blew her nose and let out a sigh. "Yeah. An Emmy or a Peabody would look pretty sweet in my cube, right?"

"Okay, so are we agreed? No surfing bulldogs?" Casey asked.

"No surfing bulldogs." They clinked glasses.

It's not just about my ambition, Casey thought. It's about not giving into bullies. It's about covering the stories that need to be covered.

And … so what if it *was* about ambition? What was so terrible about her wanting to make her mark on the world?

But that image came into her mind again, of that woman several generations dead, defiled and killed by men who either hated her or must have thought she was not fully human, that they were entitled to her body and could do whatever they wanted to her. How else could you do that to someone?

Whoever sent that to me isn't serious, she told herself. They do it because they can get away with it, get their lulz without consequences.

But if they *could* do something like that … and get away with it … would they?

41

THE TWEETS AND POSTS went out in waves, hundreds of them, starting at 2:34 a.m., surging around six and again at nine. Posted on the
campaign's Facebook page, on the pages of news organizations and
gossip sites, tweeted out with their handles, with hashtags for
#MattCason, #CasonShooting, #AJLA, and #TrueMen.

First they'd sent out the video, which wasn't that hard to find—
nothing was ever entirely gone from the internet. Blurred the boys'
faces so you could not see them, only hers, and put the sounds from
a porn film over their voices.

The text they'd used was: "SARAH" IS BETH RYDER. RIDE HER
@REPMATTCASON EVERYONE ELSE HAS! #BETHRYDER

Casey wasn't sure what woke her until her phone's text alert went
off, the loud orchestra sting by her ear jerking her upright, her heart
pounding. Stupid me for not putting the thing on Do Not Disturb,
she thought, fumbling for it.

5:55 a.m. There were three text messages showing on the lock screen. She'd somehow managed to sleep through the first two, from the morning show producer and Rose.

The most recent text was from Sarah Price.

YOU CAN RUN THE SEGMENT NOW.

There were two police cars parked in front of the headquarters, along with several news crews.

The news crews weren't a surprise, even though it was just after seven and the headquarters wasn't open yet. But the police cars?

It only took a moment for Sarah to see what had brought them. Red and white paint splatters and blotches, all over the building's brown stucco wall, the windows, the planters, and the dense, dusty shrubs flanking the walkway.

Their lot in front of the headquarters building was taped off. She drove around the back. The damage looked worse there, including scorch marks from a fire—a Molotov cocktail, maybe? That lot was taped off too. She kept going down the street to the next industrial building and parked in the lot for the brewery there.

She had no choice except to walk past the news crews. Three reporters with cameramen hovered by the walkway. Sarah didn't see Casey or News 9.

"Hey, it's Sarah, right? Would you have a moment to speak with us?"

"Are you Beth Ryder?"

"Sarah, could we get a statement from you?"

"Not right now," Sarah said, ducking her head. She walked toward the entrance, staring at the cement pavers that were spattered with red and white paint. Then she raised her head and stared back at the news crews.

What was the point of trying to hide? Everything was out in the open now.

That's when she saw someone from News 9—just a cameraman, the burly Latino she'd seen before. He stood back from the others, panning across the building, not focused on her.

For a moment, she felt a flood of gratitude like a warm bath, that at least News 9 was leaving her alone.

Of course they've already gotten what they wanted from me, she thought. They can afford to be generous.

"You work here?" the security guard at the door asked.

"Yes. Yes, I do."

"Name, please?"

For a moment, she couldn't speak. "Sarah. Sarah Price."

He made a sound somewhere between a cough and a snort and looked her up and down. A big guy with a thick neck and a blunt crew cut. "Oh, yeah," he said, the corners of his mouth sneaking into a grin. "I recognize you."

————

"Security cameras don't really show anything," Angus said. "Just guys in masks with paint guns."

"We're going to have to have twenty-four-hour guards," Jane said, shaking her head. "I can't see any way around it."

"Will the party pony up for the security, do you think?"

"Let's hope. I think at this point we can make a good case for it. Capitol Police are covering Matt and the district office."

"For kids with paint guns?"

"We don't know if it's kids. We don't know if they're connected to what happened at my house, or what just happened to Sarah. Or what happened in the park for that matter. We can't take the chance. People who come here to work and volunteer need to feel safe."

Sarah sat in Jane's office with Jane and Angus. They were the only people at the headquarters. Others would be arriving soon, at eight, when Natalie usually came in and opened up the doors.

"How do you want to handle this, Sarah?" Jane asked. "I have a draft of a memo to send out to the staff, but if you'd rather make a statement yourself, that's fine too. Whatever you'd prefer."

Sarah tried to think about it. Her mind was blank. "I don't really care," she finally said.

"Okay," Jane said, still watching her. "I'll send it to you for your review."

"I just want to do a good job," she said. It was all she could think of to say.

Angus smiled at her. "That's one thing we're not worried about."

She could feel the tears gathering. She hadn't cried since she'd known she was about to get outed. She didn't want to cry now, not in front of Jane and Angus.

"Thanks. I'd better get to it." She picked up her laptop bag and started to rise.

"Sarah, keep in mind that most of the work you're doing can be done remotely," Jane said. "If it gets to be too much for you dealing with the circus, you don't have to come into the office every day."

"You think I'm a distraction." The words were out of her mouth before she could stop them.

Jane was silent for a moment. I need to learn how to do that, Sarah thought, to stop myself from saying things before I'm ready.

"Well, obviously your past is something we will have to address. And people who come in and out of the office are bound to be curious. But that's just the way it goes on campaigns. Things come up, we deal with it, and we move on. What I *am* concerned about is the overall security here." She turned to Angus. "How far do we go to vet volunteers? How can we make sure none of them are moles? Or ... or worse?"

"Make sure we get ID, check our database to see what their registration is, maybe do a quick search on Facebook?"

"If we're discreet." Jane sighed. "Bad enough they have to come in past armed security. What kind of message is that giving about participating in an election?"

"Well, not like my people haven't had to go through that kind of shit to vote before," Angus said, a sharp edge to his smile. "Welcome to our world."

"Point taken." Jane paused again, frowned, as if she was going through a checklist in her head. "We're going to have to ask to search people's bags if we don't know them."

"If you're worried about guns, they don't need a bag to bring one in," Angus said.

Sarah thought about the man in the park, the gun in his hand. The shots, the ringing in her ears, a sharp, caustic smell, ammonia and sulfur.

"Pat-downs? Is that what we've come to?" Jane took off her glasses and rubbed the bridge of her nose. She looked utterly drained.

"Yeah," Angus said. "I think we have."

Sarah thought about the guard stationed by the door now, the one who'd smirked at her, thought about him patting people down.

"There is something I'd like," she said. "That guard who's outside now? I'd like him gone. He's an asshole."

Jane and Angus both stared at her for a moment. They seemed surprised. But then, she'd never really asserted herself here before. She'd just kept her head down and done her work.

"Okay," Angus said. "We'll tell the company to send somebody different. And if anyone else around here disrespects you, you come and tell us about it right away."

Sarah nodded. "Thanks."

Maybe she wasn't being fair. Maybe the guard hadn't meant anything by it. But none of this was fair, so why should *she* be?

CASON CAMPAIGN RESPONDS TO HARASSMENT OF STAFFER AND VANDALISM OF HEADQUARTERS

The candidate, staff, and volunteers of Cason for Congress stand behind our staffer, Sarah Price, who has been the target of an organized campaign of harassment and hate. It is outrageous that a past incident in which she was the victim is being used to hound and threaten her today. She is a valued member of our team, and she has our full support. We are exploring all possible legal and law enforcement avenues to bring the perpetrators to justice.

We will not be intimidated, nor will we falter. We will continue to stand up for *true* American values of tolerance, respect and democracy.

HEY CUCK @REPMATTCASON DYKE @JANE_HADDAD YOU CAN'T STOP ALL OF US #TRUEMEN WILL RISE AND WASH FILTH LIKE YOU AND SLUT #BETHRYDER AWAY #AJLA

42

#ALANJAYLIBERATIONARMY ANNOUNCES HALT OF ALL EXTREME REVOLUTIONARY ACTION DURING SAN DIEGO COMIC-CON TO HONOR @GEORGE_DRAKE #TRUEMEN #AJLA

UNLESS WE SEE FAKE GEEK GIRLS THEN ALL BETS ARE OFF LOL #AJLA #TRUEMEN

———

"George Drake said yes." Rose bounced on the balls of her feet in front of Casey's desk, iPad in hand.

Death threats or not, Casey could tell Rose was excited about the get. True Men's creator hadn't said much to the press since Casey's story broke. They'd made the pitch but Casey hadn't expected he'd agree—why would he, given the trouble their stories must have caused him. He'd been interviewed by the FBI, complaining of harassment and censorship on his website.

On the other hand, maybe he liked the attention. It had to have helped his sales.

"Awesome," Casey said. "So where and when?"

Now Rose grimaced. "He wants us to come down to Comic-Con."

"That's great. Perfect. Lots of good B-roll."

"I don't know, Case, the security situation—"

"They do a costume weapons check on everyone who comes in." Casey had covered that angle in one of last year's Comic-Con stories.

The truth was, she didn't want to think about that part of it right now. A hundred thirty thousand people attended the Con, and that number didn't include those without tickets who came downtown for the open events or just to hang out and soak up the atmosphere. All those people in costume, crowded into the convention center and the blocks of the Gaslamp downtown … hundreds of thousands of them. People in masks, in helmets, walking around with swords and blasters … You couldn't make that situation totally secure.

Thinking too much about that was just going to stress her out.

"Well, this is the thing," Rose said. "He doesn't want to meet at the convention center. He wants us to come to some event he's hosting in East Village on Thursday."

"A Comic-Con event?"

"It doesn't actually say. Just an address."

Okay, well, that's a little creepy, Casey thought. "Tell him yes. What time?"

Rose tapped out a reply on her tablet. "He's a strange dude. This is the email he sent." Rose swiped up and read: "'If she is willing to come to my territory on my terms, then I would be willing to offer an exchange of views.' What the fuck is that?"

"Pretention? I mean, you read those comics."

"Yeah." Rose tapped the back of the tablet. "Frankly, I'm surprised Comic-Con didn't cancel his appearance with everything that's gone on."

"They released a statement, 'we support the airing of diverse opinions, condemn all forms of hate speech, George Drake's work may be controversial but does not cross that threshold,' blah blah blah. And anyway, he's on a panel with two other writers that's about controversy in graphic novels, so."

A Tribble sound from Rose's iPad. "Whoa, he replied already." Rose tapped her iPad and read: "'The event begins at nine p.m. Thursday. You may also attend my panel beforehand if you would like. In terms of the actual interview, a film crew would inhibit my ability to speak naturally. Miss Cheng can interview me by herself or not at all.'" Rose slapped the iPad on Casey's desk. "No fucking way."

"Well, now, wait a second—" Casey said, because even though she knew Rose had a point, she wanted this interview with George Drake.

"*No.* Look, this guy is being at *best* a manipulative dick. At *worst*?"

Casey laughed. "A murderous psychopath? Dude, he's a comic book writer. Artist. Whatever he is."

"Writer-artist."

"The point being, he's a murderous psycho in his dreams. He sits on his butt all day and gets paid for making stuff up and drawing cartoons. Look, tell him I'll interview him all by myself, but I want you guys on the guest list, in case I need … I don't know, equipment. Or makeup." Casey grinned. "Tell him I need you to do my makeup. I bet he wants me to look pretty."

———

"That's a long line."

The queue for George Drake's panel stretched along the side of the convention hall on the second floor, all the way to the escalators.

"Well, it's not just George Drake," Rose said. "Rey Wan's on that panel, and Kenny Lassiter. They've got followings too." She gestured at a girl wearing a sort of red catsuit fringed with lace, thigh-high black leather boots, and a fedora. "Fire Sprite."

"And there's a Yumota," Diego said, panning up the line.

"You guys really *are* geeks." Casey scanned the hall, assessing her surroundings for threats, like she always did now.

The hall was crowded with people in costumes: Storm Troopers, Starfleet officers, bare-chested angels, Batmans and Wolverines and Doctor Whos. It wasn't hot, but the air felt stale, breathed too many times, the industrial blue and gray carpet giving off a faint scent of heated plastic fiber and chemical cleaners.

Someone could walk in here with a gun in their backpack, Casey thought. Or a bomb. They'd just need a badge.

There's all kinds of security here we don't even know about, she reminded herself. It's not just costume weapons check.

"You okay, Casey?" Rose asked.

She forced a smile and swept her fingers across her forehead. "Just a little hot. It's stuffy in here."

————————

George Drake grinned. He had a nice crooked-tooth smile, Casey thought, one that appeared full of amusement. Fifty-ish and stocky, his brown hair swept back from his forehead in the way she'd noticed other guys his age with a good head of hair often liked to do, showing it off. *Leonine*, you'd describe it. He wore a black vest with gold brocade and a chunky turquoise bolo tie.

"Look, I'm a storyteller," he said, in a reedy tenor voice. "I'm not writing political manifestos, I'm telling stories. And people are going to respond the way they respond. Am I happy that a couple of twisted, evil individuals were fans of my work? Of course not. But I can't choose my readers. They choose me."

Kenny Lassiter laughed. "You're trolling for those readers."

The large conference room was packed. Casey had a reserved seat toward the front on the right side, with a good view of Drake, who sat at the end of the long table, with the other panelists, Rey Wan and Kenny Lassiter, in the middle and on the opposite end. The moderator, an arts and culture columnist for a local web publication, stood behind a lectern on stage right.

"And you're not trolling for *your* audience?" Drake laughed again, this time not so amused. "You're appealing to your genderqueer polyamorous cohort, right?"

You could practically see the air quotes, Casey thought.

Lassiter was tall, thin, heavily tattooed. Rey Wan also had her share of visible tats, her hair dyed a fire-engine red.

Lassiter shrugged. "I'm writing what I want to read. The fact that enough other people want to read it to where I can make half of a modest living wasn't something I set out to do. It just happened."

"Rey Wan, what about you?" the moderator asked. "What was the main impetus for *your* work? You're engaging with some very difficult material. Where did the desire—or, perhaps more accurately, the willingness—come from to do this?"

Wan leaned forward. "Some life experience. Some observed experience." Her voice was nearly a whisper, impossible to hear without the mic. "Important things aren't always pleasant."

"So would it be fair to say that you're motivated by a sense of mission?"

Wan nodded. "That's fair."

The moderator turned to Drake. "So that leaves you. What is the thing that drives you to create True Men?"

"As I said, I'm a storyteller."

"But why *this* story? Is it a story *you* want to read?"

Drake folded his arms across his belly. A defensive posture. "Look, I'm not a fascist, if that's what you're getting at. I am commenting on a state of reality. I am not calling on these things to happen, I am only saying that they could, given the situation in this country." Now he smiled, showing his crooked teeth. "Consider it a cautionary tale."

———

"Casey. A pleasure."

George Drake gripped her hand firmly without trying to crush it. That was a plus, Casey thought. He was a good head taller than she was, with some heft and muscle, and she had a feeling he could be intimidating if he wanted to be.

"Likewise," she said. "This is Rose Armitage, our producer, and Diego Marin, our photographer."

"Lovely to meet you as well." Drake focused his attention on them. "I hope you got some good footage of the panel. It was an interesting discussion, don't you think?"

"Definitely. Really a lot of food for thought. Which is why we're still hoping to talk you into a more formal interview." Casey put on her most charming smile. At least she hoped it was. She'd gotten out of practice since The Event. "I won't be able to do as good a job on my own, and we want to do it justice."

Drake shook his head. "Actually, I was hoping you and I could have a little chat off the record."

"Off the record? Mr. Drake, of course I'm interested in whatever you have to say, but—"

"I'll still give you your interview." He grinned, showing his teeth. "I'll even let this gentleman film me while you ask your questions. But there are a few things I wanted to discuss with you that I'm not comfortable talking about publicly. Not yet, anyway. Maybe you'll convince me otherwise. In any case, I think you'll find what I have to say worthy of your time." He pointed a thumb behind him, toward a huge atrium where there were signing tables and long lines of fans waiting to get autographs from comic book artists, authors, B-movie actors, and seventies TV stars. "After I fulfill my obligations here, I thought maybe you and I could walk over to the event." He looked her up and down, his eyes lingering on Trusty the cane. "That is, if you're able. It's about a fifteen-, twenty-minute walk, if you're up to it."

Casey swallowed her rising irritation and forced a smile. She wasn't some delicate flower who couldn't manage to walk a few blocks. She was up to a mile and a half on the treadmill, uphill. "Of course," she said. "Not a problem."

"Goddammit, Casey," Rose said, as soon as Drake was out of earshot.

"What? I can walk that far, it's fine."

"He's trying to manipulate you. And doing a pretty fucking good job of it."

"Well, yeah. But I want to hear what he has to say."

"How do you know it's safe? How do you know he hasn't planned something?"

"Oh, come on, that's just … He's a comic book artist, for fuck's sake. Don't you think you're being a little paranoid here?"

"He's set this whole thing up, playing the prima donna, holding out a cookie for you if you do what he wants, insisting you walk through an unsafe neighborhood with him after dark—"

"This is downtown San Diego, Rose. Not a war zone. Besides, the sun won't set for another hour."

"Jesus Christ, Casey." Rose's cheeks flared red. "You know, sometimes I think you want to finish what that asshole who shot you started."

Casey felt an ugly surge of rage so intense that for a moment she couldn't breathe. "How dare you say that?" she managed.

"You rush in, and you always want to get too close! Look what happened the last time you did that!"

"Hey. Guys. Chill." Diego rested a hand on Rose's shoulder. "The Crooked Arrow was on both of us, okay? We both made that call. We both thought it was okay."

Rose's face was still flushed. Casey had a feeling hers was too.

"I'm sorry," Rose finally said. "I just don't want anything bad to happen to you."

Casey nodded. But how could she explain to Rose how she felt? That if she ran away from anything now, she'd just keep running?

"How about you go ahead to the venue with the equipment?" Diego said to Rose. "I'll follow Casey."

"What if he sees you?" Rose asked.

Diego grinned. He reached into his messenger bag and pulled out a dark green domino mask and a green T-shirt, which he held up. Green Lantern. "No worries. No evil shall escape my sight."

43

"**WELL, ISN'T THIS SOMETHING?**" Drake half shouted over his shoulder.

The crowd of people crossing the trolley tracks was so thick that Casey felt like she would be swept along with it. She pushed her way past a group of Batman cosplayers—three different-era Batmans and Robins, several Jokers, a Batgirl, and a Catwoman—trying to keep up with Drake, who walked ahead of her, his bulk making his passage easier.

A band dressed up in Star Trek uniforms played "Hotel California" in the outdoor patio of the restaurant on the tracks. Religious picketers waved giant yellow signboards with black letters warning of eternal damnation and salvation through the blood of Christ. Three stilt-walkers dressed up like Uncle Sam handed out event flyers, flanked by girls in bikinis and go-go boots. Up ahead she saw what looked like an entire platoon of Storm Troopers marching down Fifth Avenue, accompanied by a few Jedi Knights and a Chewbacca.

Chewie must be baking, Casey thought. It had been a sweltering mid-July day, and the temperature was only just beginning to cool. Sweat already soaked through her camera-ready silk knit T-shirt, and she wasn't someone who sweated a lot. The shirt was black at least. Maybe the stains wouldn't show.

"Let's go this way," Drake shouted, gesturing toward the ballpark. "Not so crowded."

"Sounds good!"

There were still plenty of people walking this way, though. Comic-Con events spilled out of the convention center and into the surrounding streets, taking over several blocks of Fifth Avenue, Petco Park, and the adjacent parking lot. People lined up across the street for something, Casey couldn't see what, and superheroes drifted in and out of the lobby of the Omni Hotel.

But there was enough room on the sidewalk for Drake and Casey to walk side by side as they headed around the ballpark.

"You know what astounds me about events like this?" Drake said. "How much is dependent on an assumption of goodwill. All these people jammed into a few blocks, in costumes no less. So many things could go wrong. It would be so easy to create chaos if one desired to do so. Just one man with a gun would be enough." He smiled and shook his head a little. "I guess we still have a basic faith in each other, don't we?"

"I guess we do," she said. Don't let him freak you out, she told herself. It's not like you didn't have the same thoughts earlier today. Everything is fine, and besides, Diego is following you.

Just in case.

Rose is wrong, she thought. I just want to do my job.

It wasn't like she had some kind of death wish.

"You know, your little story really disrupted my life. Though I suppose I should thank you."

"I'm sorry?" Focus, she told herself. "I'm not sure what you mean."

They walked along the path that bordered the trolley tracks to one side and the Petco parking lot to the other. There were still plenty of people here, going in and out of the fair in the lot, heading up the street toward the Petco entrance for whatever event was inside the ballpark. The parking lot was lit up with LEDs and floodlights and colored gels. But Drake was leading her away from those crowds, towards the pedestrian bridge that arched over the tracks, and past that, darkness.

It's fine, she told herself.

"Well, there was the visit from the FBI," Drake said. "That was a bit disconcerting. It bordered on harassment. I had the impression they suspected I might actually be part of some … conspiracy?" He chuckled. "Utterly ridiculous. A bunch of kids trolling on Twitter and spinning their wish-fulfillment fantasies on 4chan or Reddit or wherever it is they hang out these days."

"Well, there was Alan Jay Chastain and Lucas Derry," Casey said. "They weren't exactly trolling."

"Of course not. I don't mean to make light of what they did. But this idea that my work might have inspired them? That it's somehow responsible for what they did? That's like blaming *Catcher in the Rye* for John Lennon's assassination."

"On the one hand, that's a fair point. On the other … " Casey hesitated. They'd reached the other end of the parking lot. Drake gestured up the street that ran perpendicular to their path. A small group of men stood in the shadows there—not convention goers. Homeless, Casey guessed.

"Your work is more explicitly political than *Catcher in the Rye*. Wouldn't you agree that's an accurate assessment?"

"I suppose. Though I prefer to think of it as social realism. I'm describing. Not advocating."

They headed up the street. Casey's back and leg had started hurting, the sciatic pain starting to spark. She wasn't going to show him that if she could help it. A brewery off to the right in an old redbrick building. No open businesses other than that, at least that she could see.

"But what you're describing," she finally said. "I'll be honest with you, Mr. Drake. I've read the True Men series. You exclude women and gays and people of color from participating in any kind of positive way. They're villains or victims, if they're in your stories at all."

"And you object to that."

"As a woman and as a person of color? Let's just say I don't relate."

He shrugged. "And you don't have to. Maybe my work isn't meant for you. You're not obligated to read it. And I'm not obligated to create a vision that pleases you."

"Except that your work has become news."

"Through no fault of my own."

"You can't pretend what you write is value neutral."

He laughed. "I suspect you have a great deal of contempt for my values."

She wasn't sure how to respond to that.

The street on which they walked was lined with makeshift tents, shopping carts full of things she mostly couldn't make out, though she spotted cans and bottles in grimy plastic bags. Homeless people gathered there, drinking from paper bags, some already hunkered in their tiny shelters, others sitting on stools in front of their belongings.

"For all that you disapprove, we lose a great deal when we reject traditional American values," he finally said. "For example"—and now he looked directly at her, casting his gaze down to make up for their difference in height—"don't you feel safer walking through a neighborhood like this with a man?"

"It depends on the man."

"Oh," he said, smiling, "please tell me you aren't one of those feminists who thinks all men are potential rapists."

"I'm cautious of men I don't know," she said.

"Good men are protectors. Good *women* elicit that response in us."

"And if a woman isn't 'good'?"

"Then she shouldn't expect to be protected."

She caught a strong whiff of piss and shit. Not surprising, with all these homeless people and no toilets.

"I expect you're the sort of woman who resents the need for male protection," Drake said.

That was a little too close. "So does that make me a bad woman?"

"Just an unrealistic one."

I've got to get control of this conversation, Casey thought. Rose was right, this guy was a manipulator. She still wasn't sure what game he was playing.

"Evening, miss. Spare a dollar so I can get something to eat?" A black man wearing a coat and stocking hat in this weather, so grimy and faded that it was hard to say what the original colors were.

"Ignore him," Drake said. He kept walking.

Fuck you, Casey thought, loudly. She wore a light safari-style jacket, mainly for the pockets. She reached into one now, pulled out several bills she'd stashed there, and handed them to the man. His hand was so callused and cracked it felt like old leather.

"God bless," he said.

Drake was already a half a block ahead. Was he just going to ditch her now? She struggled to catch up, her heart beating fast, the nerve pain pinging harder now.

Diego is behind us somewhere, she reminded herself. No need to panic.

Finally, Drake halted until she reached him. "You're not helping him with your handouts, you know," he said. "He's made the choice to be here. His life won't improve until he makes a different choice."

"Or he's mentally ill and isn't capable of choosing."

"How condescending. I prefer to think that men have free will."

Don't even argue with him, Casey told herself. It's pointless. And all of this is off the record anyway.

The homeless encampment stretched on for blocks. The gentrification of downtown San Diego was spotty here, with construction sites in the middle of old warehouses and industrial buildings, a few auto shops, stacks of tires and corrugated tin siding and barbed wire in a jumble on one corner.

Maybe I can get this back on some kind of track, she thought.

"Mr. Drake, what was it you wanted to speak to me about that needed privacy? Was it about the FBI visit?"

"In part. Mostly I just wanted to get to know you better."

Great, Casey thought. She didn't think she was imagining the flirtatious note in his voice. This guy could turn on a dime.

"I see," she said.

"Do you? You know, you've really added a lot of stress to my life. I haven't been able to write; I can't decide how the whole thing should end. Now I'm late on my deadline. I resent that, Casey. I really do."

It had gotten dark, and it was hard for her to see his expression clearly, except that he showed his teeth again, and it didn't seem like a real smile.

"I'm sorry to hear that," she said. "But honestly, isn't it *your* choice?"

Drake stopped walking. "Oh, very good," he said. "You're smart, aren't you? I'll admit, I wasn't expecting that from a pretty TV reporter. I thought your job was primarily looking good on camera."

Now Casey smiled at him. "A lot of people make that mistake."

"Maybe we're both underestimated. A lot of people don't take those of us who write graphic novels seriously either." He started walking again. "You know, it's funny. If I really were some sort of criminal mastermind ... well, first, I'd prefer to call myself a revolutionary, in the traditional American sense of the word."

"Okay. For the sake of argument, let's say you are. A traditional American revolutionary."

"But one with both feet in the modern world. This whole idea that I'd order people to do things ... that's so old-fashioned. There's no need for it in the social media age. Just as an example ... say I was very angry at you. Say I wanted to get rid of you. There are all kinds of ways to approach that. I'm bigger and stronger than you are. I could easily overpower you."

"Physical evidence," Casey said, the words sticking in her throat. "Not worth the risk."

"Exactly." He lifted the edge of his brocaded vest. The butt of a pistol just showed there, peeking above the waistband of his pants. "I could use a gun. One that was obtained illegally. Toss it when I was through."

"Witnesses," she managed, thinking, Diego is watching me, he isn't far, this is a bluff, some kind of sick mind game.

Drake laughed. "These people? The mentally ill, as you put it? Drunks? On drugs? Hardly credible witnesses. But I agree with you, it would be unnecessarily risky. It would be preferable to have someone else do it. For example, one of these homeless people. But they're too unreliable. Instead why not use one of my so-called acolytes? Have him waiting here for us. Have him pull out a gun and shoot you dead. It would be over so quickly, and I'd have no time to react. No time to protect you. A terrible tragedy, but what can you expect, allowing garbage like this to pile up on the street?"

Third time's a charm, bitch.

Her heart was beating hard now, the sweat prickling on her back. Fight or flight. But you can't run, she told herself. You can't show weakness. It's a game.

"You have an interesting way of getting to know someone," she said.

He smiled at her. The charming version. "I'm a writer. It's in our nature to spin out fictional scenarios. We really can't help it." He gestured up the street. "Almost there."

Thank god, Casey thought.

"Of course, my preferred scenario would be none of those things," he said abruptly.

"Oh? What would it be, then?"

"As I said, I may believe in traditional values, but I'm a realist about the world we're living in. Until recently, True Men was almost an underground phenomenon. Admirers of the work found each other in chat rooms, on social media. Now, it's a hashtag. A meme." He snorted. "The popularity of the books has grown thanks to that. And I must say, thanks to you. That's the upside of notoriety. It's brought me a whole new set of fans. Several solid offers for film and television options, in fact. Though I doubt if anything will come of those. Too controversial."

"You're welcome," Casey said.

Drake grinned. "I'm still not sure the trade-off is worth it. But I do have more power, more influence, than I ever did before. And that's what I'd use."

Up ahead was what looked like an old warehouse that had been given fresh paint and some exterior planters. An LED sign read MUG with two mugs of foaming beer flashing below the word. A short line of people waited by the door, a doorman checking their names on an iPad. A sign on a post read *Closed for Private Event*.

"There are so many lost young men looking for missions," Drake said. "So many Alan Chastains and Lucas Derrys. They just need direction. It would be easy to provide. I would just have to make the suggestion." He turned to her. Stared down at her, meeting her eyes, daring her to look away. "'Will no one rid me of this meddlesome priest?'" he asked softly. Then he gently clasped her elbow. "Here we are."

44

"SO WHAT DID HE want?"

Rose had gotten there first and had grabbed a booth in the back of the dimly lit bar.

Casey shook her head, her heart still hammering. She badly wanted a drink. Would anyone care if she had one? She used Trusty to ease herself into the seat opposite Rose.

"I don't know," she said. "He was all over the place. But you're right, he's a narcissistic jerk. He's gotten a little taste of power, and he's drunk on it."

"What did he say?"

"Oh, that he could get one of his followers to kill me if he wanted."

She'd tried to keep her tone light, but from the look on Rose's face, she hadn't exactly succeeded.

"Are you fucking *kidding* me?"

"Also that he thinks of himself as a traditional American revolutionary."

"We need to call Detective Helton. Or that FBI guy."

"What's the point?" Casey was suddenly exhausted, feeling an ache deep in her bones. "He'll just say he was 'spinning fictional scenarios.' And odds are that's all he was doing. He's pissed off I complicated his life, and he wanted to show me he has the power."

"Hey guys."

Diego had arrived, and he was carrying three small mugs of beer. "I won't tell if you don't," he said.

"Oh thank god." Casey grabbed her mug and drank deeply. A very strong IPA. She could taste the alcohol in it.

"He sure took the scenic route to get here," Diego said. "We could have walked up Tony Gwynn and along J and missed all the crusties."

"Intimidation," Rose said. "He threatened her."

"Seriously?"

Casey nodded, scribbling notes in her pad, wanting to get as much of the conversation with Drake on paper as she could before she could forget any of it. Too bad it's off the record, she thought. But there might be some way to use it, depending...

Depending on what George Drake did next.

Right now he made his way around the long wooden tables, stopping to exchange a few words and shake hands with his fans. Inside the place was about what Casey would have expected from the exterior, showing exposed beams and heater vents, some brewing tanks and wooden barrels. From the size, Casey thought it only took up about a quarter of the building at most. By now the space was pretty full, the seats filled, the overflow lined up around the bar and at the back of the room.

"Notice anything about this crowd?" Rose said in a low voice. "Pale and male."

She was right, Casey realized. Most of the people here were white men, mostly young white men. A lot of them had buzzed haircuts and wore plain white T-shirts, black jeans, boots. She shivered. There were a few hard-looking guys with muscle, but most of them didn't seem formidable or scary, taken individually. Some acne-spotted faces. Chubby guts hanging over their belts.

Baby fat.

"Let's see if we can get some quotes," Casey said. "What do you think about those guys over there?"

"Hang on. Looks like Drake's going to speak."

George Drake had stepped up onto a tiny black stage at one end of the bar. A microphone on a stand was already set up there. Diego had his camera ready. The light wasn't the best, but it would do. They hadn't asked for permission to film here, but then, no one was telling them no, either. Casey and Rose stood up as well, Rose with the GoPro.

A few preliminary squeals from the microphone, and then Drake began. "Hello! And good evening."

A round of applause and cheers.

"I'm not going to make a lengthy speech. That's not what tonight is about. Tonight is about *you*, a chance for us to gather together, in meatspace for a change. I know that many of you came a considerable distance to get here. I can't tell you how deeply honored I am by that. Most of you couldn't even get tickets to Comic-Con, am I right?"

"Too expensive!"

"Sold out!"

Laughter.

Drake laughed back. "Don't I know it. They have to save all those tickets for the Hollywood elites that have taken over what used to be an event for fans. Fans like you! They've tried to shut you out! They don't care about you."

A murmur of assent.

"Well, we don't have to care about them. We have each other. We are strong as long as we are one."

"Megalomaniac, much?" Rose whispered in Casey's ear.

Casey nodded. But she had to give Drake credit—he was much better at this than she would have expected from a comic book writer. Or graphic novelist, rather.

"See, here's the thing. Those Hollywood elites? The political elites that run nanny states like California? They are out of touch with real Americans. With real American values. They've forgotten about men like you. But you know what they'll tell you? That you're privileged. Privileged! Come on, is that fair? Do you feel privileged, any of you? What do you have to say? Let's hear it!"

A roar of "No!" from the crowd.

"I'll tell you what, I've worked hard. I've worked hard all my life for what I have now. I bet you have too, I bet you've worked your heart out, but they make it difficult, don't they? All those liberals telling you to check your privilege." He snorted. "Assuming I *did* have it, what makes them think I'm just going to give it up? Why should I? Why should *you*? Men like you and I built this country. And we're going to take it back. America belongs to us."

Drake looked to the back of the room, to where Casey, Rose, and Diego sat.

"We've got some guests here tonight. Members of the media. Casey Cheng's here. You know about Casey Cheng?" He pointed directly at her, smiling his toothy smile. "There she is! One of Alan Jay's targets, but she's recovered nicely. She's been doing quite a job, I'll tell you. Quite a job, reporting on Alan Jay and Lucas Derry and my work. Right, Casey? Why don't you say hello to everybody? I for one am really glad you're here."

Most of the heads in the room turned to stare at her. And suddenly it didn't matter that they were young, that they were chubby and had pimples.

Casey lifted her hand in a wave. Pushed up her cheeks in an imitation smile.

They would want her to smile.

"I don't like where this is going," Rose whispered harshly. "We should get out of here."

Casey shook her head. If they left now ...

Drake was a bully. Bullies preyed on the fearful.

She got out her iPhone and opened up Periscope. Get the whole thing out live. That way if something happened ...

"Casey's going to interview me," Drake said to his fans. "I'm actually really looking forward it. As long as she's fair." He stared at her once more. "You'll be fair, Casey. Won't you?"

45

WHO IS GEORGE DRAKE? A NEWS 9 EXCLUSIVE, WITH CASEY CHENG

(BEGIN VIDEO CLIP: MONTAGE OF NEWS FOOTAGE OF ALLEGED "TRUE MEN" INCIDENTS, SOCIAL MEDIA INSERTS / TWEETS FEATURING #TRUEMEN) CHENG (V.O.): True Men. They claim to be a new movement, taking responsibility for a series of incidents across the country involving harassment, vandalism, assault, and even murder. As of today these claims remain unproven, and it's uncertain if an organized group even exists. But before there was an internet hashtag *(INSERT SHOTS OF TRUE MEN COVERS, PAGES AS NEEDED)*, there was the graphic novel *True Men Will Rise* by George Drake.

CHENG (IN STUDIO, GEORGE DRAKE "COMIC" PORTRAIT OTS): Who is George Drake? The writer / artist of the True Men graphic novel series calls himself a storyteller, a commenter on contemporary society, even a traditional American revolutionary.

(BEGIN VIDEO CLIP: DRAKE INTERVIEW AT MUGS) GEORGE DRAKE: I believe in defending traditional American values (LAUGHS). These days that makes me a revolutionary.

(END VIDEO CLIP) CHENG (IN STUDIO, DRAKE COMIC POR-TRAIT OTS): But this defender of American values has a complicated and at times troubled past.

(BEGIN VIDEO CLIP: DRAKE INTERVIEW AT MUGS) DRAKE: Was I on a few occasions an ass to some women at parties? Undoubtedly. But did my actions rise to the level of criminal behavior? Absolutely not.

(END VIDEO CLIP) CHENG (IN STUDIO, DRAKE COMIC POR-TRAIT OTS): George Drake denies any active involvement in a True Men "movement," which he claims doesn't actually exist.

(BEGIN VIDEO CLIP: ZOOM IN ON GEORGE DRAKE COMIC POR-TRAIT, THE DOTS THAT MAKE IT UP BECOMING BIGGER AS CHENG CONTINUES V.O.) CHENG: But the truth, like many things concerning George Drake, is more complicated.

(THE PORTRAIT IS NOW AN ABSTRACT BLUR OF DOTS)

CHENG (V.O.): Who is George Drake? We'll tell you what we've learned, when we return.

"What's that quote? 'Men are afraid women will laugh at them. Women are afraid men will kill them.'" Casey laughed. She thought she sounded nervous.

"That's pretty dark," Detective Helton said.

"But is it true?"

"People kill each other for all kinds of stupid reasons. Men do most of the killing, the great majority of female homicide victims are killed by their male partners, so I don't know, maybe."

She'd met Helton at a coffee place in the south part of La Jolla, near Windansea Beach. His call. She'd told him on the phone it was time sensitive, and at first he'd hesitated.

"I have a little time to meet later today, if you're okay with Windansea and you don't mind casual," he'd said. "I've got another appointment in the area."

She didn't know what he'd meant by that until she saw him. Instead of his usual suit, he wore a T-shirt and board shorts.

"You really are a surfer."

"Yeah. How'd you know?"

She'd laughed. "It was a guess."

"Yeah, I'm overdue for some PTO so I'm taking a little time today. Surf's cranking."

They sat at an outdoor table on the sidewalk. The coffee place didn't have a view of the ocean but it was close enough to hear the waves, catch a whiff of the brine.

She'd felt a surge of irritation when she realized that he was taking time off to go surfing, given what was happening in her life. But that wasn't fair, and she knew it. Everyone needed a break from this shit. She just didn't know when she was going to get one.

"So it's gotten measurably worse since you ran the segment? Beyond the normal uptick whenever you do one?"

She nodded. "Yes. The usual flood of trolls on our social media channels, except … I don't know, even more vitriolic and … personal. And just more of them. And they don't stop."

"Are you saving them? The threats?"

"Sure. Like always. Along with some of my more *interesting* fan mail. I just wasn't sure if there was any point in sending them over anymore, since nothing ever seems to happen with it." She sipped her coffee. Her hand was trembling a bit, she noted. Get a grip, she told herself. Focus on the coffee. They roasted their own here, and it was very good.

Helton drew in a breath that hissed through his teeth. "I'm sorry," he said. "It's not that we don't take this seriously. But with this many threats coming from so many different jurisdictions, we're limited in what we can do. The FBI is better equipped to deal with it than we are."

"I know," she said. "I've already contacted them."

Last week after her encounter with Drake she'd gone back to the FBI and called Kendrick, the agent she'd met who was on the team investigating the Cason shooting. "We're separating this from the main investigation of the congressman's case," he'd told her. "We've assigned a dedicated team in our cybercrimes unit here in San Diego that will be working in tandem with the Cason team in case there is overlap. An agent will be in touch with you about it. Please be confident that we take this very seriously."

"What did they have to say?" Helton asked.

"I'm still waiting for a response."

Helton shifted in his chair, grimacing slightly, and for a moment she thought he might say something critical—he'd seemed a little snarky about the FBI before, but maybe she was projecting.

"Well, it's a complicated investigation," he said. "The social media stuff … it's like chasing shadows. A lot of them use fake IP addresses, and sock puppets, so when one account gets whacked by the provider, they just set up another one."

"I don't want them whacked. I want them identified."

"I know. I get it. But that's the default response when you report an abuser—suspend the account. People see these tweets or whatever and report them. They're trying to be helpful."

She knew that, of course. News 9 had deleted a lot of them—you couldn't have website comments that violated your own terms of service, and as for her own channels, who wanted to interact with her if saying something positive resulted in its own torrent of abuse?

"Do you need to be on social media?" Helton asked.

They'd discussed it at the station. Did she, really? But her channels were popular, by far the most popular at the station, second only to the main account. The click-through rates were excellent. No one wanted to lose that exposure and revenue stream.

"Yes, I do. It's part of my job."

"Okay." Helton took a moment to sip his coffee. Maybe to figure out what to say next. Casey had the impression that he was someone who thought before he spoke.

"The problem is, it's a mob mentality going on," he said. "If it was one stalker, there's ways we can proceed. Identify the perp, see if there's enough to prosecute criminally, and you can choose to go after him civilly if not. But it isn't just one. Some guy sends out a threat and then a bunch of other people pile on with their own. Wash, rinse, repeat. There's no organized group to go after."

"How do you know that? They could be meeting somewhere online and organizing this."

"Yeah, they could be. But it's nowhere obvious. Sure, you've got some guys talking smack on some boards, but does that rise to the level of a criminal offense? Is one sick tweet something you can charge a guy for?" He shrugged. "I'm no lawyer, so I really couldn't tell you."

She could feel her frustration rising. She hadn't ever recovered her patience since The Event, and if she was being honest with herself, patience was never her strong suit anyway.

"What about True Men?" she asked.

"You mean the hashtag? Anyone can use that. It doesn't mean they're working together or that there's any real organization."

"And George Drake?"

"You think he's instigating this?"

"I know he's angry about the segment we did. He's said so in a statement and on social media."

"Because you made him look foolish, because you laughed at him, basically?"

"He's a target-rich environment," Casey said. "We didn't say anything that wasn't true."

"Has he said anything threatening toward you?"

Casey thought about it, about the things Drake had said when they'd walked to his event, the way he'd singled her out to his audience. "Only what someone like him could do to someone like me, if he wanted to."

"And he said this online, or to a reputable source, or—?"

"To me. Before we taped the segment."

"So you responded by going after him and hitting him with both barrels."

She set her cup down hard, rattling the spoons on the table. She wanted to scream. "I didn't 'go after him.'" She didn't scream but her voice was tight and angry. "I used his own work and his own words."

He held up his hands. "Look, I didn't say that well. What I meant was, you didn't hold back, in spite of his threats."

"No. We didn't." Okay, she told herself. Slow down. Take a breath and *think*, don't just react. "And ... maybe I went at him a little harder because of the threats, and because he's a big giant asshole, and because I'm a human being who's taking this all just a little personally right now. But there was nothing in that segment that wasn't true."

So much for slowing down, she thought. But at least she wasn't screaming.

"Fair enough." Helton grinned, pushing up the crow's feet around his eyes. The smile made him look younger. "It was a pretty epic take-down, actually."

She felt herself relax, just a little bit. "Thank you," she said. "We worked hard on it."

"Do you want to tell me what he said?"

When she finished, Helton let out a long breath. He'd sat there with his thumb pressed into his cheek and his forefinger curled around his mouth, listening.

"I understand why you're concerned," he said. "It sounds like he told you what he was going to do, and then maybe he went out and did it."

"Maybe?"

"Calling on his fans to let you know what they think of your re-porting isn't the same thing as making a literal threat to your safety."

"But he knew what the result would be."

"Like I said, I'm not a lawyer. But that seems like a hard case to make. We need evidence of him directly encouraging other people to harass and threaten you."

"I just told you what he said to me."

Helton spread his hands. "Look ... Ms. Cheng ... you've been in your line of work a while. How would you feel about reporting on something if you couldn't verify it? Don't you have rules about that stuff? How many sources you need before you can go on the air with it?"

"Yes," she said. "We do." She felt suddenly deflated. Anger was an energy; it had fueled this encounter, but now it had left her. Her body ached. She just wanted to lie down.

"And—I just want to be clear—this hasn't crossed into the real world, right? You're not being followed, or physically harassed?"

"Not that I'm aware of. And I spend a lot of time looking over my shoulder. But ... " She looked up, met his eyes. She wanted him to *get* this. "What happens if one of these fanboys takes the next step? Crosses over. Is that what it's going to take for someone to do something?"

"Ms. Cheng … Casey … " Helton took a moment, choosing his words, she assumed. "I'd really like to fix this for you, and we're going to do our best. But as long as you keep poking the hornet's nest, they're going to keep swarming. And I don't know what to tell you to do about that."

"You think I should quit covering this story?"

"I'm the wrong guy to give that kind of advice," he said. He half smiled for a moment, the kind of tell that wasn't conscious. She almost asked him why.

Instead, she thought about the story. What even *was* it at this point? She'd started with the Morena shootings; she was going to profile the victims, the long-term consequences. She'd started with herself, really. She'd ended up with Alan Jay Chastain, who'd led her to Lucas Derry, to that day in the park with Congressman Cason and Sarah Price. With the dead and injured.

Then to Beth Ryder, True Men, and George Drake.

She'd thought, for a while, that everything was coming together, that all those smaller stories were part of some larger whole, and she'd almost figured out what that was.

Now, not so much. She was back to the Big Empty.

"You okay?" Helton asked.

She nodded. "Just … discouraged."

"Yeah. I don't blame you."

They sat in silence for a minute or two, sipping their coffees. What am I going to do now? Casey thought. Just keep on keeping on? Quit?

"I can take a look at Drake," Helton said. "I know the FBI has. I'll see what they've got. Maybe I can add to it."

"Thanks. I really appreciate that." And she really did. Which felt a little pathetic and needy, because it wasn't that she really expected him to find anything, or to fix this. It was only that he seemed to take her seriously, and right now, that counted for something.

"In the meantime, you might want to consider hiring a private investigator. There's firms that specialize in this kind of cyber stalking and harassment. They do a good job."

Casey sighed. No way her salary would cover the cost of that. "I'll talk to the station about it."

She wondered how much the station might be willing to spend, if anything, and at what point having her attention-grabbing stories and the ratings they brought in would become more trouble than they were worth.

Helton nodded.

It was getting time for both of them to go. The conversation had wound down, and there was no more business to discuss, really. Unless she wanted to try to pitch *him* to do a segment, and that didn't seem appropriate, under the circumstances. But she didn't move to get up, and for some reason Helton lingered as well.

He's attractive, she thought. She'd been pushing that thought away and decided to just let herself feel it, test it out.

A cop. Did she just want to be around a man who made her feel safe?

"You gonna be okay?" he finally asked.

"Sure," she said. "I'll be fine."

Maybe I should get a gun, she thought.

46

A WOMAN NARRATES OVER footage of Matt Cason shaking hands with men and women dressed for a nice dinner—a fundraiser: *"Matt Cason says his military experience makes him a good leader for America. But under Matt Cason's watch, millions of taxpayer dollars went missing in one of the worst military corruption scandals of the Iraq War."*

Headlines and chyrons about millions of dollars gone missing in Iraq, a warehouse full of luxury goods, footage of soldiers on trial.

A male voice: *"There was cash just going out of there in duffle bags. Nobody was paying any attention."*

The woman again, over footage of Cason shaking hands with wealthy donors: *"If Matt Cason didn't stop corruption that was happening right under his nose, what makes you think he'll watch over your dollars in Washington?"*

A different woman: *"I'm Kim Tegan, and I approve this message."*

———

A photo of Matt Cason in full battle rattle that gradually becomes a stark black-and-white image. A male narrator: *"We support our brave men and women in uniform. They risk their lives, protecting our freedoms. But not every soldier is a credit to the uniform."* The image of Cason is now splashed with red. *"Matt Cason was in charge of a program that handed out cash to corrupt tribal chieftains."* Montage of men in keffiyeh, raising automatic weapons. *"There was no oversight and no paper trail. So what did America buy with those taxpayer dollars?"*

Photographs of dead and wounded American soldiers.

A different man's voice: *"He turned around and shot up our patrol. Just like that. No warning."*

Now the photo of Cason is entirely red and black.

"Matt Cason. Unfit for duty."

A different voice, low and quick: *"This message paid for by the Committee for American Values."*

————

Male narrator: *"Matt Cason is an American hero. He served his country with honor. But the qualities that make a man a warrior don't always make that man the best choice for a leader.*

"On December 19th, 2007, Cason was involved in an altercation with one Jesse Garcia at a local bar frequented by service members. He beat Garcia so badly that Garcia was hospitalized with multiple contusions and facial fractures." A photo of a man with a bruised, swollen face, a few stitches across one eyebrow. *"And why? Because he didn't like the way Garcia looked at his girlfriend."*

A mug shot of a younger Cason, with a black eye.

"The case was settled out of court, with Cason citing combat stress as the reason for his momentary loss of control."

Now we see the speaker. It's Jacob Thresher, walking along the cliffs with the ocean behind him. His voice is warm, his expression concerned. *"Unlike my other opponent, I'll never question Matt Cason's bravery and courage under fire. What I question is his fitness for office in dangerous times like these, when a cool head is needed more than a raging heart. America needs a healer, not a hater. We need more compassion, more kindness—not the kind of anger that problem-solves with fists."*

The close shot of Matt Cason's face and fist from the park, his features contorted and bloodied.

"I'm Jacob Thresher, and I approve this message."

"Fuckers," Matt muttered. He sat hunched over on the couch, elbows on his thighs, one hand covering the other, fingers flexing and digging into the covered hand.

"It's not like we didn't know it was coming," Jane said, unblinking. "Between their ad buys and Sarah's source."

Lindsey took a quick glance at Sarah. She couldn't help it.

It made sense to have senior staff meetings at their house, Lindsey thought, given that they had security here, but she wasn't crazy about having Sarah in her living room. She knew that wasn't entirely fair. Sarah had done a great job handling Social under difficult circumstances; she'd shown up in spite of that horrible day in the park two months ago, in spite of the torrent of abuse since she'd been outed as Beth Ryder.

She'd changed since that happened. Lindsey would have expected her to retreat further into her boxy suit jackets and awkward white blouses, but she hadn't done that. Instead, she'd bought a new jacket that fit better, was swapping out the stiff blouses for tops that were more relaxed.

More relaxed. That was it.

You couldn't exactly call her *relaxed*—she was on alert all the time, Lindsey thought, her posture tense and watchful—but compared to the way she was before? She seemed lighter, somehow.

Maybe it was a relief, not carrying that secret around.

But the harassment hadn't let up. It would ebb a bit and then come roaring back. The comments aimed at Matt were horrible. The ones Sarah got?

They'd finally given her an intern, a young man with a deep voice who said he was willing to screen her calls, that the abuse wouldn't bother him. But it *did* bother him, and sometimes the abusers slipped through his screening anyway. And then there were the comments on Social. They'd installed an electronic logger so they could send the overt threats to the FBI, but someone still had to read the posts and tweets and snaps to make that determination.

Lindsey still wasn't sure if she'd made the right call when she'd voted for Sarah to stay on the campaign. Would they be dealing with this level of abuse if they'd let her go?

Be kind to her, Lindsey reminded herself again. She hasn't done anything wrong.

Matt curled and clenched the fingers on his injured hand, testing the fist. "Those guys that were ripping us off weren't in my chain of command. They had nothing to do with me. Why not make me responsible for the fucking war while they're at it?"

"I think we've played good prevent defense on the whole Anbar thing with the 'Leadership' spot," Presley said. "We're well positioned to go on offense there."

"What do you have in mind?" Jane asked.

"We focus on the positive things Matt was trying to accomplish, suggesting that if we give him the chance, he'll be able to do positive things here."

Matt let out a snort. "Oh, great. So the message is, 'Hey, all the shit I tried to do in Iraq got blown up, but trust me, I'll do a better job here.' Or is it, 'This country's as fucked up as Iraq, and I've got the right experience for failed states.' Jesus Christ, what a shitshow. People don't want to hear about *failure*."

She could see it building up in him, the storm of anger and self-loathing that was never too far offshore. "You didn't fail, Matt. You did your job, and you did it well. This is no time to refight the war, okay?"

How many times had she said it? How many times had Jane said it too? But his anger was what had gotten him into politics in the first place, and they both knew it.

"Do you have any suggestions, Matt?" Presley asked. If *he* felt any defensiveness, he didn't show it. But then he never did. He was a gun for hire, Lindsey knew. He'd work for anyone who'd pay him.

"Hit back! These are lies. I want to call them what they are."

Presley nodded. "We can do that too."

"It will be expensive," Angus said. "We'll need to increase our ad buys."

"Matt's right," Jane said abruptly. "We need to hit back hard, right now. This is a swift boat, and we know what happens when we ignore them. Also? I think we ought to revisit that tape Sarah's contact sent—the one where little Kimmie insults Henry Echeverria and the entire Mexican-American community with her 'Assland' joke." She turned to Sarah. "And see what else your friend's got. If this is how Tegan's going to play, we'll play too."

"Okay." Presley glanced down at his tablet. "So what about Jesse Garcia?"

Matt shook his head. Lindsey could see the anger dissipate, leaving only the self-loathing. The sorrow.

"I don't know," he said. "It was over a decade ago. I'd just come back from my, what was it, my second deployment, and things had gone to hell over there, and I didn't handle it very well. Neither did Jesse. We were *friends* for fuck's sake. He got in some punches too. He was just drunker than I was. We both felt like shit about it after. That's why it all got dropped and you never heard about it."

Lindsey could see the scene still, the rage on Matt's face, the two men shoving and grappling and punching until Jesse finally went down, falling against a Harley in the piss-stained parking lot.

That had been a very bad night.

"What changed?"

It was a small shock to hear Sarah's voice. She rarely spoke up in these meetings, and when she did, it was almost always only to clarify requests made of her.

Matt looked up. "What do you mean?"

"You said you weren't handling things well. You went back to Iraq twice after that." Sarah blushed. "You've done a lot of great things since then. How did you get better?"

Matt smiled at her. It almost hurt Lindsey to see it, that smile. Small. Thoughtful. Real. He looked at Sarah like she was the only other person in the room.

"I got help," he said. "Not my choice. The last thing most soldiers want to do is admit they're having problems because of the job. But the CO told me I wasn't going on another deployment until I talked to someone. So I did. And it helped."

"And that, ladies and gentleman, is our ad," Presley said, spreading his hands.

Matt looked up, the smile gone, replaced by a dark irritation. "What?"

"You. Talking about your experiences, just like this. Intimate. Speaking directly to the viewer. And then how you've worked to get help for service members in distress. Because everyone who served our country deserves the chance to get better."

For a moment, the room was silent.

"Yeah," Jane said. "I think that's a good play."

Matt didn't like it, Lindsey could tell. But finally, he nodded. "I guess it's the best one we've got with this shitty hand, right?"

———

They adjourned shortly after that.

"I'll catch Ben up," Sarah said, as she stood and slung her messenger bag over her head.

They were in a strange position with Ben. Two months after the shooting, he was better, but not a hundred percent. He couldn't do the job he'd been hired to do. The campaign still paid his salary. It was the right thing to do, of course, but there were legal questions as well. On the one hand, the campaign couldn't really afford to keep someone on at Ben's level who couldn't do the job. On the other, he was injured while on the job, so they were looking at a worker's comp case at the least. It was already September. By the time it all got straightened out, the campaign would be over. Thankfully, there was a substantial uptick in donations after the shooting. That helped.

Ben had only come into the office once. Understandable, Lindsey thought. Between the armed guards, the press gauntlet, and feeling that you had a target on your back every time you walked out the door, it wasn't surprising that Ben didn't want to spend time there. She sure didn't, and she hadn't even been in the park that day.

She supposed she should be grateful to Sarah. If she hadn't been so pissed off at Matt for hanging all over her, she would have been right there too, in the park next to Matt, with a shooter taking aim at them both.

"Oh? Are you going to see him?" Lindsey asked.

"Yes, I'll stop by there later," Sarah said. The hint of a blush.

That was an interesting development. Good, Lindsey thought. She'd rather have Sarah interested in Ben than Matt. The thing about campaign romances was that their potential for disruption was limited. One way or another, the campaign would end, as this one would.

Two months to go.

We'll make it, Lindsey thought. We'll probably even win. The numbers still looked good, even with the race tightening in the last couple of weeks. There was plenty of time left for momentum to swing back their way.

But those ads would leave a mark.

What worried her most was the mark they'd leave on Matt. They were pushing his buttons in places that hurt. If his self-control faltered, if he lashed out...

Passion was good—people liked that about him, the polling showed. Unrestrained rage was not.

———

Sarah never went directly home after any kind of campaign work. Whether she went to the office, to Matt and Lindsey's, to the hotel the staff had met in last week, any kind of campaign function, she never went directly home.

If they were watching her, that's how they'd find out where she lived.

She'd changed her hair again, wore a baseball cap and sunglasses when she went out, and she wasn't sure if people even recognized her. But she wasn't taking any chances.

Tonight she went to Trader Joe's to pick up a few things for Ben, easy and convenient food to have around the house. He still wasn't feeling well. Or at least he had a hard time leaving his apartment. She got that. And he worried about having things delivered, like she did.

He'll get used to it, she thought, grabbing a bag of cheddar cheese popcorn off the shelf.

At the last minute, she decided to stop at Crooked Arrow Brewery for a small growler fill. She wasn't sure how much Ben could drink, with the kidney damage. She'd read conflicting things when she researched it on the internet, with some studies even showing that beer was good for your kidneys. In any case, she knew how much he loved Crooked Arrow beers. Maybe he could at least have a glass.

They'd made a small garden in one of the parking spaces in front of the brewery, out of wooden half-barrels. There was a sculpture too, a brightly colored figure spackled with pieces of colored glass and mirror—a leaping dolphin. On the tallest barrel was a plaque made out of wood and stamped metal that said *In Memory of Our Fallen Friends*, with a list of seven names. The victims of the Morena shooter.

It was weird to think about it. All those people had died. Casey Cheng had been shot right around here. She wondered if you could see any evidence, any bloodstains, or had those been hosed away, ground into the grease and oil and asphalt?

Aside from the garden, it looked completely normal: just another brewery in a small industrial park, at eight p.m. on a weeknight, three-quarters full with people drinking flights of beer on wooden paddles.

She went up to the end of the bar where there were the fewest people and waited for one of the beertenders to spot her.

"Hey."

Sarah jumped and turned. Matt sat at the bar. She hadn't noticed him; his back had been to her. He wore a Padres cap, a faded T-shirt, and shorts, transformed from the candidate she'd spoken to just over an hour ago.

"Hi," she said.

Matt indicated the seat next to him. "Can I buy you a beer?"

"I…" Not a good idea, she thought. She wasn't even sure why she thought it.

"No worries, if you're with someone…" he said.

"No, I'm not. I mean…I just stopped in to pick up a growler."

"Well, I don't want to keep you."

Stupid, you're being stupid, she thought. She was still waiting for the beertender to come and take her order; standing here was just dumb. She slid into the empty stool next to him.

"I have some time," she said.

Matt bought her a flight. "Don't feel like you have to finish it," he said.

"I probably shouldn't. I have to drive."

"Over to Ben's?"

"Yes. To brief him."

"And bring him some beer." Matt grinned. "An essential part of any campaign briefing."

Sarah felt her cheeks flush. "He just really likes this beer, and he's still not getting out much."

Matt nodded, the grin relaxing into the hint of a smile. The way he'd looked at her in his living room. "Yeah. Sometimes I feel like I just want to find a cabin on a mountain someplace and stay there. Or maybe a hut on some Mexican beach somewhere."

It was funny, but she didn't feel that way. Everyone knew the worst about her now. What was the point in hiding? She wanted to make a mark. To change things. That's what she wanted.

"You were really kind today," he said.

She was blushing again. "I wasn't ... I mean ... it was the truth."

"Maybe. But you know, no one's ever asked me that question, what changed." He sipped his beer, the double IPA, she guessed. "Maybe because I never wanted to talk about any of it. I was such a dick back then. It's not a time I like talking about."

"Sometimes you have to," she heard herself say. "It's not as bad as you think. Sometimes you feel better after you just ... unburden yourself."

Matt laughed and drank his beer. "Sounds very Catholic."

She felt that almost physical sensation of being slapped; she'd said something stupid, something wrong, and he was laughing at her.

No, she told herself. There's nothing wrong with what I said. It's him, not me.

Maybe I should just fill the growler and get out of here, Sarah thought.

"Hey," he said abruptly, "that's just me being a dick again. I'm sorry. I really admire you. The way you've kept going through all this ... it's amazing. And I really appreciate it."

There it was, that look of his, the high beams on, all his attention focused on her. Her heartbeat quickened. She felt a rush of pleasure, enough that she thought she might have made a small sound when she breathed out.

That's why you can't be here, she thought. You can't feel that. Not about him.

She was just so tired of not feeling it.

"Thanks," she said. "You don't need to apologize. I'm doing what I want to do. I'm glad I'm able to help."

He rested his hand on the bar. Very close to hers. He wants me, she thought. All I'd have to do is stretch out my fingers.

She reached for one of her tasters and raised it to her lips and took a deep sip. "What happened to Jesse?" she asked.

Matt looked away and picked up his glass. "Jesse? He died. Motorcycle accident about … I think it was four months after we got into that fight."

"I'm so sorry," she said.

He shrugged. "Yeah. That's the thing. Not everybody gets the chance to get better."

―――――

This was the third time she'd gone to Ben's home. He lived in a tiny bungalow behind a larger house in Normal Heights, which he claimed he paid too much for every month.

It took him a minute to answer the door; he was still using two walking sticks to get up and down when Sarah had seen him a week ago. She heard the sound of a deadbolt sliding back, the rattle of a door chain.

"Hey," he said, opening the door. He wore a faded T-shirt and thin pajama pants. It had been a hot day and was still a warm night, the breezes still. She could hear the helicopter buzz of the overhead fan.

She stepped inside. The living room was dark, dominated by a wall of books and a desk with an expensive laptop and big flat-screen monitor. "I game sometimes," he'd told her on her first visit, seeming embarrassed by it. Sarah wasn't sure why. "I like some games," she'd said, which was true enough, though she'd quit playing halfway through high school.

"Should I put this in the kitchen?" she asked now, indicating the Trader Joe's bag.

"What's that? You didn't have to bring that."

Was he grateful or irritated? Sarah couldn't tell. "Just a few snacks." She held up the growler. "Plus I stopped at Crooked Arrow and got that Belgium tripel. I wasn't sure if you could have it, but ... "

At that, he smiled broadly. "Oh, wow, thanks. Yeah, I can have it."

———————

"Shit."

They'd sat on the couch and watched the hit ads on Ben's gaming laptop, setting it on the little coffee table there.

"How did Matt react to this?" Ben asked.

"Okay. I guess. I mean ... " She thought about it. "He wasn't happy. At first he was mad, and then I think he got depressed. I ran into him at Crooked Arrow, when I was picking up the beer." She felt herself flush, thinking about the way Matt had looked at her, of his hand so close to hers.

"Oh yeah?"

There it was, that note in his voice that came up when she talked about Matt, that slight edge. Was Ben jealous?

She worked with Ben; she'd tried not to think of him that way, and it hadn't been hard. She'd closed that part of herself off, mostly, when she'd become Sarah Price. She hadn't felt much of anything the few times she'd tried to date, the times she'd told herself she should be more open, give them a chance. Not until Matt. And there was no way anything could ever happen with Matt.

She poured Ben some more beer. He'd lost weight since the shooting, his cheekbones sharpened, the soft curve of his belly hollowed out. It was wrong to think this way, but he looked handsome.

I just want to feel something, she thought. The way she'd felt in the brewery, like she was caught up in an electric current, still lingered, and she thought, maybe I could feel that again.

"How are you doing?" she asked.

"Better. The leg's better. The doctor says I got lucky there, believe it or not. Wound's healing up, I'm not going to need another surgery or anything like that."

"That's great," she said.

He laughed. It sounded bitter. "I'll probably be a hundred percent just in time for the election."

They were sitting close together, it was a small couch, a loveseat she guessed you'd call it, designed for two people. She could smell the tang of Ben's stale sweat. He hadn't shaved in a few days and she was guessing he hadn't showered either. It was probably hard with his injury.

"Everybody misses you," she said.

"You seem to be doing okay."

"We're managing. It was better when you were there though." She stared at him, waiting for him to notice; he was sipping his beer and looking straight ahead.

Finally he turned to her and met her eyes. His were hazel brown, with flecks of gold. "I don't think you mean that," he said.

"Why wouldn't I?"

"Because you've got my job, and you're killing it." He looked away.

So he's not interested, she thought. He's jealous that Matt likes me, and he's pissed that I'm doing his job, and doing it well.

"Fine," she said. She looked away too and reached for the growler in its koozie that sat on the coffee table. And saw that Ben was hard. She could see the bulge in his flimsy pajama bottoms.

Two spots of red appeared on his pale cheeks, and he covered his erection with his hands.

"Sorry," he muttered.

"Don't be," she said. "I don't mind."

She wondered what to do. She put her hand on his shoulder. The sleeve of his T-shirt was damp with sweat. She could feel her heart speed up, the warmth gathering in the center of her chest, in her groin, and she thought, I could feel something for him.

"No," he said, not looking at her. "I don't want to."

"We don't have to … we could just … "

Maybe he doesn't feel up to it, she thought, but she already knew in her gut that wasn't why.

He thinks I'm dirty.

Now he looked at her. His erection was fading. "You feel sorry for me. I get it."

"That's not … that's not why."

He shook his head and laughed. She felt like she'd been slapped.

"Look, let's just call it a night, okay? I'm sorry for … for making you feel uncomfortable. I'm just … " His eyes suddenly glistened with tears. "I'm tired, and I don't feel that great. Thanks for bringing everything over."

He's sad and hurt and confused, she thought. You shouldn't be angry.

"Okay," she said. She gathered up her messenger bag and headed toward the door, but something stopped her after she opened it, and she turned back to face him.

"You know, I should have just fucked Matt. I didn't, because it would have been stupid. But maybe I should have. It's what you think of me anyway."

"Sarah, wait," he said, "just wait a minute, that's not what I think at all—"

Bullshit, she thought, and closed the door behind her.

47

"We've Reached A Tipping Point for Justice"
An interview with George Drake
By C.N. Murphy, Ed., "Alt-Culture"

Q: About your character, Senator Linda Capaldi. Did you base her on a real-life politician? Because there are some things about her that seem familiar.

A: (laughs) She's inspired by a few, perhaps. But she is my own creation. Senator Capaldi cares only about power for the sake of power. All her warm words toward the so-called oppressed are for show. She has no moral center, and she'll turn on you in a heartbeat.

Q: Is she the center of the conspiracy? Because that seems to be where the story is heading. She's definitely #1 on fans' Most Hated list.

A: (smiles) Well, then fans will be happy to know, without giving anything away, that I have something very special planned for her.

"I just want to say again, the work you are doing today is so important. There's nothing that has a greater ability to move a voter from 'undecided' to supporter than person-to-person contact. Really!"

Smile, Lindsey reminded herself. Look at your audience. Make eye contact.

It was a good turnout, enough volunteers that they'd had to move two of the bull pen's long tables out of the way to fit them. A third table was loaded up with bagels, donuts, and coffee—fuel for today's precinct walks.

"How many of you had someone from the campaign come to your door, either this election or the one before?"

About a half dozen of the volunteers raised their hands.

"See? It works!"

The volunteers seemed enthusiastic, even though they'd gotten her instead of Matt for the precanvass pep talk. "I'm not gonna make it in time," he'd said on the phone from DC. "But I'll be there when everybody gets back from the walk."

"Part of what we're trying to do with this round of canvassing is to determine what precincts Matt should try to walk himself. That makes a *big* difference."

Nods of agreement. A few chuckles. She wondered how many of them were here for a chance to meet and hang out with Matt later.

"Assuming our data is accurate, you'll be targeting soft supporters and persuadables today, so most of the people you'll be talking to will be receptive—don't worry, we're not trying to convince hardcore Tegan fans that she's awful. Occasionally you'll get a persuadable who really doesn't like your candidate and wants to tell you all about it. But it doesn't happen that much, and in my experience, most people are polite. I like to start by telling them I'm a neighbor. I live here just like they do."

More nods.

"The app will give you policy scripts if people have questions, and it's super easy to use. But please feel free to use your own words. You don't have to be perfect. People respond when you're speaking from your heart. Even if you're someone like me, who's not very good at it."

Now people did laugh. She knew what her reputation was.

"You're great, Lindsey!" someone shouted.

"And you are much too kind." She smiled, and realized that she actually meant it. "The main thing is? Have fun with it. It really is fun, once you get the nerves out of the way."

Maybe not "great." She'd never have Matt's level of comfort with talking to crowds. But she'd gotten better.

The campaign office was quiet now, save for an occasional ringing phone. The tablets had been handed out, one per pair of walkers, and the volunteers were on their way to their assigned precincts—all except Rachel Eisenstat, the senior volunteer who had helped coordinate today's event.

"Guess I'm on my own," she said. She looked ready to go. She wore a Cason for Congress T-shirt, sports sunglasses, and one of those floppy Tilley hats you'd take on a hike or a safari.

Rachel had logged so many hours on Matt's first campaign that they'd offered her a paying job on this one, but she'd turned it down. "I don't need the money," she'd said, "and I have the time." A sturdy woman on the older side of middle-aged, with sun-streaked graying hair, she was one of those volunteers who kept a campaign going—so many political organizations would fall apart without them, this legion of middle-aged-to-older women.

"Would you mind some company?" Lindsey asked. Not because Rachel needed a partner. If anyone was equipped to canvass on her own, it was Rachel Eisenstat.

It was just that she wanted to be outside, for a change. Get away from the numbers and the endless databases and the fundraisers and see what people in an actual Clairemont neighborhood had to say. See how she did, talking face-to-face with voters, without Matt. Even if she was doing it *for* Matt.

"That would be great!" Rachel said. "Do you want a T-shirt? I think there's an extra."

Lindsey thought about it. "I'll stick with the button." Something about the candidate's wife wearing a T-shirt with the candidate's name on it seemed a little corny to her.

————

"You know, I don't care what anyone says." Rachel mopped her head with a kerchief. "A dry heat ain't necessarily better."

"Agreed."

Rachel handed Lindsey a bottle of water. Another hot, late-September day, a Santa Ana without the winds. This precinct didn't have a lot of trees to block the sun; it was on the mesa and didn't get canyon breezes either.

At least it was flat.

No one answered the doorbell at the first house, a small stucco ranch like most of the houses in the neighborhood. "Not home," Rachel said, pressing her index finger on the tablet. "Or they're hiding."

Lindsey laughed. "Their loss." She got out a door-hanger and a foldout, which she placed just under the edge of the doormat, since the house didn't have a screen door.

One not home. One soft supporter, a nice woman who wanted to know what Matt's stance on "no-kill" animal shelters was. "Because I know they *say* it's no-kill, but animals still get put down there, every day."

"I think we all want to get to a no-kill county," Lindsey said. "And the best way to do that is to fund trap-spay-neuter-release programs. Matt is a big supporter of those. Have you approached your city councilperson and county supervisor? Because this is the kind of issue where local involvement really makes the biggest difference."

———

"You're good," Rachel said. They'd stopped under a rare tree for a water break.

Lindsey felt her face flush, from the heat as much as the compliment. "I've gotten better, I guess. But I don't know if I'll ever be comfortable talking to strangers like this. Not like Matt. He thrives on it."

Rachel smiled. "You've got your own style. You don't have to be Matt."

"Thanks."

Maybe I don't, she thought. But it was still all about Matt.

And you knew that, she told herself. You're a team. No one made you throw yourself into supporting his career. You did it yourself. Because what he's doing is important, and you thought it was the best way to do good things, because he's better at it than you are.

Do I want to keep doing it?

Later, she thought. After this election is over. Then she'd figure out what made sense for her to do.

"Okay," she said. "Who's up next?"

———

The next house was marked persuadable but had a Jacob Thresher yard sign to the left of the driveway. *Thresher for a better tomorrow*, it said, with a stylized sun and surf graphic.

"I don't know, do we try?" Lindsey asked. "What's your experience with Thresher supporters?"

"Probably not worth it. Those Thresher people tend to be true believers. 'Be the change you want to see, and we'll create a tidal wave of progress.'" Rachel snorted. "It doesn't matter that he can't win. They're one step away from clapping for Tinker Bell."

She looked at her iPad, tapped, and swiped. "I guess we should double-check. There's two people living there, maybe one of them is the persuadable. You want me to take it, and you get the uncommitted across the street? The sooner we get this done, the sooner we can get out of this heat and go for margaritas."

"I like the way you think," Lindsey said. Her blouse was soaked with sweat. Maybe she should have worn the Cason T-shirt after all.

The house across the street was gray stucco and white trim, a small front yard with flower boxes and a patch of Astroturf. "Mrs. Francine Madison," Lindsey muttered. "Age sixty-seven."

The front door was open, the entrance guarded by a white metal security screen. Lindsey rang the doorbell and took two steps back. You weren't supposed to stand too close to the door; it could make the potential voter feel uncomfortable.

A woman came to the door. From what Lindsey could see through the security screen, she looked to be the right age for Francine Madison: a thin woman with shoulder-length light-colored hair.

"Hi, my name is Lindsey Cason, and I'm here on behalf of the Reelect Congressman Matt Cason campaign. Are you Francine Madison?"

"Yes."

"Great!" Smile, she reminded herself. "We're canvassing today because Congressman Cason wants to get a better idea of what issues people are concerned about here in District 54."

"Did you say your name was Cason too?"

"I did. I'm Matt's wife, actually. And we also live in Clairemont. Just west of here."

"Really? You're his wife?" She sounded ever so slightly impressed.

Now that Lindsey's eyes had adjusted somewhat, she could see that Francine Madison had dyed blond hair, wore pink chino shorts, and a scoop-necked white T-shirt. "I voted for him before," she said. "I like that he's a veteran and served our country."

"That's great! And I couldn't agree more," Lindsey said, remembering to smile. "It's especially important for this district. We have so many veterans and active service members here."

Francine Madison opened the screen door. "It's easier to talk this way."

Good, Lindsey thought. Francine wanted to talk, that was a good sign.

"So, Matt wanted me to ask you what issues are the most important to you."

"Well, there's a few. But one reason I'm thinking I might not vote for him this time is because of the illegals."

Shit, Lindsey thought. This was going to be hard. There were few issues that tripped people's switches like immigration, especially illegal immigration. You could talk about history and about migration in border regions, about crime and economic statistics, but none of it generally made a difference.

"I mean, I don't have anything against Mexicans or people like that. But the whole thing's out of control. They come here illegally and they're breaking the law, they're getting all these benefits from the government and taking jobs away from Americans by working so cheap, and I don't understand why Congressman Cason doesn't care about it."

"Well … of course he cares," Lindsey began. She felt a fresh wave of sweat break out on her scalp and back. "We live on a border, and those issues are extremely important to our district. It's something Matt deals with a lot in Congress."

"I'll be honest with you, I like what Kim Tegan has to say."

"I can understand that. If you have some time, I'm happy to talk to you about what Matt's proposals are." Smile, she told herself. "Maybe he'll even come back and tell you about them himself—"

A loud engine sound behind her, a car with a bad muffler maybe, loud enough she didn't want to try to talk over it. The engine revved again. She could smell the exhaust.

"Oh for god's sake," Francine Madison said. "That should be illegal."

Well, there's something we agree on, Lindsey thought.

She turned. A rusted-out bronze beater, some big, old American car, across the street. The engine revved again, and she heard the engine backfire, once, twice. The engine revved once more, like an exclamation mark, and the car sped down the block, tires squealing.

Then Lindsey saw Rachel lying on the ground, head and torso on the sidewalk, legs sprawled over the curb and into the asphalt street.

48

News 9 San Diego @News9SanDiego
LIVE Volunteer on @RepMattCason campaign
shot and killed while walking precinct @Casey-
ChengNews9 has campaign's reactions KASD.
us.Wgu9X

Casey Cheng News 9 @CaseyChengNews9
Campaign confirms Lindsey Cason, the congressman's wife, witnessed shooting, is unharmed.

"Lindsey wanted me to assure all of you that she's doing okay. She's tough, she always has been."

Matt Cason had that distant look in his eyes, slightly stunned. Staring at the reporters but not seeing them. Casey recognized it from the press event at the hospital back in June.

"But emotionally ... she's devastated. We all are."

He stood in front of the campaign headquarters, flanked by Jane Haddad and a young black guy in tortoiseshell framed glasses—assistant campaign manager Angus Wheeler. The shaved-head bodyguard stood behind them.

The late-afternoon sun bathed Matt's face in a golden light—the perfect shot for a campaign commercial, Casey thought, if it weren't for the occasion.

"Rachel Eisenstat was an amazing person. I walked precincts with her the first time I ran and assumed we'd be doing that again next week. I can't believe she's gone. I can't imagine the depth of grief her friends and loved ones are feeling right now."

He paused for a moment, his eyes brimming with tears. If he didn't mean it, he was one hell of an actor, Casey thought.

Now Matt seemed to gather himself. "But I want to be clear about something. Attacking a campaign volunteer like this ... it's an attack on the foundations of our democracy. Democracy requires citizens to participate. This is an attempt to sabotage that process." He was focused now, and angry. You could see it in his face, hear it in his voice. "But it's not going to work. Because come next Saturday, I will be out walking precincts myself." His voice shook. "And I know Rachel will be walking right by me in spirit. Thank you." He turned to go inside.

"Congressman," she shouted out, "are you saying someone deliberately targeted your campaign?"

He turned back, fixed his gaze on her. He knew who she was. "Are you asking me to believe that it's a coincidence at this point?"

"The congressman needs to get home to his wife," Jane Haddad said, as Cason headed inside, followed by the bodyguard. "Angus and I will try to answer your questions as best as we can."

KIMBERLY TEGAN STATEMENT ON MURDER OF RACHEL EISENSTAT

We are heartbroken and furious to hear of the vicious murder of Rachel Eisenstat. Our deepest sympathies to her family, her friends, and everyone at the Cason campaign. The sick thug who did this will be brought to justice. This kind of violence has no place in our political system.

———

American Eagle 1992 @AmericanEagle1992
TOO BAD ABOUT THAT BITCH BUT THIS IS WHAT HAPPENS IF YOU HELP TRAITOR @REPMATTCASON #TRUEMEN #AJLA

49

"**WE NEED TO DO** something for ... for the family." Jane's stare, for once, wasn't fixed on anyone. Instead, she seemed to be looking at the digital photo frame on her desk, the ones with photos of Charlotte and baby Lola. "I don't know what. What's appropriate in a situation like this? Does anyone ... Angus, do you have any ideas?"

Angus shook his head. "I'm sorry, hon. I'm all out right now." He looked as lost as she did.

Headquarters was overheated today. Sweat trickled down Sarah's back.

"I know this is very difficult for everyone," Presley said. It was one of the few times he'd made an appearance at the office. "But ballots start going out in less than two weeks. That means *voting* starts in less than two weeks."

More than half of California voters were registered to vote by mail, Sarah knew. Instead of Election Day here it was closer to Election Month.

"Yeah, Presley, we're aware of that," Angus said. "Seeing as how Jane and I have been working on California campaigns for a couple of decades in her case and eleven years in mine."

Unlike you, he might as well have said.

"Fine." Presley sounded irritated, which was rare. "But we were planning on an all-out precinct blitz, a person-to-person approach. Is that even still on the table?"

Jane shook her head. "I'm meeting with Tomás and Sylvia and I'm setting up calls with Billie at CalDems and Mac at the D Triple C, but ... I don't see how we can ask people to walk precincts, at least while whoever did it's still out there."

"And that's assuming there's just one guy doing it," Angus muttered.

"Even if they volunteer ... if something happened ... " Sarah had never seen Jane look like this—exhausted. Defeated. "I don't want that on the campaign, or on me."

Presley sat up straight, like he was correcting his posture. "All right. So what's our game plan? What are we going to do instead?"

Silence. Presley was supposed to be a big-picture strategy guy, and he was asking for game plans?

No one knew how to respond to what had happened, Sarah realized.

"Matt said he was going to walk precincts next week," she said.

Angus threw up his hands. "Oh my god, that kind of circus? With an army of police and news crews stomping all on people's lawns? That is not gonna help." He turned to Jane. "You're going to talk him out of that, right?"

"I can try. That's not a promise. You know Matt."

"I know that the Capitol Police, the SDPD, and the FBI are not going to be crazy about the idea, so maybe we can prevail upon *them* to tell Matt it's a bad idea. Even if he doesn't care about his own risk, he can't be endangering other people's lives by insisting on doing it."

"Wait," Presley said. He paused. His eyes closed for a moment. He was about to make his pronouncement. "I think he should do it."

"What?" Angus snapped. "Why?"

"Because he said he would on national television. Because that clip will get played over and over again if he doesn't. He's *got* to be strong here. He can't back down." Now Presley smiled and clasped his hands. "Besides … he's not just keeping a promise. He's defending democracy."

Sarah walked out of Jane's office and headed for her cube. She sat down, closed her eyes, and leaned back in her chair. Jane's exhaustion, Angus's despair, Presley's cynicism—she felt like she'd taken all those emotions in, and they'd left a stain of something toxic.

I have to get to work, she thought. The social media feeds … Matt's statement. The video. Something.

Her phone rang. The Communications trill. She didn't want to pick it up.

"Sarah. Hi. It's been a while."

"Wyatt. Yes, it has."

She didn't know if she had the energy to deal with Wyatt and his weird agenda, whatever it was. But maybe he knew something. He did somehow *know* things. And he'd dropped hints about who their enemies might be.

"I'm sorry about that," he said. "Got some things going on this end. But I haven't forgotten you. I saw you on that news show. You did really well."

"Thanks." Like I need *your* approval, she thought suddenly.

"And … I heard about your volunteer. I'm really sorry that happened."

Fuck this, Sarah thought. She *had* been doing really well, but suddenly she could feel the weight of it all crushing her down, making it hard to breathe.

"Yeah, we all are. Is there anything you can do about it?" Her voice shook. "People are shooting at us."

"I wish I could help with that part, Sarah. I really do. If there's any chatter about it, I'll let you know, I promise."

"*Chatter*? But … all that stuff you said about black swans … that there might be a group … "

"Oh, there's *groups*. There's like-minded people talking about things they'd like to see happen. Most of them aren't going to do much more than spout their hate and cheer on the ones who take the next step."

Sarah felt herself go cold. "But some of them do. Take the next step."

"Right. But as far as I can tell, no one's ordering anyone to do these things. No one has to. They're already motivated. They just needed some encouragement."

Of course. In a way, she'd known this all along. "How do we stop it?" She was pretty sure she already knew the answer to that question.

"I don't know. It'd be a lot easier if there was a villain, right? A mastermind we could take out of the equation. Instead it's more like wacko whack-a-mole." He laughed, just once. "Maybe it just has to burn itself out."

How are we supposed to deal with it in the meantime? she wanted to ask. But she figured there was no real point in asking. She already knew the answer to that too.

We'll raise more money, buy more ad time, she thought, hope there were still good slots left that Tegan hadn't grabbed. Send out an extra round of mailers. Microtarget on Facebook. Phone bank like crazy.

"I can help you with one thing," Wyatt said. "Jacob Thresher. How'd you like to know who his dark money backers are? I think you'll find it pretty interesting. Especially when you compare them to Kim Tegan's. Which I can also help you with."

"That would be great," she said. And then she wondered if that was even information they could use when they didn't know where it came from.

Dark money wasn't a matter of public record. That was the whole point. Donors' identities were shielded. If Wyatt had obtained their identities illegally, if he was some kind of whistleblower or spy, if they used this information and it had been hacked from someplace…

"Things like this always find their way back," Jane had said.

"Look for something in the mail in the next couple of days," Wyatt said in her ear, and before she could say anything, he disconnected.

50

WATCH THOSE HEEL STRIKES. *Land on your midfoot. Even strides. Breathe in, breathe out. Relax the shoulders. Relax the hands. One foot in front of the other.*

Don't think. Just keep running.

A half stride behind her, Morgan was breathing hard.

Well, he was a big man. In decent shape, but built like a linebacker, not a runner. Good for short bursts and beating the crap out of someone, but she knew she could outrun him.

He carried a gun in a fanny pack. Lindsey had seen it. She'd asked what kind it was. "A Sig Sauer P226, ma'am." It probably didn't weigh him down much. But she wondered how much good a gun would do, if, say, a car drove up alongside them and started shooting. He took the position closer to the street so his bulk would shield her from the fire, but if he was shot first, would he be able to draw the gun in time?

The smell of exhaust. Francine's hand clutching her arm: "You can't go over there, what if the car comes back? Come inside the house!" That was a good idea, definitely a good idea, but then she thought, you are the candidate's wife. How will it look if you run away and hide? "He won't come back, he knows we're calling 911, and he won't come back." And then she ran across the street, and it was too late to do anything at all.

"Let's turn around," Lindsey said.

There was no point in going on. She couldn't turn off the thoughts in her head, not with a living reminder panting next to her, his heavy footfalls louder than her own.

When she got home, Matt was there waiting for her, standing in the middle of the living room, still dressed in his suit from the flight home. The Padres game was on, but muted. "Where have you been?"

Lindsey spread her hands. "Where does it look like? And hello to you too."

"Welcome home, Congressman." Morgan stepped forward, sticking out his hand. Matt took it, not smiling. "I'll just head to the hotel, then," Morgan said.

"Don't be silly. I made you run with me. At least have a shower first."

"Thanks, ma'am. If that's your preference." He trotted off to the guestroom.

"Jesus, Linds, you went running?" Matt paced around the room. "Is that what you've been doing while I was gone?"

First he'd said he'd stay in San Diego and miss the vote. She'd talked him out of that. He was one of the sponsors of the bill, and it was important, even if they didn't have the votes to pass it. Then he'd tried to convince her to come with her. "What, and sleep on the hide-a-bed in your office?" They really didn't have the money for a DC apartment. He was next in line for a room in a shared condo with two other congressmen from California—that is, *if* he got reelected. "We'll stay in a hotel," he'd said. "Someplace nice. Let's make it a getaway."

She'd turned him down. "There's a vigil for Rachel tomorrow night. One of us needs to be there. And she wouldn't want you missing the vote."

"Fine," he'd finally said. "Then Morgan stays."

It hadn't been worth arguing about, and if she was being honest, having an armed policeman around was some small comfort, under the circumstances.

"There's a shooter out there," Matt said now, "and you're going *jogging*?"

"I took Morgan." She listened for the sound of running water. "Can we wait until he's gone to do this?"

Do what?

She wasn't even sure.

By the time Morgan left and she'd showered too, Matt had changed into shorts and a T-shirt and parked himself on the couch in front of the TV, 394 Pale Ale in hand. Tony Gwynn's beer, and Matt's favorite game day choice. "For luck," he'd say. "Maybe it'll inspire them to hit."

Great, Lindsey thought. So we'll be having this conversation with the Padres. If we're even having it at all.

She sat down next to him. "Are you still planning on doing the precinct walk?"

Matt muted the game. "Yeah. Yeah, I am."

"Then I want to go with you."

"What?" He stared at her in open-mouthed astonishment. "Absolutely not."

"Why? Because if you're going to tell me it's not safe, then you shouldn't do it either."

"Of *course* it's safe, I wouldn't do it if it wasn't safe, it's just ... I don't understand. Why do you want to do this, after what happened?"

"*You're* asking me this, Matt? *You* are? The man who almost got *shot*?"

"*I'm* the reason they're shooting! I'm the reason Rachel got killed!" He was yelling now, his cheeks flushed.

She couldn't tell him to calm down, that never worked, and she'd been close to yelling too. She drew in a deep breath.

Why *did* she want to go?

"Matt. If you're doing this to honor her, then I'm certainly entitled to as well. And if it's safe enough for you, then it's safe enough for me."

He shook his head. Rested his forehead on the heels of his hands. "It's better if I go by myself."

"Why? Why do you need to do this on your own? Do I send the wrong message or something? You can't be a hero if I'm around?"

Silence.

Oh my god, Lindsey thought. That was horrible. *I* am horrible.

"I'm sorry," she said. "That was a shitty thing to say. I'm not … I'm not in control right now. I haven't been sleeping. I'm just … "

"That's why." His voice was flat. "You shouldn't have to know what it feels like. And now you do." Now he looked at her, his eyes red and glassy. "I don't think anything's going to happen. But if something does … I don't want you to be there."

She felt two things at once: a swell of affection and a fresh surge of anger.

"I appreciate that you want to protect me. I do. But … look, we're either partners or we're not. I can't keep doing things this way. I just can't."

"What do you want me to do, Linds? Just tell me." He sounded weary.

"I want …" What *did* she want? "I want us to stop fighting so much. I want to feel like we're in this together. I want us to be close again."

He let out a deep sigh. "How can I when you're angry all the time?"

She almost stood up and left the room. She wanted to tell him to fuck off, then put on her shoes again and run until she was tired.

He was right.

"I'm angry because you're unavailable. And you're unavailable because I'm angry. Great."

He closed his eyes for a moment and chuckled once. "That's funny."

You started it when you screwed around on me, she wanted to say, but she stopped herself. Was that really fair? Did it even matter at this point, who "started it"? She deserved a portion of the blame, and she knew it.

"Yeah. We're a pair."

He turned to her. "So, what are we going to do?"

It was a good question. She thought about it. Tried to count up the reasons she was angry. They didn't all have to do with Matt. She was missing something, something that had to do with *her*.

Maybe she should try to get pregnant. Or adopt.

Or … run for city council. The seat in their district would be open in two years. There were so many things that could be improved in their community, in this city. She'd enjoy doing that.

Lindsey felt something in her chest start to relax.

"We finish the campaign," she said. "We try to get along. When the election's over, we can worry about the rest of it."

He nodded. He was sitting with his elbows on his thighs and his hands clasped between his knees. "I don't want to split up," he said.

"I don't either."

"Then let's not." His voice was soft. He reached out his hand and rested it on top of hers, slid his thumb between her thumb and index finger, stroked the crease of her palm.

All his attention was on her, for once.

51

"**If we aren't careful** how we handle this, it's going to look like a stunt." Jane took off her glasses and rubbed the bridge of her nose.

"You mean it isn't?" Angus popped open a bottle of Stone IPA left over from a fundraiser, handing a bottle and the opener to Sarah.

"Not as far as Matt's concerned."

It was late, after ten. The volunteers had gone home. The three of them sat, not in Jane's office, but in chairs near the kitchen. Angus had switched off the overhead fluorescents and turned on the various desk lamps instead—"mood lighting," he'd said.

Sarah knew she should be tired. The hours had been brutal lately, and she hadn't slept well last night. But she was too wired to feel her own fatigue right now.

Wyatt sent the packet to her house. It had arrived yesterday. How had he known where she lived?

Don't bother asking, Sarah told herself again. As long as no one else knows.

Whatever Wyatt was about, she didn't think he wanted to hurt her.

She'd opened the mailing box—it actually had Wyatt's name and a post office box as a return address. So the name's fake for sure, she'd thought. A six-inch-thick stack of documents that looked like tax returns. She'd flipped through the pages, torn between wanting and not wanting to know.

Dark money made its way into campaigns through 501(c)(4)s, "social welfare" organizations that were allowed to do political work. They could not legally coordinate with candidates' campaigns, but that was about the only thing they couldn't do, and they skirted those laws all the time. And with donors' identities shielded in 501(c)(4)s, it was nearly impossible to tell where the money came from. One 501(c)(4) could donate to another, obscuring the money trail even further. And they could also donate to 527s, organizations that could support candidates directly.

There was one organization she'd recognized right away: the Committee for American Values. They'd been pumping out the worst of the hit pieces on Matt, even nastier than Tegan's.

If she went through all the documents, she'd find links between the donors who funded the Committee for American Values, the donors funding Tegan, and the donors funding Jacob Thresher, she was certain. Wyatt had pretty much come out and said it.

But she hadn't gone through all of it. If this stuff had been illegally obtained— and how could it have been *legally* obtained? The only source of donors' names would be the 501(c)(4)s themselves and the IRS—then maybe it was better if she didn't know.

The documents took up most of the space in her big messenger bag, a literal heavy weight on her shoulder. There was no way she wanted to leave them at home.

"What do we do about media?" Jane asked. "We want coverage, but we don't want a circus."

"You think there's that many clowns in the clown car who'd be interested?"

"With everything that's happened? Sadly, yes." Jane stood up and opened the door to the minifridge for a bottle of beer. "They're going to want to see how Matt handles himself. How people react to him."

"And hey, there's always a chance someone else might get shot. They wouldn't want to miss that." Angus stretched out his long legs, tilted his head back. "I gotta say, this is a shitty way to get earned media."

"Yes, it is." Jane sat down and took a sip of her beer. "But we're just going to have to try to turn it into something positive." She sighed heavily. "Presley's not wrong. It's a branding opportunity."

"Okay. So what do we do, send out a press release?"

"I don't know. I don't think so. What if we get too many responses?"

"Optimistically," Angus said.

"Optimistically. Say there's a lot of interest. We really don't want a half dozen news crews following Matt around a precinct. There's security considerations, for one thing."

"How's that piece going to work?" Angus asked. "SDPD and the Capitol Police and, I don't know, the FBI are all going to get together and game plan? That's not really going to happen for a precinct walk, is it?" He shook his head, huffed out a laugh. "Because that'll look like a great use of public resources. It'll feed right into Tegan's narrative about a wasteful Washington insider and Thresher's line about a paranoid warmonger with anger-management issues."

Jane chuckled. "Yeah. Isn't this fun?" She closed her eyes for a moment. "It won't be that elaborate. We'll let all of them know and maybe ask for a squad car. We just need to find a precinct with limited entrance and egress and keep the location quiet till the last minute."

"And disguise that Morgan dude as a volunteer?" Angus was giggling now. "Can you see him canvassing voters? 'Stand clear of the door, ma'am, and keep your hands where I can see them. Now tell me how important you think a clean energy economy is to District 54. Don't you think it will enhance our national security as well as create good jobs in our community?'"

Jane snorted, spraying a little beer. She lifted her hands, struggling not to laugh, finally managing to swallow.

Sarah found herself smiling too. It really was funny, in a horrible way. And seeing Angus and Jane like this, seeing who they really were …

This is what it feels like to belong to something, she thought suddenly. To care about other people.

Then she remembered Wyatt's package, stuffed in her messenger bag.

"Okay, okay." Angus was still grinning. "We don't want too many news crews. So what do we do, give someone an exclusive?" He turned to Sarah. "Our pal Casey Cheng?"

"Well, Casey's definitely been friendly to us," Sarah said. Her mouth was dry from nerves, thinking about what was in her bag. She took a sip of her beer. "And her stories give some context to Matt's claim that the campaign is being deliberately targeted to advance a political agenda."

There was a moment of silence.

"Yes," Jane said. "That's what's going on, isn't it." Like she hadn't really thought of it in exactly those terms. "Okay." Jane straightened up. Refocusing. "We definitely want Casey, assuming she's interested. But I think we need to be careful that we're not playing favorites here. Or that we're not being too obvious about playing favorites."

"How about a pool?" Angus said. "You know, tell them because of security we can't have too many crews, and see if they'll agree to pool the coverage. Then offer a press event with Matt after."

"I like it. One camera. They can take turns if they want and share the footage." Jane turned to Sarah. "Why don't you get in touch with Casey, give her a heads-up?" She smiled. "We can give her a little extra access, on the down-low."

And suddenly Sarah knew what to do with Wyatt's package.

———

"Another campaign worker has been shot in a hotly contested congressional election, this time in Florida—"

"Shit," Casey said.

Rose paused the video on her laptop. "Yeah. At least this one didn't die."

The story had made the national news. Probably because of the Cason shooting, Casey thought. Cason was national news now, something similar happened elsewhere, ergo…

"Do you think there's a connection?"

"You mean, are those assholes tweeting and posting with the True Men and AJLA hashtags?" Rose leaned back in her swivel chair. "Yeah. Your guess is as good as mine what that actually means."

Rose had photos of her and Diego up in her cube now. One was the classic heads-together selfie, with Rose holding a particularly over-the-top umbrella drink in a tiki mug. The cube walls had a metal surface, so you could stick things up there with magnets, which Casey had always liked. You could put up documents pertaining to a story, notes, cartoons, kid's drawings. Casey had even had a photo of Paul up in her cube, briefly.

"So what are we up to?" she said. "A campaign worker shot in Florida, firebombing of a campaign headquarters in Flint, shots fired at a congresswoman's car in Pennsylvania, racist flyers in…?"

"I think it's North Carolina."

"And we've got people praising all these actions using the hashtags."

"Yeah. But we don't know what that really means. Are any of them involved with the incidents themselves? Are any of them *connected* or are they just randos who jerk each other off online?"

Casey found herself staring at the photo of Rose and Diego. Diego had on a Hawaiian shirt with giant tiki heads on it. Rose wore what looked like a Hawaiian print dress from the sixties and a chunky Bakelite bead necklace. Maybe they'd gone to the annual Tiki Convention at the Hanalei Hotel in Mission Valley.

I want someone to go with to a tiki convention, she thought. Except maybe not to a tiki convention. More like, a trip to Bhutan.

"Obviously we can't speculate too much on that," she said. "But we can talk about the connections that we do know about. The phenomena. Why do they use the hashtags? What do these guys support? Who do they hate? Maybe we can get a couple of the people tweeting this stuff to talk to us."

"Just message them and see who bites?"

"Sure. Why not?" She had a flash of that pompous ass George "I'm just a storyteller" Drake. "There's going to be somebody in that crowd who's enough of a narcissist to want to spout his nonsense on TV. There always is."

Her phone rang—the *X-Files* theme, the ringtone she used for sources.

She looked at the screen. Sarah Price.

"Hello?"

"It's Sarah." Her voice was low, but it wasn't weak, or hesitant. "I have something for you."

52

"IF WE DIDN'T THINK it was safe, we wouldn't be doing it."

Lindsey Cason stood next to her husband, their bodies nearly touching. Funny, Casey thought, in all the campaign events she'd covered so far, she'd never seen the two of them together like this. She knew that Lindsey was very much involved—the finance director, if Casey remembered right, and money was what made campaigns run. But she'd only ever seen Lindsey at a distance.

The campaign suggested doing the take at the park—the South Clairemont park where Lucas Derry had killed five people and tried to kill Matt Cason. Matt and Lindsey stood by a picnic table, where the bright sunlight was muted by the shade of a big tree—a hot, dry day for the last weekend in September. To the left and behind them was a memorial to the dead and the wounded, a small fountain with a stone obelisk in its center where the names of the victims were inscribed, the water burbling from it gently. Casey couldn't believe the city had moved so quickly on it, even though the money had been donated.

The memorial was just visible in the shot, which was a nice touch, Casey thought. Diego had made sure to get some B-roll of the fountain on its own—it would be a good visual for a voice-over, Casey thought. "A poignant reminder of the true cost of hatred." Something like that.

What the camera didn't show, and wouldn't, were the campaign staffers in the background: Angus, Sarah, and the big man with the shaved head—"Our driver, Morgan," Matt had said.

Driver, Casey thought. Hah.

For a moment, Matt seemed to scan the park. Looking for trouble, maybe. Or just remembering that day, and what had happened here. He circled an arm around Lindsey's shoulders, and she wrapped hers around his waist. He wore a white, open-necked shirt, rolled up at the sleeves, and chinos, she a colorful print blouse and capris. They were both a little taller than average, both fit, Lindsey with a blush to her cheeks that wasn't about makeup.

If you wanted a picture of a solid, supportive couple, this was it.

Funny, Casey thought again.

"But you must be a little worried," she said. "We've just had a report of another campaign volunteer shot at in Texas, in another battleground district. Thankfully no injuries this time, but—"

"And that's exactly why we're determined to walk." Lindsey's voice was strong. Steady. "We're not going to let thugs who are afraid of democracy intimidate us. Not in our city."

She sounds like a candidate for something, Casey thought.

"I couldn't put it better." Matt gave Lindsey's shoulders a squeeze. "Casey, we'd love to chat a little longer, but we need to get going. See you at the press op later?"

"Definitely."

She watched as "driver" Morgan escorted them over to the car, a black SUV with tinted windows. Sarah and Angus followed, Sarah turning once to acknowledge Casey with a small wave.

She'd see Sarah later too.

"The press op's at the North Clairemont Community Park—it's next to the precinct we're walking," Sarah had said on the phone. "I'll leave the walk early and meet you there ahead of time. There's a picnic table behind the restrooms in the southeast corner. Bring a backpack or a bag—you'll need one to carry them."

"What?"

"Documents."

That was all Sarah would tell her.

"I better head out," Diego said.

Casey felt a knot of dread in the pit of her stomach. She knew it was irrational, that Matt Cason wouldn't be doing this walk if it were dangerous, but she didn't want Diego to be the pool photographer. Rose was freaking out about it, for one thing.

"You don't have to do it," she said again. There were four local news orgs participating in the pool, last she'd heard. Let one of them supply the photographer.

"Too late now." Diego shrugged. "I flipped Charlie at News 12 for it. I lost. It's no big deal."

If he was feeling nerves about going, he didn't show any.

"So, what do you want to do?" he asked. "Come over with me and Jason in the truck and wait for the press op?"

"Ugh," Casey said. She didn't really want to sit in the van for a couple of hours while the walk went on, but the campaign had made it very clear: One photographer. No reporters.

"Actually, maybe you should hang at the Starbucks in Clairemont Square, someplace like that," Diego said suddenly. "It's close to the park."

That sounded good. She could get some work done and walk over for the press op when it was time. On the other hand, if something *did* happen ... shouldn't she be as close to the scene as possible?

"Truck's fine," she said. "At least it's not the Prius."

Diego looked almost embarrassed. "I don't know. Maybe you shouldn't wait in the truck all that time."

She thought about it. "Right," she said. It hadn't occurred to her until he'd said it. She was still getting death threats, and sitting for an hour and a half in a van clearly marked NEWS 9 was probably not a great idea.

She gave him a quick hug, his backpack and the camera still balanced on his shoulder making it a little awkward. "Just be careful, okay?"

"No worries," he said. "After we wrap tonight, Rose wants to go for a beer and a bite. You in?"

"Sure," she said. "Definitely."

It's fine, she told herself, watching him head to the van. But she still didn't like it.

Everyone thought she was crazy for volunteering to go on the walk.

"Honey," Angus had said, "you really do not need to do that."

"I just want to get some Snaps and things for Social. And I'm not worried." Not about getting shot at, anyway.

"Okay," he'd finally said. "As long as none of it's live. We don't want to clue any haters in to the location."

She'd nodded, though she knew a precaution like that only went so far. What would stop someone they met in the precinct from tweeting out where they were?

But she was really more worried about Angus having decided to come with them. "Somebody's gotta candidate wrangle, and I'm not asking a volunteer to do it," he'd said.

She didn't want any questions asked when she needed to slip away and go to the park to meet Casey Cheng.

She knew she was taking a risk. Things like this could get back to the campaign. But if it did, it couldn't go any further than her. The damage could be contained.

Mail ballots went out in less than a week. By the time Casey and her crew researched what Wyatt had given her and prepared a story, voting would most likely be underway.

If it somehow got traced back to her, hopefully the election would already be over.

Maybe she was screwing up her chance for a future with Matt's office in DC, but maybe she didn't have a chance at that anyway.

After everything that had happened, with everything that was still going on, what mattered was that he won.

53

"CONGRESSMAN, I RECOMMEND YOU let me knock on the doors and do a quick check for security before you engage with the household members."

Matt snorted. "Okay, these are people who are committed supporters, soft supporters, and persuadables. I might not be able to convince every one of them to vote for me, but I really don't expect any of them to greet me at the door with a shotgun."

"Well, you never know with some of those persuadables," Angus said, his voice sliding low.

"He's joking," Lindsey said. "Morgan, we really do appreciate your concern. But I think we can handle the knocking on doors."

Watching Matt and Lindsey, Sarah felt a hollowness in her chest, a tightness in her throat. That could have been me, she thought briefly. I could have had him. The moment came and went, and she'd done nothing.

But you wouldn't have had him, she thought. Not like that, and not for long.

What was their relationship about? she wondered. Why did they stay together? She didn't know if she'd ever understand how people made it work.

Morgan had parked the Expedition at the beginning of the block, on the border of the precinct they were going to walk. A police car slowly cruised the street. Another was stationed on the corner. This was the biggest street in the precinct, the street you'd take to get to the boulevard that led to the freeway. The most likely place that someone would enter the neighborhood.

It's fine, Sarah thought. We wouldn't be doing it if it wasn't okay.

"Do you want to do a Snap?" she asked. "Just a quick one, before we go to the first house."

Matt grinned. "Snap away."

Sarah pressed the red Record button on her iPhone screen. Matt circled his arm around Lindsey's back, resting his hand on her deltoid.

"It's a beautiful day, and we're ready to knock on some doors," he said, smiling.

54

A ~~POIGNANT~~ ~~STARK~~ *TOUCHING reminder of the true cost of* ~~hatred~~ *political extremism*

What was it? *Was* it political extremism that motivated Lucas Derry?

Casey leaned back in her chair, sipped her coffee, and stared at the words on her screen, words she'd typed. She'd found a seat at a small table at the back of the Starbucks, where the hiss and steam of the espresso machine and the grinding of the blender competed with the soft Brazilian jazz playing on the sound system. A good place to work, but she was struggling with the script.

Focus on Lucas Derry, she told herself. What did she know about him? That he hated Matt Cason. Hated his immigrant coworker. Hated two of his neighbors enough to shoot them down in cold blood. Hated her, for that matter.

From the literature they'd found in his apartment and what he'd posted online, he'd hated a lot of things. Women. People of color.

"The State." He'd liked gaming, and comics, and guns. A lot of people liked those things, and most of them weren't crazy, murderous assholes. What made Lucas different?

She supposed you could construct an ideology of sorts from the scraps Lucas had left behind, from the people he'd killed and tried to kill, from his targeting of Matt Cason. Depressingly predictable stuff.

He wasn't getting what he deserved.

Other people were taking things from him.

True Men Will Rise.

But the main residue was anger. Raw rage that had attached itself to disconnected slogans. Maybe that was all it was.

Hatred.

Her phone buzzed—a text from Diego, sent to her and Rose.

So far some good shots of Cason and his wife, a couple cool reactions from voters. Nothing exciting.

Good!!

That one was from Rose.

Casey checked the time. 2:36.

The press op was scheduled for an hour from now. Backtiming, if she hit at 6:15 (they weren't going to lead with this package, unless something awful happened), the script needed to be in and approved by 5:15. In a perfect world, that meant the footage they were using should be logged and reviewed by 4:15.

Well, this wasn't a perfect world, but they could probably make it. Diego would have an idea what the best takes from the walk were, which gave them an advantage over the other members of the pool, even though they'd all have the same footage to work from. Rose was on deck, ready to shape what was in the can while they covered the press op.

This wasn't a big story on its own, Casey thought. It was news because that poor woman had died and campaign workers in other parts of the country had been wounded or shot at, because at this point, the campaign was such a circus that anything associated with it was news of a sort. But "Matt Cason heroically walking a precinct in the face of threats and violence"? They were basically being set up to broadcast a press release from the campaign, no matter how artistically they cut the segment together.

Kim Tegan's probably wondering who she has to shoot to get this kind of coverage, Casey thought.

Were the other perps inspired by Lucas Derry, or by the unknown killer who'd shot Rachel Eisenstat? Were they organized in any way? Did they share a common ideology?

Did a hashtag or two constitute an ideology?

We can make it a story by raising the questions, Casey thought. But they weren't going to be able to provide the answers. There wasn't enough time for that, and if Detective Helton or the FBI knew, they weren't telling her.

Rose would have to take the script from here. She needed to head over to the park to meet Sarah Price.

———

Casey took a Lyft to the park. Otherwise it would have been a fifteen-minute walk, and though she was walking a lot better these days, she didn't want to get too sweaty if she could help it, since she'd be on camera later. The day had grown hotter, with dry winds kicking up—a Santa Ana on the way.

She had the driver drop her off in the main parking lot. A News 12 van was already waiting there, an hour ahead of the press op. She wondered who else would show up for this. So far, it wasn't like there was a lot of news to report.

Casey headed across the park, toward the southeast corner and the restrooms where Sarah wanted to meet. Funny, she thought. The last time she'd been to this park, to this neighborhood, it was when she and Rose had ambushed Alan Jay Chastain's mother, Helen Scott. She'd had a terrible time walking then, or standing for any length of time, or doing much of anything, really. Now, she was still carrying Trusty for the intermittent spasms and the times she got really fatigued, but she could do without the cane for short walks like this. How long had it been since she spoke to Helen? Three, four months?

She thought of Helen Scott, pictured her heavy, strained face, her faded brown hair, the two dogs pulling on their leashes. How was she doing? Casey wondered. What was her life like? Had the outrage circus moved on to newer targets? Could there ever be such a thing as a normal life for her?

Here were the restrooms Sarah had mentioned. Plenty of people were out in the park today, playing on the tennis and basketball courts, picnicking on the grass, tossing Frisbees around. She passed what looked like a kid's birthday party, with bunches of aluminum balloons marking the occasion. But Sarah was right, this particular corner was relatively quiet: there were people coming in and out of the restrooms, but no one wanted to hang out there for any length of time.

Behind the cinderblock building, it was even quieter. There was nothing here but a lone table and two trashcans, one for recyclables. A clump of trees formed a sort of screen behind that.

Casey sat down on the bench with her back to the table and checked her phone. She'd erred on the side of being a little early for the meeting, since Sarah wasn't exactly sure when she'd be able to get away.

What did Sarah have for her?

Her phone buzzed—a text from Rose. EVERYTHING OKAY? HAVEN'T HEARD FROM DIEGO SINCE LAST TEXT.

FAR AS I KNOW, Casey typed. I'M SURE IT'S FINE. THEY'RE ONLY WALKING ANOTHER 45 MIN.

YOU IN THE PARK?

YEAH, JUST WAITING

"Casey?"

She almost dropped her phone. Her heart slammed against the wall of her chest.

Maintain situational awareness, she heard Helton say in her head. But she hadn't done that.

Standing in front of her was a young man. She blinked a few times—the sun was behind him, and it was hard to make out his features at first. Pale but not entirely white. Mixed race, maybe white and Asian. She felt a little relieved by that.

Then he sat down next to her, and she saw the gun in his hand.

A small pistol. Black.

"I saw you go into the Starbucks. I waited for you outside. You didn't even notice." He sounded excited. Happy. "I followed you on my bike."

Their legs were angled toward each other, their knees almost forming the base of a V. Like we're doing an interview, Casey thought briefly, the way you cheat your angle on a couch.

She could hear in the distance the slap of basketballs on cement, the rattle of the wooden backboards and chain-metal hoops.

So this was the Big Empty. Average height, average build, with hunched shoulders. Younger than she was. Practically a kid.

Why hadn't he killed her yet?

"I thought about doing it at the Starbucks, but I decided to wait," he said.

"Why?" she managed. Her mouth was so dry that the word caught in her throat.

"Because of what A.J. said. That he wished he'd seen their faces." He was staring at hers, now. Taking it all in, his eyes wide with a kind of wonder.

Maybe he didn't really want to do it.

Keep him talking, she thought.

"Did you know A.J.? You were friends?"

He nodded. "Yeah. Me and him and Lucas. We used to hang out sometimes."

He wore a T-shirt, and she could see a square of Saran Wrap on his forearm, the one that held the gun, kept in place by semitransparent tape.

"What's your name?"

"Brandon," he said, almost shyly.

What do I say now? she thought briefly. *It's nice to meet you?*

"Brandon. Look … A.J. … .A.J. is dead. And Lucas might as well be. You don't have to end up the same way."

"Who says I will?" His voice sounded harder.

You're losing him.

"Prison, then? For the rest of your life?"

He shrugged. "At least I'll have done something big."

This isn't working, she thought. It's not working. Think of something else.

She tilted her head toward his bandaged forearm, trying not to look at the gun, at his finger moving on the trigger. "Is that a new tattoo?"

He nodded again. "You want to see it?"

"Sure," she said. "Yeah."

He pulled off the wrap and the bandage. "I got it for Lucas," he said. "And for you."

A circle with two crossed lines inside, like a plus sign, with a starburst in its center, the colors bright, the lines red and raw.

The gun in his hand was facing sideways, so he could show her the tattoo. Now it slowly righted itself, the barrel aimed at her chest.

From over his left shoulder, Casey saw movement: a person, someone approaching.

A woman. Sarah.

Casey quickly glanced away, back to the gun.

Had Brandon noticed?

Don't look at her. Keep his attention on you.

Casey focused on Brandon's eyes. They were bright, and he was smiling. "True Men, right?" she said.

"Uh-huh. He's a genius. He talks about what's really going on."

Sarah was just a few yards away now. Out of the corner of her eye, Casey could see her blurry figure advance, making a wide circle toward the front of the bench.

Oh god, what do I do? If I yell, he'll shoot.

Could Sarah see the gun? His right hand, the one that held it, was the hand farther away from her, closer to the table's edge.

Sarah stood in front of them now, and Casey still wouldn't look at her.

Please god, please let her notice something's wrong.

"Casey? Am I interrupting something?"

Brandon turned, the barrel of the gun swinging along with his head, toward Sarah.

There was no time left. Casey let out a scream that came from deep in her gut, grabbed Brandon's wrist with both hands, and pushed as hard as she could, slamming the back of his hand into the edge of the table, and the gun went off, an explosive *crack,* and she slammed his hand into the table again, but he didn't let go. Now his free hand formed a fist and smashed into the side of her head, and she saw a burst of stars but she kept her grip on his wrist, and that was when Sarah jumped on him with a grunt, knocking him down onto the bench, his head dangling off the end. Casey saw her dig her knee into his belly, wrap her hands around his neck, and Casey tightened her grip on his wrist, forcing his arm down until something popped in his shoulder, and he made a sound in his throat, a choked-off scream.

His fingers unclenched, and the pistol dropped to the ground.

"We got him," Casey gasped. "We got him."

55

(BEGIN VIDEO CLIP: BRANDON GATES IN GREEN JAIL SCRUBS, ARM IN SLING, APPEARING IN COURT) CRAIG BROOKES, NEWS 9 ANCHOR (V.O.): As expected, Gates was charged with the murder of campaign worker Rachel Eisenstat and the attempted murder of reporter Casey Cheng. In the case of Cheng, his lawyers argue that he harbors an obsessive fixation on her and his intent was merely to frighten, not to harm. Casey Cheng, however, insists that she owes her life to Sarah Price's intervention.

(END VIDEO CLIP) CASEY CHENG, WITH SARAH PRICE (IN STUDIO). CHENG: It's safe to say I would not be here if it weren't for Sarah *(SHE LOOKS AT PRICE, GIVES HER ARM A SQUEEZE)*. She was incredibly brave. She just tackled him like she was a mixed martial arts star or something *(LAUGHS)*.

BROOKES: Do you have any martial arts training, Sarah?

PRICE: No *(SHRUGS)*. I bench-press.

BROOKES: Casey, I understand you have some news about the perpetrators of the online harassment you've been experiencing. An arrest has been made, hasn't it?

CHENG: Yes, it has. This gentleman appears to be one of the ring-leaders, and I will say that the frequency of the threats has dropped considerably since his arrest. His name is Stephen Orlov, and as it turns out, he runs George Drake's fan club.

BROOKES: Wow. And ... is there any evidence that George Drake himself was involved?

CHENG: I think it's too early in the investigation to say (SMILES). But I'm sure the authorities will be looking very closely at that possibility.

BROOKES: Casey, after everything that's happened ... how are you coping?

CHENG: Well ... right now, I'm taking a few days off. And after the election's over, I plan on taking a long vacation. Maybe to Bhutan. I hear it's the happiest place on earth.

BROOKES: And you, Sarah? You've been through a lot in the last few months. What are your plans?

PRICE: Finish the campaign.

BROOKES: Finish the campaign. You're okay with going back to that? You've been in serious danger now, twice. You're not afraid to keep going?

PRICE: I actually feel better than I did. Because that first time, in the park, there wasn't anything I could do about it. This time (SMILES), this time, there was.

———

"Casey Cheng has got to be the luckiest bitch in local news."

"No kidding."

392

"Three times, man," Charlie said as he swapped his camcorder's battery. "Three guys with guns. That's just freaky. I mean, not if she was covering Afghanistan, but San Diego?"

Gabrielle felt her cheeks flush. "Well, this is embarrassing. I thought you were talking about the stories she's been filing."

"That too."

Charlie had worked in Afghanistan and Iraq for a couple of years, and even though he swore he'd come to San Diego to "chill and collect a paycheck," she sometimes thought covering this beat was a big bore for him.

Casey worked hard for those stories, Gabrielle told herself. You shouldn't think of hard work as luck. She didn't want to be one of those women who cut down other women, just because she was ever so slightly jealous.

Also, let's not forget that that shit's terrifying, she thought.

She wondered how Casey was handling it all. They weren't exactly friends, but they'd met a few times on stories and at functions, had chatted over drinks. Everybody pretty much knew everybody in this business. Gabrielle still couldn't get over the way that Casey had kept going after the same damn things that had nearly gotten her killed in the first place. But then, Casey was a little intense.

Not that Gabrielle had anything against her. When she'd gotten shot covering Crooked Arrow, Gabrielle had cried. She'd thought about it for weeks, thoughts like, "that could happen to me, that could happen to any of us," and she kept asking herself if what she was doing was worth it.

But the fact was, nothing like that was likely to happen to her. What happened at Crooked Arrow, what happened at the park, things like that hardly ever happened in places like San Diego, just like Charlie had said. They were a statistical anomaly.

What had seemed like a huge conspiracy was just three sick losers with guns.

If something like that happens to somebody else, then it's not going to happen to you. Just like if an airplane crashes, the flight you're taking the next day won't, because that roll of the dice already came up.

Which she also knew was not how probability and chance actually worked, but whatever.

"You ready to go do this thing?" she asked Charlie.

Charlie slammed the News 12 Expedition's door shut and clicked the lock in his key fob. "Yeah, let's do it."

Another day, another Kim Tegan campaign event.

———

" ... and we're gonna continue to do great things together!" Kim Tegan pumped her fist. "We're gonna protect our borders and protect our American values!"

Tegan's headquarters was decked out in red, white, and blue bunting and star-spangled balloons. There were the usual big bowls of super-sized Costco snack mix, some wine and beer and soft drinks. She'd gotten a good turnout. The volunteers and staff were a mix primarily of older white women and younger white men, with a few older men and young women mixed in. Some of the younger guys were from the local and state party, Gabrielle guessed. Both sides were putting in everything they could throw at this race.

Most of the local news affiliates had sent a camera or a team out to cover Tegan's appearance, a quick hit at most for the 11 p.m. show. As Tegan finished speaking, several of the photographers were already headed for the door. Gabrielle would have loved to pack it in herself, but as tempting as that was, they'd already come out here and Tegan promised press availability.

Anyway, it was too late. Tegan's media guy was approaching.

"Hey there," he said, all smiles. "We thought we'd do the press availability out back—there's still some nice light."

"Sounds good."

She and Charlie followed him through the party and through the back door, out to the parking lot.

———

Three crews had stuck around for Tegan, including News 9.

"So how's Casey doing?" Gabrielle asked Hunter, their on-air guy.

"You know, she seems okay. A little wound-up, I mean, more so than usual," he added, his voice dropping a couple of notes.

So she wasn't the only one who thought Casey was a tad intense.

"She took a couple days off but made sure to give us the interview first. Now she's back. Swears she's taking a long vacation soon as the election's over. Personally I think she's interviewing for a national gig."

Good for her, Gabrielle thought. She didn't want to be Casey Cheng, when it came right down to it. She had a husband and a five-year-old, and what she really wanted at this point in her life was less stress, more money, and better hours.

A seat at the anchor desk, that would be good.

"Hi, guys!"

Kim Tegan smiled and waved at the assembled crews. The media staffer guided her toward the building's wall—a terra cotta–colored stucco, it would make an unobtrusive backdrop for the shot. Otherwise you risked having someone walk into the shot from the parking lot.

The light *was* nice, the setting sun casting a diffuse, golden glow. A few campaign staffers and volunteers stood to one side, watching.

"Hi, Kim," Gabrielle called out right away. "You've made some remarks recently about the dangers of extremist language, and you've decried the negativity going back and forth on this campaign. But we haven't seen any real letup in attack ads coming from you or from Cason. In this last two weeks before the election, will we see a more positive tone from you?"

Tegan hesitated, her forehead wrinkling. "I think so," she finally said. "Yes. I mean ... I can't do anything about the PACs supporting me. The tone they take isn't something we can control. But ... " She shook her head. "I meant what I said before. We're not enemies, we're opponents."

"True men will rise!" someone screamed, and Gabrielle turned and saw a young man standing with the volunteers, clutching a pistol, opening fire.

56

SAN DIEGO, CALIF. (AP) — CONGRESSIONAL candidate Kimberly *Tegan was shot and killed today outside of her campaign headquarters by a campaign volunteer who opened fire as Tegan prepared to take questions from reporters. A warning: the footage in the following links contains graphic images and may be upsetting to some readers.*

———

There were three versions of the killing, three takes from slightly different angles, the camera moving at different moments, depending on how the photographers reacted, capturing different nuances of the same event.

Casey watched them all on her laptop, sitting on her couch at home, a place where she felt safe.

In one you saw the young man's face clearly; in another, it was easier to see the gun. One captured the bullets tearing into Kim Tegan's torso. The reputable news sources blurred that part, but you could find the unedited video on the web if you searched for it.

Then comes a point where the streams diverge. Two cameras hit the ground, the photographers taking cover the way they'd been instructed in their risk-management seminars. One manages to resume taping, a blur of feet and bodies, shots and screams. One does not, but the other camera captures what he does: crawls to Tegan's side, tries to comfort her, because there's nothing else to be done, you can see the blood pooling around her body, and there's too much of it.

The third camera captures what happens to the gunman after Tegan is shot. This one was operated by Charlie from News 12, who doesn't take cover, who remains upright, because he worked in Afghanistan and Iraq and is known to be a little crazy. One of Tegan's security staff comes briefly into frame, a big man with a shaved head and gym-built shoulders, his weapon clasped in both hands the way professionals are taught to hold a pistol, and he pops off two quick shots, and the gunman spins and drops.

———————

The gunman was 22-year-old Jeremy Evan McIntyre, who'd come to San Diego from Phoenix less than a month ago, specifically to volunteer on Tegan's campaign.

"We never suspected a thing," tearful staffers said. "He was a nice, quiet young man who seemed like he just wanted to help."

His family and friends paint a more troubling picture, of a young man who as a college sophomore had been treated for suicidal ideation and paranoid hallucinations, but who was nonetheless able to buy a gun in Phoenix two years later and take it with him west to San Diego.

He'd been obsessed with the Phoenix cinema massacre, according to several witnesses, and he mentioned wanting to work for Tegan because she promised to do something about terrorists.

He'd bought the gun "for self-defense."

"We were concerned when he left home but thought he was finally getting on track in a new city," his family said. "We didn't know about the gun."

As to what McIntyre thought he was doing, why he decided that Kim Tegan needed to die, the best anyone can do is guess. McIntyre left few clues, and he is not alive to answer.

57

RIP #KimTegan That cowardly murderer was not #TrueMen. You will have justice #Remember-KimT

LOL u dumb cucks, #KimTegan pwned U she was so busy blowing matt cason because theyre on the same side it was all a show #TrueMen

#KimTegan wasn't perfect but she was on OUR side, she wanted a pure America and to kick out the trash #TrueMen #RememberKimT

#KimTegan is just a traitorous bitch who sold us out, walking with Cason, saying we're not enemies, polishing cason's knob #TrueMen

This is what they want, they're trying to divide us. McIntyre wasn't #TrueMen. #KimTegan killing was #FalseFlag

Agree was #FalseFlag. Shit's gonna hit the fan now. They will get what they deserve #RememberKimT #TrueMen #TrueMenWillRise #ElectionDay

They will get what they deserve #KimTegan #FalseFlag #TrueMen #TrueMenWillRise #ElectionDay

58

"**Dead candidates have a** pretty good track record. Just sayin'."

Jane let out a moan. "Thanks for that, Angus. Please let's not say it outside this room."

"There's five that died, their names stayed on the ballot, and they got elected to Congress," Angus said. "I checked."

Presley lifted his hands. "We're ahead in every poll. Thresher is fading. I don't think Tegan's death changes the essential dynamics of the race."

"Five for five. If you're dead and on the ballot, you win."

Presley shrugged. "Well, worst-case scenario, she wins, there's a special election and we get another crack at it."

"No." Jane slapped her hands on the desk. "No, no, no. We are not doing this again. I have a baby I want to play with. We're winning tomorrow. End of story." She rose. "It's eight fifty. Matt and Lindsey will be here in about fifteen minutes. Let's shut down the phone bank and get the party started."

The volunteers deserved a party, Sarah thought, making her way to her desk. Not that she'd interacted with any of them much, other than Joshua, the intern helping her with Social. But she recognized some of the faces. What motivated them, she wondered, the mostly middle-aged and older women who kept showing up, after everything that had happened, submitting to bag searches and pat-downs, dealing with bomb threats and vandalism and murders?

In light of Tegan's death ten days ago, they weren't planning anything crazy for the party. No group sing-alongs or dancing. She could just see how something like *that* would look on social media. So the music would be mellow, Angus would turn on his "mood lighting," and they'd load up a couple long tables with drinks and snacks, which they'd spent a little more on than usual. Some of the volunteers had brought potluck too, and from the dishes now appearing on the tables, it looked like there would be more than enough food for the hundred or so people expected to show up.

She made her way to her cubicle. It was quiet over there. One last check of the social feeds, she thought, before the party gets started.

"Hey."

Sarah jumped, but the voice was familiar. Ben. She turned.

"How's it going?" he asked.

He looked better than he had the last time she'd seen him. Still a little thin but not as pale. He didn't have a walker or a cane, so his leg must have healed well. Just in time for the election, like he'd said.

"Okay. It's been … " How to even describe it? "Busy."

He snorted a laugh. "I bet."

I don't have anything to say to you, she thought. And you don't have anything to say to me. Why are we pretending?

"You look … like you're feeling better."

Now he shifted a bit from foot to foot. "Yeah. I feel pretty good."

"It's nice to see you," she said, and then she turned back to her desk.

"Wait a sec," he said. "I just ... " He stood there, not quite looking at her, his hands balled into fists, knuckles of one hand pressed against the knuckles of the other. "I wanted to apologize. For being an asshole when you came over to visit me. I want you to know ... " He shook his head, smiled in a way that was more of a grimace, tilted his head to look at the ceiling for a moment before meeting her eyes.

"I think you're great," he said. "I've thought that since we started working together. Here's this smart, beautiful girl, and I didn't want to say anything, or do anything, I wanted to keep it professional, and ... " He looked away again. "I didn't think you were interested."

"Oh." She thought he was telling the truth. The way he'd been during the campaign, sometimes she'd thought he was interested and other times she was certain that he didn't even like her.

And she'd done her best to keep him—everyone—at arm's length.

"Then why ... ? When I came over ... "

He let out a sharp laugh. "Oh, man. Look, if we're being honest? I've seen the way you looked at Matt. I don't blame you, a lot of people look at him like that. But ... I can't compete, you know? He's Matt. I'm the loser who's having a hard time leaving the house right now."

Ben swallowed hard, his eyes glistening. "That night you came over ... I figured you just felt sorry for me."

"I don't know what to say," she finally managed. Because it was true, what he said.

But Matt was a fantasy. Ben was real.

"You don't have to say anything. I just wanted apologize, that's all." He turned to leave.

"Ben," she heard herself say. "We could go out for a beer later. When you're feeling better."

For a moment he stood there, his back to her, and she thought, well, I tried.

He glanced at her over his shoulder. Flashed a quick smile. "That'd be great. After tomorrow. Let's do it."

She watched his retreating back as he made his way over to Jane's office. Would they really see each other after tomorrow? She realized that she wanted to. Just to see what they might be like together, outside the campaign.

But she didn't know what she was going to do when the campaign ended. Whether there would be a job for her, whether she even wanted to take it if there were.

Wait until after tomorrow, she told herself. Wait till this is over, and then you can figure it out.

As she approached her desk, the phone rang—the Communications trill. A direct call, not one that had been transferred—Natalie had already sent the main line over to voicemail.

Not that many people had her direct line, and most of the people who did were already at the headquarters.

She had a pretty good guess as to who it was.

"Sarah?"

"Hi, Wyatt."

"I saw you on the news, of course. I'm sorry I didn't call sooner."

Sarah felt a rush of irritation. "Then why didn't you?" Not that she really cared that he hadn't called, but she was tired of people being sorry for things they could have easily avoided.

"Well..." A pause. "I feel responsible for some of what's happened to you."

"Why should you? You're not."

At least, she didn't think so. But how could she know for sure? Maybe he was the one who outed her. He'd obviously known who she was, who she'd been. But what reason would he have for doing that?

"You were taking those documents to Casey Cheng in the park that day, weren't you? I assume that's what you were doing, anyway."

So what if I was? she wanted to snap, but instead she remained silent. He hadn't told her what to do with the papers. What she'd done with them had been up to her.

"Which is fine," he added. "That was a smart way to handle it."

She didn't know what to say. If she agreed, that was an admission she'd done it. And even though logically he'd know she had—how else had Casey Cheng gotten that information?—there was no need to put herself on the record about it.

"Well, the election's tomorrow," she said. Just to make conversation.

"Yes. Have you voted?"

"The day I got my ballot." After what had happened in the park with Casey Cheng, filling out her ballot and mailing it in as quickly as she could had seemed like an imperative.

"Good." A pause. "Listen. I promised you I'd tell you if I heard any chatter."

Sarah felt a cold shiver and then a prickle of sweat. "What have you heard?"

"Nothing specifically about your boss, or you. But in terms of the big picture ... the pattern analysis points to a high likelihood of incidents with the intention of disrupting the election."

"What kind of incidents?"

"Violent ones."

There was a sudden swell of cheers and clapping over the ambient jazz. Sarah turned her head.

Matt and Lindsey had arrived. They were dressed much the same way as they had the day of the precinct walk, Matt in khaki chinos and white shirt, Lindsey dressed in a bright blouse and capris.

They looked beautiful, she thought.

"Hey!" Matt called out. "Great to see all of you here!" He saw Sarah and waved. She smiled and waved back, pointing at the phone.

"Hang on a second," Sarah said to Wyatt. "Can you …? There's … it's loud in here."

"I'll hang on."

Someone, Angus probably, turned off the music. "Don't stop the music on my account," Matt said quickly. "No speeches tonight. No speeches. Just … a thank you. Thanks for everything you've done. Thanks for being here."

More cheers. The music came back on.

"I'm back," Sarah said.

"That Cason?"

"Yes."

"Just tell him to be careful. Okay? You've got security there, right?"

"Yes. Even more since Tegan."

"Good."

She took in a deep breath, and then another. She wanted to scream. This was supposed to be over. "The boy who killed Tegan was crazy. These True Men, they can't even decide who the enemy is now. And we got the one who killed Rachel. Casey and I did. We beat them! Why do you think it's going to get worse?"

"Sarah, every time one of these guys goes after a high-value target and misses, it makes them even angrier. And what you and Casey did? They could accept what happened to Lucas more easily than that."

"Why?"

"You know why. Lucas was taken down by a former soldier. A man. But Brandon Gates? Beat up by a couple of girls? And sure, some of them will deflect by making fun of him, but don't you think for a minute they aren't enraged. And the more furious they get, the more likely some of them are going to pick up guns, or Molotov cocktails, do whatever they can think of to do some damage. That's where we are now."

It can't be, she thought. Things can't keep going on this way. Matt was going to win tomorrow, and then it was going to be over.

But she knew in her gut he was right.

"Okay," she said. "Thanks. Thanks for the heads-up."

"You'll be okay, Sarah. You're smart. You're talented. I know you'll go far. But be careful out there. I just don't know if it's going to be safe."

Sarah almost laughed. When had it *ever* been safe?

"I will," she said.

With all the things she didn't know about Wyatt, she could only think of one thing that she really needed to ask right now.

"Are we going to win?"

A pause. "Yeah, I think so. I'm actually pretty sure."

Then it's going to be okay, she thought.

We're going to win, and it's going to be okay.

"Oh, by the way ... " Wyatt said. "That invasion board. The one that's been after you. I hear it's been shut down. I gather the guys behind it are going to be a lot more careful about how they conduct themselves online in the future. At least that's one thing you won't have to worry about right now."

PIPE BOMB IN MANASSAS POLLING PLACE KILLS 2, INJURES 7

Casey stared at the alert on the lock screen of her phone. "Well, that's not good," she said.

4:19 a.m.

Election Day was going to be brutal.

She lay back down on her pillow. Her alarm was set for 6:45 a.m.—earlier than she usually worked, but they wanted her to cover Matt Cason going to vote this morning, scheduled for around nine. Her last hit would be after the polls closed, at his victory party downtown, preferably after there was a projected winner and a speech. Odds were good that would be on the early side. Polling showed Cason comfortably ahead. Which was good when your opponents were a dead woman and a third-party TV star.

Sleep, she told herself. Another couple of hours wouldn't be enough, but it would help. She closed her eyes.

Another alert on her phone.

Maybe I should put it on Do Not Disturb, she thought. She just hadn't wanted to risk missing anything important, not today.

Drive-By Shooting Kills Three, Wounds Five, at Georgia Church Serving as Polling Place.

"Shit." Her heart started to pound.

When the third alert came in fifteen minutes later, she was wide awake.

Grenade Attack Destroys Cars in Parking Lot of Scranton Polling Place.

Casey threw off the covers and swung her legs over the side of the bed. Too quickly—the sudden movement sent a shot of pain from her lower back down to her calf and back again. *"Shit!"*

She took a few deep breaths, pushed herself to her feet with Trusty—getting out of bed in the morning was the one time she still really needed the cane—and hobbled into the kitchen to make coffee. No point in trying to sleep.

Video came in on the Manassas attack while she poured water over her beans.

Smartphone footage. It must have been shot right after the explosion; you could still see smoke, hear screams and moans from the victims. An elementary school auditorium. Construction-paper cutouts on one wall, children's drawings of flags and smiling people holding ballots.

A crying toddler sitting next to a bloodied woman sprawled on the ground.

Casey stared at the images.

The station called a minute later.

"Casey?" It was the morning show producer. "Can you get down here ASAP?"

She was surprised it had taken them that long.

She did her live shot as a stand-up in front of Cason headquarters, hitting at 6:09, right after the morning anchors, Mark and Sherrie, ran down what they knew about the Election Day violence—"Death at the Polls" was the bumper. She waited while they ran video that had just come in of a firebombing in Dallas, then a cut to a long shot of Cason headquarters in the gray dawn, several police cars parked in front, Sherrie's voice in her ear saying, *"Casey Cheng is live at Matt Cason campaign headquarters,"* and then she was in the box.

"All appears calm here as Cason campaign workers and volunteers prepare for a long day of getting out the vote," she said, gesturing behind her, at the knot of people waiting to be searched by the armed guards at the door, "and as you can see, it's already pretty busy."

Calm. That was a poor choice of words.

"And by *calm,* I mean that so far today in San Diego, we have not experienced any of the violence that is affecting so many other places in the country."

"Any explanation why, have there been any reports, any indications of plots disrupted in the planning stages?" she heard Sherrie ask.

"Not that I know of, Sherrie. But it's still early."

Maybe it won't happen here today, she thought. Maybe we've already had our share.

Mark's voice: *"Casey, you've been on this True Men story from the very beginning. Is what we're seeing today the emergence of an organized effort to subvert American democracy?"*

For a moment, Casey's mind went blank. But she was supposed to be the expert. True Men was *her* story. That was how News 9 had branded it: True Men, Casey Cheng reporting.

"At this point, it's difficult to say how organized they are. From my experience, they lack a coherent ideology or clear goals."

She glanced over her shoulder at the police cars, at the armed guards frisking volunteers, rifling through their bags.

"What they do have in common is rage. And the ability to disrupt. The extent to which that damages our democracy says more about us than it does about them."

"Wise words from Casey Cheng," Sherrie said. *"We've just gotten word of another attack, this time in Wisconsin."*

"You're out, Casey," the director said in her ear.

Her story. Her monster.

You didn't make this happen, she told herself. You didn't. You just helped give it a name.

———

"What's the latest?" Jane asked as Angus entered the office.

"Nineteen dead, a lot of injuries. More reports of shots fired. It's spread to twenty-five states. Mostly assholes throwing firecrackers, thank the lord."

"What is this going to do to turnout?" Sarah asked.

"Depress it, of course. People are afraid to go to the polls." Jane sighed. "Luckily with mail-in ballots, it's not as big a factor here as it is in a lot of other states. But still, we need every vote we can get. Polling's good but I don't want to count on it."

The campaign office was full up. Volunteers sat in every available spot at the long folding tables arranged in ranks in the bull pen, making phone calls. She could hear the hum of activity through the closed door and glass window of Jane's office, phones ringing, a blurred murmur of people making their pitches.

"We've got every volunteer we can round up doing phone calls," Angus said. "We've got the phone bank here, there's a couple being held in people's homes, county headquarters is busy, and Tomás says so far the people he's lined up to drive voters to the polls haven't backed out."

"And Matt?" Sarah asked. "Is he still planning on going to his polling place?"

"Of course," Jane said. She sounded resigned.

Just after nine o'clock was the latest plan. Originally he'd wanted to vote right when the polls opened in hopes of getting some coverage on the early morning shows, but with everything else that was going on, they'd decided to wait. A couple stations had local news at nine, including News 9 ("Your News 9 at 9").

He didn't have to, Sarah knew. He could mail in his ballot instead of dropping it off in person. The mail-in ballots only had to be postmarked by today. Or he could take it to a different polling place, or to the county elections office.

"Then I'll go too," she said. "To get some things for Social."

She wasn't sure why she wanted to be there. It wasn't because she wanted Matt, not anymore. It was just seeing it through. And maybe if she got some images out on Social, a short video or two, it might encourage people who were afraid.

"I am guessing there's no point in trying to talk you out of that," Angus said.

Sarah felt herself smile. "No, not really."

"Well, hell, I'll go too." He stood up and stretched. "Be nice to get some fresh air."

"Oh, fine," Jane said. "Let's all go." She shrugged. "A show of support. I don't know. It'll probably be the safest polling place in San Diego, anyway."

"I wish we weren't still trying to make this a horse race," Casey said. "Because at this point, it's truly beating a dead horse."

Rose snorted. "Oh my god, what I wouldn't give to have you say that on air."

"Don't tempt me. I'll be in Bhutan for the fallout."

The blocks around the elementary school where Matt Cason would vote were lousy with live trucks and news vehicles: local, national, global. This was "The race that ignited the True Men movement," and everyone wanted coverage of the ending. Police SUVs parked on the blocks leading to the school as well. Casey had counted three of them, with another sitting in the parking lot by the entrance to the elementary school auditorium that served as the polling place.

An elementary school auditorium. Casey thought of the footage from Manassas attack, the kids' drawings on the walls, the smiling voters sketched in crayon. Maybe they could use that shot somehow, for this segment.

Oh god, she thought. There's something wrong with me. There's something wrong with all of us. How do we fix it?

She wasn't even sure what "it" was.

Reporters and photographers stood clustered on the sidewalk, at times drifting into the front yards of the remodeled ranch houses, yards planted with huge, spiky succulents, bark beds with rose bushes, gravel, the occasional vegetable garden. Residents of the area had started to congregate as well, some on their way to vote, others drawn by the circus that had camped out in their neighborhood.

Casey stared out at the bay. It was a clear, blue day, and she could see all the way to the ocean on the other side of Mission Boulevard.

I just want this to be over, she thought.

It wouldn't be, though, she knew. Just because the election would be over didn't mean that this all would end.

"Look who's here," Diego said. Casey and Rose looked in the direction his camera pointed.

Coming up the sidewalk were Sarah Price, Jane Haddad, and Angus Wheeler, followed by a knot of about a dozen people she didn't recognize, carrying CASON FOR CONGRESS signs, some wearing campaign T-shirts, several news crews in their wake.

"Sarah, hi!" Casey called out, waving. She wanted to give Sarah a big hug, but she didn't want to do it on camera. It might be the perfect "poignant moment" for the package, but she didn't want to supply it. There were complaints about her objectivity as it was.

Sarah broke away from Haddad and Wheeler and trotted over to Casey.

"Hi, Casey. It's good to see you." She smiled, a real smile, and Casey thought, *Oh what the hell?*, and hugged her anyway.

Sarah hugged her back. Here's your perfect poignant moment, Casey thought, and here are some tears to make it even better, because now she was crying.

She let go of Sarah, pressed the bridge of her nose between her thumb and forefinger, and smiled shakily.

"Sorry," she said. "Long day already."

Sarah nodded and gave Casey an awkward pat on her shoulder, and Casey could see the muscles move in her throat as she swallowed hard.

"It has been," Sarah said. She glanced around, at the cameras and microphones now surrounding them, drawing closer, weirdly silent.

Well, not *weirdly*. They wanted to hear what the two of them were saying.

Okay, Casey thought, patting the tears on her cheeks so she wouldn't smear her makeup. Time to get it together. Because god knows how many photographers were shooting them by now, and she was not the story. She had a job to do.

She gestured at the crowd. "What's going on?"

"Just a little show of support," Jane Haddad said from behind Sarah. "With everything that's going on ... we felt that it was important. Of course we won't get within one hundred feet of the polling place."

"Of course."

Rose was already mingling with the group carrying signs and wearing Cason T-shirts, looking for likely interviews, two steps ahead of the other news teams. "Do you want to make a statement?" Casey asked Sarah.

"Not really." She didn't look away. She seemed calm. Steady. "I don't have anything new to say." She glanced back at the Cason supporters. "You should talk to Carol—that older woman in the climate march T-shirt? She'll give you a good bite for sure."

"Thanks," Casey said. "And ... thanks. It's really good to see you too."

———

(LIVE SHOT: WESTERN BAY PARK, ON STREET NEAR EINSTEIN ELEMENTARY) CAROL OLSEN, CASON VOLUNTEER: I'm 83 years old, and if one of those little punks wants to take a shot at me, let them. I'm not afraid. I'm here to support my candidate and our democracy.

CASEY CHENG, NEWS 9: And you, sir? As I understand it, you're not a Cason supporter.

MIKE KELLEY, AREA RESIDENT (49 YEARS OLD, WEARING USMC T-SHIRT): No, ma'am, I am not. I'm pretty conservative, to tell you the truth. I already voted for Kim Tegan. But my feeling is, people should be able to vote without being scared. So I just thought, maybe I could help keep an eye on things (GESTURES AT THE PEOPLE LINING THE SIDEWALK). I think a lot of us are feeling that way.

"Is that Cason?"

A black SUV with tinted windows cruised slowly down the street, heading toward them. It looked like the SUV that had ferried Cason around for the precinct walk, but Casey wasn't sure.

Jane and Angus started clapping, Angus waving at the Cason volunteers, who began to cheer. Sarah held up her iPhone.

It had to be him.

The black SUV slowed, then stopped just a few yards in front of them. Matt Cason hopped out, followed by Lindsey. He wore a navy suit today with an open-necked light blue shirt. Lindsey was dressed in a pantsuit, cream, with a chocolate brown blouse.

"Wow, look at this!" he said. He approached the volunteers. Diego was on it, grabbing the spot with the best angle, even as two other photographers jostled for position.

Matt shook hands, gave hugs. "I wasn't going to just drive by without stopping to say hello," Casey heard him say. "And to thank all of you, for all your work, for being here … this is just … " He seemed to choke up. He pressed his index and middle finger against his forehead, his eyes closed. "It's pretty overwhelming."

Casey pushed her way to the front of the scrum. "Representative Cason—Matt—"

"Hey, Casey." He was smiling again.

"Matt, how does it feel to be here, coming to vote, after everything that has happened on this campaign, with all that's going on in the rest of the country right now?"

"That's a tough one."

They stood close together now, nearly toe to toe, close enough for Casey to see that he wore something under his blue shirt. Not an undershirt. A light Kevlar vest.

"I'm angry. I'm … sad. And I'm really grateful." He gestured at the volunteers holding up signs, at the people who'd come out of their houses and now lined the sidewalks. "These are the people I'm doing this for. And the fact that they're out here, today … you know, our democracy is under attack. I mean, literally. But this is the defense. Right here."

Abruptly, he turned away. His hand found Lindsey's. The black SUV, which had been waiting behind them, engine running, pulled up and the driver's window rolled down.

"Representative Cason?" the driver called out.

"That's okay, Morgan," Matt said. "We'll walk."

Matt and Lindsey started down the street, toward the school. The cameras followed alongside. So did Sarah. She held up her phone, staring at the image of Matt and Lindsey on its screen.

Casey watched them head down the block to the auditorium, stopping along the way to shake hands with people on the sidewalk. She'd need to reposition herself down there as well. She started walking, passing two police cruisers, the officers standing by them, watching. A helicopter circled overhead, the circles increasingly smaller, the blades sounding oddly like beaters against the side of a metal mixing bowl.

For a moment, the noise and the crowds receded, and she saw only the school, the American and California state flags fluttering from a tall mast, the asphalt parking lot, the chain link fence that surrounded the playground.

Everything looked normal, if you just looked straight ahead.

ACKNOWLEDGMENTS

Writing acknowledgments is always stressful for me because I know I will forget someone. And I really want to thank everyone who helped me with this book, both directly and in terms of being amazingly supportive of me while I was writing it. This was not an easy book to write, and I needed all the help I could get.

First, many thanks to all the folks at Midnight Ink who have ushered this book out into the world, especially acquiring editor Terri Bischoff, editor Nicole Nugent, and cover designer Shira Atakpu (I love this cover so much!). Thank you for believing in this project. Your fearlessness and support mean a great deal to me.

My deep appreciation to my agent, Katherine Fausset. Publishing is not an easy business, and I could not ask for a better person to have in my corner. Always supportive, always kind, and always battling for a better deal. Thanks as well to all the other hard-working folks at Curtis Brown, in particular Holly Frederick, Kelly D'Agostino, Sarah Gerton, and Olivia Simpkins.

Huge thanks go out to author Tom Abrahams, who gave so generously of his time and expertise in broadcast journalism. He patiently answered all my questions, even the stupid ones, with a writer's understanding of what I needed to know and why I needed to know it. Meeting people like Tom made me want to create a character like Casey, who cares deeply about her job and about doing it right. Any mistakes I made (and I'm sure I made a few) are the result of my own incompetence, not from any errors on his part.

The same goes for the San Diego political experts / campaign workers who talked me through the nuts and bolts of local elections. We tend to be very cynical about politics in today's United States, with some reason. But at the same time, in my experience there are many dedicated people working in politics who care passionately about the potential of our system to do good and to accomplish good work. This book is in large part an appreciation of all the elected officials, campaign staff, and volunteers who work so hard to do the right thing. (That includes the Squirrels. You know who you are!)

As always, special thanks to my family, especially Bill, Dana, and Dave. Have I mentioned how awesome it is to have writers for a sister and brother-in-law? I'm probably going to have to thank them twice. Gratitude as well to my cousins Jill and Sandy.

Speaking of writers, I am truly blessed with a fine circle of writer friends. Thanks especially to Dana Fredsti, Allie Larkin, Jo Perry, Catherine McKenzie, Kim Fay, and Richard Burger for their beta reads; Bryn Greenwood and David Fitzgerald for their general support; along with the Fiction Author's Co-op, Purgatory, and so many wonderful folks in the crime fiction community that I couldn't begin to list them all. I'm convinced that crime fiction writers must get all their demons out on the page, because they are such an incredibly nice group of people.

And where would I be without Billy Brackenridge, my partner in sushi, wine, and fine conversation? Far poorer in the things that really count: experience and friendship.

Finally, to everyone at two of my locals, Amplified Aleworks and Dan Diego's. Writing can be an isolating profession. At the end of a long day where I mostly talked to my screen and to my cat, I can't tell you how much I appreciated being able to go have some great food, fine beer, and good times. You all rock.